DIEHARD FAN

by

Lenny Levine

J K PUBLISHING

Diehard Fan
Publisher: J K Publishing
Published: January 2021
Printed in the United States of America
ISBN: 978-0-578-78341-3

This book was published with the assistance of Self-Publishing Relief.

Cover design by Self-Publishing Relief

To Lana, Zack, Vivian, James, and Katie

"Some things can affect you so disproportionately, it makes you wonder. When Bobby Thomson hit the home run, I was driving back from the Catskills with my friend Roger Goldstein, who was a rabid Giant fan. Russ Hodges' voice was coming out of the radio, yelling, 'The Giants win the pennant! The Giants win the pennant!' and Roger was pounding on the dashboard, whooping and hollering and laughing hysterically. I remember having a powerful urge to stomp down on the accelerator as hard as I could, run the car off the road, and smash it into a tree. Can you imagine? At that moment I actually wanted to die, as long as I could take him with me."

—My father, a Dodger fan, recalling the October 3, 1951 "shot heard 'round the world."

CHAPTER ONE

Tuesday, September 25, 1951

The mist drifted out of the Boston night onto ancient Braves Field, wisps of it swirling like yellow cotton candy in the glare of the light towers. It settled on the grass and seeped into the heavy grey-flannel uniforms of the Brooklyn Dodgers as they stood in the field, mixing with their sweat.

At shortstop, Pee Wee Reese kicked the infield dirt in disgust and then smoothed out the divot. With their luck, the next ground ball would have found it; that's how things had been going. And to confirm it, he took a peek at the scoreboard. The Giants had taken a 3-0 lead in Philly.

Earlier in the inning, Pee Wee had done what he hadn't done in a thousand chances. He'd booted a routine ground ball, and without the help of a divot. It had been the wet grass and Buddy Kerr, the Boston baserunner, flashing by him at exactly the wrong moment. What else was new? He set himself and looked in to see what pitch Campy was about to call.

Carl Erskine stood on the mound and stared in at Roy Campanella for that same sign. Three runs had already scored, there was still only one out, and the bases were loaded.

In the radio booth, Red Barber was telling his listeners, "Friends, it's only the second inning here in Boston, but we are already at the crossroads."

It wasn't like the Dodgers had been playing badly. Since August 11th, when they had a thirteen-and-a-half game lead, they hadn't been world beaters, but they weren't beating themselves either.

It was the Giants. They never seemed to lose. The Dodgers would split a double-header and the Giants would win one. If the Dodgers took two out of three in a series, the Giants won all three in theirs. They'd been slowly gaining on them for the last six weeks, and now, as Erskine stood on the mound with the bases full around him, the Giants were only two games behind.

Left-hand-hitting Brave first baseman Earl Torgeson settled into his stance and pumped his bat.

"One out," Red Barber reminded his listeners, "and the bases are F.O.B. That's 'full of Bostons' this time, folks, not 'full of Brooklyns.' If the Dodgers are going to stop the bleeding, it has to be now. They've already lost the first game of the double-header, and if this one gets away, and the Giant score in Philly holds up, their lead will be down to one wafer-thin game. Who'da thunk it?"

Erskine had to be careful with Torgeson, who liked 'em down and in. Fast ball away, said Campy's sign. Carl nodded his agreement and delivered a called strike on the outside corner.

At second base, Jackie Robinson tried to ignore the pain in his chest from the pitch that hit him in the first inning. He pounded his glove and picked up the next sign, curve down and in. That was where Torgeson liked it, but it would be out of the strike zone, and if he made contact he'd hit a ground ball to the right side. Jackie got ready to move to his left if it happened.

Erskine's arm came around in its familiar, over-the-top motion and almost delivered a wild pitch. It bounced in the dirt at Torgeson's feet, caroming off Campy's chest protector as he slid in front of it and blocked it.

"Okay! Okay!" Campy called out, clutching the ball, his eyes roaming the diamond, making sure the runners stayed put. "That's what I'm here for."

Jocko Conlon, the home plate umpire, muttered, "Nice stop," as he took the scuffed ball and handed him a new one.

Campy settled into his crouch again and called for the same pitch. Erskine made it perfect this time, but Torgeson didn't bite. He let it go by for ball two.

Charlie Dressen, the Dodger manager, paced the dugout, looking more like a bantam rooster bobbing back and forth than a tiger stalking up and down. He'd once told his team, "Just hold 'em close, boys; I'll think of something." It was funny then, but the jokes had been few and far between lately. A scant two weeks ago, he was making plans to rest his pitching staff for the World Series. Now, the only pitchers he'd rest were the ones he didn't trust, which was everyone except his big three: Newcombe, Erskine, and Roe. They'd be doing it all from here on. Newk was pitching tomorrow and then again on Saturday with only two days' rest in between. Carl Erskine, no matter how many pitches he had to throw tonight, would be working again on Friday. Like a jockey in the stretch, Charlie was going to the whip.

"Two-and-one, the count on Torgeson," Red Barber reported. "Runners taking their leads, Kerr on third, Wilson on second, and the speedy Sam Jethroe on first. Erskine winds and delivers…"

A fastball meant for the outside corner, but right over the heart of the plate. Torgeson swung.

"Foul straight back," said Red Barber, as the ball clanged off the facing just below him. "You know, fans, people get excited about long, foul home runs, but it's the fouls straight back that scare pitchers the most. Torgeson was right on that pitch and missed hitting it on the button by a fraction of an inch."

Next came a curve ball, just missing outside. Now it was three-and-two.

Barber wondered if Boston manager Tommy Holmes would have the runners moving on the next pitch. "With one out he'd be taking a chance, but his Braves are in fourth place with nothing to lose, and they can be the spoilers. Sam Jethroe, the runner on first, is one of the fastest men in baseball. Let's see if they try it."

Campy called for another fast ball, up and in. With two strikes, Torgeson could go for it and miss, or pop it up.

"Erskine into his motion," said Red Barber, "and there go the runners. The pitch is swung on…"

***

The borough of Brooklyn in 1951 was home to two million people and one million radios. Road games were not televised back then, so most of those radios, if they were on, were tuned to WMGM and this game. One in particular, a 1939 Philco tabletop model, sat on the kitchen counter of an apartment on Bay Parkway in the Bensonhurst section.

Eddie Fein stared across the table at it as if, by looking hard enough, he could see the players right through the maroon cloth that covered the speaker. His seventh-grade social studies report on the Incas, which he was supposed to be writing, sat in front of him, as far from his mind as Peru.

("You know, fans, people get excited about long, foul home runs, but it's the fouls straight back that scare pitchers the most.")

"C'mon, Carl," he said, with all the heartfelt urgency of a prayer. "Strike this guy out."

Barry Fein sat across the table from his son, grim-faced, his hands clenching and unclenching in his lap. A bottle of Schaefer beer stood on the table in front of him, a pile of empties in the sink. He'd been working on the beers since they'd started listening to the game. Scotch was before dinner, and sometimes during, but ballgames were for beer.

Sounds drifted in from the TV set in the living room, the Milton Berle Show. ("We have a celebrity in the audience tonight, folks, Monty Wooley. What? He's not? Oh, sorry, madam, your beard fooled me.") Laughter from the TV and from Eddie's mother.

"Jesus." Barry threw a disgusted glance toward the living room and turned up the radio.

"C'mon, Carl," Eddie repeated, hoping that if he said it again it might help.

("Sam Jethroe, the runner on first, is one of the fastest men in baseball. Let's see if they try it…")

Julia Fein, sitting in the living room, heard Red Barber's voice get louder and thought for the umpteenth time how her husband was almost as much of a child as her son. She looked back at Milton Berle.

("Please give a big hand, ladies and gentlemen, to Allen Roth and his United Nations orchestra. Someday, they may all get together.") Julia smiled and the studio audience laughed.

Eddie looked over at his father, about to ask him if he thought Sam Jethroe was faster than Jackie Robinson, but the look in Barry's eyes stopped him. It was the kind of look he'd had the time Eddie and his friend Lionel accidentally smashed someone's windshield while throwing a baseball around in the middle of Bay 29th Street.

"Let's go, Carl," he said, changing it to "let's go." Maybe that would work better than "c'mon," which sounded a little whiny.

("Erskine into his motion, and there go the runners. The pitch is swung on and lined into the gap in right-center field…") Eddie held his breath, as Barry muttered, "Shit!" ("…It's a base hit. Kerr scores, Wilson scores. Here comes Jethroe, he'll score…and now the throw from Furillo sails over the head of the cutoff man and Torgeson pulls into second. Ohh, doctor!")

"God damn it!"

Barry slammed his fist down on the table. The bottle teetered for a precarious instant and then fell over, spilling a stream of beer onto Eddie's report.

"God damn it!" Barry said louder, swiping at the overturned bottle with one big hand and sending it flying across the room and against the wall, where it shattered.

("Our special guest tonight is that fine British actor, Nasal Bathroom, I mean Basil Rathbone,") said Milton Berle, as Julia leaped to her feet. She rushed to the living room door and stared into the kitchen in disbelief.

"What the hell is going on in here?"

Eddie held the soggy Inca report in the air as it dripped onto the table and stared at her helplessly.

"It's okay!" Barry said, glaring at her. "I'll clean it up. Don't start."

"Don't start? Who has to start?" she said, her voice rising. "You're already well into it. What's the matter, they're losing?"

"I said I'd clean it up!"

"Are you also going to rewrite his report?" She gave an angry glance at Eddie.

"It's okay, Mom…"

"No, it's not okay!" Her voice had that tone that always turned his guts to mush. "You weren't even supposed to be listening to the goddamn game until you finished your report. Did you finish it?"

"Yeah," Eddie lied, "but it got wet. So I just have to recopy it."

"Let me see it," Julia demanded.

"Aw, Mom…"

"Let me see it."

"Leave him alone!" said Barry, his eyes glinting. "I'm the one you're after. Pick on me."

Red Barber continued to speak from the radio, as Eddie watched them stare each other down like gunfighters. Even while telling you the Dodgers were losing, the Ol' Redhead sounded warm and soothing to him, especially compared to the angry silence flashing between his parents.

Barry unlocked his eyes and looked over at him.

"Go to your room and recopy your paper. Then go to bed."

"But, Dad…"

"Go to your room," Julia told him. "And dry off that report first, so it doesn't drip beer all over your floor."

("I saw the Sugar Ray Robinson-Randy Turpin fight," Milton Berle was saying in the living room. "Do you know why they call him Sugar? Because when he stepped into the ring, he asked Turpin, 'One lump or two?'")

Eddie mopped his report with a dish towel, then headed down the hall toward his room. Red Barber's voice was cut off in mid-word behind him. He was sure his father did it, because his mother wouldn't dare.

He closed the door, plopped down at his desk, and stared at the wall. He hated this.

Muffled, angry voices came from the kitchen.

"… you really scare me when you get this way." That was his mother. There was a loud bang that made Eddie jump. His father must have smashed his fist down on the table again.

His mother said something else, and then something about "your dead-end job." There was another loud bang, and the front door slammed.

Then it was silent.

He took out his notebook and started copying his three sentences about the Incas, but he couldn't stand it. He opened the door and looked out.

The kitchen was deserted, beer bottles still in the sink, broken glass on the floor. The door to the living room was open and the TV was still on.

He carefully crossed the kitchen and looked in.

His mother sat on the couch in the dark, staring coldly at the screen. On it, Sid Stone, the Texaco pitchman for the Milton Berle Show, was standing behind a little table, selling Havoline motor oil. In one hand, he was holding a can of it, and with the other, he was trying to get rid of a diminutive young man in knickers.

("Go away from me, kid, ya bother me.")

"Where's dad?" said Eddie.

"Don't ask me." Julia's eyes never left the screen. "And don't ask me who he is, either."

***

("…Torgeson pulls into second. Ohh, doctor!")

In the dining room of an apartment two blocks from the Feins', Sandra Weinstock smiled delightedly.

"Ohh, boy!" she said, as she softly applauded the radio. Moments before, she'd heard Russ Hodges, doing the Giant-Phillie game on WMCA, describe Alvin Dark's solo shot, putting the Giants up 3-0. The inning had ended and, during the commercials, she was switching to the Dodger game. It had been her unbelievably good fortune to get there just in time for Torgeson's base hit.

"Six-nothing!" she said to herself, unable to contain her joy. "They're losing six-nothing!"

Then, as at similar times these past weeks, she thought about how her dad would've loved this. She looked over at her mother's china cabinet, to a photo from ten years ago of a teenage Sandra and an overweight, balding man in a dark suit, both of them grinning like fools in front of their apartment building in Manhattan's Washington Heights, both of them in their Giant caps.

("Our special guest tonight is that fine British actor, Nasal Bathroom, I mean Basil Rathbone.") In the living room, Yetta Weinstock laughed "haw, haw, haw," in that braying sound that always set Sandra's teeth on edge.

It was a mistake to come and live here. Even the good things happening in the game couldn't keep that thought away. After her dad died, it seemed like the natural thing to do. Her mother needed her and she had no particular ties to her bookkeeping job or her small apartment in the Village. No boyfriends either, for that matter.

And it was okay at first. Her mother's apartment was large and airy, with a view of Bensonhurst Park across the street and, in winter through the trees, Gravesend Bay. She'd quickly found a job at Faber's Sporting Goods on 86th Street under the el, keeping the books for old Mr. Faber and helping him deal with the customers.

But it was three years now, and her life was slipping away. She missed the vibrancy of Manhattan, the theaters, art galleries, and coffeehouses only minutes from her door. And her mother, let's face it, was a first-class pain in the rear.

"You're still listening to that game? What's the matter with you, you're missing a very funny show."

She stood in the doorway, a vision of uncombed gray hair, pouchy cheeks, and stained housecoat. A cigarette dangled from her lips. Her voice had gotten deeper over the past few years from smoking, and salesmen on the phone sometimes thought she was a man.

"I'm doing fine, Ma," Sandra said. "The Giants are winning and the Dodgers are losing a double-header."

"Big deal, there's lots of baseball games," said her mother. "Milton Berle is only on once a week."

("…'One lump or two?'")

She looked back into the living room, then at Sandra.

"Listen, you're making me miss it. Do you wanna come in and watch it or not?"

"I've got the game on, Ma," Sandra said, stifling a cough.

Yetta Weinstock gave her daughter one of those "what can I do with you?" looks. "Suit yourself," she said, and went back into the living room.

Sandra turned her attention to the radio just as Red Barber was calling Willard Marshall's base hit, scoring Torgeson.

"Seven-nothing!" she said to herself in wonder. "This is so great."

A cool breeze drifted in through the dining-room window at that moment, bringing with it the smell of the leaves, and she suddenly needed to be outside. She wanted to enjoy this moment, and her mother's apartment wasn't the place to enjoy anything. In fact, she'd made up her mind; she was going to move out.

But right now she had to get into the air, away from here even for a little while. The games were going well, and she could leave them that way for now. She'd take a short walk through the park, maybe go down to the bay. She wouldn't be gone long, and she could check in on the scores when she got back.

"Ma, I'm going out for a while," she called toward the living room.

"You shouldn't go out with that pneumonia of yours," her mother's voice called back.

"It's not pneumonia, Ma, it's bronchitis."

Yetta appeared again in the doorway. "Weren't you told it could turn into pneumonia?"

Sandra looked heavenward for a moment and tried to be calm.

"If it's okay for me to go to work, it's certainly okay for me to take a little walk," she said. "Now, stop worrying."

"Whatever you want," muttered Mrs. Weinstock, as she turned and went back into the living room. On the screen, Metropolitan Opera star Patrice Munsel was singing an aria, and Milton Berle, wearing a wig and an evening gown, was sneaking up behind her.

***

The tall, heavyset man strode down Bay Parkway toward Bensonhurst Park, his headache pounding even harder than his feet against the pavement. There was no denying it; his life was complete and utter shit.

The woman he'd married, the woman he'd once been stupid enough to love, was an ugly, abrasive bitch, whose only joy in life was to make him miserable. Day after day, without let-up.

It was hard enough most of the time, but it was really hard if the Dodgers were losing, and she knew that. She saved herself especially for those times. He didn't know what would have happened tonight if he didn't get out of there.

He thought of the Dodgers again, because they always seemed to be on his mind. In a way, they were all he had left. The only thing in the world he could summon up any passion for.

How pathetic he was.

And even more pathetic, loving the Dodgers was like loving a beautiful woman who gets you all excited, brings you almost to orgasm, then spits in your face.

They'd done it to him so many times, he'd lost count. But this time…this time, they were doing it to him royally. They were blowing the biggest lead any team had ever blown, and it wasn't to the Cardinals or the Phillies.

It was to the fucking Giants! The fucking Giants!

His headache flared and it made him wince. He increased his pace, pounding even harder as he strode past the park and into the underpass beneath the Belt Parkway.

The sounds of the cars above him echoed down the walls. At one point, a truck rumbled across some metal construction plates, making a loud and unexpected boom that ricocheted off the walls around him like artillery fire.

He almost screamed.

A cry came from his throat, but he cut it off, clenching his teeth and quickening his pace, finally emerging onto the promenade along Gravesend Bay.

He made it to the rail and gripped it with both hands, staring down at the black water below, his chest heaving.

Then a woman's voice called his name.

At first he thought it was his imagination. He looked up and saw her, a small, trim figure walking down the promenade toward him. She was smiling.

It took him a moment to realize who she was.

"Sandra," he said, forcing a smile of his own that must have looked like a rictus. If it did, she didn't notice.

"Is it Friday already?" she asked.

"What?"

"We weren't supposed to see each other again until Friday."

"Oh, right."

God, his head was killing him.

"Isn't it beautiful out here? And we're the only ones smart enough to enjoy it."

He looked around and saw that there was no one else on the promenade.

"You see? Nobody," she pointed out. "I guess we're the only two people who aren't fans of Uncle Miltie."

"Uncle Miltie?" He had no idea what she was talking about.

"You know, Mr. Television, Milton Berle. Every Tuesday night, the streets are always empty like this. Everyone's glued to their TV sets, watching that dopey show, including my mother."

Including his wife. He tried to keep his voice steady and get through this. "I know what you mean; I feel the same way. He makes me want to wrap up the box."

She smiled tentatively.

"Wrap up the box? I don't understand."

What was he doing? First, he'd had another of those Normandy flashbacks in the underpass, and now here he was, lapsing into his private sense of humor.

It was secret little jokes to himself that got him through life as a child on the Upper West Side. It was why he rooted for the Dodgers instead of the Giants. To set himself apart from all the jerks in the neighborhood, which was everyone.

"'Wrap up the box' is just an expression of mine," he explained. "It means 'turn off the TV.'"

It took her a moment, and then she laughed.

"Very clever." She looked at him in admiration. "I think you're actually funnier than Milton Berle."

"Well, that's not saying very much, is it?"

She laughed again, and he liked the sound. Was his headache starting to ease up a little? He thought so. Maybe it was good that he'd run into her.

"Wrap up the box," she said, "can I use that? I'll give you credit for it, I promise."

"Be my guest." Now he was smiling himself. "You seem to be in a good mood."

"Do I? I guess it's because it's a beautiful night, the Giants are winning, and the Dodgers are losing a double-header."

If she'd suddenly pulled a knife and stabbed him, it wouldn't have been more unexpected. He stared at her.

"I'm a big Giant fan; you can probably tell," she went on. "It's been like a miracle!"

She interpreted his look as one of interest and gave him a mischievous grin.

"You know, I almost feel sorry for the Dodgers. Because they know my Giants are gonna catch 'em. Because they always blow it in the end."

She laughed again. It made her look like a gargoyle. He winced, but she didn't notice.

"It's like a tradition with them."

His headache was back now with a vengeance, bursting into excruciating waves of pain.

"They do it every year, like clockwork. If it's September, you know it's time for the Dodgers to do their September swoon. And they do, they certainly do. They fold like a cheap…"

Her voice grated like fingernails on a blackboard. His head was exploding. He had to stop her. She was killing him.

"Shut up," was what he meant to say, but instead, he found himself reaching for her.

"What are you…?" was all she could manage, and then his hands were around her throat. He pulled her toward him, her eyes wide in disbelief. To anyone passing at a distance, they might have been lovers about to kiss. But there was no one in any case.

"Shut up! Shut up! Shut up!" The words shrieked in his mind, but no sound came from his lips.

She flailed desperately in his grasp, struggling to breathe, her fingers clawing at his hands, trying to pull them away. He was oblivious to it, as he was to everything but the voice inside him, screaming, "Shut up! Shut up!" His fingers tightened around her neck.

Her right hand caught on his watch and tore it off in a spasm, clutching it like a final souvenir of her life, the life that was slowly being squeezed out of her.

Moments later, he stood gaping into her unblinking eyes, her body slumped against his. The sounds of the cars rattling the plates on the highway came from far away, and he could hear the lapping of the water below. In the distance, across the bay, the lights of the Parachute Jump in Coney Island winked red, blue, and green.

What just happened? he thought. A chill took hold of him, like an icy fist, grabbing his heart. *What in God's name just happened?*

He was still holding onto her. Fearfully he looked around, but saw no one. He lifted her, carried her to the rail, and lowered her over the side, hearing the splash as she fell into the bay.

He was shaking, but, incredibly, the pain in his head was diminishing. On wobbly legs, the man began to walk back down the promenade toward Bay Parkway.

He gritted his teeth through the underpass and was just past the park and starting to get himself together, when a new kind of panic hit him. His Hamilton watch was gone.

Was it on the promenade? Should he go back and look? No, too risky, and besides, he probably left it at home. At least he'd better have.

But he had to wait. He couldn't go home yet, not until he was sure his wife was asleep.

His mind in turmoil, the tall, heavyset man kept walking.

CHAPTER TWO

Wednesday Evening, September 26th

Barry shuffled the cards and glanced at the other three men sitting around the kitchen table. "Okay," he said, "which one of you guys is going to pay me the most?"

Everyone at the table laughed, but Eddie, standing behind him, didn't like it when his dad talked that way. He thought he was jinxing himself.

"Hey, wise guy," said Nick DiFazio, sitting opposite Barry, his wide frame shaking the kitchen chair, as well as the gun in its holster hanging from the back of it. "Where'd ya come up with all this false bravado, fella? You feel lucky 'cause the Dodgers won today for a change?"

"They won by ten runs, Nick," Ben Gluck said proudly from the end of the table, pointing a long, thin forefinger at Nick and then using it to push his glasses back up on his beak of a nose. His tone of voice was the same as when he talked about his son Lionel, who was Eddie's best friend and the pitcher on his Little League team. "We're back on the track and rollin'."

"Yeah?" said Nick, "I think the track's goin' off the cliff." He indicated the radio on the counter. "Turn it on. Let's see how the Giants are doin'."

"Uh uh," said Barry. "We don't listen to Giant games here. Next week, when we play at your place, we can listen to anything you want."

Seymour Herschfeld, sitting opposite Ben, spoke up. "Next week is the World Series, ain't it? So we'll be listenin' to the Yankees."

Ben Gluck laughed. "They don't play the World Series at night, ya yutz! Typical Yankee fan."

Seymour Herschfeld shrugged and several pounds of flesh moved in the process. His son Ronald, another friend of Eddie's, wasn't quite as corpulent as his dad, but he was working on it.

"All I know," said Seymour, "is the Yankees won three out of the last four World Series."

"You're right," said Barry. "That's all you know."

Eddie turned toward the sink and was handed a wet plate by his mother. "I never got a chance to look at your report on the Incas," Julia said. "How did it turn out?"

"Great, Mom, I handed it in today."

Actually, he'd wound up copying the first three paragraphs of what the Encyclopedia Britannica had to say on the subject. Maybe Mr. Farnsworth would think "societal mores" was an example of Eddie's unique style of writing. In the meantime, he wasn't going to worry about it, as he piled up the dried plates and, with the aid of a step stool, began stacking them on the upper cabinet shelf.

"I don't know what you Dodger fans got to be so smug about," Nick said, reaching back behind his chair into the pocket of his leather jacket and taking a newspaper out of it. "Now here's the *World Telegram and Sun*, the paper you work for, pal," he said to Barry, as he leafed over to the sports section, "and it says they're ruinin' their pitchers' arms. Here it is; it says, 'Pitching Showdown Puts Dodgers in Peril.' Except it don't exactly say that. It says 'Pitching Show<u>drown</u>.' Now, who was the guy that proofread it, you?"

"Me and several others," said Barry, not taking the bait. "And you wouldn't be able to fool them either."

"Hey, Nick," said Ben Gluck, "are you savin' that paper 'cause you're in it?"

Nick became serious. "That don't matter."

"No, really," said Ben, "pass it over. I couldn't believe this when I saw it."

He took the paper from Nick, turned to page three, and placed it in the middle of the table. Half-way down was the headline "Woman's Body Found On Rocks In Gravesend Bay." Ben pointed to the second paragraph.

"There it is, 'Homicide Detective Nicholas DiFazio.'"

"Is it misspelled?" Barry asked.

"No," said Nick, sounding tired. "Tell the truth, I'm sorry they used my name."

"Sandra Weinstock," said Seymour Herschfeld, looking at the article. "It says she lived with her mother on Bay Parkway and Cropsey, but the name don't sound familiar."

"She worked at Faber's Sporting Goods," said Nick.

Eddie practically fell off the step stool. He recovered just in time to save the plate he was holding.

"It's Sandra, Dad," he said. "Remember her?"

Barry looked at him blankly.

"She was the one who sold us my glove."

One day last spring, at the start of the Little League season, Barry had surprised him as they walked along 86th Street by suddenly suggesting they go into the store. He'd then bought him the Rawlings Pee Wee Reese model Eddie had been pining for all year.

"She was?" said Barry.

"Sure, Dad, don't you remember?"

He seemed to think about it. "I remember buying you the glove, but I can't say as I remember her."

"It says she was strangled," said Ben Gluck, "and that's all the police know. Is that true, Nick? You guys got no clues at all?"

"You're readin' it in the *World Telegram and Sun,* ain't you?" Nick said, folding up the paper and putting it back in his jacket pocket.

"Nick can't talk about police business," Barry explained to Ben, shuffling the deck one last time and passing it over to Seymour for cutting.

"The man speaks the truth," said Nick. "Now let's play poker."

Barry began dealing out two cards down, one card up.

Eddie was still trying to absorb it. Not counting his grandmother, who was very old and who he hardly remembered, this was his first experience of someone dying. She was really nice to him too, not like Mr. Faber, who was always warning him not to touch the merchandise.

She was murdered, he thought. *Somebody strangled her.*

He'd once seen a picture of a woman being strangled in a *Tales from the Crypt* comic book he'd bought and snuck into the house. At the end of the story, she came back to haunt the man who'd done it. Her face, which was beautiful when she was alive, was all bug-eyed and rotting away.

"How're you doing there, kiddo?" his mother asked gently, but it still startled him.

Julia noticed, and wished these men would keep in mind there was a boy in the room. She hoped he wasn't going to have nightmares.

"I can finish the dishes myself, honey. Why don't you go in and see what's on TV?"

Eddie thought she looked especially pretty at that moment. Julia's face, framed by her long, auburn hair, didn't look like a movie star's, but then, how many faces did? None that he knew. Her nose had a little bump in it and her jaw was maybe a touch too pointy, but her eyes were big and brown, and when she smiled she was the most beautiful woman in the world.

"I'm all right, Mom," he said. "I'd rather watch the poker game."

"Yeah, he's okay, Julia," said Nick, putting his cards down and lighting his cigar. Eventually, all four men would be lighting up and the kitchen would turn blue with smoke. Eddie loved the smell as much as his mother hated it. Cigarette smoke was okay with her but not cigar smoke.

"Let him stay and observe," Nick suggested. "He can watch his old man and learn how to be a good loser."

Ben laughed. "I hope he doesn't learn it from the way you coach." Nick coached the Cougars, the P.A.L. Little League team Eddie and his son Lionel played for.

"He has to learn to be a good loser from somebody," Julia said, pointedly looking at Barry.

Barry said nothing, his eyes drilling into his cards. Eddie was afraid they'd start going at it in front of everyone, but the moment passed. He glanced across at Nick, who was frowning as he studied his hand, and wondered if he'd noticed.

Nick had always inspired his awe. Physically, he seemed no bigger or stronger than his dad, but he was somehow much larger.

He'd taught Eddie how to play shortstop, keeping him after practice and hitting grounders at him on the rocky infield. They'd be soft and easy at first, but then they'd get harder and harder, until they were absolutely wicked. But Eddie stuck with it because he wanted to be a good shortstop. Also because he was more scared of telling Nick he was scared than he was of the baseball.

But the thing that scared him the most, more than any bad hop, was running into Nick's son Carmine. He kept a wary eye out for Carmine DiFazio the way midwesterners look out for tornadoes.

Carmine was generally regarded as the toughest kid in the school. He was two years older than Eddie, 30 pounds heavier, and a hundred times more vicious. It was Eddie's mission in life to avoid him. Whenever he couldn't, he'd be in for it one way or another. If he was lucky, it was just insults. Otherwise, it was insults and pain.

Only once had he ever said anything about it to Nick, and the next day Carmine was waiting for him after school. He'd told Eddie, the next time he said anything about him to his father would be the last time he said anything to anybody. Eddie believed him.

The dishes were now finished and Julia, fanning the air to keep the smoke away from her face, retired to the living room and turned on the TV. Eddie could hear the theme music for the Arthur Godfrey Show coming through the door.

Meanwhile, the card game was in full swing. They never played for much, 50 cents to a dollar, but every once in a while things got dramatic, and a week's salary could be on the table.

His dad once told him that the players' styles were as important as the cards. For example, Seymour Herschfeld was a conservative player, folding early a lot of the time. He probably regarded himself as shrewd, not throwing good money after bad, but he was also predictable, which put him at a disadvantage.

Ben Gluck's style was more aggressive, forcing the action. But sometimes his competitiveness got in the way of his reason, and it would cost him. If he was down a few bucks, he'd try to win it all back in one hand, and Barry looked for such opportunities to try and take him for even more.

Eddie attempted to keep all this in mind as he watched over his father's shoulder. When he was younger, he used to walk around the table to get a glimpse at the others' hole cards when they looked at them, but Ben Gluck eventually objected, saying he was giving Barry signals. It wasn't true, but Barry had made him stop.

"So Newk went all the way today for his nineteenth," Ben was now saying, as he shuffled.

"See?" said Nick, "that's what I'm talkin' about. He ain't gonna have an arm left. Why'd they leave him in the game when they had a ten-run lead? It's stupid, right, Eddie?"

Nick always tried to needle him about the Dodgers, but by now, Eddie could handle it.

"It was a twelve-run lead for a while," he said. "But I don't think they were stupid to leave him in. Newk won't get tired; he's a big, strong guy."

"So whataya gonna say then about Preacher Roe?" Nick teased. "He ain't big and strong. He's as skinny as a rail, and old besides."

"Don't use him as an example," Barry interjected. "He's got the best record on the staff. Tell him what it is, Eddie."

"Twenty-two and two."

"And what's his earned run average?"

"Three point oh one."

Ever since his father taught him how to keep score when he was eight years old, he'd been fascinated by baseball statistics. He remembered them the way other people remembered faces or good stories. His mother often said she wished he knew his schoolwork the way he knew baseball statistics.

"Well, his arm's gonna fall off too," Nick warned. He looked once again at the radio sitting on the counter. "Hey, can't we put on the Giant game for two seconds? Just to get a score?"

"Yeah, why don't you do it, Barry?" said Ben. "I'm curious myself."

Barry shrugged. "Flip it on, Sport," he said to Eddie.

Eddie did so, moving the dial from 1050, where it had been set for the Dodger game that afternoon, to 550. The smooth, baritone voice of Ernie Harwell issued forth.

("…in the bottom of the sixth here in Philadelphia, as Larry Jansen once again takes the hill for the Giants.")

Another announcer with a drawl or a twang, Eddie noticed. If he was ever going to become the sportscaster he dreamed of being, he'd have to learn to talk like that. But he'd have to practice in secret. He once tried out his southern accent on Lionel Gluck and was mocked and ridiculed for days.

("Larry had some problems early in the first inning…")

"Problems, problems," sang out Ben.

("…but he was helped out by a sensational catch by Willie Mays…")

"Say hey!" said Nick.

("…and since then, he's been cruising.")

"Maybe the cruise ship is about to sink," Barry suggested, just as Ernie Harwell administered the coup de grace.

("And now, he's got a ten-run lead to work with.")

"Ten-run lead," mused Nick. "Where've I heard that before?"

"Shut it off," said Barry in disgust. Eddie was happy to comply.

"It doesn't matter," said Seymour. "The Yankees are going to win the World Series anyway, no matter who gets in against them."

"Who's their second baseman?" Ben yelled across the table at him.

"It's not important that I know…"

"Who's their second baseman, goddamn it?"

"Whose deal is it?" Barry interrupted.

"It's Jerry Coleman, ya smug, superior know-nothing!" Ben sneered.

"It ain't Jerry Coleman, it's me," Nick said, picking up the deck. "And calm down, Ben, for Chrissake; you're gonna have a coronary. Jeez, Dodger fans."

"Giant fans will have their coronaries in due time," said Barry. "Now, deal the cards."

Eddie watched as his father was dealt two hole cards, but he couldn't see them. Barry hid them in his palm as he flashed a quick peek and then put them down. He was then dealt a six of hearts, the lowest card showing, so it was up to him to open. He pushed two quarters onto the table.

"Raise you," said Ben, who had the king of spades showing. He slid out a dollar. Nick chipped in his own buck, and Seymour frowned at his cards. After a brief pause, he slowly put in his dollar bill.

"A man with nerves of steel," remarked Nick.

The hand progressed, Nick dealing and calling out the possibilities as they appeared. Seymour soon folded. Ben, with a pair of kings now showing, kept raising Nick, who had an ace and queen showing, and who kept raising him back. Eddie figured that if Nick kept raising, he must have at least another ace and maybe a queen hidden. His father, who had picked up a seven of hearts to go with the six, quietly stayed in.

After the fifth card, Barry still showed only the six and seven. Nick had picked up another queen, so he now had a pair of them sitting there along with the ace. If he really did have another queen and ace in the hole, Eddie thought, he'd have a full house. Quite a pile of money was accumulating on the table.

Ben gritted his teeth and peeked at his hole cards yet again. His two kings had not gotten any better, but they were still the best of the cards showing. Was Nick bluffing, with only the pair of queens? And why the hell was Barry still hanging around? He finally decided to put in, and Nick immediately raised him and Barry raised him again.

"That's it for me," he said disgustedly.

"Looks like there ain't no one here but us chickens, huh?" Nick said slyly. "Who's gonna be the bigger one?"

He dealt Barry his sixth card, the five of hearts, giving him the five, six, and seven.

"I've never seen a straight flush," Seymour observed.

"And you won't see one tonight," said Nick, as he dealt himself a seemingly innocuous nine of clubs. "Right, Barry?"

"In or out?" Barry's face and voice betrayed nothing.

"I ain't goin' nowhere," Nick said affably, adding to the pile.

"Raise you," said Barry.

"See you," said Nick, grinning at him, "in your dreams."

He slid out some more money from his dwindling holdings, picked up the deck, and dealt the seventh card, down. Barry again hid it from Eddie as he glanced at it.

"Dad," Eddie complained.

"Sssh," said Barry.

"Whatsa matter?" said Nick. "You're afraid if he sees what you got, he'll tip your bluff?"

Barry slid five dollars more into the pile and looked at Nick invitingly.

Nick wasn't worried about a straight flush. Just a plain old flush would beat what he had, which was two measly queens (he was a pretty good bluffer himself). He did some quick figuring. With Ben and Seymour folding, a total of 23 cards had been dealt. There had been one heart showing in Ben's hand, none in Seymour's, and he had only one in his own hand. So, along with Barry's three, that made five hearts he knew about, with eight unaccounted for. What were the odds of two of them turning up among Barry's three hidden cards? Whatever they were, he decided, he didn't like them.

"Forget it," he said, throwing in his cards.

Eddie let out a whoop, as Barry quickly combined his cards with the others and then reached out to haul in the pot.

"Dad, were you really bluffing?" he asked him.

"That's between me and God," Barry said, smiling.

"I thought you didn't believe in God," said Ben.

"Then it's between me and me."

Barry scooped up the bills and coins as the living room door opened and, to the sounds of Break the Bank with Bert Parks in the background, Julia came into the kitchen.

As Barry continued to rake in the take, Nick noticed something.

"Is that a new watch?" he asked.

There was a barely perceptible pause in Barry's arm movement as he hauled in the last of the money.

"It is, as a matter of fact," he said, a little sheepishly. "I stupidly left my old one in the men's room at work today, and by the time I realized it, somebody swiped it. So I got this new one during lunch hour."

"Hmm, that's too bad," said Nick. "The watch you had before was a real nice one, wasn't it?"

"Yes, it was," said Barry. "And speaking of time, it's after ten o'clock, Eddie, and you've got school tomorrow. Time for bed, Sport."

"Aww." This was Eddie's instinctive reaction to any reference to school or bed. "Can't I watch the end of the poker game?"

"You just did, as far as I'm concerned," said Ben, gathering up what was left of his money. "I've got work tomorrow." He glanced at Seymour accusingly. "When is your wife gonna let you out on weekends again, so we can switch back to Fridays and have a real game?"

Seymour shrugged.

Nick continued to regard Barry, who seemed preoccupied with clearing the ashtrays. Finally, he stood up and started to put on his shoulder holster.

"Help your old man count his dough, Eddie, but don't let him spend it. It's really mine, and he's gonna give it back to me."

Julia frowned at the overflowing garbage pail.

"I see Nate Preston forgot to collect the garbage again."

Their superintendant and his family lived in the basement apartment of the building, one of the older ones in the neighborhood. It used a dumbwaiter system for its garbage collection. Every evening, sometime after dinner, Nate Preston would send up the cart, buzzing each apartment in turn, and the tenants would put their bags of trash on it. Occasionally, for one reason or another, he missed a night, and this was one of them.

"I'll have to take it downstairs," she said resignedly.

"Leave it; I'll do it," said Barry.

"No, I'd rather you and Eddie stay here and finish cleaning up. The less time I spend in all this smoke, the better."

"Hey, Dad, tonight's your night to clean up, huh?" Eddie joked, looking at the pile.

"Heh, heh," Barry said weakly.

***

Out in the hall, Nick relieved Julia of the two bags of garbage as they started down the stairs. They all reached the lobby, and he told the others to go on ahead and he'd catch up with them. He and Julia continued on down to the basement.

"I got it," he said, opening the basement door for her with one hand while holding the soggy paper bags away from his clothing with the other.

"Thanks, Nick, this is very kind of you." She gave him a smile. "But I didn't think I'd need an armed guard to help me take out the garbage."

He shrugged. "You never can tell; there could be rats down here."

"If we see one, are you going to shoot it?"

"Nah, I'll just scare it away with my face."

They entered the dimly lit basement.

"I wanted to talk to ya anyway," he said. "How's he doin'?"

She knew he meant Barry, not Eddie. "He seemed okay tonight," she said. "I guess life would be beautiful if the Dodgers won every day and he always did well at poker. But I don't know, Nick. He drinks a whole lot more than he used to, and he gets so angry. You should've seen him last night, before he stomped out of here."

"Yeah?" Nick carefully kept his voice matter-of-fact. "He went out last night?"

"It started with the stupid Dodgers. They fell behind by a lot of runs, and he couldn't stand it. He actually threw a beer bottle across the room. Thank God Eddie wasn't hit by the flying glass. Then we sort of had words and he walked out."

Nick could imagine them "sort of" having words. Seeing their marriage wear down like this made him feel sad, and helpless. He dropped the bags into one of the large cans that were lined up against the wall.

"How did he seem after he got back?"

"I don't know; I was asleep by then. I tell you, since he came home from the war it's just getting worse and worse."

Nick held the door open for her, and they began to climb the stairs back to the lobby.

"The war was rough on a lot of guys," he said.

"You don't seem to have problems, and you were right there with him. He couldn't have gone through worse than you did."

"Some people react different than others."

Julia stopped at the head of the stairs.

"And some people just become different altogether," she said. "Barry wasn't the same man when he came back from that war; you can't deny it. He was always easygoing, not brooding and secretive like he is now. He was going to be a top reporter, like his dad. But here he is, working as a proofreader and not wanting to be any more than that. What's wrong with him, Nick? You probably know him better than I do."

Probably better than I want to, he couldn't help thinking.

"Maybe he needs professional help, like from the V.A. or somethin'. I know it sounds like I'm passin' the buck, but I'm only a cop, not a psychiatrist. I love the guy, but I don't know what to do neither."

They passed in silence through the lobby, until they came to the front door of the building. Nick paused with his hand on the knob.

"Oh, I wanted to ask ya," he said. "Teresa's always after me to tell her things I want for Christmas and stuff, 'cause she never knows what to get me. I always liked Barry's watch, and I was gonna tell her to buy me the same one, but now he lost it. Do you know what kind it was?"

To his surprise, he saw tears well up in her eyes.

"I certainly do," she said. "It was a beautiful watch. I got it for him for our anniversary, the first one after he came home."

Then she uttered the very words he didn't want to hear.

"It was a Hamilton."

CHAPTER THREE

Thursday Morning, September 27th

Teresa DiFazio clattered noisily about her kitchen, setting the cereal bowls and silverware on the table as loudly as she could, as a message to her son in his room, who should have been dressed and ready for breakfast but who never was.

"Carmine!" she yelled. "You're gonna be late for school. What are you doin' in there?"

Her 13-year-old daughter Mary sat at the table and winced each time her mother slammed down another utensil. It didn't help that she'd practically screamed in her ear just now, and Teresa had a voice that could shatter glass. Mary was the one who was ready for breakfast on time, so she was the one who was suffering. Wasn't that always the way in this family?

"I know what he's doing in there," she said, glancing up at Teresa with a salacious look.

"You better watch your mouth," she was warned.

"What did I say?" Her eyes opened wide in offended innocence.

Nick, in shirtsleeves, came into the kitchen adjusting his tie.

"Listen to your mother," he said automatically. He had no idea what it was about, and, in truth, preferred to remain ignorant.

"Why does she always pick on me?" Mary whined.

"'Cause you're the chosen one."

He leaned over and gave her a kiss on the cheek, from which she pulled away. Mary didn't mind her father kissing her, but she wasn't going to give up a good pout this easily.

Nick and Teresa exchanged a peck on the lips.

"Mornin', babe," he said, noticing that her roots were beginning to show again. He liked his wife as a blonde, but wished she'd be more attentive to it sometimes.

"You need to get more sleep," she said, feeling her own tiredness. Whenever Nick had a restless night, so did she, from all his thrashing about.

Once, early in their marriage, she'd gotten up and tried to move to the couch, but he wouldn't hear of it. *A typical Italian man,* she'd thought. If a woman left his bed, it was an insult to his virility. Not that she'd ever slept with any man but Nick, Italian or otherwise, but she'd heard stories.

She gave an exasperated look in the direction of Carmine's room.

"Would you go in there, please, and tell your son to get a move on? His oatmeal is getting cold."

"Oatmeal, ick," Mary muttered. "Why do we always have oatmeal? I hate it."

Nick and Teresa ignored her.

"Carmine," he shouted, "get in here!"

"Just a minute," came a muffled voice through the wall.

"No, now!" Nick barked. "Don't give me that 'just a minute' crap."

"Awright, awright."

After a few moments, they heard Carmine's door slam as he stepped into the hall. He slouched around the corner, slunk into the kitchen, and sat down sullenly at the table.

Carmine was 14, but could have been taken for 16 at least. His arms had become muscular this year, with the help of weights he kept in his room, and his facial hair was coming in almost to the point where he'd be ready to shave.

It was all ruined, of course, by the acne that raged over his cheeks and forehead. He'd beaten up a kid the other day because he'd been told the kid called him pizza face. He didn't know if it was true or not and didn't care. The main thing was, it gave him an excuse to work out on somebody.

His hair was combed neatly now, parted on the side, but as soon as he left the house he would immediately re-comb it into an upswept pompadour with a "duck's ass" in the back. He would also re-tie his tie, which was currently arranged in the standard fashion, into a gigantic Windsor knot as big as a fist, with only two inches of material hanging from it. The top three buttons of his shirt would be undone, and his sleeves would be rolled up past his biceps.

"What did I tell you about slamming that door?" Teresa said to him.

"I dunno," he mumbled.

"I dunno? What's that supposed to mean?" She put down a bowl of oatmeal in front of him.

"I dunno," he repeated, adding a shrug this time.

"Don't you get smart with your mother," Nick barked at him.

"If he doesn't know, then how can he be smart?" Mary giggled.

"Shut up," Carmine said to her, which made her giggle more.

"Shut up the both'a yez!" Nick said, disgusted.

He didn't know exactly when he'd lost control of his kids, but he most definitely had. His son had always been a problem, to put it mildly, but now it was both of them. Teresa said it was just because they were teenagers, but that was no answer. It only put a name to what he couldn't understand.

"Shut up and eat," he told them. "I don't wanna hear another word at this table."

They like that, he thought. *It gives them an excuse not to talk to anybody.*

He watched for a moment as they resentfully picked at their bowls of cereal, fidgeting in their chairs, their faces set in matching expressions of defiance. He'd interrogated murderers who looked like that.

Which made him think again that maybe he was going off the deep end about Barry. The investigation was only a day old, and who knew what they were going to find? For all they could tell, Sandra Weinstock had any number of bitter ex-boyfriends lurking around in her life.

It had all the earmarks of that type of crime. She'd been carrying no money, not even a handbag, and hadn't been sexually assaulted. Usually, it's some poor slob whose lovesickness had turned lethal.

But he couldn't get over the strong feeling of déjà vu he'd had when he first saw how she was killed. And that watch, that fucking watch. Why couldn't Julia have said he lost a Benrus, or a Bulova?

"Were you thinkin' about the case last night, honey?" Teresa asked, interrupting his thoughts. "Is that why you couldn't sleep?"

"Huh?" He looked up at her, and then noticed that the kids had paused in their oatmeal ordeal and were staring at him.

"You got a new case, Dad?" Mary asked with sudden interest. "Somebody got murdered?"

"Anyone we know?" asked Carmine hopefully.

"Jesus Christ!" he exploded. "Whadaya think this is, some sort'a game? What kind'a human beings are you growin' into?"

He looked at the clock.

"It's twenty after eight already; you got school. Now get your books and get outta here."

They hesitated, then groaned and pushed their chairs away from the table. A minute ago, neither of them had wanted to be there. Now, they were being kicked out just when it was getting good.

Nick and Teresa sipped their coffee and listened to them banging around in their rooms, getting their things together. Finally, they heard them at the front door, Carmine mumbling something and Mary saying, "Why, so you can jerk off?" and then going "Ow!"

"Leave your sister alone!" they hollered simultaneously. The door closed and there was silence.

"Where does she learn about things like that?" Teresa wondered.

Nick didn't answer because he couldn't. They finished their coffee and she began taking the dishes off the table.

"So, what's the story? You gonna keep me awake every night this week? Most of them don't get to you like this, so it must be a bad one."

He shrugged. "It shouldn't be, but I might have extra problems here."

It always felt kind of funny talking about cases with Teresa, but sometimes it helped. Speaking his thoughts out loud tended to clarify them, and there were things he could say to her that were harder to say to his partner. There were several aspects of this case that were like that.

No, he thought, just one aspect, but it was a beaut.

"I don't want this to go no further, you understand me?"

She nodded. "It never does, Nick, you know that. When have I ever...?"

"Yeah, yeah," he interrupted. "It's just that this time it's especially important. I got a feelin' about who might'a done it, and I hope to hell I'm wrong."

She waited for him to go on. He chewed his lower lip.

"How'm I gonna explain this? There are certain things I know about Barry…"

"Barry?" she said in amazement. It just came out of her. "You're tellin' me you think it was Barry?"

"Would you keep it down?"

He gave a nervous glance out the window toward the Feins' apartment. The DiFazios lived on Bay 29th Street, a block away from Bay Parkway, but the rear of their building was lined up directly with the rear of the Feins' building, and their two apartments faced each other as if across a narrow courtyard.

Teresa had a voice that tended to carry, and Nick was always aware of how strident she could get.

"Let's just say I know certain things about him and leave it at that, okay?" he said. "Anyway, I found out he got real mad Tuesday night and walked outta the house right around the time of the murder. This wouldn't'a meant nothin', except I noticed he happened to lose a particular item. He claims he lost it yesterday mornin', but there was somethin' funny about the way he said it. I think he may be lyin'.

"I think he might'a lost it Tuesday night, and in a very bad place. And the problem is, we found it."

This wasn't working. Telling her the whole story was out of the question, and not telling her didn't work either.

She waited, then realized he was finished. Neither of them spoke for a moment.

She'd always been curious about Barry. As much as she loved Nick's earthiness and how open he was about his feelings, she had a secret fascination about strong, silent types. There was something unknowable about people like that, and it made them all the more interesting. But to think of Barry as a murderer…

"Jeez, Nick," she said, "he's your best friend."

"More than that," he said grimly. "I owe my life to the guy."

***

Crouching in his bedroom closet, Carmine suddenly glanced up from the deck of pornographic playing cards he'd been looking at by the beam of light that came through the partially opened door. He'd taken it off a kid at school the day before and hastily threw it in the closet this morning when his old man had called him for breakfast.

He'd forgotten about it until just before he and his bratty sister were out the door, so he'd snuck back into his room to get it. He wanted to bring it to school to show his friends.

No, forget that. They were his flunkies, not his friends. He had no friends.

He'd been thinking about whacking off while he waited for his old man to leave and his old lady to start doing the dishes so he could sneak out, when he'd heard her say, "Barry? You're tellin' me you think it was Barry?"

It had immediately put his libido on the back burner.

He'd crawled deeper into the closet and put his ear closer to the wall that separated it from the kitchen. He'd been eavesdropping like this ever since he was little and discovered how the sound could travel through the wall and be amplified by the acoustics of his closet.

What he was hearing now thrilled him even more than the pictures in the "French deck" would have. He was almost getting hard from it. This was gonna be great.

He couldn't wait to get a hold of that little piss ant Eddie Fein and deliver the bad news personally. And you can bet he was going to deliver it in a very special way. Oh yeah.

CHAPTER FOUR

Thursday Afternoon, September 27th

Preacher Roe, one of the worst-hitting pitchers in baseball, stood at the plate with two down in the top of the sixth and the game tied at two apiece. He waggled his bat and squinted out through the bright Boston sunshine at Braves rookie pitcher Chet Nichols, as Gil Hodges, the potential go-ahead run, took a cautious lead off second. Preach was a lousy hitter, but he was a pretty good bunter, and he'd helped himself in the fourth inning by bunting in a run on a squeeze play, Duke Snider streaking in from third. But this was not a bunt situation. Now, he needed to come up with something extremely rare for him, a base hit.

Nichols checked the runner and delivered. It was a sharply breaking curve that fooled Preach, but his bat somehow made contact and he hit a chopper back to the mound. The ball barely eluded Nichols, whose follow-through had left him out of position, and bounced once, twice, three times up the middle of the diamond just past the diving attempts of Sisti and Kerr, the second baseman and shortstop, and on into center field. Hodges, in full gallop, scored easily, putting the Dodgers up 3-2.

Preach stood at first base and allowed himself a grin. Maybe things were starting to go right.

***

Things were going far from right for Eddie, as he sat in his social studies class and read what Mr. Farnsworth had written on his Inca report: "Encyclopedia Britannica: A+, Edward Fein: F. See me after class."

At the blackboard, Mr. Farnsworth was droning about the conquistadors, while Eddie forced himself to breathe slowly and evenly, trying to untie the knot in his stomach. He was pretty sure he'd have to have one of his parents sign this handwritten testament to his laziness and shame. His dad figured to be the easier one, but not if he was in a bad mood. All the more reason to worry about the Dodgers this afternoon.

His thoughts were interrupted by the sensation of his seat moving beneath him. All the desks in the classroom had seats that folded up when you stood, and now, his was doing it by itself, against his will and against his buttocks, slowly standing him up.

He forced it back down with his arms and flashed a glare back at Lionel Gluck, who was sitting behind him and looking at Mr. Farnsworth in seemingly deep concentration.

"Cut it out," Eddie hissed.

"Edward," said Mr. Farnsworth, as Eddie's stomach snapped to attention.

Mr. Farnsworth was wearing his tweed sports jacket with leather elbow patches today. He fancied it made him look collegiate, something he would have preferred his career to be, rather than stuck here in a public school teaching the children of Philistines.

"You should pay less attention to your friend Lionel there, and more to Francisco Pizarro. Maybe you can tell us what he did in 1533 against Atahualpa."

"Went three for five," Lionel whispered, as Eddie ignored him.

"He went to war?" Eddie guessed.

Mr. Farnsworth considered it.

"I guess you could put it that way. But how did he go about doing it?"

"By attacking his fast ball and laying off his curve."

Lionel's lips barely moved, and only Eddie could hear him. For all intents and purposes, Lionel was looking straight at Mr. Farnsworth with an expression of intelligent interest.

Eddie had no idea of what to say.

"He went to war against him…with his soldiers?"

The whole class cracked up laughing. Mr. Farnsworth allowed it to play out, waiting until it had died down.

"I think we can assume he used soldiers, Edward, rather than telling Atahualpa's mother on him." This got some tittering from the class.

"What I want to know is how it took place? What exactly did he do?"

Eddie, of course, had no idea, but he did know that Mr. Farnsworth would bleed this moment for everything he could. Finally, with one last look of condescending disappointment, Mr. Farnsworth turned his attention away.

"Can anyone tell me?" he asked.

Ronald Herschfeld's pudgy hand immediately shot up.

"He invited Atahualpa to a peace conference, and Atahualpa only brought a few guards with him 'cause he thought he was a god, and invincible. Then Pizarro's soldiers killed the guards and took him prisoner."

"Very good, Ronald."

"Very good, Ronald," parroted Lionel into Eddie's ear. "Fucking teacher's pet Yankee fan. He should yank my doodle, it's a dandy."

The bell rang. Instantly, there was a flurry of desks opening and books being shoved into briefcases. For the previous ten minutes, the rest of the school had been going from their final classes to their home rooms and getting ready to leave. But since Mr. Farnsworth was both their social studies teacher and their home room teacher, they alone had the privilege of ten extra minutes of social studies.

"Do it quietly," said Mr. Farnsworth. "If you keep acting like Pavlov's dogs every time the bell rings, I'll have you write a report about him."

"What do you think?" said Lionel. "It's probably around the seventh inning. Preach is going for his twenty-third."

"I have to stay after school and talk to Fartsworth," Eddie said, using the name they always called him. "It's about my Inca report."

Lionel reached his arms into his desk, pulled out a bunch of books, and shoveled them hurriedly into his briefcase.

"Whoo, boy! I'm glad I decided not to copy mine from you."

"Who gave you the choice? And what idiot would let you copy his report anyway?"

"An idiot like Moronic Ronald the Yankee Wank," he said smiling smugly, "in exchange for two stupid Joe DiMaggio cards you could find in half the bubble gum packs in the stores. He gave me his report and I just added my own charming style to it. Fartsbreath didn't even know the difference."

Lionel was tall and lanky with large hands, the perfect tools of a dominant 12-year-old Little League pitcher, which he was.

"So I guess it's tough titties for you. I'd love to wait around and hear the gory details, but I've gotta get home and hear the gory details of the Dodgers slaughtering the Braves. Good luck, and don't let him get you under the desk."

He gave Eddie a wicked grin, lifted his briefcase, and took his place in the line that was forming to be escorted by Mr. Farnsworth to the stairwell.

Eddie stayed in his seat, conspicuous to all, as they filed out.

When they'd gone, he got up and paced the aisles of the empty room, idly slapping the desks, wishing he could get home to the game like Lionel was doing. If this didn't take too long, he still had time to catch the last couple of innings. Preacher Roe against a rookie, so the chances were good.

They could really put the Giants away if they won today and tomorrow. The Giants weren't playing until Saturday and the Dodgers could clinch at least a tie before the Giants even took the field. But before any of that could happen, Mr. Farnsworth had to happen.

When he returned, Mr. Farnsworth was in no particular hurry. He told Eddie to wait a minute, as he sat down and began reading a general notice from the principal that he hadn't had a chance to look at earlier. This had been a hell of a day. The kids were especially edgy and restless, refusing to pay attention, and chattering incessantly about the Sandra Weinstock murder. They reminded him of sharks smelling blood in the water.

The whole school seemed to be talking about it, even though most people didn't even know her. It made him sad. There were so many more important things in the world for them to be concerned about, like the war in Korea. Why didn't we just use the A-bomb and get it over with? But don't get him started. He looked up from his desk at Eddie.

"Your mother teaches school, if I'm not mistaken. Is that true?"

Eddie was familiar with this tack. Every teacher he'd ever had, once they'd found out Julia taught fourth grade at a school in Greenpoint, insisted on throwing it in his face.

"Why are teachers' children always the worst students?" they wanted to know. First of all, he wasn't the worst student. And second of all, why ask him? They were the teachers.

"Yes, she does," he answered.

"I met her on Open School Night, and she seemed like a very nice lady. Doesn't she help you with your schoolwork?"

Eddie could hear Julia in his head. *Oh yes*, she would say in answer to that question, *every chance I get. Just as soon as I come home from my hour-and-a-half subway ride from the other end of Brooklyn, make dinner for Eddie and his father, who has a job that pays next to nothing, which is why we don't have a car and I'm still teaching, since somebody in this family has to earn a living; and then clean up the dishes, do my lesson plans, and fall into bed.*

"Sure, she helps me," he said.

"Well, maybe she should help you more often."

He took the report from Eddie's hand, turned to the end, and began writing something at the bottom of the page.

"This is a note to your mother, asking her to sign this disgrace of a report. I'd also like you to look up the word 'plagiarism' in the dictionary." He wrote the word in large letters at the top of the page.

"Write out the definition and bring it in, along with your mother's signature, tomorrow. Then, over the weekend, you'll write the report on the Incas that you were supposed to have written."

"Okay," Eddie murmured.

Lionel had the right idea, of course. Instead of just copying it from the encyclopedia, he should have added his own "charming style" to it, even if he didn't understand half of what he was writing.

But actually, now that he was thinking about it, there was something he did understand.

"Pizarro was wrong, wasn't he?" he asked.

"Excuse me?"

"He lied to Atahualpa about that peace conference, and then his men wound up killing all the Incas and stealing their country from them. He didn't have the right to do that, did he? It was their country."

Mr. Farnsworth looked at him with the sort of interest a scientist might give a new strain of virus.

"Stole their country? Where did you get that idea?" His eyes narrowed. "Are your parents Communists?"

"What?"

Mr. Farnsworth studied him at length.

"On second thought, she shouldn't help you with your schoolwork, not if that's her influence. And the report you're writing had better not say anything like the Marxist propaganda you've just spouted at me. You may go now; you're dismissed."

Eddie was confused, but thought he saw an opportunity. At least it was worth a try.

"If you don't want her to help me, do you still want her to sign this report?"

"As far as I'm concerned," Mr. Farnsworth said distractedly, beginning to reread the principal's notice, "if that's the sort of help she provides, you can wallow in your ignorance."

Good enough.

"Thanks, I'll do that. So long, Mr. Fartsworth," he said, slurring the last part.

He grabbed his briefcase and got out of there.

* * *

"So, where is he?"

Vito Peccarino idly cleaned his fingernails with the point of his switchblade as he crouched behind the bushes next to Frankie Fontana and Carmine DiFazio. They were diagonally across 21st Avenue from Bensonhurst Junior High School, ideally situated to take Eddie down whether he chose to walk along 84th Street toward Bay Parkway or along 21st Avenue toward 85th Street.

"We been watchin' the whole fuckin' school go by," Vito complained, giving Carmine a look of belligerence.

"Keep your pants on, and put the fuckin' knife away," Carmine said, peering intently through the bushes. Where was the little prick, anyhow? He knew he was in school today because he'd seen him earlier.

Squatting next to Carmine, Frankie fidgeted, his right leg moving nervously back and forth, occasionally touching Carmine's and practically driving him berserk each time. Finally, Carmine gave him a good, hard elbow to the ribs.

"Whatsa matta wit' you?" he demanded. "You gotta go to the bat'room or somethin'?"

"No, no," Frankie protested, clutching his side. "Why? What'd I do?"

"You were rubbin' your leg against me like a friggin' dog in heat, that's what," Carmine informed him. "You wanna get fucked like a dog?"

"No, no," Frankie protested again, moving over slightly and putting some distance between them. "Jeez."

Carmine turned around and projectile-spat a large piece of phlegm against the brick wall of the apartment building behind them, where it clung nicely. He certainly didn't need these bozos with him to take care of a little pipsqueak like Eddie. He just preferred to have an audience, that's all, but if they kept getting on his nerves he was gonna tell them to piss off.

One thing had worked out, at least. He knew who his old man had been talking about this morning, because it was all over the school. He thought he remembered her, that prissy little bitch who worked at the sporting goods store, but the only thing that bothered him was the fact that Vito and Frankie had known about it before he had. Who would've thought that by being late for school, he'd actually miss something?

But he still knew more than they did, and it comforted him as he waited for that little asshole to show himself. Whoops, there he was.

Eddie was crossing 21st Avenue, lost in thought about telling his mother Mr. Farnsworth had actually loved his report. In fact, he could truthfully say it had gotten an A+, and now he was doing another one for extra credit. It was amazing how things worked out sometimes, and maybe they were working out right now for the Dodgers.

He began to walk faster as he got to the sidewalk, turned right, and was heading toward 85th Street, when a pair of hands reached out from the bushes and grabbed him.

"Join the bush club!" Carmine said with a smirk, yanking him through the shrubbery to the accompaniment of snickers from Vito and Frankie.

He pulled Eddie down to the ground and planted a knee firmly on his chest.

"How're ya doin', ya little shrimp?" he asked, leering at him. "Are you Fein?"

This got another laugh from his stooges.

Eddie couldn't believe his own stupidity. He always made sure to walk on the outer part of the sidewalk near the curb, away from bushes and alleyways, but he didn't this time because he was feeling good. Which was dumb of him.

"I got news for ya," Carmine said, "and you're gonna be real innerested in knowin' what it is. But first we're gonna have us a little Show and Tell. Ya like Show and Tell?"

He didn't like the question. Were they gonna make him take down his pants, or something? A bead of sweat trickled down his neck.

"I don't know," he said.

"Ya don't know? Hey, this guy don't even know what he likes." Carmine laughed. "How're ya supposed ta get whatcha want if ya don't know what it is?"

He laughed again and gave Eddie two playful slaps, forehand and backhand, across the face, just hard enough to hurt a little.

"I'll show ya whatcha want since ya don't know," Carmine went on. "This is the 'Show' part of Show and Tell. Whatcha really want is to see the nice present Vito's got for ya."

"Hey, I don't got no…"

"Shaddup and show it to him."

"Carmine, what…?"

Why do I hang around with these morons? he thought.

"The fuckin' thing you got in your pocket. Capeesh?"

"Oh yeah," Vito said slowly, recognition dawning. He reached into his pocket and pulled out the closed switchblade.

"Ain't it nice?" he asked, kneeling down near Eddie's face and grinning at him with yellowed teeth. "Ya want me ta give it to ya?"

"No," Eddie said softly, trying not to panic. This was something new. They'd done some bad stuff to him, but never with a knife.

"No?" said Vito, leaning in closer.

Vito Peccarino was a small kid for his age, just slightly bigger than Eddie even though he was two years older. But what he lacked in stature he more than made up for in crazy. "Mad Dog Peccarino" was what the other kids called him, and he was actually proud of it.

What he wouldn't have been proud of, had he known, was the other nickname Carmine and the rest had for him: "Pecker."

"Ain't you got no manners?" he asked, the smell of garlic and mozzarella cheese on his breath making Eddie almost gag. "When ya refuse a gift you're suppos'ta say 'No, thank you.'"

"Besides," said Carmine, "here ya are turnin' it down and ya didn't even see it opened yet. G'head, Vito, open Eddie's present."

Vito flicked his wrist and the knife snapped open, the point narrowly missing Eddie's left eye as he jerked his head away from it.

Frankie Fontana, anxious not to miss any of the action, leaned in over Carmine's other shoulder to put his two cents in.

"How d'ya like it, fag?" he started to say, but only got as far as "how d'ya…" before Carmine, annoyed at his proximity, sent a forearm into his nose.

"Ow! Shit!" he cried, stumbling backwards as his eyes teared up.

Carmine paid him no attention, enjoying the frightened look on Eddie's face.

He'd hated Eddie Fein for as long as he could remember. The snooty way him and his parents talked, with no Brooklyn accents like regular people. It was like they were smarter than everybody.

But what *really* started him hating Eddie happened two years ago, the day Carmine played his final Little League game.

Nick was there. He wasn't Carmine's coach because they didn't let fathers coach the teams their sons played on, but he was standing on the sideline anyway, watching the game with the little squirts he did coach, waiting for their turn to use the field.

It was the bottom of the seventh, the last inning in Little League games. The score was tied, and the other team had the potential winning run on second. Carmine, standing at his shortstop position, was unaware of the score or the situation.

And so what if he was? There was no scoreboard on that dinky field, and there were a lot of runs scored in the game. How was he supposed to know?

And he wasn't the only one; the right fielder didn't know either. The batter for the other team hit a line drive into the gap in right-center and it rolled all the way to the fence, easily allowing the winning run to score. The right fielder ran it down anyway and then threw it in to Carmine, who was covering second, even though the game was over.

Carmine turned to see the runner coming up on him with a stupid grin on his face, slowing down and not sliding. So he did what he was supposed to do; he tagged him. So what if it was hard? So what if it was in the stomach?

The kid was a fuckin' baby anyway. He doubled over, fell down, and started crying.

The other team was celebrating at home plate and didn't see it, but Nick did. He charged across the field and grabbed Carmine before he could even think, slapping him in the face, cursing him, taking him by the neck, and marching him over to the sideline, where he told the coach he was pulling him off the team.

Standing there, getting a great big kick out of it, at least as Carmine saw it, was that little prick, his old man's "Teach a Scrawny Loser How to Play Shortstop While His Own Son Can Go Fuck Himself" project, Eddie Fein.

Not that he would want to learn anything from his old man anyway, but that didn't matter. Only Eddie Fein mattered.

Eddie Fein, the biggest smartass Dodger fan in a whole neighborhood full of 'em. Carmine distinctly remembered standing at recess one day last spring, with the Dodgers in first place and his Giants in last, and hearing that fuckin' voice coming from all the way across the yard. Well, things were changing.

"We're gonna turn you into a Giant fan," he announced. "Whatta ya think'a that? Maybe we'll even carve an 'NY' on your ugly face."

"Yeah, yeah, let's do it," Vito giggled, and Carmine realized he'd just made a mistake. All he wanted was to have a little fun before he delivered the message. The last thing he wanted was to give this lunatic next to him bright ideas.

"Take it easy," he said, throwing a sharp warning glance at Vito, who took note of it and looked away.

It was no comfort to Eddie. He was getting more and more scared by the minute.

"We're gonna see how much of a Giant fan you can be," Carmine said. "This is the 'Tell' part of Show and Tell. You're gonna tell us about the greatest team in baseball, which is who?"

He had to give it at least one try or he could never look at himself in the mirror.

"The Dodgers," he said resolutely.

Carmine slapped him, hard this time.

"Wrong," he said. "Ain't you the one who's supposed to know all about baseball? Who's leadin' the league in RBI's?"

"Monte Irvin," Eddie muttered.

"And what team is he on?"

"The second-place team."

He got another slap, to the delight of Vito and Frankie, who'd, by now, absorbed his rebuke and was back to enjoying Carmine's performance in his usual servile way.

"Gimme the *name*, asshole," Carmine said, emphasizing "asshole" with another backhand.

"The Giants," Eddie sputtered.

"Right, and who leads the league in doubles?"

"Alvin Dark."

"And what team is he on?"

"Shit, the Giants. All right?"

That earned him another slap.

"Watch your language, fuckbrain," said Carmine, getting howls of laughter from the other two.

"Who's the best pitcher in the National League, and you better not say Don Newcombe or Preacher Roe, or I'm gonna let Vito here shove his knife up your ass."

For a brief moment of resistance, Eddie was tempted to say Warren Spahn of the Braves or Robin Roberts of the Phillies, but he said nothing, rather than give the answer Carmine expected.

"I'm waitin'," he said ominously.

Eddie remained silent.

"Ya want a hint? Gimme the knife, Vito."

"Aww…"

"Gimme the fuckin' knife."

Vito reluctantly handed it over, as panic rose within Eddie, but all Carmine did was to place the flat side of the blade against his face. Then he ran it down his cheek, like a straight razor.

"What's this remind you of, you little scumbag? I know you know the answer."

Eddie knew only too well, as he'd known the moment Carmine had asked the question. It was the name of the one Giant pitcher who could strike terror into the hearts of even the greatest Dodger hitters just by taking the mound. He was the man with the perpetual scowl, who never shaved on the day he was pitching because it made him look that much meaner. But, of course, he had more than just a mean look. He had a mean curve, a huge rainbow that started right at your head and broke a foot-and-a half over the plate. It would freeze right-handed hitters because, in that split second, they couldn't tell it from the fast ball. And the fast ball was devastating. It would explode at them, whipping by under their chins as they flinched away, another close shave from the man known as "The Barber."

"You know who I'm talkin' about," Carmine snarled. "Say it."

This is all bullshit anyhow, Eddie decided. *I'll just play his stupid game and then maybe he'll let me go.*

"Sal Maglie," he mumbled.

"I couldn't hear you. Who's the greatest pitcher?"

"Sal Maglie," Eddie said louder.

"That's right," said Carmine, "Sal Maglie. And he's Italian, like me." His omission of Vito and Frankie was, of course, intentional.

"The greatest pitcher in baseball, and his name is Salvatore…" He gave Eddie three light slaps, in rhythm with the three syllables. "…The Barber…" slap, slap, slap "…Maglie!" he shouted triumphantly, punctuating it with the two hardest ones yet.

Where are all the adults when you need them? Eddie wondered desperately, as his face stung. Why doesn't someone walk by? They were right next to a building; doesn't anybody look out their windows?

Meanwhile, Carmine was deciding that, as far as his two idiots were concerned, the show was over and it was time to get rid of them.

"Vito," he said, turning toward him and shifting his weight on Eddie's chest in the process, making him grunt, "take Frankie and go over to Al's Soda Fountain. Bring me back an egg cream."

"What!?" Vito couldn't believe his ears. "Whatta ya want an egg cream for?"

"To pour down your fuckin' pants; why d'ya think I want an egg cream? 'Cause I'm thirsty, that's why. Just lay out the money; I'll pay ya back. Take Frankie and do what I said."

"Why do I gotta go?" Frankie whined.

"'Cause you'd rather be pickin' up an egg cream for me than pickin' up your teeth."

Vito hesitated.

"What about my knife?" He looked at it longingly.

"It'll still be here. I can't guarantee ya that it'll be clean, though," he added for Eddie's benefit. "G'head."

After a moment of indecision, the two of them slowly stood up and started to push their way through the bushes out onto the street.

"Hold it!" Carmine commanded. "Go around to the end so it'll look like you're comin' outta the buildin'. Jeez, I gotta tell you everything?"

They did as they were told, turning and looking over their shoulders one last time before disappearing around the hedge.

Carmine grinned wolfishly down at Eddie, who was really terrified now. Why did he send them away? This was getting worse by the second.

"Okay," Carmine said, "now we get to the innerestin' part."

He held the point of the knife close to Eddie's Adam's apple, just to make sure he had his undivided attention.

"Your old man lost somethin', right?"

If Eddie had been given a hundred guesses as to what Carmine was going to say, he wouldn't have come close.

"Huh?" was all he could manage.

"I said, your old man lost somethin'," Carmine repeated patiently. "Right?"

"Yeah," Eddie answered slowly. How did he know that? And where was this going?

"Did your old man say he lost it yesterday mornin'?"

Carmine was really enjoying the look on Eddie's face. He could see why his old man had become a detective; this was fun.

"He did, didn't he?" he insisted.

Eddie nodded.

"Lemme see if I can tell ya somethin' else." Carmine felt like a magician who'd just succeeded in hypnotizing the whole audience. "On Tuesday night, your old man got mad. He got real mad. In fact, he got so mad he walked out. Is that true?"

What the hell is happening? Eddie thought. He nodded weakly.

"Sure, he did."

Carmine's voice sounded almost soothing, even though he could barely contain himself. Shit, this was even better than he'd imagined.

"Well, guess what?" he said. "Your old man is a liar. He didn't lose that thing yesterday mornin', like he said. He lost it Tuesday night. And in a very bad place. Whaddaya think'a that?"

Eddie didn't know what to think. This was getting more and more bizarre.

Carmine moved the knife closer, until the tip of it was right against Eddie's throat.

"He lost it Tuesday night, and my old man found it Wednesday mornin'. Ya know what that means?"

He waited for an answer, but all he saw was the stunned look on Eddie's face.

"It means your old man is in big trouble. It means your old man killed that Sandra Weinstock lady."

He was pressing the knife so close now that a tiny bead of blood was forming under the tip.

"Your old man," Carmine said, drawing out each syllable like a judge pronouncing a death sentence, "is a fuckin' murderer."

CHAPTER FIVE

Eddie, his mind swirling, used his key to let himself into the empty apartment. His mother wasn't due home until after 4:30, which was how it had been since he was in the first grade. Last year, they'd finally decided he was old enough to stay in the apartment by himself after coming home from school, rather than downstairs in the care of Nate and Rosalie Preston, the super and his wife. He'd attained the status of what later generations would call a latchkey kid.

As he dropped his briefcase and headed for the refrigerator, he could hear the muffled sound through the kitchen floor of a radio playing "Loveliest Night of the Year."

It was their downstairs neighbors, the Haberman sisters, two elderly spinsters who'd been elderly spinsters the day Eddie was born. They were the first tenants to move into the building when it was finished sometime during the '20s, and the volume of their radio playing had increased with their hardness of hearing.

Eddie took bare notice of it. He was on automatic pilot, his mind everywhere but where his body was. At first, he'd wanted to flat-out disbelieve what Carmine said. Carmine was completely full of shit, that's all there was to it.

But he couldn't, because he always came back to the question of how Carmine knew the things he did. And there was only one answer, no matter how hard he tried to think of another: Nick.

Nick must have been talking about it.

Okay, but that still didn't mean his dad was a murderer. He couldn't accept that, couldn't even conceive of it. And if he was, which he wasn't, why would he kill Sandra Weinstock? He didn't even remember her. At least, that's what he said.

He took a bottle of milk out of the refrigerator, picked up a glass from the dish drainer, and poured some into it. As far as he could tell from what Carmine was hinting about, they must have found a watch and it had something to do with the murder.

But just because his dad happened to lose a watch, why would Nick think it was the one the cops found? People lose watches all the time. And why would Nick suspect his dad? He's his best friend.

So it couldn't be. Carmine must have heard him talking about something else.

Maybe Nick was just saying his dad was absent minded, and he mentioned losing the watch. The connection with the murder was Carmine's idea. That was it.

But that wasn't it. Carmine also knew about his dad getting mad on Tuesday night and walking out. How did he know that?

And why didn't Carmine know it was a watch, if he knew so much? He kept referring to it as a "thing." Why wouldn't Nick have used the word "watch" if all he was talking about was absent-mindedness? Why would he be secretive?

And there was something else. It was the way Carmine just let him go after he told him. He suddenly folded up the knife and got off him, almost like he was taking pity.

And that strange thing he said just before he turned the corner and disappeared around the bushes: "My old man knows certain things about your old man." What did that mean?

Whatever it meant, and whatever "certain things" Nick knew about Barry, there was a lot about his dad that Eddie did not know. He'd been only two years old when the war began and his father enlisted, and he had no recollection of him from those days. There were visits home during the first year, before Barry was sent overseas, but Eddie had only vague memories of those.

For the most part, he existed as a mythical figure, a hero who was fighting to save our country. There were photos, of course, and the letters his mother would read to him, but above all, there was the Dodgers.

In letter after letter, Barry would say he hoped Eddie was being a good boy and listening to his mother, and rooting for the Dodgers.

Julia had told him they were his father's passion, and taught him some of the players' names, at least as many as she knew. They'd listen together to games on the radio, and she'd help him write letters to Barry, telling him how the team was doing.

He remembered the day his dad came home, how he and his mom had waited at the foot of the stairs to the Bay Parkway station. Barry had come bounding down the steps, swinging his duffel bag to the pavement, and sweeping them both up into his arms.

That was one of the few happy moments he could recall. Eddie was only six and didn't know what was wrong, but something sure was.

He'd catch his mother crying sometimes. He knew she was upset about his dad not wanting his old job back, taking another one that wasn't as good. His dad would get real quiet, sitting in his chair with a beer or a glass of that brownish, funny-smelling stuff he later learned was scotch. He'd stare at nothing and tell Eddie to leave him alone.

When Eddie began Little League, his dad came to the first game. He struck out four times and made three errors, and, the next week, Barry said he wasn't going.

He said it was because he didn't want to make Eddie nervous, didn't want to jinx him. Eddie pleaded with him, but Barry said, "Go out there and play, and then come home and tell me all about it. Tell me everything, good and bad. Don't leave anything out."

Eddie thought it was a lousy idea, but he had a better game that week. He even got his first hit, a ground ball that snuck through an inept infield.

Afterwards, he ran home to tell Barry, who was overjoyed and wanted to hear him tell it again and again. Eddie decided he still wanted his dad to come, but this wasn't so bad.

Next week, Eddie went hitless again and struck out twice. He didn't want to talk about it, but Barry insisted.

So he began, and, funny enough, even though he was telling him bad stuff, it was okay. Just having Barry's absolute attention made up for a whole lot.

It became a weekly ritual. At first, Eddie only talked about his own part in the game, but his dad wanted to know about the rest of it, so he tried to remember other things. It made it even better, because he could make it last longer.

After a while, he could do a virtual play-by-play, like the announcers when they re-created games on the radio. He couldn't remember everything, of course, but he was good at capturing the highlights, the drama of it.

He realized he actually enjoyed doing that as much as playing ball. Sometimes, during a slow moment in the field, he'd be tempted to rehearse how he was going to describe something, trying to get the words just right for his dad. And that's the way it had been for four years now.

Then, of course, there was the Dodgers. And, as no boy ever would, he'd never forget the first game his dad ever took him to. He had the date memorized: April 15, 1947.

It happened to be not only the first Major League game for him, but also the first for a certain Jack Roosevelt Robinson. In fact...holy shit, he'd completely forgotten. The game!

He reached over to the radio and turned it on, all else pushed aside by the need to know what was happening. The voice of that new guy, Vin Scully, filled the kitchen.

("...all tied up at three apiece here in the bottom of the eighth.")

Scully's voice was smooth, like the other announcers, but had no southern accent or country twang to it.

Maybe if I could develop a nice, even tone like that, he thought, I could...

Forget it. Three-three in the eighth, he just said, and Boston was batting. Was anyone on base? Despite everything, Eddie was right into it.

("Addis takes his lead off first...") Well, that answered his question. ("Preacher Roe checks the runner and delivers.)

("Jethroe swings and sends a sharp bouncer up the middle, into center field for a base hit. Addis is rounding second, headed for third. He'll make it standing, and the Braves have runners on first and third with no one out.")

Eddie took a nervous sip from his glass of milk. They can't lose this game; they just can't. And, goddamn that fucking Carmine, his father can't be a murderer.

But did Nick think he was?

("Earl Torgeson is the batter. The Dodger infield has moved in close, hoping for a play at the plate. Roe comes set and delivers. Fast ball on the inside corner for strike one.")

Okay, wait a minute. Maybe Nick was just worried about his dad's temper as well as his forgetfulness, and that's why he was talking about both those things.

And why should he assume, just because Carmine didn't overhear him say it was a watch, that Nick was being secretive? Why couldn't Carmine have only heard the part after Nick already said it was a watch, and was now calling it "it"?

("Roe staring in for the sign. Addis leading off third and Jethro off first. Here's the pitch…strike two. A curve over the outside corner and a beauty.")

There we go, much better. He wasn't gonna fall for Carmine's bullshit. His father would never hurt anybody.

Then, in his memory, he heard his own voice. *Dad, I think you really hurt that guy.*

It caused him to almost drop the glass of milk. He didn't know which was worse, the memory or that he hadn't thought about it since, well, since it happened.

***

It was almost a year ago at Ebbets Field, on the final day of the 1950 season. The Dodgers had caught fire at the end of September, while the first-place Phillies had collapsed, and now they were only one game behind. If they could beat the Phillies on this last day, they'd force a three-game playoff.

Barry had told him they were going to the game. Absolutely. No matter how early they had to get there to get tickets.

***

("Torgeson swings…")
His mind was suddenly pulled back by Vin Scully.

("...and sends a high chopper to second. Robinson fields it and fires toward home. Here comes Addis. He is...") Please, please, Eddie prayed. ("...safe!")

No!!

("The Braves take the lead, 4-3!)

("And now Campanella is arguing with plate umpire Frank Dascoli, and Dascoli has just thrown him out of the game! Campy has just been ejected from this game!")

Rap. Rap. Rap.

Their neighbor, Mr. Schwartz, was knocking on the door to the dumbwaiter shaft. Sam and Myra Schwartz lived on the other side of the building, but they shared the same shaft with the Feins, which made them virtual next-door neighbors.

Rap. Rap. Rap.

Eddie got up from the table, walked over, and opened the dumbwaiter door.

Instantly, the music from the Haberman sisters' radio got louder, wafting up the shaft toward him.

"Hi, Eddie, I hope I'm not disturbing you," Mr. Schwartz said above it. "I just wanted to tell you that your mother doesn't have to make dinner for me tonight, because I'm visiting Myra and I'll catch a bite to eat at the hospital."

Mr. Schwartz's wife had been in and out of the hospital, and Julia had been cooking extra food for him from time to time.

"Sure, Mr. Schwartz, I'll tell her," he said, still trying with one ear to hear what was going on in the game. He thought he heard Vin Scully say there was one out.

"You have the Dodger game on?" Sam Schwartz asked. "How are they doing?"

He was in his 30's, with a face that always reminded Eddie of a soft-boiled egg, round with slightly runny eyes and drooping cheeks. In fact, everything about Mr. Schwartz seemed to sag.

"Are they winning?" he wanted to know.

"No," Eddie said, unable to keep the edge out of his voice. He hated it when people asked him the score if the Dodgers were losing.

"It's 4-3. Campy just got kicked out of the game."

"Oh, they can't afford to lose him, can they? He's good."

"Yeah."

He strained to hear what was happening on the radio, anxious to get back to it.

"I haven't been able to follow it much, you know, what with Myra being ill, but I heard he's having a great year."

"Yeah."

Cooper had just made out, so now there were two away. Mr. Schwartz went on, seemingly unaware of Eddie's inattention. Willard Marshall was up now. Where were the runners, first and second?

" ...met your father on the subway this morning, and he was telling me what a year Campanella's having..."

Eddie nodded his head automatically.

" ...saying he might even win the M.V.P...."

Marshall, on the first pitch, hit a come-backer to the mound and Roe threw him out at first to end the inning. Okay, one run behind, that's not too bad. They've got to make up for it in the ninth. Who was due to bat?

" ...your father is a killer."

His stomach fell like a lead sinker.

His mouth opened and he gaped across the shaft at Mr. Schwartz, who looked back at him benignly.

"What did you say?" he croaked.

"I said Roy Campanella, according to your father, is a killer. They really need him. Do you think he'll be suspended?"

It was as if his heart had stopped. Now it was pounding.

"I hope not," he said weakly.

"Well, I'll let you get back to the game. Remember to tell your mother what I said, okay?"

"Yeah." He slowly closed the dumbwaiter door.

He sat back down at the table and sighed as he sipped at the glass of milk during the Schaefer Beer commercial.

Dad, I think you really hurt that guy.

***

They'd gotten up at five in the morning and, fortified with a bag of sandwiches Julia made for them, they'd taken the train to Ebbets Field, changing at Coney Island from the West End to the Brighton line and getting off at the Prospect Park station.

The sight of the ballpark as they turned the corner onto Empire Boulevard had always been thrilling, but at sunrise that day it was especially so. Nearly a thousand people were already there, even though the gates wouldn't open for another four hours. It was to be the biggest crowd of the season, over 35,000.

They managed to get seats in the lower deck out in left field, three rows from the front, just above the sign on the outfield wall that said "The Brass Rail." Barry, as he usually did, took a seat on the aisle, so he'd have leg room.

After writing down the lineups, Eddie tucked his scorecard under one knee and slipped the pencil into his shirt pocket, as his father did, so that his hands would be free in case a ball came their way. None ever had, but he always did it just in case. As for bringing a glove, Barry always said that would be cheating.

The stands seemed to vibrate with anticipation as game time approached. Everyone could sense they were going to roll over the Phillies today, even though they were going up against Robin Roberts. The great right-hander had been suffering through a terrible stretch, not having won a game in his previous six starts, and Don Newcombe was just the man to make sure it continued.

The only sour note was the guy sitting behind them. He was fat and greasy, with a foghorn for a voice, and he announced to all and sundry that he was a Giant fan who was only there because he wanted to see the Dodgers suffer.

***

Vin Scully's voice pulled him back to the present as, on the radio, Reese led off the ninth with a ringing double down the left-field line.

Okay, tying run on base and in scoring position. His focus was now back to the game at hand.

He listened, as Robinson hit a ground ball to the right side, moving Reese to third with only one out. Just a fly ball would tie the game.

But Roy Campanella was supposed to be the next hitter, and he'd been thrown out of the game, so who's batting?

Vin Scully informed. ("Wayne Terwilliger coming up to the plate to hit in Campanella's spot,") he said.

Wayne Terwilliger, Eddie was aware, was a light-hitting reserve infielder.

He began chewing on the inside of his cheek, as Terwilliger, sure enough, grounded weakly to third. That brought up Andy Pafko as the Dodgers' last hope.

And while Pafko knocked the dirt from his cleats and settled into the batter's box, Eddie's thoughts, like it or not, drifted back to that final game of last season.

***

It had been as tense as you could want, a real knuckle-biter. They were still scoreless in the sixth, when the Phillies pushed across a run. But the Dodgers got it right back on Pee Wee's fly ball homer, which barely made it over the right field fence.

Throughout it all, fueled by multiple beer purchases, the Giant fan behind them never let up, with a steady stream of insults for the Dodgers and loud exhortations for the Phillies.

After three innings of this, Barry turned around and asked him to tone it down. He was told it was a free country.

"Then why don't you give the rest of us some freedom and shut up?" Barry said, to the approval of all within earshot.

The Giant fan, of course, was not to be stopped.

Barry said nothing after that, showing few signs of his own multiple beer purchases.

His dad never acted like those drunks Eddie saw in movies and on TV, sloppy and falling all over themselves. He could get angry, or get tired, but never seem drunk like other people.

But as the game and the Giant fan wore on, Eddie could tell his dad was getting steamed. At one point, he muttered, "I can't take much more of this."

It moved into the bottom of the ninth, still tied.

Cal Abrams, the Dodger left fielder, led off. Barry had always told him they should be proud of Cal Abrams because he was one of the few Jewish players in baseball.

He justified that pride by taking a very close three-and-two pitch and working out a walk. An ovation from the crowd accompanied him to first base. The potential winning run was on.

"He's gonna die there!" yelled the Giant fan. "The Jews are gonna say kaddish for him!"

Eddie could feel his dad tense up and start to turn, but stop himself.

Pee Wee was next, and he tried to bunt but was unsuccessful on two pitches. So he did one better, lining a single into left center, as Abrams stopped at second.

The crowd was screaming their support now, and, for the first time all afternoon, the Giant fan said nothing.

Another bunt was in order, as Duke Snider stepped to the plate and the Philly infield crept in. But Duke crossed them up, rifling the first pitch into center field for a base hit, as the crowd rose to its feet. This was going to be it.

Abrams rounded third, heading for the plate. Milton Stock, the third base coach, windmilled his arm frantically, urging him on.

From the left field stands, they had a perfect view of it, Richie Ashburn, the Philly center fielder, charging the ball and fielding it cleanly, uncorking a perfect throw toward Stan Lopata the catcher, with Abrams barely past third base.

"No, no!" they both yelled, almost in unison. "Hold up! Hold up!"

But Abrams, following Milton Stock's orders, kept going, lumbering toward Lopata, who by now had caught the ball and was waiting for him. He was out by 15 feet.

In the sudden silence, the cackling of the Giant fan sounded like fingernails on a blackboard.

They all took their seats again and, as they did, the Giant fan said one more thing, so softly only Barry and Eddie could hear him.

"Jews can't run fast," he said. "Otherwise, Hitler wouldn't have killed so many of 'em."

Barry turned in his seat and faced him.

"How would you like," he asked, his voice soft and icy calm, "to have your anti-Semitic brains bashed in?"

The Giant fan blinked and looked away.

Barry fixed him with a stare for a moment more, then turned back to the field, where, despite all, things were still promising. The Dodgers had men on second and third, and still only one out.

But they walked Robinson intentionally, then Furillo swung at the first pitch and popped out to the first baseman, and Hodges hit a harmless fly to right.

The crowd let out a massive groan and settled in once more. Extra innings.

As Cal Abrams trotted out to left field, some boos could be heard, but Barry called out, "That's okay, Abie. We'll get 'em next inning!"

The 10th inning started out badly, with Robin Roberts singling up the middle, as the Giant fan began cranking it up again.

Waitkus, after making an attempt to bunt, swung at the next pitch and dropped it perfectly into short center field, just beyond everyone's reach, Roberts stopping at second.

With one out, Dick Sisler, who'd already gotten three hits in the game, strode to the plate.

"Prepare to meet your doom, ya bums!" yelled the Giant fan melodramatically, as people began to stir in their seats.

Sisler took a big swing at the first pitch and missed. Then he fouled one off.

With the crowd begging Newcombe to strike him out, Sisler watched one go by wide for ball one.

Newcombe stepped off the mound for a moment to gather himself. Then he looked in, checked the runners, and the big right arm came around.

Fast ball down the middle. Sisler swung and lifted one toward left.

"Fly ball," said Barry immediately, as they watched it rising into the air, coming in their direction.

Abrams in left field must have thought so too, because he stood still for an instant. Then he turned and began sprinting for the wall, as a bad feeling crept into Eddie's stomach.

"It's gone!" the Giant fan predicted.

Eddie stood up with the others and stared at the ball descending toward them out of the sky. The Giant fan kept screaming, non-stop.

"Here it comes! C'mon, you beautiful baby. Come to Papa!"

But it wasn't coming to him. It was coming to Eddie. He raised his arms among a sea of arms and stretched toward it. What happened next happened in a flash.

Barry's hands darted in front of his. In one motion, he caught the ball, turned, and immediately released it, slamming it straight into the face of the Giant fan.

It struck the man in the center of his forehead and ricocheted, sailing off to the left into another cluster of reaching hands.

The Giant fan's eyes rolled up into his head. He fell backward heavily and slid down in his seat, the back of his skull striking the top of it as he did.

Eddie stared at him in horror, as he felt his father grab him by the arm and pull him into the aisle.

"Come on," Barry said, practically dragging him up the steps toward the exit ramp.

The crowd's concentration was completely on the home run and the shock of what it meant. Only Eddie had seen what really happened.

He hustled to keep up with his father, as he strode down the zig-zagging ramps under the stands, the crowd above them now, murmuring. The game was still going on and, at the moment, they were the only ones leaving the park.

They came to the deserted exit gate and walked out onto Montgomery Street, behind left field.

"Dad, I think you really hurt that guy," Eddie said breathlessly, as they hurried along toward the subway.

Barry didn't answer for several seconds, and then it was about something else.

"They're down by three runs," he said. "The game's as good as over."

"But Dad, you..."

"I'm sorry I took away your home run ball, Sport. But we wouldn't have wanted to keep it anyway."

***

Vin Scully's voice drew him back, out of his reverie.

("One and two the count on Andy Pafko, and the Dodgers are down to their last strike. If they lose today, the Giants will be only a half-game behind them.")

My dad could've killed that man, Eddie realized, and he didn't care. He didn't care one bit. Oh, God, what if he did kill Sandra Weinstock?

("Reese, the potential tying run, takes his lead off third.")

He couldn't think about it. It was too much.

His eyes strayed to the radio sitting on the counter above him, the light on its large dial glowing from the center of its domed shape, making it look like a shrine.

Please let something good happen, he thought.

He needed a sign that everything would be all right. He felt like his whole world was in chaos. Something good had to happen or he'd go crazy.

His hand tightened around the glass of milk. He silently pleaded to Pafko to get a base hit. Just one base hit, that's all.

("Nichols into his windup. And here's the pitch. Pafko swings and misses. Strike three!")

"No!!"

Eddie slammed the glass of milk against the table. It shattered into his palm.

He hardly felt the pain. He looked at the broken glass, the spilled milk, and his bleeding hand as though they were an exhibit in some kind of freak show.

I have to do something, he thought dully.

But he knew it wasn't just that he had to get a towel, clean up the mess, and see about his hand. It was something much, much harder.

He had to find out the truth.

CHAPTER SIX

("One and two the count on Andy Pafko, and the Dodgers are down to their last strike.") Nick put the phone back in its cradle as he caught the snippet of play-by-play from the radio on Joe Flannery's desk.

"You tryin' to torture yourself?"

"Screw you," Joe said, his freckled face tightening in annoyance. The freckles, combined with his carrot top, made him look younger than his 39 years of age.

His desk was across from Nick's. Joe had been bringing in the radio for the past two days, keeping the volume low so as not to disturb the rest of the 62nd Precinct squad room. Right now, he was the disturbed one.

"Fuckers," he murmured.

"What's the score?" Nick inquired. "How much they losin' by?"

Joe shot him a dirty look just as Pafko struck out.

"Fuckers," he repeated, as he reached over and shut off the radio so emphatically the knob came off in his hand.

He stared at it, as Nick laughed.

"I love watchin' you Dodger fans; ya take it so serious. Listen, forget that for a minute. I just got through talkin' with Macy's about the watch."

Joe put down the knob and slid his chair across the aisle. Nick checked his notes.

"They confirmed what Hamilton told us about the serial number. It was part of a shipment of two hundred watches in October of '45. But there were only ten that were this model, the Hamilton Martin."

"I don't suppose Macy's kept a record of the serial numbers when they sold 'em."

Nick gave him a "what do you think?" look.

"We're lucky they even kept track of the models. All they had were ten sale dates."

"And all for cash, I bet," said Joe.

"You expected our guy to be nice enough to write a check? All we got is the names of the five people workin' the jewelry counters back then."

"Great. When we find 'em, we can ask 'em if they happened to remember ten different people from six years ago."

So far, nothing. They had plenty of finger prints from the watch, including a partial palm print, but the only clear ones were Sandra's.

There were other things they'd been able to learn, though. They knew the size of the guy's wrist by the hole he used in the watch band. It was thick, and according to the bruise patterns on her neck, he had large hands.

And he was tall. At one point in the struggle she'd been lifted off her feet; the patterns showed that too.

Julia bought Barry's watch for their first anniversary after the war, she said, which put it at around November of '45. He didn't know if she bought it at Macy's, or even if it was a Martin model, but he knew there was no way he could casually bring it up again.

"Wasn't that Weinstock dame somethin'?" Joe slid his chair back to his side of the aisle. "When d'ya think was the last time she washed that house coat?"

"C'mon, give her a break. The woman just lost her daughter."

"She lost the laundry soap way before that."

He began trying to push the knob back into the radio.

Just before midnight on Tuesday, the police had gotten a call from a frantic Mrs. Weinstock, saying her daughter hadn't come home. They'd sent over a patrolman to take her statement, treating it as a missing person. All of that changed a few hours later when they got another call.

A man who'd been taking a sunrise stroll on the promenade had spotted her body, caught on the rocks as the tide went out and now in full view. That's when Nick and Joe had come into it.

Since then, they'd interviewed a number of people, including Yetta Weinstock and Sandra's boss, Mr. Faber. They'd taken a trip into

Greenwich Village that morning to talk to her former neighbors and fellow employees at the clothing store where she'd been the bookkeeper.

He'd had the thought, perhaps the hope, that maybe something had been going on, some kind of embezzlement she'd been part of, or that she'd discovered. It was three years since she'd worked there, but that didn't mean anything.

Joe's remark about Mrs. Weinstock was about the follow-up interview they'd just done with her. It was to see if she remembered anything else, or maybe, would say something inconsistent with her previous statements.

It was a long shot, of course, but she could have been involved in it herself. He'd seen stranger things than a mother hiring someone to kill her daughter.

But, of course, none of that seemed likely.

The bitter ex-boyfriend theory was also fading since no one could remember Sandra dating anyone. If there was an ex-boyfriend anywhere, no one knew about it.

Nick looked over his notes again. The Mrs. Weinstock interview was mostly routine stuff about Sandra's habits and interests. He'd written down the word "Giants" at one point, and now he recalled it.

When he asked her if there'd been any changes in Sandra's behavior during the last couple of weeks, she'd said no at first, but then thought a minute.

"Except, maybe, baseball. She was real happy and excited 'cause of the Giants. She and her father used to…" At that point, she'd started to cry.

"They make these fuckin' radios with such cheap parts," Joe complained, tossing the knob into his waste basket. "Now I'm gonna have to turn the goddamn thing on and off with pliers."

"Joe, let me ask you somethin'; how come it gets you so pissed off? It's only a game, right?"

Joe looked at him the same way he'd just looked at the knob.

"Easy for you; you're a fuckin' Giant fan. Everything's goin' your way right now."

"Sandra Weinstock was a Giant fan too; did you notice?"

"Then she died happy. Listen, save all that 'only a game' crap for them."

He waved his arm at the pictures on the wall behind Nick of "Our Best PALs," the five people who were the largest neighborhood contributors to the Police Athletic League. There were also photos of the teams Nick coached. Eddie and Lionel stared out from a few of them.

Nick didn't want to argue, but he knew Joe was wrong, at least in his case. It would be great to see the Giants pull this off, but it was nothing compared to what he got out of teaching baseball to those kids.

Like turning Eddie from a scared rabbit into a slick little shortstop that attacked ground balls and gunned throws across the field. Or James Preston, the super's kid from the Feins' building and the only Negro face in the team picture, who played a good, solid first base and could occasionally hit one out.

Then, of course, there was Lionel, who might even have big league potential someday, though Nick wasn't crazy about how his old man bragged about him. But he could forgive Ben. He understood Little League parents. What he didn't understand was why people acted like their lives depended on whether a bunch of strangers won or lost.

"You should know better than anyone," Joe said. "If Bill Terry hadn't pissed off the Dodger fans all those years ago, you never would'a become the legend you are."

He was talking about what happened in 1934, the year Giant manager Bill Terry uttered the fateful words, "Is Brooklyn still in the league?" Nick was only 23 and in his second year on the force, walking a beat in Flatbush.

Terry was his favorite Giant, not only because he was one of the best hitters in baseball, but because he took shit from no one, not even the dictatorial John McGraw, who made Terry player-manager despite the fact that the two of them never got along.

The Giants were the defending World Series champs that year, and, during an interview in February, a reporter asked Terry how he thought their rivals, the Dodgers, would do in the upcoming season. Terry then facetiously posed the question that would come back to haunt him.

A few days before the sixth-place Dodgers walked into the Polo Grounds and beat the Giants two straight, costing them the pennant and sticking it to Terry, Nick happened to be glancing through the FBI's Ten Most Wanted list.

It was posted in every police station in the country, but most cops were too busy with their own problems to bother studying people who were probably someone else's.

But that's just why Nick was interested. If they weren't his problem, he was free to wonder about how some of them could elude capture for so long.

Number Three, for instance, a murderer and child abductor named Albert Glanville, nicknamed "The Gruesome Grease Monkey" because he sometimes worked as an auto mechanic. He seemed to know just the right moment to move on, before enough people started to notice their children were missing. His activities took place in different parts of the country, and years would go by between them. The FBI had only recently identified him, after he'd been at large for over 15 years.

Nick noticed that Glanville had worked as a mechanic in the Memphis area in 1922, and it made him think of Bill Terry. That was the year Terry signed with the Giants. And, as Nick remembered, he owned a filling station in Memphis.

There weren't many cars on the road in those days, so how many filling stations could there have been in the area? What were the odds that Glanville, at some time, might have worked as a mechanic for Bill Terry?

It was a connection like something out of *Ripley's Believe It or Not*, and it stayed in the back of his mind.

It was still there, nestled in his subconscious, as he rode the Ninth Avenue elevated line up to the Polo Grounds on Sunday, September 30th, the last day of the 1934 season, bought a box seat ticket behind first base, and hoped Bill Terry and the Giants would beat the Dodgers and save themselves.

Not all of the 45,000 people with him shared that hope. In fact, at least half of them were Dodger fans. They were all around Nick in the seats near first base, where Terry stoically played his position, and they screamed at him every chance they got.

One row in front of Nick and one seat over was a large man wearing a gray cloth cap. He didn't yell and call Terry a bum like the people around him, but he didn't cheer for the Giants either, even when they jumped ahead with four runs in the first. He didn't seem to be rooting for anyone, just watching the game.

Nick was only marginally aware of him, but then something happened in the top of the sixth. The Giant shortstop fielded a ground ball and threw it wildly over Terry's head, all the way to the box seat railing.

Terry turned and bolted toward the seats, and that's when the man said something.

"Why don't you fire that shortstop, Bill, since you're so fond of firing people?"

His accent was hard to place, but definitely not New York. Nick wondered who Terry had ever fired. As a manager, he'd traded people but never actually kicked anyone off the team. Before that, he was only a player.

The man got more vocal as the game went on. It was nothing compared to the abuse that other fans were hurling at Terry, but Nick found himself leaning forward, trying to catch it.

What he heard wasn't anything special, unless you took it a certain way. For instance, when Terry called time out in the top of the eighth and slowly walked over to the mound to relieve his pitcher, Freddie Fitzsimmons, who'd obviously had it, the guy yelled, "Out of gas, Bill, out of gas!"

Then he'd laughed.

A few minutes later, after a wild pitch let in the tying run for the Dodgers, he said, "Tighten up those lug nuts, Bill, 'cause the wheels are comin' off."

It went on like that, right through the Dodgers' three-run rally in the 10th that put the game away. At one point, the crowd reacted to the scoreboard, where the first-place Cardinals, commonly known as the Gashouse Gang, were winning their game to further seal the Giants' fate.

"Hey, Bill," the guy called out, "remember the old *Gas* House Gang?"

Glanville was supposedly husky, like this guy. Nick tried to recall his mug shot. He could only see the back of the guy's neck and part of his face in profile, and the cloth cap was pulled low over the eyes, but he decided, what the hell. He'd follow him for a while after the game to see where he went. He had nothing better to do.

The great Mel Ott, in a slump he'd have to wait until next year to get out of, grounded to third to end it. The players on both teams poured out of the dugouts and made their way toward deep center field, where the clubhouses were located, a peculiarity of the Polo Grounds.

The crowd, as was the custom, spilled out onto the infield in their wake.

Nick hung back and watched, as the guy made his way over to first base, where he bent down, scooped up a handful of dirt, and put it into his pants pocket. He walked back to the stands, and then down an exit ramp, Nick only a few yards behind. They came out of the ballpark onto 155th Street.

It wasn't hard to keep track of him in the crowd because of his size and the gray cap, as he walked west for a couple of blocks to Amsterdam Avenue, crossed it, and then turned north.

Evening was approaching, and the streetlights began to come on. The crowd had thinned out by now, and as they left Harlem and entered the area known as Washington Heights, there were fewer people on the street. It was Sunday, near dinner time, and most of the residents were in their apartments.

Nick crossed to the other side, to put more space between them, and watched from a quarter-block behind. The man was walking purposefully but in no particular hurry.

Washington Heights was a neighborhood of Irish and Jewish immigrants, with bars and taverns mixing in among storefronts that had signs in Yiddish. Out of one of those, a tailor shop, Nick saw a young boy emerge. He was wearing the traditional long black coat and felt hat, and looked to be about ten or eleven years old.

The guy noticed him too. The boy had come out of the store directly in his line of vision and was now walking ahead of him. Nick watched the guy stay back for a block, then catch up to the boy at the corner of 162nd as he waited for the light, and tap him on the shoulder.

They talked for a moment, the guy gesturing, seemingly asking for help with something, reaching into his shirt pocket and taking out a dollar bill, offering it to the boy, who took it.

The two of them turned the corner and started walking west.

Nick crossed the avenue again and followed, keeping to the shadows of the buildings as they walked up the long block toward Broadway. The guy glanced back once or twice but didn't spot him.

Midway down the block was a closed Tydol Flying "A" gas station.

The man led the boy there, past the pumps, toward the garage at the far end, where a 1925 Stutz sedan stood parked in front.

Nick realized that if he was going to make a play it better be now, while they were in the open, before they reached the car. Even then, he hoped to God it wouldn't turn into a hostage situation.

With his badge in one hand and his service revolver in the other, he closed the distance between them.

"Police! Stop right there!" he hollered. "Get away from him, son. GET AWAY FROM HIM!"

The boy froze, staring wide-eyed at Nick for a moment that lasted forever. Then he jumped to the side, out of reach.

Nick kept his gun trained on the man, who'd made no attempt to grab the boy, but had raised his hands and was looking back at him with a lopsided grin on his face.

"You're Albert Glanville," Nick said to him.

The man merely nodded.

It turned out that Glanville had only worked at Bill Terry's gas station for one week and was fired, not because Terry suspected his sinister underside, but because he did sloppy work. Terry hadn't given him another thought but, of course, Glanville was well aware of Bill Terry over the years, though he'd never seen him play.

He'd gone to the game that day because of all the publicity and the fact that he'd recently begun living less than a mile from the Polo Grounds.

As he told police, he'd never particularly liked Terry, but, even while sitting in the stands and delighting in the man's failure, he realized how miserable his own life was in comparison, and how much he truly hated him.

Glanville's capture elevated Nick to detective and made him, at 23 years of age, the youngest in the history of the NYPD.

As he was leaving the official press conference announcing the capture, a reporter took him aside and introduced himself as Barry Fein of the *World Telegram*.

"What about the infield dirt in Glanville's pocket?" he wanted to know. "Did he ever tell you what he intended to do with it?"

Nick paused and gave him a respectful once over.

"He was gonna throw it in the grave with the next kid he killed. Like he was buryin' Bill Terry's ashes. You know you're the first guy that asked me about that?"

It seemed like many lifetimes ago, as he now looked across the aisle at his partner.

"If I'm such a fuckin' legend," he said, "how come I'm sittin' here next to you?"

Joe gave a good natured snort.

"Meanwhile," said Nick, "you got any ideas about this, any hunches? Why do you think Sandra Weinstock died?"

Joe gave the broken knob on his radio another hostile look.

"Maybe it was 'cause she was a fuckin' Giant fan."

Nick threw his head back and laughed.

"Joe, you kill me," he said.

***

Eddie couldn't stop the bleeding. He'd tried dabbing at the palm of his hand with a wet towel and it hurt like a sonofabitch, so he carefully held onto another wet towel while doing his best to clean up the broken glass one-handed.

At the same time, he was trying to work up a good story. Julia would have a conniption if she knew it was because the Dodgers lost. And she'd have a Major League conniption if she ever knew the rest of it.

He heard her key in the front door, turning as if to unlock it and finding it already open.

"Eddie, why didn't you lock this door?" Julia said peevishly, as she pushed it further open. "I keep telling you…"

She stepped into the kitchen and came upon the scene.

"Oh my God, look at your hand! What did you do to it?"

"It's okay, Mom," he said instinctively.

How many times in his life had he used that phrase? Thousands? Millions?

"I was carrying the glass of milk from the refrigerator and I must've slipped on something, 'cause my hand hit the table and the glass broke."

She cautiously took hold of it and lifted the towel away.

"You were only just now having your milk? When did you get home, anyway?"

Bad choice. He wished he'd had more time to think.

"At the regular time. But I didn't feel like having it right away."

"Then you shouldn't be having it now, when it's so close to dinner."

She frowned worriedly at his palm, which was seeping blood.

"It spilled before I could drink any, so I guess it all worked out," he said, trying to make a joke.

She looked more closely at his hand.

"Oh, honey, you really hurt yourself. This is bad."

He could hear the panic in her voice.

"Come on, we have to get you to Dr. Glazer right away."

She took him by his other arm and he barely had the chance to pick up the towel again as they headed for the door.

"Hold your hand above your head," she instructed him, as they plunged down the stairs toward the lobby. "That way the blood will flow away from the wound."

With her arm around him, she hustled him up the street to Benson Avenue, which they crossed against the light.

Eddie allowed himself to be carried along, as he wondered how he could even start to do what he had to. This was real-life detective work. He was a seventh-grader.

"We're lucky the doctor's only a block away," Julia gasped, as they hurried past the synagogue on the corner and charged up the porch steps of the house next door to it.

There was no one in the waiting room.

"Dr. Glazer!" she yelled. "It's an emergency! Eddie needs help!"

The double doors to the examining room opened immediately, and Lenore Glazer came out with a look of concern on her face.

"What happened, Julia?" she asked, and then spotted Eddie behind her, his right arm above his head, holding the bloodstained towel like the Olympic torch.

"Oh, I see. Come on inside, Eddie, and let's have a look at it."

Lenore was Dr. Glazer's wife. They'd married shortly after they met, while he was in med school and she was in nursing school. Eddie thought she was a sweet woman who was everything a nurse should be: calm, reassuring, attentive.

"Let's take that towel away," she said as she led him inside and helped him onto the examining table, Julia following in their wake. Dr. Glazer came into the room.

"Thank God I got home in time, Dr. Glazer; he could have bled to death," was how Julia greeted him. "I don't know how much blood he's lost already. There was another towel and it was full of it."

"Now, take it easy Julia," Dr. Glazer said, as he took Eddie's hand.

He looked at his palm, shining the bright overhead light on it.

"This doesn't look particularly life-threatening. Get me the magnifying glass, would you, Lenore?"

She reached into one of the cabinets and got it out for him. He peered through it at Eddie's hand.

"You've got some glass in there. How'd you manage that?"

"I was holding a glass of milk, and I..."

"It's going to need stitches, I'm afraid," Dr. Glazer went on.

Sometimes, Eddie noticed, Dr. Glazer would ask you a question and then not wait to hear the answer. It was probably the most objectionable thing you could find about him. His voice sounded a little tired, he thought. Maybe he was just taking a nap.

Julia's nervous energy still hadn't burned off, even though she no longer imagined Eddie as a bloodless corpse.

"I wanted to take those steaks out of the refrigerator," she thought out loud. "We rushed over here so fast, I didn't have the chance."

Which reminded Eddie. "You don't have to make dinner for Mr. Schwartz tonight, Mom. He told me he was going to the hospital to see Myra and he'd eat there."

"Get me a pair of tweezers, would you please, Lenore?" said Dr. Glazer. "It's a shame about Myra Schwartz, isn't it?" he said to Julia.

She cut a nervous glance at Eddie. She and Barry had never said anything in front of him about Myra's cancer, because they felt it would upset him. At least Julia felt that way.

"Well, they live right across from us, you know," she said, trying to steer away from the subject, "so I've been cooking an extra dinner for Sam. Eddie usually passes it over to him through the dumbwaiter shaft, right honey? But he has to stand on a step stool to reach."

She looked over at Eddie, and then back to the doctor.

"He's so short for his age. Why do you think that is? His father is so tall."

Why is she talking like this? "Mom," Eddie said uncomfortably.

"Well, Dr. Glazer knows more than we do about biology, honey. I just thought he might have an answer."

"It doesn't take a biologist," the doctor said with a smile. "Kids grow in spurts, especially around his age. Eddie's almost a teenager. Who knows, in a few months he could grow six inches and that step stool will just be a childhood relic."

He turned his attention back to the hand.

"Now, I'm afraid what I'm going to do will hurt a bit, Eddie," he said. "But I'll bet you'll show us how much of a grownup you are already."

How much of a grownup? He was still a kid an hour ago, and he'd had a knife pressed to his throat. And that wasn't even the worst of it.

"I'll be all right," he said.

"Oh, I can't look," said Julia.

"Why don't you sit down, Julia dear?" Lenore suggested. She took the magnifying glass from her husband and held it over Eddie's palm, putting her other hand on his shoulder.

"You don't have to watch. In fact, nobody does except the doctor. Turn your head away, Eddie, and we'll all have a nice conversation while it's happening, all right?"

She looked at him confidently.

"Sure," he said and winced, as Dr. Glazer extracted the first tiny bit of glass.

"I'll bet that's your throwing hand," she said. "You play baseball, don't you?'

"He certainly does," said Julia. "His team, the Cougars, won their P.A.L. division championship last year."

"Really," said Lenore. "What position do you play?"

"Shortstop," Eddie answered, wincing again.

"Tell them how you ended the game," Julia said proudly.

"I was just lucky," Eddie said.

They'd been leading 1-0 in the bottom of the final inning. Lionel, as usual, had dominated the game. He'd hit a home run for their only score, and he was working on another of his no-hitters.

Suddenly, with three outs to go, he began to struggle. He walked the first two batters and, with the other team's best hitter at the plate, went to a full count.

"Watch the runners!" Nick called out to Eddie, who signaled to the second baseman that, in the event of a steal, he'd be the one to cover second.

Lionel went into his set position and then delivered.

Determined to throw a strike, he threw a fat one right down the middle, as, sure enough, the runners took off.

The batter, who'd been waiting all day for a pitch like that, swung and hit a sharp line drive headed for center field, the only solidly hit ball off Lionel the whole game.

Eddie had been moving to cover second, and his path took him right into it. He barely had to stretch out his arm before the ball smacked into his glove as if drawn there. Without breaking stride, he stepped on second, chased down the runner, who was desperately trying to get back to first, and tagged him on the shoulder.

Then he just kept going, running off the field in celebration, jumping into Nick's open arms as he was mobbed by the rest of the team.

"Wow, an unassisted triple play!" Lenore said. "I'll bet you want to be a ballplayer when you grow up."

"No, actually, I want to be a play-by-play announcer."

Dr. Glazer tweezed out another little sliver of glass and put it on the tray.

"I thought every boy wants to be a Major Leaguer," he said.

"I'm a good fielder, but I'm not such a good hitter. Lionel is the real star of the team."

Lionel had once offered to help him with his hitting. They'd gone down to the park with a bunch of balls and he threw him "batting practice." In the middle of it, Lionel got bored and decided to practice his curve instead. Eddie, at least, made him pick up all the balls.

"I'm a better announcer," he said. "I know a lot about players' statistics and game strategy."

"Sounds like you'd make a good coach," said Lenore. "Does your dad do any coaching?"

Eddie looked over at his mother. It was still a sore point that Barry didn't come to his games, even though he'd told her time and again it was okay. In fact, when he'd described the triple play to his dad, it was like making it happen all over again.

"His father has a hard time getting around on weekends," Julia said.

"Oh," said Lenore.

"All right, we've gotten all the glass," said Dr. Glazer. "Now, just a few stitches, so hang in there, Eddie."

"How about the P.A.L. raffle?" Lenore asked him. "Are you selling a lot of tickets?"

The raffle was something he and Lionel had dismissed as totally useless. The grand prize for the drawing was two season box seats at Ebbets Field for next year, which would have been wonderful if only they were eligible for it.

Since they were selling the raffle tickets, they couldn't participate. The only prize they could win was for selling the most, and that was an autographed picture of Charlie Dressen.

"It's a booby prize," Lionel had said. "The only thing it's good for is to prove he can sign his name."

But it was easier not to go into all that with Lenore Glazer, and to just say, "I've been selling 'em pretty good." He flinched from the pain in his hand.

"I always liked to sell raffle tickets," Lenore said. "It can be fun. You get to meet people and see their homes, if they let you in."

This was really hurting now. He wondered how much longer it was going to take.

"Even if they don't let you in, you still get a glimpse of their lives. You can learn a lot about people by selling raffle tickets."

A stab of pain obliterated everything for a moment, and that's when he had the vision.

He saw himself standing in someone's house, note pad in hand. Except, it wasn't a note pad, it was a pad of raffle tickets, but no matter.

He was going from house to house, talking to people, asking them questions. Just like a det...

"Mom," he said suddenly. "After we get home, I'm going out for a while. I need to sell some raffle tickets."

CHAPTER SEVEN

"It's ridiculous," Julia said, as she peeled potatoes over the sink. "Where do you get these ideas?"

"I've gotta sell more raffle tickets than Lionel; I've just got to. I can't let him beat me. I want to win this contest so bad I can taste it." He'd heard that expression somewhere; it had the right note of desperation.

"You've never told me anything about this. And now, just before dinner, you want to go outside and run around the neighborhood with your injured hand? I don't understand you."

"I didn't want to bother you; that's why I never said anything about it. And my hand is all right. All I have to do is write down people's names, and Dr. Glazer said I could do that without hurting it. And I'll be back before dinner."

He didn't actually know that, but he'd deal with it later.

"Did you finish your homework?"

He could sense he was getting closer. She was falling back on old strategies, which meant she was running out of things to throw at him.

"I did it as soon as I came home. That's why I didn't drink the milk right away."

"Oh yeah?" She turned from the sink and gave him a knowing look. "How did the Dodgers do?"

Shit. He should never underestimate her.

"They lost 4-3. But I only had arithmetic homework, so I did it while the game was on."

Now he had her. He knew she wouldn't ask to see it while she was rushing to get dinner ready. She might want to look at it later but, again, later didn't count. Besides, he'd just thought of the clincher.

"Oh, and I wanted to tell you. My Inca report got an A+."

She stopped peeling the potatoes and looked up at him with such joy on her face that he suddenly wanted to cry.

What's the matter with me? he thought, fighting it.

"Oh honey, that's wonderful," she said. "You'll have to show it to me."

"Well, it's at school right now 'cause Mr. Farnsworth put it up on the bulletin board. But I'll bring it home as soon as he takes it down."

"That's just great. I'm so proud of you."

He fought the tears again.

"So," he said, "can I go out and sell raffle tickets?"

Julia looked at her watch. "I don't know how much time you'll have. Your father will be home in less than an hour."

"I'll sell as many as I can before then. Thanks, Mom."

He headed for his room to get the raffle book. Where the hell had he put it? He hadn't seen it in weeks.

It was under a stack of Captain Marvel comic books. He snatched it up, grabbed a pencil, and took the stairs two at a time down to the lobby.

Outside, he started to turn right toward Bay Parkway and Cropsey where Sandra's mother lived. At least that's where Seymour Herschfeld said she lived when he was reading from the paper.

He'd figured on checking all the directories in the lobbies and the names on the bells, but now he had a better idea.

He turned left and headed toward Al's Soda Fountain on 86th Street, and the telephone book that was attached to the phone booth there. It was a half-block out of his way but it would be a lot quicker.

A West End train from Coney Island was rumbling into the elevated station above his head as he stepped cautiously through the doorway. This was where Carmine had sent his two goons to get him an egg cream, and Eddie was prepared to turn around and get out of there if he spotted either of them.

It was possible, since Al's Soda Fountain was a hangout for neighborhood kids. It was a modest place, three booths and an eight-stool counter, with a newspaper and magazine stand just inside the entrance. Al Schaefer, the proprietor, was in a great mood at the moment.

"Eddie Fein!" he called out from behind the counter, where he was putting the finishing touches on two vanilla frappes for the teenage girls sitting in the center booth.

"Whatta ya think, huh? The Giants are only a half-game back."

Al Schaefer was a thinnish man of modest height. He was in his early 50's, with prematurely gray hair in the places where he wasn't prematurely bald. Eddie often wondered how a guy whose last name was the same as the Dodgers' beer sponsor could be a Giant fan, but he never could get a straight answer out of Al.

He was the only adult Eddie knew who it was okay to talk back to. He respected Al for that, but right now, he didn't have time to think up a smartass retort, so he merely grunted. He made his way to the rear of the store and started paging through the phone book.

"Got a heavy date?" Al called after him, making the teenage girls giggle.

Eddie ignored it. There were three Weinstocks in the book that lived on Bay Parkway. One was a Y. Weinstock at 8800, which would put it right on the corner of Cropsey Avenue. Bingo.

He snapped the book shut and headed toward the door, enduring Al's taunts along the way.

"Did you hear the Dodger game? I had it on in here. You should've come in and listened to it with me, and had some ice cream. I would've given you a free scoop."

Eddie paused at the door.

"Here's a free scoop," he said. "The Dodgers will win this weekend and the Giants will lose. Then I'll come in and watch you cry in your ice cream, which is watery enough."

The two teenage girls went "ooh," as he closed the door behind him.

He turned onto Bay Parkway and ran the three blocks to Cropsey Avenue, panting as he arrived in front of Yetta Weinstock's building. Catching his breath, he went into the lobby and rang her bell.

A few seconds went by. Then what sounded like a man's voice answered the intercom.

"Yes?" it said.

"Um, is Mrs. Weinstock there?"

"This is Mrs. Weinstock, who is it?"

What a voice! He hoped his voice would get that deep when he grew up. She could do play by play with that voice.

"My name is Eddie Fein, Mrs. Weinstock. I'm selling raffle tickets for the Police Athletic League."

"Oh God, no. I can't even think about anything like that now. I'm sorry."

What was he doing? This wasn't the right way. Say something about her daughter.

"I was a friend of Sandra's, Mrs. Weinstock," he said quickly. "In fact, she was the one who encouraged me to sell these raffle tickets. That's why I wanted to see you. Can I come up for a minute?"

There was a pause. "What did you say your name was?"

"Eddie. Eddie Fein."

There was another pause. "All right, I guess."

The buzzer went off and the lock sprung to let him in. He took the elevator to the fifth floor and was about to knock on the door of 5F, when it opened.

A large woman in a house dress, with mad-scientist hair and cigarette smoke curling from her nostrils, stood in front of him, giving him the once over.

"My Sandra wanted you to sell raffle tickets?" she asked skeptically.

"Yes," Eddie said, "she told me that selling raffle tickets was how you could meet interesting people and learn from them. I really liked her a lot, Mrs. Weinstock. She was always nice to me and let me stay in the store. I can't believe this happened to her."

That last part was the truth and he hoped it made up for the bullshit part.

Mrs. Weinstock's appraising look softened.

"She wanted you to sell those tickets, huh? So I guess she would've wanted me to buy one. Why don't you come in, Eddie?"

She opened the door the rest of the way and led him into a cluttered dining room with newspapers and magazines strewn about the table.

"What kind of prize do I get if I win?"

"Two season tickets to Ebbets Field for next year," he said, following her inside.

She stopped so abruptly, he almost ran into her.

"Why would she have wanted you to do that?"

Uh oh. How could he have forgotten what a Giant fan Sandra was? As if to drive it home, there she was in a picture with her father, wearing her Giant cap and smiling at him from the china cabinet.

"I know what you mean," he said, trying to recover. "I root for the Giants, too. In fact, that was the first thing we had in common. We both really hated the Dodgers."

He was aware he might be jinxing them for all time, but what choice did he have?

"The money goes to the P.A.L., not the team, and Sandra and I sort of hoped that a Giant fan would win the raffle and go out there to boo the Dodgers for a whole season." He was turning red. Would she notice?

The explanation seemed to satisfy her, or at least, it didn't matter.

"I never cared much for baseball myself," she said. "It was really her father who got her interested in it." She sighed and looked around. "Now where did I put my purse?"

"My father was the one who got me interested too. In fact, I wonder if Sandra knew him. Did she ever say anything to you about Barry Fein?" He held his breath.

She thought a moment. "No, I can't recall she ever did."

He exhaled. "Then I guess she didn't know him."

"I don't know if she knew him or not," Mrs. Weinstock said distractedly, still searching under all the magazines and newspapers for her purse. "I'd imagine there were lots of people she didn't tell me about. I guess we didn't talk as much as we should have."

She picked up a small piece of paper that had been caught between two of the magazines.

"Oh, look," she said, her eyes starting to fill with tears, "it's the prescription for her bronchitis medicine. She never even got the chance to have it filled."

Mrs. Weinstock stared at the piece of paper for a moment and then began crying softly.

Eddie stared at it too. He felt terrible for Mrs. Weinstock. But he couldn't let himself be distracted. Feeling bad was not going to help him.

"This is a beautiful apartment," he said, looking around. "Sandra used to tell me how big it was."

Mrs. Weinstock mopped at her cheeks with the back of one hand.

"Well, there was certainly plenty of space for her. She should've been very happy here."

"I always thought she was. She used to tell me what a great apartment she lived in. She said she loved her room."

"She did?" Her eyes took on a confused hope.

For a moment he was repelled by what he was doing. But if he was making her feel better, then what was the harm?

"She said she really loved it a lot," he said. "Do you think I could...? No, never mind; I'm sorry."

"You want to see her room, don't you?" Mrs. Weinstock said gently, putting the prescription down on the dining room table.

"Could I?"

"Sure, of course you could."

She led him through the kitchen and down a short hallway. There were two bedrooms, one to either side, and Sandra's was the one on the right. It looked like a cross between a girl's bedroom and a teenage boy's, with a frilly, pink bedspread and heart-shaped throw pillows, and a Giants pennant on the wall next to pictures of Bobby Thomson, Monte Irvin, and Willie Mays. A ball and glove adorned the top of her bookshelf. Against the far wall was an oak desk with a captain's chair in front of it.

Eddie noticed that the desk blotter was actually a large calendar, with a square for each day of the month. He'd never seen one like it before.

"This is really neat," he said.

Sandra had written several things on it. He tried to make them out, but Mrs. Weinstock kept talking to him, and he had to look up at her.

"What am I going to do with this room?" she was saying. "I'd hate to move anything." Her eyes started to tear again. "I don't know, I just get the feeling that if I leave it as it is, she might show up again, somehow."

She made a soft whimpering sound and then got control of herself.

"I shouldn't talk about things like that to you; you're just a boy."

"That's okay, Mrs. Weinstock, I understand."

"No you don't, and I hope you never do." She sighed. "Meanwhile, let me find my purse and buy that raffle ticket. I think I remember where I put it now; it's in the kitchen."

She turned and left him alone.

Eddie couldn't believe his luck. Hastily, he read what Sandra had written on the calendar. There were only four entries, which either meant she wasn't very busy or she didn't write everything down. He read "Mom – B'day" on the 12th, "Store inventory" on the 17th, "Pick up shoes" on the 20th. Then his eye moved to Friday the 28th, which would have been tomorrow, and he suddenly felt nauseous.

It said "Lunch – B.F."

"I found my purse, Eddie. Come on in here," Yetta called from the kitchen.

"Great, Mrs. Weinstock," he called back, still staring at the notation. It was in pencil. He had a pencil in his hand, along with the raffle book.

Before he could think, he reached out and added a short, curved line to the second letter, so that it now read "Lunch – B.P."

"I'll be right there," he said, moving quickly down the hallway toward the kitchen.

CHAPTER EIGHT

Thursday Evening, September 27th

The three of them sat watching television in the living room, Barry in his chair, Eddie on the couch, and Julia next to him. On Channel 2, George Burns was holding his cigar at a jaunty angle as he warbled, ("Tho' April showers, may come your way...") while Gracie looked on admiringly.

("Oh, George,") she effused, ("you have such a beautiful voice. I can't think of another singer who's one-tenth as good as you.")

George paused in his singing to point out modestly, ("Frank Sinatra's a pretty good singer.")

Gracie scoffed. ("Him? Why, you make him look sick! At least that's how he looked when he heard you sing.")

"How's your hand feeling, Sport?" Barry cradled his glass of scotch as he looked over at Eddie.

"Not too bad."

"I still don't understand how you did it," Julia said. "Were you rushing around or something?"

"I told you, Mom, I slipped."

Gracie said something else at that moment and the studio audience laughed, pulling his mother's attention back to the TV.

Eddie's attention was entirely inward. He sat and pretended to watch the show as he mentally kicked himself over and over. Why did he change those initials? It was so dumb. The police must've already seen the calendar. They'll know it was changed.

Stupid. Stupid.

He'd realized it right away, even as he stood in the kitchen with Mrs. Weinstock, barely able to write out the raffle ticket in his distraction. At first, he tried to think of some excuse to go back into her room and erase it, but it wouldn't have mattered. Any erasure would still show up. What had he done?

The Burns and Allen Show went into a commercial for Carnation Evaporated Milk.

"How long do the stitches stay in?" Barry asked, getting up and moving over to the breakfront to pour another splash into his drink.

"At least a week," Julia said as she picked up Eddie's empty cream soda glass along with her own and carried them into the kitchen. "But Dr. Glazer wants to look at it on Tuesday, just to make sure it's healing right. He's going to come home from synagogue during a break in the services."

I've got to be more careful, Eddie thought. *I've got to stop doing stupid things.*

Barry settled back into his chair. "Synagogue? Services?"

"Tuesday is the second day of Rosh Hashanah, you might remember, and there are actually some Jews that celebrate it."

Oh, God, they weren't going to argue about this again, were they? He'd heard it over and over, how his father was an atheist and would tolerate no "hypocrisy." He could not go through rituals he didn't believe in and neither, by extension, could they. Eddie, alone among his Jewish friends, had never spent a day in a Hebrew school and was soon going to miss out on the great Bar Mitzvah cash-in.

It bothered him and it didn't. It was nice not to have to run off to Hebrew school after regular school like some of them, and to sleep late on Saturdays. But if his father didn't believe in Judaism, why were they supposed to be proud of Cal Abrams for being Jewish?

And goddamn it, was Sandra really planning to meet him for lunch tomorrow? If she was, did that mean something was going on? Was she his secret girlfriend?

Last week, they'd all watched an episode of Fireside Theatre, where Don Ameche played a man with a secret girlfriend. He'd sneak away from his wife to meet her. Eddie was bored because it was a love story and not a western or a mystery, but now he remembered and it made him uncomfortable. He glanced over at his father and tried to imagine him kissing Sandra Weinstock.

The commercial was over and Burns and Allen resumed. They were doing a sketch with their announcer, Harry Von Zell, who had some sort of stomach problem they were afraid he'd gotten from Gracie's cooking.

Eddie stopped thinking about his father and Sandra kissing and concentrated on how they could've planned to have lunch together, if it was true.

He worked on Barclay Street in downtown Manhattan, while she, of course, worked right here on 86th Street. He had a strict hour for lunch. Eddie knew that because his dad complained about it enough.

So she'd have to take the train into Manhattan to meet him. It would also make sense if they didn't want to be seen together in the neighborhood.

In that case, she'd have to tell Mr. Faber she needed a longer lunch hour. If she didn't, then maybe it wasn't his dad.

How could he find out? He could pay a visit to the store tomorrow under the guise of selling raffle tickets.

This was good; now he was thinking again. He thought of something else. It would be brazen, but should he try it? Why not?

"Dad, did you really lose your watch in the men's room?" he said, just putting it out there.

Julia stiffened beside him. Barry looked over in annoyance.

"What brought that up?"

"Uh, nothing..."

No, not nothing, you idiot. Think!

"I don't know; I just remembered the time I left my Lone Ranger watch in the bathroom at Riis Park. Is that what you did?"

Barry looked past him toward Julia, who stared at the TV. "That's right, Sport," he said. "Although, your mom doesn't believe me. She thinks I lost it while I was inebriated."

On the screen, the sketch had finished and George and Gracie were back in front of the curtain.

Barry gave Julia a small, rueful smile.

("I love Humphry Bogart movies,") said Gracie. ("He really knows how to handle women. You know, George, whenever I see Humphry Bogart in person, he reminds me of you.")

("He does?")

Gracie's head bobbed up and down.

("Uh huh. He always says, 'How's George?'")

"Is that what you think, Mom?"

Julia's pinched expression didn't change.

"Sometimes when your dad gets 'inebriated,' he gets careless, as well as uncaring."

They both looked straight ahead at the screen.

"But why don't you believe he lost it at the office?"

"Maybe it's because I don't want to believe he gets 'inebriated' at the office."

Barry slowly shook his head.

"I don't want to talk about this anymore," said Julia.

("Say good night, Gracie.")

***

Nick, sitting on the sofa next to Teresa, glanced out his living room window at the Feins' apartment. He could see their TV screen flickering, but it was too far away to tell what they were watching. His own family happened to be watching Stop the Music on Channel 7. Bert Parks was crooning, ("If your sweetheart sends a letter of good-bye, It's no secret, you'll feel better 'la di dah.'")

"'Cry,'" said Mary, lying on her stomach in front of the set, scissorng her legs in the air behind her. "It's so easy. This show is stupid."

"Quit kickin'," Carmine complained. He was sitting cross-legged on the floor next to her and her right foot had almost hit him, or so he'd decided. "And if it's stupid, why are you watchin' it?"

"Will you two pipe down?" said Teresa. "We're all watchin' it 'cause it's a good show. Besides, Mary, don't you think Bert Parks is cute?"

"I think he's ugly."

"What would he think of you?" Carmine stuck a finger up his nose, pulled it out, and pretended to shoot a booger at her. Or didn't pretend, you couldn't tell.

"Shut up," she said, flinching away from him.

Nick wasn't listening to them, or to Bert Parks. He looked out the window toward the darkened living room across the way with its flickering blue dot, and remembered a seething June night in 1944, when he and

Barry had crouched together in a field near Saint-Laurent and desperately tried to figure out what their story would be.

As for the case, Forensics could only say Sandra died sometime before midnight, but he knew it had to be closer to 8:30. That's when she told her mother she was going out for a walk, and it didn't figure she'd wander around the neighborhood for three hours.

So that meant the guy had been on the streets between 8:30 and 9:30.

If he'd used a car, someone might have seen him get in or out of it. There were a lot of houses and apartments in the area and it would take a while to cover them all, but people in the neighborhood tended to look out their windows, especially on a nice night like Tuesday.

Bert Parks was introducing Harry Salter and his orchestra as they launched into an unnamed instrumental.

"'Blue Tango,'" Mary said after five notes.

"Why don't you keep your mouth shut?" Carmine suggested.

"Carmine!" Teresa snapped at him.

"Who cares if she knows these dumb songs?"

Nick knew that neither kid wanted to be sitting there. They both wanted to be out running around with their friends, but he wasn't going for it, not at their age, not on a school night. And it didn't matter what show they were watching because they weren't going to like it, so the circus went on.

There was no avoiding it; he'd have to do some things on his own, things that would get him in major trouble if anyone found out. He'd already started taking notes about the case in a little book he carried around that Joe didn't know about.

In the same way he'd studied the FBI Most Wanted list when he was younger, Nick studied the "murder book" they kept as part of every investigation. Guys at the precinct would kid him about it, and he'd remind them there was no use keeping records if nobody looked at them.

Now he had his own little murder book. He took it out of his shirt pocket and glanced through it, his eye falling on the list of sale dates for the watches. He noticed again that two of them had been sold on the same day. This probably meant nothing, but when they eventually tracked down the salesman he might remember something because of it.

Meanwhile, and more immediately, he thought about Barry. Nick was

well aware of his own part in the insanity that took place in that field. If
the shit ever hit the fan, who knows how Barry might feel about throwing
in one more confession.

He'd have nothing to lose.

("Ring! Stop the Music!!")

He looked up and noticed that Carmine was staring at him.

"What?" he said.

Carmine's acne turned an even deeper red and he said nothing. Bert
Parks answered the phone and began chatting with a lady in Omaha.

"What?" Nick said again.

"Nothin'," Carmine mumbled. "I was just wonderin' if you were
gettin' any closer to findin' out…"

He stopped, because he suddenly realized he'd strolled out onto a
tightrope. What the fuck was he doing, asking his old man about the case?
He didn't want his old man to know he even gave a shit.

But Nick was staring at him and he had to, somehow, finish the
sentence.

"…who's pitchin' for the Giants on Saturday."

("No, I'm sorry, Mrs. Buchanan, it's not 'The Blue Mambo.'")

"What a nincompoop," Mary said.

Nick looked at his son like he was crazy.

"Closer to findin' out who's pitchin' for the Giants? What are you
talkin' about?"

"I dunno; never mind," Carmine muttered.

By now, Mary had sensed his discomfort and was staring at him too.

"What are you lookin' at?" he said, and instantly realized his mistake.
She jumped on it.

"I'm lookin' at an imbecile. A moron, an ignoramus. A complete
dodo. Who cares who's pitching for the stupid Gi…"

He shoved her, knocking her onto her back, and was immediately on
top of her, cocking his right arm, ready to punch her lights out.

"Hey!" Nick and Teresa yelled together, as Nick sprang from the
couch.

He grabbed Carmine and yanked him off his sister. "I hate her!"
Carmine screamed.

Nick pulled him across the living room and braced him against the wall.

"The next time you raise your hand to her, tough guy," he growled, "I'm gonna kick your ass from here to Canarsie."

He turned toward Mary, who was crying.

"And you. You stop provokin' him, ya hear me? This is your fault just as much as his. Now the both a yez, go to your rooms. I'm sick'a watchin' ya."

Mary choked back her tears, while Carmine simmered in silence. They both slunk out of the living room, turned into their rooms, and slammed the doors in unison.

"I'm sorry, babe," Nick said to Teresa, who was still in shock. "I gotta get outta here for a little while. Buy some smokes."

"But Nick…"

"They'll be okay; they're just teenagers," he said, unable to resist her favorite phrase. "I just need some air, all right?"

"Sure," she said resignedly.

On the TV screen, Bert and June Valli were into a swinging rendition of "If I Were a Bell I'd Be Ringing."

("Well sir, all I can say is la di da, la di da, la deee da.")

If he was going to do what he planned, Nick thought, why put it off? It was still early enough to pay another visit to Mrs. Weinstock.

"They'll be okay," he repeated to Teresa, "don't worry."

He slipped on his leather jacket and headed for the door.

In her room, Mary lay on the bed crying and pounding her fists in frustration against the mattress. She wished she could kill them both, her piggy brother and her horrible beast of a father. Telling her it was her fault, the nerve of him!

And Carmine. She kept hearing his repulsive, grating voice. "Who's pitching for the Giants?" The Giants, the Giants, the goddamn, almighty Giants. Even the name was disgusting. It made her think of big, swaggering bullies, stomping around, having their way with people, just like her brother and her father. Boy, wouldn't she love to give it to those bastards, just once, about their miserable freakin' Giants!

Then she realized, maybe she could. Maybe she could be the biggest, most obnoxious anti-Giant fan in the world. Why not?

She'd have to know what she was talking about, but she could learn.

She already followed baseball a little, so how hard could it be? Any moron on a street corner could argue about baseball. She'd seen it time and again, how furious they got, screaming like they wanted to rip each other's heads off.

And that was just the effect she wanted. She could imagine the both of them, steam pouring out of their ears as she confidently and knowledgeably reduced their Giant heroes to lumps of shit.

And the thing was, she knew where she could she get this information, this ammunition that would lay them low. It was funny, in a way, because she'd always thought of him as a little twerp. But boy, was he ever going to come in handy now. Eddie Fein didn't know it yet, but he was about to be the architect of her sweet and devastating revenge.

***

The tall, heavyset man lay on his back, alone in the darkened bedroom, hands laced behind his neck, staring at the shadowy cracks in the ceiling. He'd retreated here, claiming to be tired and wanting to lie down, but it was just to get out of that living room with all its tension.

He never liked sitting around watching TV, even in the best of times. The only thing on television that interested him was baseball, and these days, even that was just another way to be tortured.

A soft moan came from his throat as he tightened his fingers around the back of his neck.

He remembered when he was a teenager, deciding to root for the Dodgers to show all the Giant and Yankee fans among his so-called friends and family what he thought of them. It was 1927, the year Babe Ruth hit sixty home runs, and the Dodgers were pathetic. Their version of Babe Ruth was Babe Herman, a good hitter, but a clown to whom the most ridiculous things happened. A fly ball once hit him on the head. A reporter once observed him carrying a lit cigar in his pocket.

In the beginning, none of it mattered, since his rooting was only symbolic, a protest to set himself apart. But eventually, he realized that he'd committed himself, and to ever back down would be humiliating. As time went on, it became all the more important that the Dodgers succeed and the Giants and Yankees fail.

It never happened. Not until he was in his late twenties and just starting to realize he'd never accomplish the things his father did, that he was always going to be mediocre, just like the old man said he was.

In 1939, the Dodgers began to improve. They fired their manager Burleigh Grimes and promoted their shortstop, Leo Durocher. The same Leo Durocher who now managed the Giants.

He used to love Leo Durocher. Leo was the man who'd spurred the Dodgers' turnaround, along with players like Dolph Camilli and Cookie Lavagetto.

It was the same year he'd moved to Brooklyn with his wife and newborn son, and it was like the Dodgers were a welcoming committee. They had their first winning season in seven years, finishing ahead of the Giants for only the second time in his life.

They may have been improving, but he never would, not in the eyes of his father. And presenting the old man with a new grandson did nothing to help, as a tasteless joke or two about talent skipping a generation made clear.

But the Dodgers, they were another story. The next year they finished second, fifteen-and-a-half games better than the sixth-place Giants. And in 1941, they finally won their first pennant in twenty-one years.

The entire borough went crazy, celebrating into the night from Brooklyn Heights to Coney Island. Then it was on to the World Series, and the Yankees.

It did not start off well. The Dodgers lost two of the first three, all close games.

Then came October 5, 1941, his own personal day of infamy, two months before Pearl Harbor. And it had started out as the best day of his life.

He'd done something extraordinary that morning, something spectacular, something that, for the first time in his life, was going to win his father's respect. He'd long ago given up on winning his love. Now it was only his respect he wanted, and could never have.

But he'd get it today. It would be grudging for sure, but there was no way his father could deny him. A woman was alive because of him. His own good judgment and quick action had saved a life. It was a great day, until it suddenly wasn't.

At Ebbets Field, Game Four of the World Series was beginning. He'd settled in at the kitchen table to listen to it, reflecting on what an incredible morning it had been. Saving someone's life. You can't do better than that.

He'd been in the habit of phoning his parents on Sundays. It was for his mother's sake, and it had always been an ordeal. But not today. He couldn't wait to talk to his father.

The imaginary conversation played out in his head, in accompaniment to the game on the radio.

And it was a beautiful accompaniment. The Dodgers were about to nail down the final out and tie up the Series.

They'd taken a 4-3 lead into the ninth, with their ace reliever Hugh Casey on the mound, and were now only one strike away, as Tommy Henrich stood at the plate with two out and no one on base. Mel Allen was calling it.

("Three and two the count on Henrich," he said. "Joe DiMaggio on deck.")

The phone rang in the living room. He heard her answer it.

("Casey goes into the windup. Around comes the right arm, in comes the pitch. A swing by Henrich…he swings and he misses, strike three!")

Game over!

He leaped to his feet with a shout and pumped his fists in the air, as Mel Allen's voice went on, drowning out the gasp coming from the living room.

("But the ball gets away from Mickey Owen!")

("It's rolling back to the screen. Tommy Henrich races down toward first base! He reaches it safely! And the Yankees are still alive, with Joe DiMaggio coming up to bat!")

He stood frozen, his arms half-way above his head in a celebratory pose never completed. His wife stood in the doorway, ashen faced.

"It's your mother," she said, her voice breaking. "Your dad was working in the garden. He suffered a massive stroke. He's…he's dead."

In a daze he followed her into the living room and took the receiver. He listened to his sobbing mother, as she tried to describe what had happened.

All he could think was that his father had, somehow, done it to him again. And this time it was forever.

He felt no sadness. All he felt as he gripped the phone was a hollow, impotent rage.

The play-by-play still floated in from the kitchen. In one ear, his mother wailed pitifully. In the other, the Yankees were scoring run after run, piling them on like shovels full of dirt, burying the Dodgers.

Burying all hope.

Two months later, the Japanese bombed Pearl Harbor and he was in the Army.

CHAPTER NINE

Noon, Friday, September 28th

"When Cortez landed near the site of Veracruz," Mr. Farnsworth intoned, "in order to prevent his men from even thinking about retreating, he did a very unusual thing. What did he do?" Several hands went up, none of which were Eddie's or Lionel's. "Yes, Ronald?"

"He burned all his ships," Ronald Herschfeld piped up smartly.

"He also burned his britches," Lionel whispered to Eddie, who paid him no mind. Three more hours to get through before he could go over to Faber's Sporting Goods and see what he could learn about Sandra's lunch plans.

Which gave him a sudden idea. Maybe B.F. was Mr. Faber! Of course. She was having lunch with her boss. What was Mr. Faber's first name? He didn't know, but he'd sure find out this afternoon.

"Edward!"

It was like being awakened by a slap.

"Huh? I mean, yes, Mr. Farnsworth?" He'd almost said "Fartsworth."

"You didn't bring me your mother's signature as I instructed you to."

What was going on here? This was the one thing he thought was under control.

"But you said she didn't have to sign it."

Mr. Farnsworth's eyes zeroed in on him like a D.A. catching a witness in perjury. "Why would I have said anything like that to you?"

The rest of the class swiveled in their seats like a tennis crowd, looking back and forth.

"You said it didn't matter, because you thought my parents were Communists."

He knew this would get lots of "oohs" and murmuring, and it did. Oh well, so what?

There was a flicker of recognition in Mr. Farnsworth's eyes, followed by the more familiar flicker of annoyance.

"I did not accuse your parents of being Communists, Edward. If you remember, all I did was ask you if they were, which is not the same thing. Nice try, but I still want to see your mother's signature on Monday, as well as your new report."

The little bastard, he thought. *Trying to get me in trouble like that.* He could just imagine the rest of them telling their parents about it. Some of those self-righteous idiots would be only too happy to get him fired.

He returned to the lesson.

"In November of 1519, Cortez reached Tenochtitlán, which is now called what, class?"

"Mexico City," most of them answered.

"Psst," Lionel said, "look down."

Eddie did and saw a baseball card being pushed up through his seat crack. It was of Spider Jorgensen, a long-time utility infielder with the Dodgers who had been traded to the Giants last year in mid-season. He was wearing a Giants uniform on the card, and Eddie had never seen it before. He picked it up and glanced back at Lionel, who gave him a satisfied grin.

"I'll take that, Edward," said Mr. Farnsworth, striding up the aisle and snatching it away from him. "And since you're more interested in baseball cards than history, I'd like that report to be at least a thousand words."

The bell rang.

Eddie nodded morosely, as the sounds of seats being pushed up filled the air around him. He joined the others as they all formed a line at the side of the room.

"If he wants a thousand words, draw him a picture," Lionel suggested. "Actually, I'm glad you have to write that thing because you deserve it, you sonofabitch. You lost my card."

"You lost your own card. And I should make you write it for me. Who asked you to show it to me right then? Couldn't you wait two more minutes?"

"Okay, now, no talking in the hall," Mr. Farnsworth said, as he always did.

He watched the class file out of the room and stepped out the door after the last of them, closing it behind him. He gave a look of disgust at the baseball card in his hand. Spider Jorgensen in a Giants uniform.

They all clattered down the Down staircase, two flights to the street. Those who were going home for lunch peeled off from those who were continuing on into the basement lunchroom, which included Eddie and Lionel.

"Mmm, chow mein today," Lionel said, sniffing the air.

"You're smelling the boiler room," said Eddie. "You only know it's chow mein 'cause it's Friday."

"Did he really say your parents were Commies?"

"Hey, Lionel, hey, Eddie, wait up!"

Ronald Herschfeld arrived at the double doors behind them just in time to catch the backswing, which he absorbed mostly in the stomach and face. He staggered back, then finally got in synch and pushed his way through.

"I'm not going home for lunch today," he explained. "My mom's helping my dad out 'cause his secretary's sick." He fell in step beside them. "Hey, I heard the Yankees can clinch this afternoon."

"What's Joe DiMaggio's batting average?" Lionel asked him.

"I don't know," said Ronald. "Three-hundred something?"

"Two-sixty something," said Eddie.

"How about that rookie who's supposed to be so great, Mickey Mantle?" said Lionel. "What's he hitting?"

"Listen, I don't have to…"

"Two-sixty something," said Eddie.

"If you don't even know that, how do you know they can clinch today?"

Lionel gave him a playful left jab to the arm and faked a right to the midsection that made Ronald cover up.

They got their trays and queued up at the steam table to be served their plates of chicken chow mein, two slices of bread with butter, and a small container of milk.

"In China, do you think they eat their chow mein with bread and butter?" Lionel wondered.

"In China," said Eddie, "they don't eat chow mein."

They took their seats at one of the long tables packed with kids, yelling, laughing, and screaming at each other, with occasional interruptions for swallowing.

Lunchroom veterans like Eddie and Lionel ate defensively, hunkering down and surrounding their plates with their forearms, protecting them from sudden attacks by others. In this atmosphere, an unguarded plate of food was just begging to wind up in your lap.

Ronald, not used to eating in school, made a mistake right away. He held up his container of milk to take a sip.

Eddie immediately lunged at the underside of it with his fork and stopped just short of puncturing it.

"Hey!" Ronald yelled, pulling the container away and splashing some drops onto his shirt.

"You should never drink your milk like that," Eddie told him. "You should always keep it on the table and bend over it. If I weren't your friend just now, that milk would be pouring out of the bottom."

"And if you weren't HIS friend, Ronald," Lionel advised, "you'd be holding it over his head the minute he did it to you. In lunch warfare, every move has a counter-move. It's called a lunch counter." Lionel cracked himself up.

"Hi, Eddie."

It was a girl's voice, just behind him. He turned around.

"Hi, Mary," he said in surprise. "When did you start eating here?"

"I didn't, and I've gotta get home soon. Can I talk to you for a minute?"

Since the end of summer Eddie had seen Mary DiFazio a couple of times from a distance. Now he noticed how much she'd changed. Before, she'd been a tall, gangling tomboy, and not all that pretty. But right here, standing over him, she looked almost beautiful, with long, dark hair and sultry, gray eyes. It was almost like she'd become a different person.

"Sure," he said, and waited for her to go on.

"I mean, in private." She glanced at Lionel and Ronald, who were gawking at her. Then, with a tilt of her head, she indicated the far corner of the lunchroom near the tray disposal window.

Could this be a trick? Eddie looked around to see if he could spot Carmine or his friends anywhere, but he didn't see them.

"Watch my food," he said to Lionel as he got up.

By now, Lionel had regained his tongue.

"Ohh, Mary, baby, you're breaking my heart. Why do you want him when you could have me?"

She turned and flashed him a withering look.

"'Cause you're Lionel Gluck, the dumb cluck, the stupid schmuck, not worth a…" She leered meaningfully at him, as Ronald giggled.

"C'mon, Eddie," she said, turning away.

He followed her over to the corner, noticing that one of the student lunchroom monitors was looking their way. He thought that was good. For all he knew, Carmine was hiding on the other side of the partition, waiting to pull him through the tray disposal window, or at least try.

She stood close to him. He could smell her perfume and wondered whether her mother let her wear it or she was doing it on the sly. In any case, it smelled good.

"You know everything about baseball, right?" she asked him.

"Well, not everything."

"But enough," she said with a trace of impatience. She evidently was not impressed by his modesty. "If you were arguing with a Giant fan, what would you say?"

"That would depend on what he said."

"What if you started the argument? What would you say?"

"I usually don't start arguments."

She looked up at the ceiling and sighed.

"Okay, here's the thing: I want to be an anti-Giant fan, and I want you to teach me how."

"You want to be a Dodger fan?"

"No, I want to be an anti-Giant fan."

He thought about it for a moment. "So you don't care about the Dodgers; you only want to know bad things about the Giants that you can use in an argument."

"Exactly!" Her eyes lit up and she broke into one of the prettiest smiles he ever saw. "Can you do it?"

"I guess so," he said. "But why do you want to go through all the trouble?"

The smile vanished and her expression hardened.

"'Cause I hate the Giants. And I hate my brother and I hate my father."

Eddie knew that kids were always saying stuff like that, but there was something extra in the way she said it.

"I know what you mean about your brother," he said. "I'd hate him too, if I were you. In fact, I already hate him and I'm still me. But your father…"

"He's just as bad. Now, I don't wanna talk about it." She folded her arms in front of her. "Are you gonna help me or not?"

"Okay, okay, give me a minute."

He was beginning to get an idea, a risky one, but maybe it could pay off.

"All right," he said, "I'll do it. But only if you'll do something for me."

"What?" she said, on guard.

"Does your father ever talk about his cases?"

"Sometimes, a little, why?"

"Listen," he said softly, making her lean in closer, which wasn't too bad either, "Sandra Weinstock was a good friend of mine. I want to know what your father's been doing about it, and if he suspects anyone yet. Could you find out something like that for me, without anyone knowing?"

Her eyes widened, which was not at all the reaction he expected.

"You mean, spy on him?" she said with a mischievous grin. "Oh, that would be great!"

"Okay," he said, "you've got a deal."

He held out his right hand so they could shake on it, forgetting about the bandage.

She noticed it just in time, before she was about to grab hold of it, and pulled back.

"What happened to your hand?"

"This is from being a Dodger fan. But never mind that, just take hold of my fingers."

She did so, gently with her fingertips, which felt kind of nice. They stood that way for a moment.

"Tell me something bad about the Giants," she said.

"Sal Maglie has trouble with left-handed hitters," he said, looking into her eyes.

"Terrific!"

She gave his fingers a little squeeze. Of course, he knew the Dodgers had only one left-handed hitter in the lineup, but she hadn't asked him that.

***

Faber's Sporting Goods was under the el on 86th Street, directly across the trolley tracks from Al's Soda Fountain. It was a small place that had been struggling of late since a new and larger Davega's Sporting Goods franchise had opened on 20th Avenue. This recent development hadn't exactly lightened Mr. Faber's general mood, which was sour to begin with.

Eddie entered the store shortly after three o'clock and found him behind the counter, unpacking a carton of footballs and muttering to himself.

"Hi, Mr. Faber."

The old man looked up and squinted at him through thick, rimless glasses.

"Oh, it's you. If you're just here to look around, you could grab a broom and help me clean up the goddamn sawdust they pack these things in. Why they pack footballs in sawdust is beyond me."

He straightened up and leaned against the counter.

"Or are you actually gonna buy something for a change?"

Eddie was about to say he was selling raffle tickets for the P.A.L., but suddenly remembered Mr. Faber hated the P.A.L. because they bought their equipment from Davega.

"I was thinking about a new Dodger cap," he said, "but I'd be glad to help you out."

This was good. This might be an even better approach.

"Nah, forget it; I'll clean it up myself. I did everything before and I can do everything now. If I need help from the customers, I might as well go out of business. You are a customer, aren't you?" He looked at Eddie accusingly.

"Sure, sure." He picked up a Dodger cap and gave it a speculative glance.

"I was really sorry to hear about Sandra, Mr. Faber," he said.

"Yeah," the old man said quietly, taking a football out of the carton, wiping it off with a rag, and placing it on a shelf behind him. "Such a sad and terrible thing. You know, it would've been three years ago today that she started working here."

Three years ago today. Would that be an occasion for lunch with the boss?

"Can I ask you a question, Mr. Faber? What's your first name?"

"Bernard. Why?"

Yes! Yes! "Nothing, I just never knew it."

This was looking good, but it still didn't prove anything. He thought maybe he could take it a step further.

"You know, I think I remember Sandra telling me it was going to be three years," he said. "Was she supposed to have lunch with you today?"

Mr. Faber was about to place another ball on the shelf, but he stopped.

"Funny you should ask me that. Do you know the police asked me the exact same thing?"

His stomach did a little flip.

"They did? What did you tell them?"

"That it was the first I'd ever heard of it. And now you're saying she told you we were going to have lunch? Maybe you should tell the police that."

Oh God, what had he done?

"Well, I'm not really sure," he tried to backtrack. "I thought I remembered it, but I could be wrong."

And it also meant, he realized sickeningly, that B.F. could still be his dad.

But that wasn't the end of his problems. Mr. Faber, it seemed, wasn't going to let it go.

"If you don't tell the police about it, I will." He squinted even harder at him, his eyeglasses glinting. "It could be important. You must have remembered it right. Otherwise, how would you even know about it? You wouldn't just make something like that up."

"No, no. Of course I wouldn't."

And then it got even worse.

The door banged open and Carmine and Vito Peccarino came into the store.

They glanced at Eddie for a moment and then Carmine turned his attention to the rack of baseball bats against the side wall. He began to rummage through them.

"Here, lemme show ya somethin', Vito," he said. "I got Bobby Thomson's new stance down perfect."

Eddie could sense Mr. Faber tensing up behind the counter.

"Leave those bats alone," he said. "They're for sale, not for playing around."

Carmine ignored him. "Look at all these crappy models here. Carl Furillo, Duke Snider; these ain't no good. Ah, here we go, Bobby Thomson." Vito looked on in smirking admiration.

Mr. Faber started to come out from behind the counter.

"Did you hear what I said? Leave them alone."

"Oh, hi, Mr. Faber," Carmine said, as if noticing him for the first time. He drew a bat out of the rack and hefted it.

"I'm thinkin' of buyin' this one, but I gotta try it out. You let people try things out before they buy 'em, don't ya?"

He turned to Vito, who was now giggling.

"See, when Bobby Thomson was standin' up straight, he was only battin' .230. Now, he's been killin' the ball 'cause he crouches down like this while he's waitin' for a pitch."

He got into a crouch and began to leisurely swing the bat back and forth at waist level, coming up just short of a glass cabinet.

"Put it back, I'm warning you," Mr. Faber said, as he stepped behind the counter and reached under it.

Eddie moved away, trying to get as far to the side as he could, looking for the shortest path to the door if he needed it.

Carmine took another casual swing in the direction of the glass cabinet. Then he turned the bat sideways and held it out toward Mr. Faber, like a peace offering.

"Gee, Mr. Faber," he said, smiling at him and slowly walking up the aisle to the counter, "I don't wanna cause no problems. We were just goin' by and I saw my friend Shrimp Boat over there." He indicated Eddie. "So I came in to say hello."

Mr. Faber, his hand still under the counter, gazed at him evenly.

"You're not gonna say hello to him with a bat in your hands. So I'm telling you for the last time. Put it back."

"Okay, okay," Carmine laughed, moving over to the bat rack and sliding it in. "Just wanted to talk to my friend over there." His other friend Vito was finding this hysterical.

"Then you're gonna talk to him outside."

Mr. Faber made a sweeping motion toward the door with the hand that wasn't still under the counter.

"Let's go. Out!" He looked over at Eddie. "You too."

Carmine had moved over to the entrance, and now he stood there making a courtly bow and swinging his arm toward the street in a "you first" gesture, convulsing Vito in the process.

Eddie looked back helplessly at Mr. Faber, who glowered at him.

"And don't forget what I told you. If you don't do it, I will."

Carmine continued to hold the door open, as he gingerly moved by him. He had a quick impulse to fake toward Bay Parkway and then bolt down the street toward 21st Avenue, but Carmine grabbed his arm and put an end to that idea.

He was marched up the block, with Vito trailing along, past the Famous Cafeteria and Thom McCan Shoes, to an entryway just beyond, that led to some apartments above. Carmine pushed him against the door, and they stood, blocking him off from the street.

Were they going to pull the knife again?

Carmine leveled an angry gaze at him.

"Somebody told me somethin' about you, you little cocksucker. What were you doin' tryin' to hold hands with my sister in the lunchroom?"

Eddie blinked. The question was so surprising, and so stupid, that he didn't know what to say. And then he realized how ridiculous this was.

Here, he'd gone and tampered with evidence in a police investigation. Then, instead of just keeping his mouth shut, he'd gotten Mr. Faber to make him go to the police and lie. And for all he knew, his dad still could've done it.

Now, on top of it all, here was Carmine, probably about to beat the shit out of him. And for what, holding hands with his sister? No, no, wait, TRYING to hold hands with his sister?

The sheer lunacy of it overwhelmed him. He started to laugh, and then he couldn't stop. It just poured out of him in torrents, like a fountain of raucous, whooping cackles. He practically shrieked with laughter.

Carmine and Vito took a step back and looked around nervously.

"Hey, shut up," Carmine said. "What the fuck's the matter with you?"

Compared to the cops, compared his real problems, this was pathetic.

"Vito," he said, still laughing, "you know why Carmine wanted to be alone with me yesterday? 'Cause he wanted to talk about you."

Vito shot a look at Carmine, who continued to stare at Eddie.

"What the fuck are you tryin'a pull?" he said.

"It's true, Vito. Ask him what he told me about you."

He was ad libbing, but then he remembered something he'd once heard Frankie Fontana say.

A feeling surged through him, like Popeye draining a can of spinach.

"Ask him what his nickname is for you."

Carmine's face flushed, and Vito saw it.

"He calls you Pecker," said Eddie. "And if you don't believe me, ask Frankie."

Vito's eyes narrowed. He glared at Carmine, who started to say something. Eddie used this instant of distraction to duck between them and take off.

He ran down the block, sprinting toward Bay Parkway. The light turned in his favor just as he reached the corner, and he never broke stride, racing across the trolley tracks, between the posts of the el to the other side of 86th Street.

He sped down Bay Parkway, finally daring to slow up as he approached his building, quickly looking back over his shoulder. They were nowhere in sight.

As he turned his head forward again, he practically smashed into Ronald Herschfeld.

Ronald was ecstatic.

"Eddie," he said, his voice filled with wonder, "I just saw the greatest Yankee game of my life. It was on TV just now, the first game of the double header. Allie Reynolds pitched a no hitter. His second no hitter of the season! Ted Williams was the last guy he had to get out. Ted Williams! He hit a foul ball behind the plate and Yogi Berra dropped it. Can you believe it? So they still had to get Williams out. Then, guess what! Williams popped it up behind the plate *again*. *Again!* And this time Yogi caught it! Allie Reynolds pitched a no hitter! It happened just now, and if they win the second game, they'll clinch the pennant!"

Eddie was thinking furiously, as Ronald babbled on. Actually, there was a way out of one problem, a big one. He didn't really have to go to the cops; he just had to tell Mr. Faber he had. The old man would never know. He'd drop by the store tomorrow and do that very thing.

He stared down the block again and made sure Carmine and Vito really weren't coming. Then he turned back to Ronald.

"You know?" he said. "That's the most unimportant thing I've ever heard."

***

Nick navigated the unmarked '43 DeSoto into the parking area behind the precinct house as Joe Flannery removed a piece of gum from his mouth and flipped it out the window. Nick had once asked him why he didn't wrap it up in a piece of paper and put it in the ashtray like a human being, and Joe had replied that, as a public servant, he was helping out his fellow public servants, the street cleaners, by keeping them employed.

They'd just spent the last several hours questioning neighborhood residents whose windows looked out on the streets leading away from Bensonhurst Park, talking to dozens of people, leaving dozens of cards with their phone number. So far, no one had remembered seeing anyone matching the general description.

"You gonna listen to the Dodger game tonight?" Joe asked him, as they got out of the car and started walking toward the precinct house.

"Nah. Why should I listen to a Dodger game?"

"'Cause it matters to the Giants. If the Dodgers win tonight, they'll be a full game up on 'em with two to go. They'll still be in control of the situation."

"And if they lose, the Giants are tied with 'em."

"That ain't gonna happen. The Phillies are pitchin' Karl Drews and they always kill him."

"Suit yourself."

It had been a very bad moment for Nick last night at Mrs. Weinstock's. When he'd gotten there, the apartment was full of friends and relatives who'd arrived earlier in the evening to pay their respects. For privacy, he took her into Sandra's room to talk.

He was about to show her a photo of Barry and ask if she'd ever seen him, or if Sandra had ever mentioned his name, when he glanced down at the desk calendar.

It was like being kicked in the groin.

They hadn't taken the calendar with them out of respect for Mrs. Weinstock's wish to keep the room intact. Nick had suggested that, at that point, they didn't need to be hauling stuff away unless they knew it was relevant. Joe had gone along.

Now, as the letters "B.P." stared up at him, it was like someone had invaded his home and painted them all over his walls. He almost lost it for a moment.

"Who's been in this room?" he thundered.

It startled Mrs. Weinstock, who got all flustered.

"Nobody," she said defensively.

Then she remembered the boy who was selling raffle tickets. She may have left him alone in there, she said, but only for a minute. She tried to recall his name, but couldn't.

Nick demanded to see the raffle ticket. She didn't know where she'd put it. Finally, after he watched her frantically search the kitchen, she found it.

On the back was the signature of the seller: Eddie Fein.

"I'm gonna be glued to the radio tonight," Joe was saying, as they reached the front of the building and trotted up the steps to the main entrance. "It's too bad they can't televise the road games. I've been listenin' to the radio my whole life, but once you get used to seein' it, it's not the same."

"You should be glad it ain't on TV," Nick said. "Carolyn would be wantin' to watch her favorite shows tonight, and you wouldn't get to see the game."

"Bullshit!" Joe said, louder than he had to. "I can watch any fuckin' game I please, any fuckin' time I want."

Nick was sorry he'd joked about it. Joe and his wife had a testy relationship, and they'd probably had a fight about the very thing.

He got to his desk and saw there was a pile of messages waiting. One of them was from Bernard Faber, wanting to talk to him. He wondered what that could be about.

CHAPTER TEN

Friday Evening, September 28th

As they began the bottom of the ninth in Philly, Carl Erskine's right arm was on its metaphorical last legs. He hadn't been pinch-hit for in the top of the inning, even with the score tied and the Dodgers desperately needing a run, because Charlie Dressen had lost all faith in his bullpen and was riding Ersk to the finish.

He'd been staked to a 3-0 lead, which could have been a lot more, since his teammates had been whacking Karl Drews around pretty good. But Drews got out of jam after jam, dancing through raindrops in practically every inning until the seventh, when he was relieved by Andy Hansen.

Andy was a Giant castoff who'd been picked up by the Phillies earlier in the season and, now in this game, was doing more for the Giants than he ever did as a Giant. He'd given up one measly single in three innings.

A 3-0 lead would've been plenty for Erskine in most games, but Carl was pitching on two days' rest and was wearing down. Little by little, the lead had evaporated. Now, as he started the ninth in a tie game, he had to summon all the strength he had left.

***

("Richie Ashburn stepping to the plate for the Phillies. This game, friends, is as tight as a new pair of shoes on a rainy day.")

Red Barber's drawl drifted into the living room as Julia turned off the TV. The Aldrich Family had finished and now Boxing From St. Nicholas Arena was coming on, signaling the end of her Friday night's viewing.

She came out into the kitchen, where Eddie was slowly pacing back and forth between the stove and the refrigerator, drumming his fingers on the table as he went by it.

"How're they doing, Sport?"

"Tied 3-3. Do you think Dad's listening at work?"

"It's hard to say. Depends on when he gets a break."

Barry had called shortly after 4:30, telling her the *World Telegram* had sprung a 70-page supplement to next Saturday's edition on the proofreading department and everyone had to stay late. There'd be galleys coming in all evening. He didn't know when he'd be home.

("Ashburn settling into the batter's box. He's gone oh-for-four tonight.")

Julia sat down at the table. She realized she hadn't listened to a game with Eddie, just the two of them, in a while. This might be fun.

("Erskine winds and delivers...a fast ball inside.")

Eddie, as he paced back and forth, had been thinking about the watch. He decided that Nick did not know for sure if it was his dad's, because, if he did, he would've arrested him already. That was something to hold onto.

("Erskine wheels and deals. Change-up in the dirt for ball two.")

"Mom," he said, just throwing it out there once again, "what kind of watch did Dad have?"

Julia gave him a weary look.

"Again with the watch? Why does everyone want to know about the watch?"

"Everyone?"

("Clyde King is starting to heat up in the Dodger bullpen.")

"Well, Nick. He wanted Teresa to buy him something like it for Christmas."

Really, Eddie thought. So Nick asked her about the watch, but he didn't tell her the real reason.

"What kind was it?"

"A Hamilton Martin."

("The two-oh pitch to Ashburn,") the radio intruded, ("is swung on and blooped into shallow left field. Pafko coming over, Reese and Cox going out. It could be trouble...and it is; it drops in for a base hit. The

Phillies have the potential winning run on.")

He couldn't let the game distract him. Hamilton Martin, he had to remember that.

"Why did you get mad when I asked you last night?"

She sighed. "Oh honey, I wasn't mad at you. It's just that I got it for your dad on a special anniversary, and I was upset that he lost it."

Eddie thought about it. Special anniversary.

"Was it engraved?" he asked.

If it was, then his dad was innocent. Nick couldn't have found a watch that was engraved, or there'd be no doubt. Please, let her say it was engraved.

"No," she said.

("Dick Sisler is the batter, and the Dodger infield is playing in for the sacrifice bunt.")

"It doesn't matter," Julia went on. "It was our first anniversary after he came home from the war, and it was special."

"Why did you think Dad wasn't telling you the truth about it?"

"What's going on here? Am I being interrogated or something?"

"No, no," he said, as Sisler laid down a perfect bunt, moving Ashburn over to second, "it's just that I'm trying to understand."

Julia got up from the table and went over to the counter. She fumbled in her purse for her cigarettes.

"Believe me, kiddo, I'm trying to understand too."

("Lefty-swinging Bill Nicholson is due up and it looks like they're going to walk him intentionally and pitch to the right-hand-hitting Puddin'head Jones. Campy is signaling for four wide ones.")

She tapped a Chesterfield out of its pack, lit it up, and sat back down, as, on the radio, Nicholson trotted to first and Willie Puddin'head Jones, the Phillie third baseman, approached the plate.

"You know, when I first met your dad he hardly drank at all."

("Erskine comes set and deals...a curve ball on the outside corner, strike one.")

"In those days, he was really something, your dad. You don't remember this because you were only a baby, but, one time, we were taking you to the Prospect Park Zoo. We were standing on the platform of the Bay Parkway station, waiting for the train, when we heard someone scream."

("The 0-1 pitch to Jones…fast ball, just missing inside.")

"A woman had fallen onto the tracks. Some stupid kids were chasing each other around and they accidentally bumped into her, and she lost her balance. When she landed, her foot got wedged between the ties, and she couldn't get it out. She was flailing around and didn't see how close she was to the third rail."

He stared at his mother, as Red Barber told everyone listening, which was not them at the moment, that Jones had already gotten two hits in the game.

"We could hear the signal bells going off downstairs. A train was about to pull into the station. There must've been thirty people on that platform and everyone was in shock, except your father. He yelled at the woman not to move, and then he jumped down onto the tracks."

("Erskine looks in for the sign…")

"We could hear the train coming. If I wasn't holding you in my arms I don't know what I would've done. He kept telling her to stay calm, and, amazingly, she was doing it. But I wasn't calm. I wanted to jump out of my skin, I was so scared.

"Finally he got her foot free. Then he helped her up and started to lift her onto the platform. We could see the train by then, coming into the station, right at them."

("A check of the runners…")

"He was incredible. He even made sure she was safe before he started to climb up himself, and then he just made it."

("And here's the pitch…")

"Oh, honey, your dad was so wonderful. I wish you could've seen it."

("…swung on and lined between third and short, into left field for a base hit! Ashburn is rounding third and heading home. Pafko's throw is…not in time! Ashburn slides in, and the Phillies have beaten the Dodgers four-to-three!")

The words went past him. He stared at his mother in amazement.

("Friends,") said Red Barber, his voice filled with wonder, ("as impossible as it seemed just a short time ago, that thirteen-and-a-half-game lead is now the stuff of history. The Dodgers and the Giants, with two games to go, are in a flatfooted tie. Now what do you think about that!")

***

Two blocks away, in a bar called the Bath Avenue Tavern, Barry's fingers tightened around his glass of Johnny Walker Red as he stood in the crowd of men listening to the game. He'd come in during the eighth inning, and it was the third bar he'd been to since he left work.

He didn't usually hang out in bars. Drinking, to him, was not a sociable activity and it was easier and less expensive to do it at home, as long as Julia didn't nag him about it. The call he'd made to her earlier, lying about having to stay late, was because he didn't want to see her just yet.

Not until after he'd sufficiently blotted out the events of that afternoon.

To say he only drank at home wasn't entirely accurate, since he generally allowed himself a drink or two at lunch. Today, he'd allowed himself one more, which was his first mistake. The second, third, and fourth mistakes were the blatant typos that got by him.

His supervisor had called him into his office, and what followed was humiliating, to put a polite word on it. Among other things, he'd been told that people in the department were calling him "the hundred-proof reader."

The rest of it, though, was what he was working the hardest to forget.

John O'Houlihan, the proprietor of the bar, scanned the crowd. He wasn't a baseball fan himself but he liked what was happening. The closer things got, the more people seemed to want to experience the games in the company of like-minded individuals.

The best investment he'd ever made was the television set he'd put in at the beginning of the season. Even the games that were only on radio seemed to draw a crowd now, since the pennant race heated up.

As he glanced around the room during the odd moments when he and the other bartender weren't busily serving drinks and collecting money, he thought that tonight could come close to a record.

There were a lot of new customers in the joint, faces he didn't recognize, but one that he did belonged to Jimmy Riccio. Jimmy was a part-time taxi driver who lived around the corner on 21st Avenue and was one of the Friday night regulars. He was also a Thursday night regular and most of the other nights too.

You had to keep an eye on him, even though he was a little guy. He could be pugnacious as hell when he'd had a couple.

"How about my Giants?" he said for the fifth time to the man on his right, who was giving him the cold shoulder. "Tied for first and they didn't even have to do nothin' to get there. The Dodgers just rolled over and gave it to 'em. Right, pal?"

"Yeah, sure," said the guy.

"Bums. That's what they call 'em and that's what they are. Who here says they ain't?" he shouted, looking defiantly around him.

"Shut up," somebody said.

John O'Houlihan reached up to switch off the radio and turn on the TV to Channel 4, where the Friday night fights from St. Nicholas were in progress.

"Watch out Jimmy don't start nothin'," he told the other bartender.

He had a place full of pissed off Dodger fans, and he would have preferred to keep the fisticuffs confined to the TV set.

Jimmy Riccio didn't like being told to shut up.

"Who the hell said that?" he demanded to know, glaring at the crowd of men milling around him. "Say it to my face, you Dodger asshole. Who the hell said that?"

"Take it easy, Jimmy." John reached across the bar and put a hand on his arm, both to calm and to warn.

It worked for the moment.

"Hey, John, whatever ya say." Jimmy turned away from the others and favored him with a gap-toothed grin. "Ya know why I like you? 'Cause you ain't a friggin' Dodger fan. Lemme show ya somethin'." He reached into the back pocket of his trousers and took out his billfold. "You ever seen my lucky two-dollar bill?"

"Yeah, Jimmy, many times. Why don'tcha leave it in your wallet, keep it safe?"

"This here's a special two-dollar bill."

Jimmy took it out and waved it in the air, starting to address the crowd again.

"I got it August 13th at the Polo Grounds, when the Giants beat the Phils a double-header, and they ain't lost since. I bet you mugs never saw nothin' like this here piece'a legal tender."

"Yeah?" said the guy on his left, a large, swarthy truck-driver type. "Lemme see it."

He snatched it out of his hand, to Jimmy's shock, and held it just out of reach, giving it a dirty look.

"Hey!" Jimmy yelled.

He tried to climb the guy, but the truck driver held him at bay with his other arm, while he passed the two-dollar bill along to his buddy, who also gave it a dirty look, and passed it on.

Shit! O'Houlihan thought. *Someone's gonna tear it up and we're gonna have a fuckin' brawl on our hands.*

"Give it back to him!" he shouted over the hubbub. "Give it back to him or I'm clearin' the place. You hear me?"

Nobody seemed to. Jimmy had gotten down off his barstool and was cursing and clawing his way through the crowd, desperately chasing his prized possession.

Each guy who looked at it frowned or sneered or muttered an insult. The last one pretended to spit on it, before finally giving it back to him.

"Here," he said, "you hang on to this. It ain't over yet; we got two games to go. You're gonna eat that thing."

Everyone within earshot broke into cheers.

"Fuck yez all," Jimmy muttered, as he pushed his way back to the bar and got on his stool.

He carefully folded the bill, returned it to his wallet, which he patted once for reassurance, and signaled John for a refill.

For the next half-hour, he punctuated his drinks with a stream of invective about the Dodgers, their mothers, their wives, and their sanitary habits, all but unmindful of the pleas and threats from John O'Houlihan to knock it off.

Finally, he'd used up his money, except for the two-dollar bill. He dismounted unsteadily from the stool and elbowed his way to the rear of the club, pausing at the door for a parting shot, which he couldn't seem to come up with.

After a moment of unsteadiness, he blurted out, "The Dodgers are choke artists!"

He held his hands around his neck to illustrate the point.

"Choke artists!"

It wasn't much of a taunt, but he was running out of steam by then. He leaned heavily against the door and it opened, his momentum carrying him out onto Bath Avenue, where he staggered for a moment, righted himself, and then started to make his tipsy way toward 21st Avenue, oblivious to everything.

Included in his oblivion was the man who'd come out of the bar behind him, and was now following him down the street.

CHAPTER ELEVEN

Saturday Morning, September 29ᵗʰ

Nick and Joe carefully squatted in the tall grass of the vacant lot on 21st Avenue, midway between Bath and Cropsey, trying to disturb as little of the scene as possible. Some of it had already been trampled on by the cop who'd discovered the body, unavoidable, since he had to wade through the underbrush after having seen the victim's leg sticking out of a clump of weeds.

"Definitely strangled," Joe said. "And we know this guy. This is Jimmy Riccio, the drunk that keeps gettin' into fights at that place around the corner from here, the Bath Avenue Tavern."

"Smells like that's where he might'a been," Nick said. "And it wasn't much of a fight from the looks of it. Somebody must'a taken him by surprise, or he was too drunk to know what was happenin'."

Both of them realized that what they were seeing was very unusual. Most homicides in the neighborhood came out of domestic quarrels, as a result of beatings, blunt instruments, knives, things like that. Sometimes there was a shooting, but robbery was usually involved. Strangulation they almost never saw, and now it had happened twice in three days.

"Whattaya think?" Nick said. "Is this tied in with Sandra Weinstock?"

"Could be, although I gotta tell ya, I can't see what connection she'd have with a guy like Jimmy Riccio."

Joe took the piece of gum out of his mouth, carefully wrapped it in a tissue, and put it in his pocket, respecting the integrity of a crime scene now, not donating work for the street cleaners.

Nick moved around behind the body, which was lying on its side. He could see that the back pocket had been pulled inside out.

"Guy's wallet was taken," he said.

"So maybe it was robbery."

"Don't make sense if it's the same perp. What's that over there?"

He'd just noticed a square, black, wallet-like object in the weeds a few feet away. He moved over and carefully picked it up with his gloved hand. It was Jimmy Riccio's.

"No money," he said, looking through it.

"So, like I said, maybe it was robbery."

"Hmm."

A young uniformed cop approached them. "The M.E. is here. Do you want me to escort him over?"

"Give us another minute," Nick said.

He looked once again at Jimmy Riccio, the eyes staring, mouth slightly open, tongue protruding between his lips. There seemed to be a small spot of green just inside his mouth.

Nick leaned over and separated the lips a bit further. There was something in there, all right, a small, crumpled up piece of paper. He reached in and took it out.

"How about this?" he said, unfolding it. "A two-dollar bill. Either he was carryin' his money in his mouth, or our perp left him a tip."

He looked at it more closely.

"Holy shit."

"What?" Joe said, coming over to look.

Nick shook his head at the insanity.

"I think we might'a found what Sandra Weinstock and Jimmy Riccio had in common."

He remembered what had set Barry off on Tuesday night before he left the apartment. The Dodgers were losing a double-header. They'd lost again last night, a big one.

Nick couldn't stop staring at the two-dollar bill in his hand, and the autograph written on it, "To Jimmy, a great Giant fan! Sal Maglie."

***

"Eddie, wake up."

Julia gently shook his shoulder.

"You have a phone call. Mary DiFazio wants to talk to you, although I can't imagine what she'd want."

He slowly emerged from a dream in which he'd been standing on the platform of the Bay Parkway station, watching his father trying to rescue Sandra Weinstock from the tracks as the train was pulling in. Suddenly, Barry had stopped and looked up at him. "Save me," he'd said.

Eddie blinked and his mother's face came into focus.

"Mary DiFazio?" he said in a thick voice.

"Yes, and speak softly while you're on the phone. Your dad's still sleeping."

The phone was in the living room, which shared a common wall with his parents' bedroom. He looked at his watch and saw that it was only 8:30 as he padded down the hall, Julia right behind him.

"Tell her not to call so early on a weekend next time," she said. "It's a good thing I got to it before it woke up your father."

"H'lo?" he said into the receiver.

"Something's happened," Mary said in a whisper, "and I can't talk about it. Can you meet me at Al's Soda Fountain in fifteen minutes?"

"Um. I guess so."

Julia was standing over him, listening. What reason could he possibly give her for putting on his clothes and just walking out of the apartment? He'd think of something.

"Sure," he said.

"Okay, I'll see you there." The line went dead.

He stood for a moment with the phone in his hand and then hung it up.

"Mom," he said, "Mary has some reference material I need for my social studies report, and she just found out her family's going away for the weekend, so she has to give it to me now. I'm going out to meet her."

"Right now you're going out? You haven't even had breakfast."

"I know, but they're leaving soon. It won't take long."

He started walking down the hallway toward his room and his clothes.

"Wait a minute, what social studies report? I thought you did it already and it got an A+."

"I'm doing another one for extra credit," he said as he took his pants out of the closet and got into them. "Mary had Mr. Farnsworth for social studies last year and she has some great stuff for me that'll really make the report solid."

He grabbed his shirt from off the back of a chair, threw it on, and ducked into the bathroom, quickly brushing his teeth as she stood by.

"I'll be back in just a little while," he said as he emerged and walked past her.

"Teresa never said anything about them going away this weekend." She followed him down the hall toward the coat closet. "Where are they going?"

"Mary didn't tell me." He reached in and got his jacket. "I'll be back in time for breakfast, Mom, don't worry."

Before she could say anything else he stepped out the door and started down the stairs, aware that she was watching him. He'd have to figure out how to undo all this when the time came and, actually, he realized how. He'd say that Mary thought they were going away but she'd gotten it wrong.

Meanwhile, he wondered what she wanted to tell him.

He hit the street and turned left toward the 86th Street el. Nate Preston and his son James were out in front of the building, hosing down the sidewalk.

"Whatchoo doin' up so early?" Nate asked him with a sly grin. "Couldn't sleep last night after the Dodger game?"

"The Giants got 'em now, Eddie," James said, putting in his two cents. His tone wasn't mocking, like Nate's, but calm and reasonable, with an inevitability about it.

James was Eddie's age, but his voice was deeper, and he was already taller and heavier than his dad, who was small and wiry.

"Oh yeah? We'll see about that," was the best Eddie could come up with at this early hour, as he moved down the block.

Al's Soda Fountain of all places. He'd better get ready for even more abuse from Al Schaefer.

As he opened the door he saw Mary sitting in the far booth in a white middy blouse, daintily sipping a nickel coke through a straw. Al, who was making scrambled eggs and bacon for the three construction workers sitting at the counter, greeted him.

"Hey, the Artful Dodger is here. I want you to know that, in honor of what Puddin'head Jones did to them last night, I've got a special goin' on today. On every ice cream cone I'm gonna add a dollup of chocolate pudding and call them 'Puddin'head Cones.' Whattaya think?"

"I think you should make it Boston cream pie, seeing as how the Giants are gonna get creamed by Boston today."

He sat down across the table from Mary, who smiled at him around the straw.

"That was good," she said. "That's the kind of thing I want you to teach me."

"What happened?" he asked her.

She leaned across the table and spoke in a low voice. "There was another murder last night. My father got a call around six o'clock this morning. The phone's right near my room and he tried to talk soft, but I got out of bed and listened." There was pride in her voice. "It was the same as Sandra Weinstock. Somebody got strangled."

"Did he say who?"

"No, I don't think they knew, only that they found a body."

It passed through his mind that his dad hadn't come home until very late last night. Well, so what?

"Okay, that was good," he told her. "But I need to know what your father is doing about Sandra. Did you find out anything yet?"

"Hey," she said, plainly disappointed at his reaction, "it's not so easy. I can't just look in his little notebook whenever I want to, ya know."

"He has a notebook?"

"Yeah." She gazed off for a moment and started to twirl a strand of her hair around a finger. "Actually, I don't think he ever did that before."

"Can you find out what's in it?"

She released the strand of hair and looked across the table at him.

"Maybe," she said evenly, "but why should I? You still didn't teach me anything about being an anti-Giant fan and I already did something for you. And I even got up at six in the morning to do it, so now it's your turn."

Eddie looked over at Al, who was talking to the three construction workers, and thought for a moment.

"All right," he said, "let me give you an idea of what it's like. Come over to my side of the booth."

He moved further in and made room for her on the seat. She came around the table and slid in beside him. She was wearing that perfume again, which was nice.

"The Giants are playing the Braves up in Boston today," he said to her, "and they're facing Warren Spahn. Now this is what I want you to tell Al over there." He whispered something in her ear and she giggled.

"'Scuse me, Al," she called.

Al was just getting to the punch line of a dirty joke he was telling, starting to lower his voice to deliver it. He looked up in mild annoyance at the interruption.

"Yeah?"

"Do you remember when they used to say, 'Spahn and Sain, and pray for rain'?" she asked him.

"Yeah, so?"

Mary forgot for a moment what the rest of it was and turned to Eddie, who whispered in her ear again.

"Oh, right," she said, and looked back at Al. "Well, after today the Giants are gonna say, 'Spahn and pain, and down the drain.'"

It made the construction workers chuckle, and Al gave a glance of mock disgust at Eddie.

"What are you, her lawyer?"

Eddie shrugged and looked back at him with an expression of innocence.

"He's teaching me how to be an anti-Giant fan," Mary explained.

"Oh, I see," said Al. "Well, I'm not worried about Spahn. The Braves better worry about Sal the Barber. How about that?"

Eddie whispered something else in her ear and she nodded her head.

"Sal the Barber's gonna be shaving himself today. The five-o'clock shadow's comin' off early, right after his two-o'clock shower."

This time, the construction workers cracked up.

"Okay," Eddie said, "end of Lesson One."

"This is fun," Mary said. "When is Lesson Two?"

"As soon as you find out something else. Now I've gotta get back home, so here's our story: You met me here 'cause you had some information for my social studies report and you thought your family was going away for the weekend. But you were wrong; they're not going away. And the stuff you had was about Balboa and I needed stuff about Pizarro, got it?"

He could hardly get the words out right, because she looked so pretty as he explained it to her, her face all serious in concentration. She nodded and they both slid out of the booth and headed for the door.

Al was back to telling the dirty joke, as Eddie held the door open for her like a gentleman and watched her as she moved past him out onto the street.

He was about to remind her again of what their story was, when he suddenly noticed the fear in her eyes. He turned and followed her gaze.

Standing not ten feet away, coldly regarding them, was Nick.

They stood there staring at him.

"Hi, Daddy," Mary said in a little-girl voice.

"Hi, Coach." Eddie tried to sound casual.

Nick didn't answer him. He was looking at Mary.

"You, Miss Wise Guy," he said. "Get back home where ya belong, and apologize to your mother for sneakin' out and makin' her a nervous wreck." He snapped his fingers and jerked his thumb in the direction of Bay 29th Street. "I'll deal with you later."

"But Daddy, I…"

"Home!" Nick said, like a man giving an order to his dog.

Eddie realized that, of course, his mother had phoned Teresa as soon as he'd left and asked her what was going on.

Nick now turned his death-ray gaze on him.

"You I wanna talk to right here."

Mary gave him a quick, helpless glance.

"So long, Eddie," she said softly.

"Bye," he whispered as she started to walk away, his eyes following her.

"You look at me, Romeo," Nick told him.

Eddie couldn't meet his eyes, couldn't do anything but stare at the ground, knowing how guilty it made him look.

After Mary had disappeared around the corner, Nick gave another snap of the fingers and jerk of the thumb.

"Over there," he said, indicating an area beneath one of the staircases leading to the station above them.

Eddie moved over to it and found himself standing in a cramped space, the back of his head practically touching the underside of the stairs. Nick loomed over him.

"They don't treat kids very nice in juvenile correctional facilities," he said. "You might be findin' that out first-hand."

Eddie's stomach gave a lurch.

"I didn't do anyth…"

"You did plenty," Nick cut in. "And you ain't doin' anymore. I could arrest you right now for what you done, remember that. So I'd better like what you're gonna tell me. Why did you change those initials? Why did you make up that story to Mr. Faber?"

Oh God, even that. Mr. Faber hadn't waited; he'd gone ahead and called the police. Everything went wrong. Everything.

A sense of numbness began to creep into him. He heard the sound of a train approaching on the el above him and remembered the dream, the helpless look on his dad's face.

An image came to him, of breaking free, ducking past Nick like he'd ducked past Carmine yesterday. Then he'd run up the stairs to the station platform and throw himself onto the tracks in front of that train.

It was a powerful feeling. In his twelve years of life he'd never had one like it. Yet somehow it didn't scare him.

In fact, it was oddly liberating. If everything was lost, then there was nothing to lose.

He looked up at Nick.

"I don't know what you mean about initials," he said, looking straight at him. "And I told Mr. Faber the truth. Sandra did say she was gonna have lunch with him. I guess it was supposed to be a surprise, and that's why he didn't know about it."

He expected Nick to explode in rage. He braced for it, but it didn't happen. Nick's face held only disappointment, and sadness.

"Who told you to say that, your dad?"

"No!" Eddie said it so emphatically, it surprised him. "He doesn't know anything about it." He was starting to cry now.

Nick's expression hardened. "You're lyin' to me, Eddie. And that's just makin' things worse for yourself. I know you changed those initials; you're the only one who could'a. And Sandra didn't say nothin' of the kind to you." He pointed a finger in Eddie's face, making him flinch. "Make no mistake about this. I meant what I said about juvenile correctional facilities. You wanna stay outta one? You'd better stay outta this. It ain't none'a your business, and it especially ain't Mary's. What were you two doin' in there?"

"She was helping me with my social studies," he said miserably, unable to think of anything else.

"With no books, huh? Well, she ain't helpin' ya anymore with anything. Now go home. Your mother needs you."

Eddie stood there, his nose running, the tears pouring down his cheeks. "You're supposed to be his friend," he sobbed. "You should know better than anyone that he didn't do anything bad!"

Nick suddenly looked tired. "You've got no idea about what I should know." He reached into his jacket pocket, took out a bunch of tissues, and handed them to Eddie.

"Now go home. And stay outta this," he said, gentler this time, but just as final.

CHAPTER TWELVE

Saturday Afternoon, September 29th

As he took his lead off second base, Willie Mays could see that Warren Spahn wasn't paying enough attention to him. He'd paid him more attention when Willie was on first a few minutes ago, but it hadn't mattered. He'd stolen second anyway.

Warren Spahn would always hold a special place in the 20-year-old's heart. His first Major League hit, earlier that season, was against the great left-hander, a home run high over the roof of the Polo Grounds. But it had come only after an 0-for-12 start to his career, and it didn't stop him from going 0 for his next 13. He'd walked into Leo Durocher's office and asked to be sent back to the minors, saying he wasn't good enough for Major League baseball. Leo told him that no matter what he did, even if Willie went 0 for the rest of the season, he was his center fielder.

That was many base hits, several clutch home runs, and a bunch of spectacular catches ago, as now, with one out in the second inning, he could sense Spahn's near-total concentration on Don Mueller at the plate.

Willie took a couple of steps off the bag, as Spahn still didn't give him a glance, checked over each shoulder, making sure the shortstop or the second baseman wasn't sneaking in behind him, took another step toward third as Spahn peered in for the sign, and just kept going.

Walker Cooper, the catcher, yelled but it was too late to do anything but watch Willie raise a cloud of dust at third with a head-first slide, losing his cap in the process. Two pitches later, Mueller plunked a soft line drive over the drawn-in infield and Willie trotted home. The Giants were on their way again.

***

Eddie looked out his bedroom window at the DiFazios' apartment, trying to spot Mary. From his desk chair, the bars of the fire escape outside his window lined up with the bars of the fire escape outside hers, and he could see past them into her room. Over the years, as boys would, he'd sometimes try and catch a peek at her. But her curtains were always judiciously closed.

They were closed right now, and he couldn't see much else in the apartment except Teresa's arm resting on the kitchen table.

He'd been banished by his mother to his room, to write his Inca report and not come out until it was done, receiving these orders to the sounds of his father throwing up in the bathroom.

Barry was awake by the time he'd gotten back. He was pasty-faced and sitting at the table in front of a glass of tabasco sauce and three raw eggs.

He'd said nothing, looked up briefly as Eddie came through the door, then went back to his contemplation of the glass. Julia, on the other hand, wasted no time.

"Why did you lie to me? What's going on between you and Mary DiFazio? Why were you sneaking off to meet her?"

He went for the easiest question. "I wasn't sneaking off. I told you I was meeting her."

"Don't get smart with me." Why did parents always say that? "What were you two doing? And don't tell me it was a social studies report."

"But it really was a social studies report, or it was supposed to be. See, she got confused and thought I needed information about Balboa, but actually it was Pizarro, and…"

"Bullshit!"

Eddie blinked in surprise, and even Barry looked up at her. She rarely used language like that.

"You're just making it up, like you make up everything. Like that story about them going away for the weekend. Teresa said Mary could never have thought that. She knew her father was out on another case."

Before he could stop himself, he glanced over at his dad, who was sitting with his face in his hands after downing his noxious cocktail.

Wherever he was last night, Eddie thought, he sure didn't get this way at work.

"And that business about getting an A+ on your report, that was a lie too, wasn't it?"

He remembered her face lighting up when he'd told her. Tears started to come again. This was ridiculous. When was the last time he cried twice in the same day?

"You never did that report in the first place. Or he's making you do it over, right?"

There was nothing he could do, he was officially crying again. How was he going to get to the truth if he couldn't even pull off something as stupid as this?

Now, he sat at his desk and his eyes drifted from Mary's curtained window to the social studies book and encyclopedia volume in front of him.

The more he read about the Incas, the more he got to like them. They, too, were children whose lives were rudely changed, who'd been forced into battle against grownups much stronger than they were, whose world they couldn't understand.

He was making pretty good progress, paraphrasing the encyclopedia, mixing in some of the stuff from the textbook, and adding what Lionel would call his own charming style. The words were starting to pile up, and he was probably half-way to a thousand when he came to the part about Machu Picchu.

He stopped writing and read it over again, fascinated. Machu Picchu was the lost city of the Incas, the holy shrine that the Spaniards could never find.

And they sure tried, because they assumed the holiest place had to contain the richest treasures. But no matter how many people they tortured and interrogated, they never found anyone who knew where it was.

Eventually, they came to believe it never existed, that it was only an Inca legend. And the whole world thought so too, for almost 400 years, until it was discovered in 1911.

So how did they keep it a secret? Not having a written language helped, and the place was so isolated that anyone who worked on building and maintaining it never left there. The Spaniards couldn't find it because no one knew about it except the people who needed to know.

He thought about Nick. Now that he'd recovered from the scariness and could think about it, something was wrong. Nick had lied to his mom when he asked her about the watch. He said it was for some kind of Christmas present. That's unusual, isn't it? Why ask his mom? Why didn't Nick just ask his dad what kind of watch it was? If the cops suspect a piece of evidence belongs to someone, they go right up and ask him, don't they? If they don't just haul him in, outright. No, something was wrong. It was almost like Nick hadn't told the other cops about his dad. Could that be?

The Incas didn't write things down, but Nick does. He keeps a notebook.

Where was Mary; how could he get a hold of her? He had to convince her to keep trying, don't stop, no matter what her father threatened her with.

He had to know what was in that notebook. That notebook was Machu Picchu.

***

Russ Hodges' voice echoed in the near-empty Bath Avenue Tavern as it issued from the radio on the bar.

("There are no two players in the league, outside of the Dodgers, who hate the Giants more than the man at the plate right now, Walker Cooper, and the man on deck, Willard Marshall. They're both ex-Giants who don't have any love lost for Leo Durocher, and either one of them could tie this thing up with one swing.")

"I don't know what else I can tell ya," John O'Houlihan said to Nick, as the two of them stood at the far end of the bar out of earshot of the four guys huddled over their drinks, listening to the game at the other end.

"Yeah, I'm sure," said Nick, "but bear with me a minute, okay? I want you to take a look at some pictures and tell me if you recognize anybody from last night."

He took out five photos he'd put together including Barry. The others were two guys from their platoon and two of Teresa's cousins.

("One out, here in the ninth, and the Braves have men on first and second. Maglie has a 3-0 lead and is just two outs away from putting the Giants into first place.")

"The joint was real crowded, like I been sayin'," said John O'Houlihan. "There were a whole lotta people I never seen before, goin' in and out all night."

He sounded almost wistful. Here he was, just starting to make decent money out of this dump, and now this had to happen. He was expecting tonight's Dodger game to be his biggest night of the year, and now customers would probably stay away in droves.

Cops coming in here to drink off duty, that was one thing. In fact that was to be encouraged, and he was glad enough to see them whenever they came to bust up a fight. But homicide detectives were another story.

"Take a look at these," Nick said, indicating the photographs. "Anybody familiar?"

("Cooper swings and sends a slow roller toward first. Lockman up with it, fires to Dark at second for the force, the throw back to first...not in time. Two out, and now here's Willard Marshall.")

"Hmm."

O'Houlihan looked over the pictures carefully.

Nick realized this was the first time in his life he'd ever watched a witness looking at mug shots, or a lineup, and hoped there would not be an I.D.

("Maglie into his set position, checking the runners. Here's the pitch to Marshall. A pop-up in foul territory, just off first. Lockman under it. He's got it!

Sal Maglie has just pitched a five-hit shutout and, fans, it took a hundred-fifty-three games to do it, but, for the first time all season, the Giants are in first place!")

"This guy. He was here last night," said John O'Houlihan, pointing straight at Barry.

***

Julia sat on the living room couch finishing her lesson plans for Monday. One of the nice things about weekends was that she didn't have to write them up when she was so tired, after two long subway rides sandwiched around five hours of trying to control a classroom of overactive nine-year-olds.

A few minutes ago, she'd heard Barry curse as he turned off the radio, muttering something about the fucking Braves beating us three out of four and now rolling over for the Giants.

He came into the living room, bleary-eyed and unshaven, a sour expression on his face. She noticed a stain on his undershirt where some of the raw egg had dripped, and had to fight the urge to cry. He looked just like a derelict.

"I'm gonna lie down for a while," he said, moving toward the bedroom.

"Why don't you ever talk to me?" she said to his back, as he closed the bedroom door softly behind him.

She looked at her lesson plans again and felt like ripping them into shreds. She wanted to scream.

Get a grip on yourself, she thought, as she stood up and walked, stiff-legged, into the kitchen to make some coffee. The doorbell rang.

She wondered who it could be on a Saturday afternoon, as she moved aside the peep-hole cover and looked through the hole. There was Nick.

She opened the door.

"Hi, what brings you around?" she said, putting on a smile.

Nick put on his own smile.

"Hey, Julia, nothin' much. I was just on my way home and thought I'd see how the master of the house was doin'.""

"He's the master of the bedroom at the moment. He said he wanted to lie down for a while, but why don't you come in?"

"Thanks."

He stepped inside and noticed that Eddie was standing in the half-open doorway to his room, staring at him.

"Hey there, Eddie," he said, the smile still in place.

"Hi, Coach," Eddie said carefully.

Julia looked at him and sensed something odd. But she figured he'd been so absorbed in what he was doing in there, which had better be writing, that it made him a little slow on the uptake.

"You want some coffee?" she asked Nick. "I was just starting to put some on."

"Nah, that's okay." He glanced out the kitchen window and said, "Jeez, ya know, it's such a beautiful day out there, I'm surprised he's stayin' inside. Ya mind if I go in and ask him if he feels like goin' for a walk or somethin'? He can always tell me to get lost."

It might not be a bad idea, Julia thought. Maybe if he unburdened himself to Nick he'd feel better. At least she hoped he would.

"Sure," she said, "why don't you go in and ask him? He might not even be asleep yet."

Eddie stood in his doorway and watched Nick make his way through the living room, open the bedroom door, and step inside, closing the door behind him.

Was this it? Would his father come out of that room in handcuffs?

"How are you doing with your report?" Julia asked him.

"Good, Mom, I'm about half-way through it." He tried to keep from staring past her toward the bedroom door. "You can even read it for yourself."

He needed her to know he wasn't lying. If she was about to see her husband being taken to jail, he at least owed her that.

The door to the bedroom opened.

Barry came out first, and not in handcuffs. He was still pale and unshaven, but he'd changed his egg-stained undershirt for a clean one and was wearing an open, short-sleeved shirt over it. There was a weak smile on his face.

"I don't know what all this 'guy stuff' is about," he said to Nick over his shoulder, "but it better not be about the Giants winning today, or I'm coming over there tonight after the Dodgers take care of Robin Roberts and dragging you out of bed."

"Don't worry," Nick said, giving him a pat on the shoulder, "I know better than to mock the unfortunate."

Eddie stood silently, as Barry said he'd be back in a little while, and they started out the door.

"Thanks, Nick," Julia said softly as the two of them went by.

Yeah, Eddie thought. *Thanks, Nick. Thanks a whole lot.*

His mouth felt dry and his stomach was queasy as he turned back inside. He sat down at his desk and looked out the window for the umpteenth time at Mary's room. The curtains were now open, and there she was.

***

The sun was getting lower in the sky over Gravesend Bay, promising a spectacular early autumn sunset in about 20 minutes. But right now it was at eye level, so bright the eye could not look at it, casting gigantic shadows of the people as they strolled along the promenade.

They were mostly young couples, some with baby carriages, some with small children who chased each other about and occasionally tried to climb the railing, getting sharp rebukes from their parents.

Nick and Barry sat on one of the benches, which were relatively unused at the moment since they faced the sun. Watching Barry squint reminded Nick of those gangster movies where the cops grilled the bad guys under an intense, bright lamp. The cops didn't do that sort of thing in real life, but it added an interesting touch now, he thought. That and the fact that they were sitting right near the spot where Sandra Weinstock was killed.

Nick had filled the time between the apartment and here mostly with small talk about movies, the weather, etc. Barry had said little, content to let him guide the conversation and decide where they were going.

"You like this place?" Nick now asked him.

"Not really. That fucking sun is just adding to my headache."

"You look like you could use some sun."

"Please, spare me." Barry covered his eyes with one hand and leaned back against the bench. "What's all this that you wanted to talk to me about?"

"We'll get to it. You feelin' all right?"

"Yeah," Barry groaned, "top of the world."

He took his hand away from his eyes and looked over at Nick.

"What's the matter, man? What can I do for you?"

Nick shifted his position on the bench, so he was facing him.

"I got a little problem maybe you could help me with. Where were you last night?"

Barry gave him a wary glance.

"Your problem has something to do with where I was last night?"

"Maybe. Where were you?"

He looked away, not a good sign.

"I was working late."

Nick let it hang there a moment.

"So," he said, "if I was to ask the people in your office, that's what they'd say?"

Barry squinted again, and then stood up.

"This sun is really getting to me; do you mind if we start back?"

"Hey, whatever you want."

They walked back along the promenade toward Bay Parkway and the underpass, Nick saying nothing. Finally, Barry spoke.

"Why do you want to know where I was? Is this something I should be worried about for some reason?"

Nick shrugged. "You act like you're worried already."

More silence, and then Barry muttered "fuck" under his breath.

"All right," he said, "here's what happened. I had some trouble at work, and they wound up insisting I leave early. I didn't want Julia to know about it, so I didn't go straight home. I stopped at this place down the block from the paper, figuring I'd kill some time until I could go home when I was expected to.

"Well, after I'd had a couple of drinks, I still didn't feel like going home, so I called her. I made up a bullshit story about having to work late, some crap about a supplement to next Saturday's edition. After that…"

They'd reached the underpass. Saturday afternoon traffic was brisk on the Belt Parkway above their heads and the metal plates were still laid out across the roadway, as they'd been on Tuesday night.

It had bothered Barry the first time they'd gone through, but now Nick saw his jaw tighten, and he covered his ears as he walked faster. A few moments later, they emerged.

"God, I hate that fucking noise," Barry said.

"After that…what?" Nick prompted him.

"After that, I don't remember much."

Ahead of them was Bensonhurst Park. There were people with kids here as well, most of them gathered in the playground, but the benches by the sidewalk were free.

"Why don't we sit down over there," Nick suggested, "and you can tell me whatever 'much' you remember."

"Listen, can't we do this some other time?"

"No, we can't." Nick was through being accommodating. "Now let's sit down, okay?"

They moved over to the nearest bench.

"So you were in this place down the block from the paper, and you called Julia. Then what happened?"

Barry squeezed his eyes shut and pinched his thumb and forefinger against the bridge of his nose, a study in concentration, or pain, or both.

"I don't know. I must have stayed a while longer and then moved on. I vaguely recall stopping at another place near there, and then I must have taken the subway home."

"You didn't stop at any of the joints in the neighborhood?"

"I might have. All I remember is waking up this morning."

"The bartender at the Bath Avenue Tavern said you were there last night. Were you?"

"I could've been; I don't know." He took his fingers away from the bridge of his nose and opened his eyes. "What's this about?"

"You remember how the Dodgers did last night?"

"What?"

"You heard me."

Barry shook his head. "I guess they lost, because today Russ Hodges said they were tied with the Giants going in. And now the Giants have moved into first place, temporarily I might add, but..."

"There was a guy at the Bath Avenue Tavern last night, a short guy named Jimmy Riccio, who kept insultin' the Dodgers. You remember him?"

"I don't even know if I was there, all right?" Barry said in annoyance. "What do you want me to say?"

He buried his face in his hands.

"Shit, my head is killing me. Can we go home?"

"You remember Tuesday night, when you left your apartment? Where did you go?"

Barry looked up, confused.

"Tuesday night? That must've been the night we had that argument. Wait a minute, how did you know I went out; have you been talking to Julia? Why do you care where I...wait a minute, Tuesday night. Wasn't that when...?"

The look of confusion became fear.

"Nick, what are you asking me?"

"I'm askin' you where you went."

He shook his head, as if in wonderment.

"You're not going to believe this," he said, "but I honestly don't remember."

He gave a bitter laugh.

"Isn't that something? I can't even remember where I go or what I do half the time. Pretty pathetic, huh? I'm a fucking pathetic drunk, that's what I am."

He lowered his head into his hands again.

"Ya know," Nick said softly, "one of the smartest things I ever did was all those years ago, when I slipped the landlord a couple'a bucks to hold that apartment on Bay Parkway when it opened up. I knew it'd be perfect for you and Julia and the kid, and Brooklyn was where you belonged, not the place you were livin'.

"But I also knew it'd be perfect for us to be neighbors as well as friends. And it still is, Barry.

"I see what you're goin' through, and I feel for you. But even if it hurts me to do it, my job is to ask you these questions. I keep hopin' you'll give me the kind'a answers that'll help, but so far you ain't doin' it. Maybe you need more time to think, and then you'll remember. But meanwhile, I gotta ask you just one more question, okay?"

Barry looked up.

"Sure, I guess so."

"You didn't lose your watch at work on Wednesday mornin', did you? How did you really lose it?"

Barry looked at him in confusion. Then his expression hardened.

"You son of a bitch."

"What?"

"You've involved Eddie in this."

"What? What are you talkin' about?"

"I knew he was acting strange, bringing up my watch out of nowhere. Is that how you do your job? You've got no fucking shame, have you."

He stood up abruptly, Nick, in surprise, a beat behind.

"Now I've got a question for you," Barry said. "We both know why you're talking to me like this, don't we? I want to hear you say it."

"Aw, for Chrissake, Barry, that's got nothin' to do…"

"It's got everything to do with it. Now say it. Say that asshole's name."

"Hey, calm down, all right? We were never gonna mention this again. Or did you forget that too?"

"Believe me, there are some things I'll never forget. And I want to make sure you don't either. Now say that Nazi prick's name."

Nick hadn't uttered it in over seven years, but he must've thought of it a million times.

"Major Gerhardt Schmidt," he murmured.

Barry glared at him.

"You were there too, Nick. You wanted it. It was both of us; that's what you said then. I think you should say it now."

"It was both of us, okay? Now take it easy."

"No, you take it easy. And while we're at it, fuck you and your questions."

He turned away and strode up the block.

"Yeah," Nick said softly, "fuck me."

***

Mary pulled the curtains aside and looked out her window. She, like Eddie, had been sentenced to her room, and she'd spent the last few hours lying on the bed dozing on and off, trying to make up for the sleep she'd missed after the six a.m. phone call and all the drama.

She'd expected her father to be mad at her, but not this angry. After all, what had she done except leave the house while her mother was sleeping and go around the corner to meet Eddie Fein? What was the big deal? She would've been back before her mother woke up anyway and nobody would've known, except that bigmouth Julia had to call and wake Teresa up. And, of course, her father had to come home just then for a quick shower.

He really blew his stack about it too. Way out of proportion to the "crime." He'd said that, from now on, he didn't want her to have anything to do with Eddie. That really surprised her.

This was way beyond just a matter of her sneaking out of the house. It was almost like he knew what they were up to, what they'd been talking about.

And why was Eddie so interested in this, anyway? She didn't believe for one minute that it was just 'cause Sandra Weinstock was a friend of his. There was something else going on.

Just as the thought occurred, Eddie appeared at his window.

For an instant he looked surprised to see her. Then he held up one finger, signaling to wait a second, and began scribbling something. He held up his loose leaf book to the window.

Written in large letters across a blank page was *I've got to talk to you. When can I see you?*

She shook her head and mouthed the word "can't."

He ripped out the page and scribbled something else, then showed it to her.

Very important!!!

Again she shook her head. "Can't."

Life and death!!!

All she'd wanted was for him to teach her to be an anti-Giant fan. How did it turn into this?

She'd been so impressed with him at Al's Soda Fountain, how quick-witted and sure of himself he was. Boys, to her, had always been crude and clumsy people, not nearly as important as her girlfriends. But lately, she and her friends had been looking at boys differently. In fact, the subject now dominated their conversations, but older boys, not someone like Eddie Fein.

Still, he was kind of cute in a way, cuter than she'd ever noticed. His face now, as he held up the piece of paper, was so sad.

But what could she do? She was really scared now. All that anger she felt when she launched her anti-Giant crusade had evaporated. She could barely remember it.

This is about murder! she reminded herself, and almost shivered.

But look at him, how sad he is. It's so hard.

The sadness in his face was mirrored by hers, as she shook her head one more time and mouthed the word. "Can't."

CHAPTER THIRTEEN

Saturday Evening, September 29th

Joe Flannery reached across his desk to the radio and turned up the volume a bit. Even without the knob he'd snapped off in anger on Thursday, he was still able to pinch his fingers around the stump that remained and turn it, as long they weren't too sweaty. He wanted to hear, because the Dodgers had a threat going in the second inning.

("Campy takes his lead off second,") said Red Barber. ("One man out. Roberts checks him and delivers to Pafko. Curve ball missing outside, ball one.")

Nick looked up. "What's the score, still nothin'-nothin'?"

"Yeah, but Campy just hit a shot off the left field wall that just missed bein' a home run. Roberts don't have it tonight."

"You're whistlin' in a graveyard," Nick said.

They'd been filing witness reports for the past hour, and there were plenty of them. Everyone they'd found that was in the bar last night said they remembered Jimmy Riccio very well. Everyone, of course, but the one guy who didn't even remember being there, and whose existence Nick's partner knew nothing about.

For now, all he could do was concentrate on the paperwork and procedural crap. Later on, when he got home, he'd have time to think.

("Pafko swings and belts one. A long, high drive out to left-center. Ashburn going after it. He's at the wall. It's gone! Pafko hits his 28th and the Dodgers lead 2-0!")

Joe silently punched an upraised fist in the air. What little he'd had to celebrate lately had to be toned down in the station house.

"Hey, why'n'tcha turn it off?" Nick suggested. "It's distractin' ya."

Joe just grinned at him, as the phone rang on his desk.

"Flannery," he said into the receiver, listened a moment, then rolled his eyes at the ceiling.

"The liquor store will still be open later," he said in measured tones. "Why are you bothering me with this?"

He listened for another moment.

"They'll still have the goddamned chenin blanc, so stop worrying."

Another second.

"People are not going to make a run in the next two hours on the goddamned chenin blanc."

Nick heard Joe's Brooklyn accent straighten out and figured it was Carolyn on the phone. You wouldn't know by the way he talked around other cops, but Joe had a Master's degree in sociology. Carolyn did too, and she taught at Brooklyn College, but Joe had shunned all that to become a cop. Nick had the feeling Carolyn wasn't too happy about it.

"Academia is all bullshit, believe me," Joe once said. "You can learn more sociology on Cropsey Avenue than in ten years at Harvard."

He hung up the phone.

"Her cousins are comin' over for dinner tomorrow," he said, the Brooklyn accent returning, "and if we don't have the right fuckin' wine, she'll get run outta the family. Goddamn bunch'a snobs."

("Roberts into his motion, and the pitch to Hodges is drilled into center field for a base hit.")

Joe grinned again. "See, I told ya. Roberts don't have it tonight."

"It's early," said Nick. "Don't get excited."

Joe leaned back in his chair.

"I see where Forensics got some good prints off the wallet, and they ain't Jimmy Riccio's."

"Let's hope we finally caught a break," Nick said, feeling slightly sick.

***

("...top of the fifth, here in the City of Brotherly Love, and the Dodgers are ahead 4-0. So far in this pitchers' duel, Don Newcombe has been firing bullets, but Robin Roberts has fired a few blanks and it's cost him.")

Eddie looked across the table at his father, who was staring into his glass like the Dodgers were the ones on the short end. There had been no Schaefer beer this time, just Johnny Walker Red all the way, and it had begun the moment Barry came home from the walk with Nick.

"Your Show of Shows is starting," Julia called out from the living room. "Anybody interested?"

After his dad and Nick had gone out, as Eddie plowed away at the Inca report, all but destroyed by Mary's turndown, he'd waited for the phone call from the police. He was sure Nick had only gotten him out of the house so he wouldn't be arrested in front of his family.

When Barry came home, Eddie was ecstatic with relief. He knew his dad hadn't done it. He must have explained to Nick whatever needed explaining, and now it was over.

The look on Barry's face, and the beeline for the scotch, put an end to that idea.

("Snider taking his lead off first, and here's the pitch. Robinson swings and sends a line drive into left field for a base hit. Sisler over to field it... and it gets by him! It's going all the way to the wall. Snider is rounding third, he'll score. An error by Sisler, and now it's 5-0 Dodgers!")

"Hey, Dad, how about that!" Eddie said.

Barry continued to stare into his glass.

"Dad?"

"What?" he said sharply. Ever since he'd walked in, he'd said almost nothing to Eddie.

"I think I'll go watch Sid Caesar for a while."

This wouldn't sound odd, he knew, because the game was in good shape at the moment, and the show was one of his favorites. But the real reason he wanted to go in there was the copy of today's *World Telegram and Sun* that was on the couch.

Earlier, he'd seen his dad looking intently at something a few pages in. He'd watched him read it, then close the paper and put it aside. Now it had found its way to the living room, and Julia was sitting next to it on the couch.

On the TV set, Imogene Coca was coming through the door of an apartment, to applause from the audience. She was beside herself with grief.

("That was the saddest movie I've ever seen. That poor woman, that poor, poor woman. How could he treat her that way?")

She took a hankie out of her pocket and blew her nose into it with a resounding honk.

("I've never cried so much at a movie in all my life.")

Julia began to reach for the newspaper to clear a space for Eddie, but he got to it first and kept it at arm's length as he sat down next to her.

"They're just coming home from a movie," she explained.

("Charles!") Imogene called out in a fishmonger's voice, as she looked over her shoulder toward the open doorway. ("What's taking you so long?")

Her face melted once again into sobs.

("Oh, every time I think about that poor, poor woman.")

Eddie tried to glance down at the paper. The main section seemed to be under the rest of it.

Sid Caesar appeared in the doorway, laughing hysterically.

("Boy, did he ever give it to her good! What a great movie! Funniest movie I ever saw!")

Julia laughed, and Eddie pretended to laugh with her, reaching out and pushing the paper further away, but only moving the other sections, exposing the main section.

Imogene was shocked and appalled.

("How could you laugh at that movie! Anyone who'd think that movie was funny has no sensitivity!")

Sid, taking great offense, made a fist that was half the size of her head.

("Don't tell me I've got no sensitivity!") he roared at her.

Eddie looked down. He knew the story was on the inside, so he was going to have to turn a few pages to find it.

("Go ahead, hit me!") Imogene taunted. ("It'll just prove what I said. C'mon, hit me!")

Sid's face seethed with frustrated twitches and grimaces.

("I've gotta hit something,") he said in a tight voice. ("I'll hit this chair!")

He stepped away from Imogene and cocked his fist next to one of the easy chairs.

("If you hit that chair,") Imogene warned him smugly, ("it'll be exactly the same as if you hit me.")

Sid's facial twitches went into overdrive. He hauled off and punched the chair.

("You hit me!") Imogene wailed.

Julia laughed, but half-heartedly. An angry, physically imposing man and a diminutive wife didn't always seem funny to her.

The skit ended, and a commercial for Snow Crop frozen orange juice came on.

"How are the Dodgers doing, Sport?" she asked. "How come you're not running out there during the commercial?"

Good question. Fortunately, he didn't have to answer it because she suddenly remembered something.

"I've got to start warming up the rest of that pot roast for Sam Schwartz. He should be back from the hospital by now."

She got up and went into the kitchen.

Eddie flipped open the paper and scanned pages two and three.

Nothing.

On page four at the top was a small item with the headline "Did He Die of Pennant Fever?"

Nick's name wasn't in it this time, but it said this was the second strangulation death in a week. It said the police "claimed to have evidence" linking the killing to the fact that the victim was a Giant fan who had spent the hours before his death insulting a bar full of Dodger fans.

He closed the paper as Julia came back into the room.

On the TV screen, Carl Reiner in a trench coat and carrying a notepad, was interviewing Sid Caesar's German Professor, who was supposedly an expert on mountain climbing.

"Oh, good," Julia said as she sat down.

("Professor, have you, personally, ever fallen from a mountain?")

("Sure,") said Sid in his German accent. ("You tink maybe you're talkin' to an amateur? I vunce took a ten-t'ousand-foot flop from the slopes of Mount Slippery.")

What did they mean by "evidence"? Eddie thought. What kind of evidence could prove something like that?

("My goodness, professor, how badly were you hurt?")

Sid held up his pinky.

("You see this?") He pointed to the tip of his fingernail. ("This is the only original part left of me. The rest is all new.")

The audience broke into howls of laughter, and so did Julia.

("I used to be a redhead,") Sid added.

"Oh, that's really great," she said, wiping at her eyes with the back of her hand. Then she noticed Eddie's lack of reaction.

"What's the matter? You're not listening to the ballgame and you're not laughing at Sid Caesar. Do you feel all right?"

"I'm fine, Mom. I guess my mind wandered."

"Hmm."

The sketch ended and Eva Gabor, that week's guest hostess, now stood in front of the curtain introducing the dance team Mata and Hari.

Julia rose from the couch and went into the kitchen to get the pot roast. "Why don't you knock on their dumbwaiter door and make sure Sam's home?" she called out.

Eddie got up and followed her into the kitchen. His father was still sitting at the table, the level of scotch in his glass the same, the level in the bottle down a bit. Red Barber was saying that the Phillies had men on first and second with no out.

"Is it still 5-0?" Eddie asked.

"Find out for yourself," Barry said, indicating the radio. "Red Barber gives the score every three minutes."

Why is he mad at me? Eddie wondered. *Ever since he came home he's been mad at me.*

"It was only an innocent question," Julia said gently.

Barry nodded his head as if he were learning something new.

"Innocent question. I'll try to remember that."

Just then, Red Barber gave the score, which was still 5-0.

Eddie didn't know what to make of any of it. He moved the step stool over to the dumbwaiter door, as Julia took the plate of pot roast, mashed potatoes, and carrots out of the oven where it had been warming up.

He opened the door, stepped up on the stool, and was greeted by an overpowering smell of rot. The garbage cart was moving past him, traveling slowly upward toward the apartment above them. One bag of particularly odiferous garbage sat on it.

"Whew," he said as he watched it go by, then looked down the shaft. The face of James Preston, the super's son, stared up the four stories at him.

"James," Eddie called down, "you're supposed to collect it, not deliver it."

During the years he stayed with the Prestons after school, James had shown him how to run the dumbwaiter cart; which rope was the "up" rope, which was the "down," and how to tell when it was even with a floor.

They'd played with it on the sly when James's father wasn't around, until the day they almost wiped out one of the Haberman sisters as she opened her dumbwaiter door and started to reach across the shaft. That was the end of that.

Now, James held up a finger to his lips.

"Shhh," he said.

"Eddie, don't yell down the shaft like that," Julia said. "The whole building can hear you."

"Yeah," Barry muttered, "don't blab any secrets to the neighbors."

Eddie waited a moment for the smell to subside, then reached across to Sam Schwartz's door and knocked.

"Just a second," a muffled voice said, and then Mr. Schwartz opened it.

"Oh, hi, Eddie."

Julia paused before handing Eddie the plate.

"It's a little hot. How's your hand?"

"It's okay," he said taking it from her.

("Sisler swings,") Red Barber's voice interrupted, ("and there's a shot up the middle.")

Eddie turned toward the radio.

("Oh, what a stop by Robinson! He flips to Reese for one, on to Hodges, double play!)

("What a sensational grab! That ball was ticketed for center field, but Jackie lunged for it, snagged it, and just as he was about to fall on his face, somehow managed to toss it to Reese to start the double play. Put a star next to that one on your scorecards, fans.")

Eddie could also hear Red Barber's voice coming from below him, up the shaft from the Haberman sisters' apartment. The pennant race was supposedly bringing all kinds of fans out of the woodwork, and now it was the Haberman sisters, or at least one of them.

"Sounds like they're doing okay," Sam Schwartz said.

Eddie gave one last sniff to make sure the odor in the shaft was completely gone, then leaned over and handed him the plate.

"How's Myra feeling?" Julia asked, over his shoulder.

Sam gave her a little smile.

"She had a good day, today."

"I'm glad somebody did," Barry said to no one.

Julia's face turned crimson.

"It's all right," said Sam.

"Well," Julia said, flustered and embarrassed, "I hope you like your dinner."

"I'm sure I will. Thanks, Julia."

Eddie stepped off the stool and closed the dumbwaiter door. He knew Myra Schwartz was dying, despite his mother's attempts to protect him from it, as he'd known on Thursday when she'd tried to get Dr. Glazer not to talk about it.

He couldn't imagine what Sam Schwartz must be going through, and he didn't want to try. It all made him feel awkward, which was why it was easier for him not to tell his mother he knew, just as it was easier for her to believe that he didn't.

Julia turned to Barry and was about to say something to him, but the phone rang in the living room. She hesitated for a second, and then went to answer it.

Eddie couldn't decide whether to join her or stay here. He wanted to try and find out why his father was acting so strange, but part of him also wanted to be away from it.

Julia's voice took the decision out of his hands.

"Oh, hello, Lionel. Yes, he is; he's listening to the game. Do you want to talk to him?"

Eddie went into the living room and took the phone from her. Lionel's voice yelled into his ear.

"Did you just hear what Robby did! Why the hell can't you make plays like that behind me when I'm pitching?"

"Unassisted triple plays don't count?" Eddie replied.

"You were lucky," said Lionel. "But the reason I'm calling is not because you can't play shortstop. It's 'cause my dad and me are driving down to Philly tomorrow for the game, and we want to know if you and your dad can come."

"Wow! You've got tickets?"

"Of course not, you fool. My dad got the idea 'cause Red Barber said there were lots of seats left for tomorrow. The Philly fans don't care; they're just winding down the season. It'll take us less than two hours to get there. They just finished this new highway, the New Jersey Turnpike, and you can go sixty miles an hour."

He felt a shiver of excitement, just like he did a year ago. Being at the final game of the season, with the pennant on the line. Same opponent, even, but with the novelty of seeing the Dodgers on the road. And things would be different this time. They'd better.

"Hold on, let me find out."

He went into the kitchen and told them. Julia was all in favor.

"That sounds terrific, Barry, why don't you go?"

Maybe it would do him good. Nick coming by earlier didn't seem to. Maybe nothing would, but why not try? And, she had to admit, she'd welcome the time to herself.

"Interstate flight, huh?" Barry mused, getting up from the table. "Okay, let me talk to Ben."

He went into the living room.

Interstate flight? Eddie thought. *Does he think we're taking a plane?*

Then it hit him. He meant running away. No, take it easy, it was just a joke. He'd been saying weird things all night.

He could hear Barry talking to Ben about what time they'd be leaving and how, of course, it was assuming the Dodgers held onto their lead and won tonight. As usual, his words sounded clear, not slurred at all.

Julia sat back down on the couch as, on the screen, Sid Caesar was doing a monologue about a newlywed husband on the phone with his mother.

("Don't worry, Mom,") Sid was assuring her. ("She's feeding me good. She's feeding me just like you used to. That's right; she puts the spoon in the food, blows on it, and puts it right in my mouth.")

Julia could relate to that. In a way, her husband was like a baby. They don't have the ability to tell you what's wrong, but they sure can let you know about it.

The difference was it was easy to love a baby. And it was getting so hard to love...

Eddie looked up and noticed her wiping her eyes with the back of her hand again, although he hadn't heard her laugh.

***

"Whoops!"

Carmine pretended to lose his balance and lowered his shoulder into Frankie Fontana as they rounded the corner of 86th Street onto Bay 29th. This caused Frankie to lose his balance too, but for real, as he stumbled hard against the window of the lingerie shop, his face and hands hitting the glass and leaving a smear.

"Jeez, Carmine."

"Sorry," Carmine chuckled. He wouldn't have minded seeing Frankie crash right through that window and wind up with a girdle on top of his friggin' head.

Earlier, the two of them had been making "trolley car bombs," peeling the cork linings out of bottle caps, sticking match heads inside, and putting back the cork. They'd laid out a bunch of them on the trolley tracks and watched as the trolleys ran over them and bursts of flame shot out from their wheels.

Carmine had gotten a big kick out of this kind of thing in the past, but tonight it all seemed kind of weak.

Look what I'm doin', he thought with disgust. Vito was who he really wanted to run around with tonight, but Vito was pissed off at him. And it was all because of that fucker Eddie Fein.

He was lucky it hadn't been worse. Vito had been ready to kill him over that fuckin' nickname. He'd actually pulled the knife, right there.

Only some fast talking had saved Carmine. He'd said he never called Vito "Pecker," and that the nickname was Frankie's idea. In fact, he, Carmine, had never liked it when Frankie said it.

Vito was stupid enough to half-believe that, so at least Carmine got him to put the knife away. But he'd lost one of his trusty lieutenants, at least for now, and Eddie was going to pay for it.

He looked over at his one remaining toady.

"Your shoelace is untied," he said to him.

"What?"

"Go over to that car, bend over by the tire, and tie your shoelace."

Frankie looked down at his feet.

"My shoelaces are tied. Whatta ya talkin'…"

"No they ain't," said Carmine. "I gotta show ya how to tie your shoes? Here, watch me."

He moved over to the car parked by the curb and squatted down, his left foot against the rear tire. Taking the metal tip of his shoelace, he pressed it against the air nozzle.

Frankie, realizing what was happening, started to laugh as the air hissed out of the tire.

"Stop laughin' ya asshole," Carmine said, "and check to see if anyone's comin'."

Frankie stifled his glee and looked up and down the empty street.

"Lemme try it, Carmine," he burbled impatiently.

"Okay, don't piss in your pants."

Carmine stood up and looked around.

"Let's move down the block a ways."

They walked down several car lengths to a green, late-model Packard, where Carmine stopped and gave one more look around.

"Ya know how them Packard commercials say, 'Ask the man who owns one'? Well, I happen to know the guy that owns this one. He's that hotshot fag Lionel Gluck's old man, and he's a fuckin' Dodger fan besides, so why don't ya tie your shoe over here?"

Grinning, Frankie kneeled down by the tire and did it perfectly.

"Hey," Carmine said, kicking the right front tire. "You didn't tie your shoelace tight enough. Come over here and do it again."

Frankie, now in full giggle, didn't even get up. He duck-walked over to the front tire and began to let the air out.

Standing over him, Carmine was sorely tempted to kick him in the head. But he didn't, and congratulated himself on being a good person.

CHAPTER FOURTEEN

Sunday Morning, September 30th

"I hate this dress!" Mary yelled to her mother in the kitchen, as she made a sour face at herself in her bedroom mirror. "It's so frilly. It makes me look like Shirley Temple."

"You're suppose'ta look like Shirley Temple when you go to Mass," Teresa called back. "Now hurry up and finish or we're gonna be late."

"Why do we have to go to the nine-o'clock?" Mary pouted as she picked up her hairbrush. "We never get a chance to sleep on Sundays."

Nick, wearing his blue serge suit, tucked his little notebook away in the inside jacket pocket as he looked into her room.

"That ain't true and you know it, so stop makin' things up. We're goin' to the early Mass 'cause I gotta work today, and you knew that too. What do you gotta do today, besides complainin'?"

He moved on down the hall, rapping once on Carmine's door as he passed it.

"You too," he hollered, "move it!" as he continued on into the kitchen to grab a cup of coffee before they had to leave.

As soon as he did, Carmine opened his door and emerged, wearing the gray suit they'd bought for him the year before. He'd hated it then because it was baggy and he hated it now because it was too tight. He slipped into Mary's room.

"Whatta you want?" she said over her shoulder into the mirror, as she continued to brush her hair.

"I wanna talk to you about somethin'," he said, closing the door behind him. "Yesterday I heard the old man tell you not to talk to Eddie Fein. How come? What were you and that little faggot doin' together?"

"None of your goddamn business." She turned to face him, defiantly slapping down the hairbrush. "And don't you ever call him that again."

Carmine gave her a wicked grin.

"Why, 'cause you got a crush on him? You like little boys?"

Mary gave him a wicked grin in return.

"Do you like little boys? Why are you pals with that creep Vito Peccarino? You're the faggot."

He would've loved to smack her, even with their parents in the next room, but he needed to find out something. He had to stay cool.

"What were you talkin' to Eddie Fein about?" he asked in an even tone of voice

"Why don't you go ask him?"

She turned back to the mirror and began brushing her hair again.

Man, he wanted to kill her.

"You never even liked him. You used to make fun of him. Now, all of a sudden, you're sneakin' off to meet him? And holdin' hands with him in the lunchroom?"

He enjoyed the fleeting look of surprise on her face in the mirror.

"That's right, I got people watchin'. Now what did that shrimp say to you?"

"About what?" she asked in an overly innocent voice.

About me! he wanted to scream. *About me being the one that told him about his old man!*

He hadn't slept all night, thinking about whether Eddie had told her. If he did, Carmine vowed, there'd be no limit to the pain he was gonna inflict on that little rat. But the important thing was to find out if it was so.

"What were you talkin' about with him?" he asked again.

She turned around.

"Why do you care? What's it got to do with you?"

She doesn't know, he realized. If she knew, she'd be rubbing his face in it, not acting this way. He was all right.

Relief washed over him.

"Nothin'," he said. "In fact, never mind. I don't give a shit."

Her eyes widened, then narrowed.

"Wait a minute," she said. "First you come in here demandin' to know what we said, and now all of a sudden it don't matter?"

"That's right," he said, starting for the door. "Why should I care about a little twerp? Besides, like you said, it ain't none of my business."

"I think it is," she said, causing him to stop with his hand on the knob. "I think you know somethin'."

In the kitchen, Nick was having an epiphany. It made him pause in mid-sip and put down the coffee cup. Ever since yesterday afternoon, it had bothered him.

Barry's reaction had been genuine, no doubt about it. He'd accused Nick of using Eddie against him. That meant he hadn't told the kid anything, that the kid really was acting on his own. But why? Was there something incriminating about Barry that Eddie knew, or had discovered?

But more than that, why did Eddie know that Nick suspected him? Why would he blurt out, "You're supposed to be his friend. You should know better than anyone that he didn't do anything bad!"

There was only one time Nick had ever said a single word about it to anyone, Thursday morning with Teresa, here in the kitchen.

"Are you through with your coffee?" she asked him now, looking up from the breakfast dishes in the sink.

"Gimme a minute," he said as he got up from the table and headed for Carmine's room.

The door was open but nobody was inside. When was the last time he'd been in here? He couldn't remember. Nick looked around at the piles of clothing, comic books, and discarded candy wrappers all over the place. He noticed a half-eaten Snickers bar on the bed, some of it melting onto the sheet.

Is every teenage kid a slob, or just mine? he wondered.

Even the clothes in the closet were mostly on the floor, with a couple of old jackets on hangers only because Carmine hadn't worn them in ages. Nick poked his head inside the closet and looked around. It immediately felt different to his ears. Something had changed. Then it hit him.

"Oh, you miserable fucker," he muttered. It was the sound of Teresa washing the dishes in the kitchen; it had gotten louder.

He went further into the closet and squatted down, putting his ear close to the back wall. It was practically as if he'd stuck his head in the kitchen sink.

***

Julia's head was in the refrigerator, as she looked for the mustard to put on the bologna sandwiches she was making for everyone to take to the game. The phone rang in the living room.

"Would you get that?" she asked Eddie, who was sitting at the kitchen table with a pencil and a ruler, making a scorecard out of a piece of notebook paper. He'd already finished one and was now working on a second.

He got up, went into the living room, and picked up the phone.

"H'lo?"

The voice at the other end sounded annoyed.

"It's Ben Gluck, Eddie, is your dad there? I need to speak to him."

"Hold on, I'll get him," he said, putting the phone down as he opened the bedroom door.

His father was facing away from him, in undershirt and trousers, tucking a large roll of bills into his pants pocket. Barry turned and looked surprised to see him in the doorway.

"What's doin', Sport?" he said.

He seemed to be in a better mood this morning, but it was hard to tell.

"Ben wants to talk to you."

"He'd better not be changing his mind or we've got bologna sandwiches for a week," Barry said as he picked up the phone. "Hi, Ben, what's up?" He listened for a few seconds. "That's terrible; do you need any help?" He listened some more. "Okay, we'll just wait here 'til you call us."

By this time, Julia had come into the living room as Barry hung up the phone.

"Some goddamned kids evidently let the air out of two of their tires," he said. "Ben has to jack up the car now, put the spare on one of the wheels, then jack it up again and leave it, while he and Lionel roll the tires over to the Esso station on Cropsey. So we won't be leaving for a while." His eyes flicked over to the liquor cabinet, then back.

"We should still be okay if it doesn't take too long."

Since they had to wait, Eddie figured he'd take the scorecards into his room, on the off chance he'd see Mary. He didn't know what more he could do than he'd already done, but if he saw her, at least he'd have another shot at it, which was more than he could accomplish in the kitchen. He noticed his mother glancing into the living room to see if his dad had gone over to the liquor cabinet.

As he put his stuff down on the desk, he wondered about that roll of bills. It had to be way more than their share for the tickets, gas, and tolls. He looked out the window.

Mary was there. She was in a white dress, standing in the middle of her room and talking to Carmine. Whatever they were saying seemed to be serious, judging by the looks on their faces. Then their heads turned toward the door.

***

"Who in the GODDAMN HELL do you think you are!"

Nick stormed into the room at Carmine, punctuating the "goddamn" and the "hell" with hard, open-handed shoves to the chest that sent Carmine reeling backward.

"What'd I do?" he said, bouncing off the dresser and trying to regain his balance.

Mary tried to get out of their way. She backed into the bed and sat down heavily in a flourish of white crinoline.

"What's goin' on in there?" Teresa called from the kitchen.

"Ya like eavesdroppin' on people?" Nick glared at Carmine, the urge to beat the shit out of him almost overwhelming.

"You like sittin' in that closet, listenin' to police business? I oughta lock ya up in that goddamn closet."

He watched Carmine's wary eyes looking furtively around the room, and remembered how people always said he and his son had the same eyes. It infuriated him. He clenched his fists.

"Dad!" Mary cried out.

Carmine's head was spinning. What went wrong? His bratty sister didn't know anything; he was sure of it. Just now she got a little suspicious, but he could handle that. He was home free. What happened?

Then he realized it didn't matter. What mattered was the gigantic unfairness of it. Eddie Fein's old man was a fuckin' murderer. What had he done, compared to that? And if it was police business, why was his old man tellin' his old lady about it?

Why was he the fuckin' scapegoat for everything? Taking all the shit? It pissed him off. It pissed him off good!

He looked at his father and for the first time in his life, thought, *He ain't so fuckin' big.*

Then he started swinging.

The first one caught Nick by surprise in the chest, as Mary screamed. He ducked the second and moved into Carmine, tying him up, but their momentum pushed them sideways. They fell against the bed, onto a horrified Mary, who screamed again, trying to roll out of the way and not quite making it, the bottom of her dress catching underneath them and ripping.

Carmine happened to wind up on top. He struggled to free his arms, as Nick struggled to keep them pinned, all the while trying to bring his knee up under Carmine's midsection.

He finally did, and put his whole weight behind it, shoving Carmine off him and launching himself from the bed in the same motion. He ducked a wild, flailing right hand, and bulled into Carmine again, sending him backward into the dresser. This time it slammed against the wall. The mirror wobbled and fell forward between them, grazing Nick's shoulder as it crashed to the floor, glass flying.

They stood frozen on either side of it.

"Oh my God!" Teresa was in the doorway, aghast. "Nick, what're you doin'?"

"Dealin' with a slime bag whose ears are bigger than his brains," he said, glaring at Carmine.

She looked over at Mary, cringing on the bed.

"Are you okay, baby?"

"Yeah, but my dress is ripped," Mary sniffled.

Teresa surveyed the shambles. She didn't know what led up to this, but she did know they were going to miss the nine-o'clock Mass if they didn't leave this very minute.

And maybe church would be a good thing. Let them both cool off for a while, and she'd get the story from Nick later on. She glanced around the room, at the pieces of mirror everywhere, at her daughter's torn dress, and decided to take charge of the situation.

"Then let's go, Nick, we're gonna be late. We can clean all this up when we get back. Joe and Carolyn are supposed to meet us out front and they're probably waitin' for us right now. Carmine, straighten yourself up and let's get movin'."

"What about me?" Mary said tearfully. "Look at my dress; it's ruined."

"Get your blue one outta the closet, the one you wore last Easter, and change into it. You can meet us inside; we'll save a seat for you. But make it quick 'cause you gotta get there before the sermon starts. And be careful of the glass. Now come on, Carmine, let's go."

She turned and headed for the front door.

"This ain't over," Nick said, as he tucked his shirt into his belt and followed a sullen Carmine toward the door.

He stopped and looked back at Mary.

"See? You hated that dress so much, now you should be happy."

He followed his son and wife out of the apartment.

Mary wasn't happy, but she wasn't really all that upset, now that it was over. It had been kind of thrilling to see the two of them fight like that.

She slowly got up off the bed and started for her closet, avoiding the pieces of mirror all over the floor.

A shard stood balanced against one of the legs of the dresser and she stepped gingerly around it. As she did, her eye caught a reflection, a small, flat object under her bed.

She stopped and tried to make it out from the reflection, but she couldn't. So she moved over to the bed, kicking little pieces of glass out of the way, and carefully bent down and looked. Her breath caught.

"Oh, boy," she said softly to herself, as she reached under and took out Nick's notebook.

***

When the mirror fell, Eddie had jumped out of his chair in shock, but the biggest shock was right now, watching her stand in the middle of the room reading that notebook.

Before he could allow himself a thought, he was moving to his bedroom door to close it.

He came back, shoved a pencil and the notepaper with the half-completed scorecard into his pocket, climbed over the desk, and opened the window. By the time he'd stepped out onto the fire escape, he figured he must have decided to do it.

He closed the window part-way behind him and quickly took the three flights down the fire escape, dropping the final six feet to the courtyard.

A tall chain link fence separated the back of the building from the rear of the DiFazios' and he climbed it. Being careful of his bandaged right hand, he lowered himself to the other yard.

For all he knew, either of his parents could knock on his door at any moment and discover him gone, or even look out the window right now and see him, but there was nothing he could do.

Mary was alone; he was sure of it. The way she was standing there reading the notebook, not hiding it, meant they'd all left.

And if they hadn't, so be it. This was his chance and he had to take it. Machu Picchu.

Mary continued to flip through the pages, not understanding a lot of it, but noticing how a few of her father's entries were about someone called "B."

"Like B at St. Laurent?" was one of the first notations. Then "B—at Bath Ave. Tav." later on, with a couple of others in between.

B must be a suspect, she thought, just before a sudden tapping noise at the window nearly scared her to death.

"Jeez, Eddie," she said in astonishment, "what are you doin' here?"

"Let me in," he mouthed from the other side of the glass.

She opened the window and he climbed inside.

"Is anyone else around?" he asked, looking anxiously toward the doorway.

"No, but..." she couldn't get over it, "what are you *doin'* here?"

"Listen, I'm sorry about this," he said, holding out his hands pleadingly and looking into her eyes, "but you've gotta let me see that notebook."

She backed away, clutching it to her frilly bosom.

"I'm not supposed to even talk to you. Why do you wanna know about all this stuff anyway?"

But even before she'd gotten to the "anyway" it had already dawned on her.

"Ohmygod!" she gasped. "'B' is for Barry. 'B' is your dad!"

***

It was a ten-block walk to St. Finbar's and they did it in eight minutes of strained silence. Joe and Carolyn were already waiting for them in front of the church, amidst a thinning crowd of people who'd begun moving inside.

Nick and Joe and their wives had been meeting on Sundays at Mass for about a year now. It gave them a chance to get together outside of work, something they did less of than other partners at the precinct.

Despite Joe's putdowns of academia, he and Carolyn still socialized quite a bit with her colleagues and their spouses. This separation of their private lives was one reason why Nick's "friend, Barry" was just a name to Joe. Nick counted that now as a good thing.

Carolyn waved as they approached the church steps. She looked terrific as always, her long, brown hair swept up and held in place by a silver clasp, her makeup perfect. Joe, standing next to her, looked impatient.

"Sorry we're late," Teresa said breathlessly. "Nick and Carmine had a little accident, so Mary has to change her dress. She's gonna meet us inside."

"Don't ask," said Nick.

Joe wasn't about to.

"Carolyn," he said, "why don't you, Teresa, and Carmine go find us some seats, so Nick and I can talk for a minute?"

Carolyn rolled her eyes.

"Cops are as thick as thieves, aren't they?" she said to Teresa. "Bradford here always needs to talk to Nick about something or other. We haven't walked into a church together since the day we got married."

She took Teresa's arm and they joined the others as they filed inside. Carmine moped along behind them.

"Bradford?" Nick said.

Joe gave a quick glance at Carolyn's retreating form.

"Yeah, that's actually my real given name, Bradford Joseph Flannery. She teases me about it."

"Bradford Joseph Flannery, huh?" Nick mused. "It's got a certain ring to it."

"Well, the next time it rings don't answer it. Meanwhile, after you left last night, we got a call from John O'Houlihan."

"Yeah?"

Nick's blood pressure jumped slightly at this. He'd taken a risk by making that little side trip to the bar and showing O'Houlihan those pictures. Now, just one casual mention along the lines of "You know those pictures your partner showed me...?" and there'd be a lot of shit coming his way.

"What'd he want?" Nick asked, keeping his voice matter-of-fact.

"He said he remembered somethin'. Shortly after Riccio left, he overheard one of the regulars, a guy named Max Herskowitz, sayin' some not-very-nice things about the value of Riccio's existence. He could'a just been blowin' off steam, but O'Houlihan said he left the bar about ten minutes later."

"Interestin', but we figured the guy followed Riccio right out. Ten minutes is a long time to go around the corner."

"Not if you're staggerin', or maybe stoppin' to take a piss." Joe paused reflectively.

"No, forget I said that. I don't wanna be testin' the whole fuckin' area for urine that matches Riccio's. Anyway, this Herskowitz guy might be worth lookin' into."

"We couldn't contact him yesterday, right?"

"Yeah, his wife said he was stayin' with his sick mother and he'd be back home today."

"Can't wait to find out how his mother's doin'. Anythin' else?"

"Nah." Joe squinted at the last few people going into the church. "Come on, let's join the ladies and get our souls cleaned."

"I'd like to clean my kid's soul," Nick muttered, falling into step beside him. "Right after I clean his clock."

He reflexively patted his jacket and discovered the inside pocket was empty.

***

"B? There's someone in there called B?" It really shouldn't have surprised Eddie, but hearing her say it still gave him a jolt.

She nodded, clutching the notebook even more tightly to herself.

"Please," he said, "you've gotta let me see it. My dad didn't do anything."

"How do you know?" She backed even further away from him. "I don't wanna get involved in this."

"But you already are. You found the notebook and you looked at it."

"So what?" she said. "I'm gonna put it right back under the bed and you're gonna leave. They're waitin' for me at the church and I've gotta change my dress and get over there."

"Let me look at it, just for the time it takes you to change," he pleaded. "Then I'll go, I swear, and you can put it back. As far as anyone knows it'll be the same."

She wavered for a moment.

"Oh God, why did I ever want to be an anti-Giant fan? None of this would'a happened."

Looking away, almost as if she couldn't bear to watch herself, she handed him the notebook.

"You stay here," she said, moving over to her closet and starting to look around in it for the blue dress. "I'll go change in my parents' bedroom. Jeez, I must be nuts."

Eddie said nothing, not wanting to waste a second. He took the partial scorecard and the pencil out of his pocket and sat down on her bed, already starting to thumb through the notebook. Whenever he saw "B" he copied whatever it said onto the back of the piece of paper.

Other things caught his eye, like the entry in the Jimmy Riccio section that said, "$2 bill found stuffed in mouth. Sal Maglie autograph."

He let out a low whistle. So that was the evidence they were talking about.

He didn't need to copy it because he knew he'd remember it, but he did copy the ten sale dates from Macy's for the watch, and was finishing the last one when Mary, in her blue dress, came back into the room.

"You look beautiful," he said. It just came out of him.

It made her blush. He really was sweet. For a moment, her curiosity trumped her fear of her father.

"Did you find out anything?" she asked.

"Maybe. I have to think about it."

She came over and sat down next to him on the bed, knowing she shouldn't be doing this.

"What are all those dates?" she said, noticing what he'd just written.

"They found a man's watch in Sandra's hand." It gave him a creepy feeling to say that, as it had when he'd seen it in the notebook. "It must've been bought at Macy's on one of these dates, but they don't know which one. See, all this started 'cause my dad had the same kind of watch and he lost it. My mom got it for him for their first anniversary after he came home from the war, and these dates are right around that time."

"Did she get it at Macy's?"

"That's what I have to find out."

Mary looked again at the list.

"October and November of '45…" She did some figuring, and then a strange expression came over her face.

"Eddie," she said softly, "your mom did buy the watch at Macy's."

"What?"

"I know. 'Cause I was there when she bought it."

***

"Joe, you're not gonna believe this, but I gotta go back home."

"You're kiddin'."

They were practically at the church door when Nick had stopped short.

"I know this is gonna sound nuts," he said, "but I just realized, I was smokin' a cigar in our bedroom just before we left and, in all the rush to get out, I accidentally left it on Teresa's night table, and I think it was still lit."

He began to back down the steps.

"And forget about the apartment maybe burnin' down, it was her mother's table and if I get a hole in it, she's gonna put a hole in me."

Joe laughed.

"Nice job, pal. Ya want me to tell her that, or should I say ya suddenly got the runs?"

"Go with number two. I'll try to get back here and sneak in during the Offertory. If I don't make it, I'll meet yez all out front afterwards."

As he was saying this, he spotted a cab coming slowly down Benson Avenue toward the church.

"Taxi!" he called, taking the rest of the steps in two big strides.

***

Julia had just put the last of the sandwiches into a large bag when she felt Barry's arms encircle her waist, as he gently kissed the back of her neck.

"I'm sorry," he whispered into her ear.

She turned in his embrace, her eyes filling with tears, wanting to say so much but unable to say a thing. There were tears in his eyes too.

"I've never stopped loving you," he said.

They kissed. It was long and deep, and Julia could not remember the last time they'd kissed that way. She clung to him, wishing it could go on, wishing she could take him into the bedroom and they could make love, the kind of wild, passionate love they used to have. But she knew they couldn't, not now, not with Eddie at home. And maybe, she thought sadly, not even if they'd been alone. She rested her cheek against his chest.

"All I want is for you to be happy," she murmured.

"I know, and I'll always love you for that," he said quietly. "But I can't be. And so all I do is make you unhappy too. You'd be better off without me, and so would Eddie."

"No, no." She lifted her head and saw the pain in his eyes. "That's not true. Whatever you may think of yourself, you're wrong. Eddie worships you. And I love you."

A tear slid down his face.

"You don't know what goes on inside me. Sometimes I think I should have died in the war. It would've made things so much simpler."

"Please don't talk like that." She reached up and cradled his face in her hands. "We'll get help. They have programs for veterans. I could find out…"

"It wouldn't do any good," he said calmly, resignedly. "No one can help; it's too late."

He couldn't stop his eyes from wandering, just for an instant, over her shoulder toward the living room and its liquor cabinet.

"Don't," she said softly, still cradling his cheeks. "Go see Eddie; see how those scorecards of his are coming along. Talk to him about the game. You know he'd love it."

He drew her close and they kissed again, long and slow.

"Okay," he said finally, reluctantly letting go of her and starting toward Eddie's room.

***

"See that date, November 12, 1945?" said Mary. "That was two days after my eighth birthday. I remember it 'cause that was the year my aunt gave me a really ugly skirt. Thank God, it was too small for me, so my mom took me to Macy's to exchange it for something else. Carmine had to come along, and it turns out your mom was there too. She took the train in with us."

"Are you sure?" Eddie said. "Where was I?" He did some quick figuring of his own.

"I was seven then, so that would be when I had my tonsils out."

"That's right, I remember that too!" Mary's eyes lit up, the thrill of discovery now pushing aside everything else. "You were in the hospital, and your mom was gonna buy you a game or something. My mom tried to make me and Carmine behave by saying we could go to the toy department with her if we were good. But it took forever, 'cause we got stuck in the jewelry department while she was buying that watch."

"Wait a minute. Just 'cause she was buying a watch, how do you know it was the same one?"

"'Cause it was such a big deal. It was for your dad and it was their anniversary, and she couldn't make up her mind. She was taking so long I wanted to kill her. Plus, I had to put up with Carmine pulling my hair."

Eddie glanced down the list.

"November 12th is here twice. They sold two of the watches that day."

"I noticed that," she said, her face suddenly taking on a far-away look. "And it seems familiar, but I don't know why."

***

"You suppose he wants some privacy?" Barry asked Julia, looking at Eddie's closed door. "Things start occurring to twelve-year-old boys, you know." He winked at her.

"Shh," she whispered, smiling, "he'll hear you."

He lowered his voice. "If he understood what I just said, it won't matter anyway." He raised his right hand, about to knock on the door.

"Hey, Sport..." he started to say.

Before he could, there was another knock, on the dumbwaiter door in the kitchen. They stood there a second, and then Julia moved toward it.

"I'll see what Sam wants," she said. "You go ahead with Eddie."

Barry again raised his hand to knock, and then slowly brought it down, an embarrassed look on his face.

"You told me I said something insensitive to Sam last night, didn't you?" he said to Julia. "I've got to apologize."

***

In the taxi, Nick tried to figure out when it could have happened. It might have been when he was kicking Carmine off him and Carmine took that extra swipe. Or it could have been any other way, but he was pretty sure the notebook wasn't just lying there in the middle of the floor or he would have seen it. Maybe the mirror had fallen on it. He hoped so.

As the cab proceeded down Benson Avenue toward Bay 29th Street, he kept his eyes peeled for Mary. If she was already on the street, then she probably hadn't found it. But as the blocks went by he began to get more edgy. She'd had plenty of time to change and be walking toward the church by now.

He told the driver to stop on the corner, instead of going all the way around the block to pull up in front of the entrance, because it would be quicker to walk from there.

The fare came to 40 cents and, not wanting to waste time fumbling for change, he gave the cabbie a buck, to the guy's delight. Fifteen seconds later he was entering his lobby.

Taking the stairs rather than waiting for the elevator, he got to the apartment, put his key in the lock, and opened the door.

***

"Who among us can truly say he knows himself?"

Father Tonelli's weathered, craggy face regarded his congregation with a look of challenge and contempt.

"Who among us is so vain?"

Carmine wondered where his old man was. Joe Flannery had come in and whispered something to Teresa, before moving past her to take his seat next to Carolyn, but he couldn't make it out.

Sitting through the Gospel reading in boring Latin, and then, since it was Sunday, again in boring English, he tried to figure out how his old man had known. His bratty sister hadn't told him anything; he'd already decided that, and, just because he discovered the closet, he still didn't know Carmine was in there listening that particular time.

There was only one other way he could've found out. And Carmine had to fight the urge to punch the back of the pew in front of him.

Eddie Fein.

"'Forgive them, Father, for they know not what they do,'" said Father Tonelli. "Those are the words of Our Lord, Jesus Christ. It is only God who truly knows us, and we must continuously ask Him who we are."

Carmine didn't know who he was and had never thought about it. He did know, however, who he wasn't. He wasn't someone who was going to sit there like a death row inmate, waiting for his old man to come back, suffering through the ordeal of the Mass until he could begin his own ordeal.

Fuck that! he thought, and felt an irrational spasm of guilt because he'd thought a curse word in church.

Father Tonelli finished his sermon and returned to the center of the altar. There, facing away from the congregation, he began to recite the Creed.

"Credo in unum Deum, Patrem Omnipotentem," he intoned.

Carmine, who because of Teresa's laxity had been sitting on the aisle, was out of his seat and out on the street by "Omnipotentem."

***

One of baseball's ironies is that doing something right can often make something wrong happen, and vice versa. A scorching line drive can be hit directly at someone for an out, or a weak dribbler can become a base hit because it dies on the grass where no one can field it.

Sometimes it happens that way in life. If Nick had waited for the elevator it would have taken him that much longer to get to the apartment, but he would have run right into Mary in the lobby as she got out of it.

Since that hadn't happened, he now walked into an empty apartment, calling out her name and getting no reply. When he got to her room, everything seemed as it was, the mirror in the center of the floor, glass scattered all over.

If he'd gone straight to the window and looked down at that moment, he'd have seen Eddie climbing the fence that separated their two courtyards, but his concentration was on the room, as it should have been.

He might have noticed that some glass had been cleared away from in front of the bed, if Eddie hadn't thought of it and moved several of the pieces back after Mary had replaced the notebook. Nick, in fact, had to clear away the glass himself before he could bend down to look, so it seemed as if he'd been the first to do it.

In baseball, the difference between lofting a lazy fly ball or launching a towering home run is only a fraction of a second in your swing. After Barry had apologized to Sam Schwartz, who'd graciously accepted it, he'd gone to the window and looked out. But Eddie was just disappearing into the shadow of the building a fraction of a second before he would have been seen.

And as baseball has long, slow intervals, like pitching changes, throws to first base to keep a runner close, the rituals between pitches, so it was a slow interval that finally did it.

Had a car not been driving up to the air hose just as Ben and Lionel were arriving at the gas station, their tires would have been filled five minutes sooner, and their phone call to the Feins would have been likewise.

Instead, the call came just as Eddie was climbing back into his room and closing the window behind him. He'd hardly sat down at his desk when Barry was knocking on the door.

"Okay, Dad, I'm ready to go," he called out, and he was. Except for the unfinished scorecard.

CHAPTER FIFTEEN

Sunday Afternoon, September 30th

Shibe Park was packed. Thousands of Dodger fans had taken Red Barber's advice, some making the trip down to Philly as soon as the game ended Saturday night and camping out by the ticket booths. By the time Barry, Ben, Lionel, and Eddie got there, an hour before the game, all the parking lots were full. They wound up having to pay five bucks to a guy on North 31st Street, a half-mile from the stadium, just so they could park in his driveway.

There were long lines at the ticket booths, and when they reached the window they were told that if they wanted to sit together they'd have to be out in dead center field near the top of the upper deck. But if they wanted to split up, the guy said he could give them two pairs in the upper left field stands, much closer to the field but two sections apart. That's what they decided to do.

"You'd better take your half of the sandwiches," said Barry as he reached into the bag. "We've got a special on bologna this week."

He and Ben wore suits, with shirt collars open and no tie, as did most of the men in the crowd. Eddie and Lionel, like the other kids, wore jeans and polo shirts, and lightweight jackets, since the temperature was in the 60's. Lionel noticed a scorecard vendor going by.

"I'm buyin' a couple," he said. "How about you? Or did you make up your own, like the cheapskate you are?"

"I make up better ones than the ones they sell," said Eddie, "but I'll buy one anyway." He handed him a dime.

"The last of the big-time spenders," said Lionel, getting his own money from Ben.

He turned and ran after the vendor, almost plowing into a man heading the other way.

"Lionel, watch out for your arm!" Ben yelled. He adjusted his glasses and squinted at the people milling around them. "Listen, after the game, let's meet by the car," he said to Barry. "It'll be easier than tryin' to find each other in this mob."

He glanced at the sky, which was starting to cloud over. "If it's raining or anything, and you guys get there first, you know where I keep the spare key, don't you?"

"Under the hood, I think you once told me."

Eddie wasn't sure how he felt about that. It was ridiculous, but he thought back to that "interstate flight" reference. He hoped his dad wouldn't do something crazy like trying to steal Ben's car. He also didn't like the thermos full of Johnny Walker Red his dad had brought along.

He'd noticed it as they were riding in the car, and he assumed that was what was in it. His dad never brought a thermos to games because there was more than enough beer around. He wondered about it until he remembered something Barry once told him about Connie Mack owning Shibe Park and not allowing the sale of beer. Amazing how foresighted his dad could be about stuff like that.

The outside of the stadium reminded him a little of Bensonhurst Junior High, which did not bode well. It had the same austere red brick facing with white concrete trim. The tall windows over the home plate entrance looked like classroom windows. In fact, as soon as they were past the turnstiles there was a short flight of steps exactly like the stairs to their gym.

But when they came out into the upper deck behind third base, all of it changed. He'd always loved that moment when you reached the top of the ramp and the field was suddenly there, laid out in front of you.

More than that, this place actually felt kind of like Ebbets Field. It held about the same number of people and had double-decked stands on the same three sides, with a right field fence featuring a large scoreboard.

No advertising on the walls, though, that was a difference. And center field was much deeper, with the stands going straight out from left field to form a distant corner with the right field fence, not bending in like they did at Ebbets Field, where you could hit home runs to straightaway center, but Duke Snider could take them away with spectacular, wall-climbing catches.

As they reached their seats above left field, the grounds crew was watering down the infield, while players on both teams soft-tossed in front of their dugouts. There were the Phillies, in their crisp white uniforms with red, oversized numbers, and the Dodgers in their somber road gray.

Eddie had never seen the Dodgers in gray uniforms, because Barry refused to go to the Polo Grounds. He decided he liked the effect; it made them look more serious, more determined.

Bubba Church, the Phillie righthander, was warming up behind home plate, and several feet away, good old Preacher Roe was getting set for the Dodgers.

Eddie was kind of sorry they'd gotten there so close to game time. He always liked watching batting practice, and especially infield practice.

All the home runs launched from the batting cage were impressive, but what he really loved was watching them throw the ball around. How effortlessly the third baseman could go behind the bag, or the shortstop deep in the hole, and then peg a strike to the first baseman, who'd turn and nonchalantly zing it straight to the catcher, as the coach standing beside him hit the next ground ball. It was always great during Little League games, after one of Lionel's numerous strikeouts or an infield out, when they could whip the ball around the infield.

The public address announcer gave the starting lineups, and Eddie copied them down on his official Phillie scorecard. He'd given his dad the homemade one.

Barry hadn't said anything about it before, but now he asked, "How come you only made one?"

"The ruler slipped and it got ruined," said Eddie. "I didn't have time to make another one."

The Phillies took the field.

There was cheering from several parts of the park, but Dodger fans were silent, including the section they were in.

No Giant fan behind us this time, Eddie thought.

The Star Spangled Banner was played, Bubba Church finished his warmup tosses, and, as Carl Furillo stepped into the batter's box for the Dodgers, the sun broke through the clouds. Eddie hoped it was a good sign.

The first pitch was delivered for a called strike, and Barry took his first sip from the thermos.

"It'd be great to get them early," he said as he replaced the cap. "The Phillies have nothing at stake, so if they fall behind, they'll be mentally packing their bags."

With that, Furillo swung and lofted an easy fly ball to right field for the first out.

Pee Wee Reese was next, and he worked out a walk on five pitches, making way for the Duke, as the fans around them began to stir.

"Get them early," Barry said.

Pee Wee took his lead, then took off on Church's first pitch, which was laced into right field for a base hit. Reese never broke stride, rounding second and heading for third, hook-sliding in ahead of the throw and bringing the crowd to its feet as he did.

That brought up Jackie Robinson.

"Let's go Robbeee!!!" Eddie could hear Lionel's voice from two sections away.

Robinson couldn't. He bounced a two-strike pitch to short, where Hamner began the routine double play to end the inning. No runs.

Eddie entered the 6-4-3 on his scorecard and sighed. Barry reached beneath his seat for the thermos.

"Nobody said it was going to be easy."

He peeked over at the scoreboard in right field. There was nothing yet about the Giant game in Boston, only the pitchers, Larry Jansen for the Giants, Jim Wilson for the Braves.

C'mon, do it, Eddie told himself. *Start asking him stuff. Ask him about that roll of bills in his pocket. This is the chance now, between innings. C'mon, don't be chicken. Do it!*

"Dad," he said softly, "how much money did you bring?"

Barry glanced over at him. "About twenty bucks. Why, what do you want to buy this time?"

"You sure? 'Cause I thought I saw you put some money in your pocket."

There was the slightest pause.

"Oh, that," said Barry, "that's separate. That's my bonus from work.

I didn't want to leave it home 'cause I don't want your mom to know just yet. There's a dress she has her eye on, and I'm going to surprise her with it."

"Oh," Eddie said, and thought, *He's lying*.

He looked back down at the field and wondered what next.

Preacher Roe was completing his last warmup pitches and Ed Pellagrini, the Phillie second baseman, was stepping to the plate.

He'd wait until the inning was over; it would give him time to think.

"C'mon, Preach!" he called. "Get 'em one, two, three!"

Roe nearly got 'em one, two, three. The only blemish was a two-out double, but Preach got the next guy to ground out to Robinson. As Jackie was throwing to first to end the inning, some extra cheering erupted from the Dodger fans.

Up on the scoreboard, the Braves had taken a one-nothing lead over the Giants.

***

"Why didn'tcha say somethin'? I would'a kept an eye on him."

Joe Flannery snapped his gum in punctuation, as he and Nick walked down Bath Avenue from the precinct house. They'd spent the last few hours doing follow-up interviews with people who lived near the vacant lot. No one had seen or heard anything, which was par for the course these days.

"It don't matter," Nick said. "My main problem is keepin' Teresa from goin' nuts."

She'd seemed pretty calm when he finally caught up with them after Mass, but he could tell she was only holding it in because Joe and Carolyn were there.

"You could let some of the guys look around a little," Joe said. "There's no shame in that."

Nick gave him a sharp glance.

"Listen, he's my kid and I'll take care of it."

He knew that would be enough to satisfy Joe, who wouldn't think he had any other reason for wanting to keep his fellow cops out of it, like Carmine telling them what he'd overheard in that closet.

Fucking little prick, he thought. He was gonna kill him when he got a hold of him.

They reached the corner of 20th Avenue, where Joe had to turn off. He looked at his watch.

"Game's gonna start pretty soon. I know how I'll be spendin' the day, flippin' that dial."

"I'll be spendin' it findin' my kid," Nick said with a tight smile.

"Hey, good luck with that," Joe said seriously. "But if you want to take a break, do me a favor and stay away from my house. I don't wanna be listenin' with a goddamn Giant fan."

"Don't worry. You're gonna be upset enough by yourself," said Nick.

A flicker of a smirk crossed Joe's face.

"We all better hope Dodger fans don't get upset today. People seem to be dyin' when they do."

***

Preacher Roe's elbow was really bothering him. It had started on Thursday as he gutted it out in Boston and he'd hoped it would ease up, but two days in between were not enough. As he threw his warmup pitches to Campy, after the Dodgers had gone down in order in the top of the second, he tried to break off a curve but just couldn't get any snap on it.

Tommy Brown, the Phillie first baseman, stepped into the batter's box.

"How're they treatin' you?" Campy asked him. "Playin' much pinochle?"

He liked talking to the hitters, partly because he was a friendly guy, partly because it spoiled their concentration. Brown, who'd played a lot of pinochle with Preacher Roe when he was with the Dodgers, merely grunted. Many of the hitters did that.

Campy signaled for a fastball up and in and Preach reluctantly nodded. On any other day he'd bend a curve on him.

Brown and everyone else on the Phillies had noticed Preach didn't have his curve. He was looking for a fast ball and he jumped on it, but was a little too quick. He lined one foul into the box seats off third base.

Preach rubbed up a new one, while Campy stood behind the plate and considered. This might actually be a good spot for the curve, even if it wasn't working. They were ahead in the count and Tommy was geared for the fast ball. He might chase a curve out of the strike zone.

Campy settled into his crouch, put down two fingers, and set the target low and outside.

Preach tried, but the elbow wasn't cooperating. The ball hardly broke and was not outside enough. Brown made him pay for it.

In left field, Andy Pafko turned and watched just like everyone else. It soared high into the upper deck, landing in a crowd of people to the right of Barry and Eddie.

"This is no good," Barry said, bearing down on the pencil as he entered the home run on his scorecard.

"It's only one run, no matter how far they hit it," said Eddie. "Isn't that what you say?"

"No good," Barry repeated. "That double he gave up last inning was scorched. And this one looked like a batting practice pitch."

Mel Clark, the right fielder, was the next batter, and Preach's change-up fooled him into hitting a fly ball to Snider. But his 2-and-0 fastball to Granny Hamner was smashed to left field on a rising line.

"Crap," Barry muttered, as they watched it rocket toward them and then disappear from view under the overhang, along with Pafko, who was going after it.

For a moment, they didn't know what had happened. Did he catch it? Was it another home run? A second later, Pafko's throw to the infield came out from underneath, as Hamner pulled into second.

In the Dodger bullpen, below them in foul territory, Ralph Branca started to get up. Barry shook his head.

"No good," he said again.

No good, Eddie thought too. The idea that his dad might steal the car and make a run for it still seemed crazy, but not so far-fetched.

That money could've come from their savings account, maybe all of it, he thought. *It could be what he's planning to live on. He knows where the spare car key is. It'd be as easy as saying he was going to get a hot dog and just leaving.*

In the meantime, Preacher Roe was trying to get out of it. He was walking the eighth-place hitter, catcher Andy Seminick, intentionally to bring up the pitcher.

I'll just stay with him the whole time; that'll take care of it. I'll never let him out of my sight.

Preach had no trouble striking out Bubba Church for the second out, even without his curve, and that brought up Pellagrini.

"God damn it," Eddie heard Barry mutter. "Look at that."

He was pointing at the scoreboard, where the Giants had tied it up in the top of the second.

In the bullpen, Branca was warming up in earnest.

Do I really think he'd try it? Eddie wondered.

And if he did think it was possible, then what did that say? Didn't it mean that he thought his dad was guilty?

"Ohh!" Barry groaned, as Pellagrini drove one past third and down the left-field line. It bounced around the Dodger bullpen, as Branca jumped out of the way and Pafko pursued it.

Hamner scored, Seminick stopped at third, Pellagrini slid into second with a double, and now it was two-nothing.

Richie Ashburn, the center fielder who'd thrown out Cal Abrams at the plate the year before, was the next man up.

Eddie decided that worrying about what his father might do didn't help. He'd just wait and see, ask him more questions between innings. He brought his mind back to the game.

"One more out, that's all we need," he said. "If he gets through this just giving up two runs, it's not that bad."

"Maybe," Barry said, as Ashburn swung and hit a chopper up the middle. "All yours, Robby."

Robinson moved to his right and extended his body to get to it. Not an easy play, but one he usually made.

Not this time. The ball ticked off his glove and found its way into short center field, where it lay there. Both runners, on the move with two out, scored one behind the other.

Four-nothing.

A pall settled over the park, at least some of it. The Phillie fans were cheering in various sections, but in the upper left-field stands there was dead silence.

Charlie Dressen made his deliberate way out to the mound, signaling to the bullpen for Branca.

Barry stared angrily at the field, then stood up. "I'm going to get us some ice cream, Sport. Keep score for me if I don't get back in time."

He had no idea what to do. Did he trust his father or not? He did trust him. He had to.

"Okay, Dad," was what he wanted to say, but what he heard himself say was, "Wait, I'm going with you."

***

("...all tied up at one apiece in the top of the third on a bright, sunny day here in Boston,") said Russ Hodges. ("And the day just got a little sunnier for Giant fans because we've gotten word from Philly that the Dodgers are now trailing four to nothing.")

Carmine could hear it coming through the window of Nate and Rosalie Preston's apartment, as he stood just outside the basement door of the Feins' building at the bottom of the ramp, invisible to anyone passing by above on Bay Parkway.

As a Giant fan it made him feel good, and as the person he was it made him feel extra good to think of that little shitface and his murdering father suffering, as they must be, three floors above him.

("Jansen on third, Dark on first with one out,") Russ Hodges continued. ("Mueller at the plate with a count of two and two. Wilson delivers...and it's a ground ball to the right side, and into right field for a base hit!")

Carmine silently celebrated.

("Jansen comes in to score, Dark goes to third, and the Giants have taken the lead, two to one!")

He allowed himself a smile. After escaping from St. Finbar's, he'd taken a circuitous route home to minimize the chances of running into his old man.

As it happened, he'd arrived at the apartment only minutes after Nick left, but, of course, he didn't know that. He'd shed his despised suit and put on a pair of jeans, a t-shirt, and a jacket. Then he stuffed a few changes of clothing into a laundry bag and looked inside the coffee tin where Teresa kept the household money. It had a little over thirty bucks in it, which he took and then got out of there.

He'd walked over to Bay 28th Street, to a house that had been empty since its owner, an old woman, died a month ago. The porch had wooden latticework underneath, and he lifted a corner of it and stashed the laundry bag behind it. He'd come back and get it later.

First, he had some serious pain to inflict on Eddie Fein.

He looked for him down by the ball field in Bensonhurst Park. Maybe he and that other faggot Lionel Gluck were tossing a ball around, which they might do on a Sunday morning, but there were only a couple of other kids on the diamond.

The sight of it, though, brought back a very unpleasant memory. One day last June, he and Frankie Fontana had been goofing around in the park, idly looking for little kids to terrorize, when they'd spotted a game going on on the ball field.

Carmine recognized his old man's team in the field by the white uniforms with the faggy royal blue trim, like the Dodgers. Even the name "Cougars," in script across the front, looked like "Dodgers" from a distance. He hated it that his old man, who was across the field on the sidelines, didn't care about a thing like that.

Carmine had taken in the scene, Lionel on the mound, the other team with runners on first and second. He didn't know the score, of course, or the inning or how many outs there were, since there was no scoreboard, but it looked like the other team had something going.

"Let's watch this a minute," he said to Frankie. "This might be good."

With that, the batter swung and sent a line drive toward center field, that Eddie snagged behind second and turned into his unassisted triple play.

With a sickening shock, Carmine saw Eddie gleefully running off the field straight toward his old man, who had a huge smile on his face. Then he leaped into his arms.

He watched the two of them hugging while the rest of the team celebrated around them, and it was as if someone had reached into him and ripped his heart out.

Everything turned blurry for a second, and he heard a sobbing sound coming from somewhere. To his horror, he realized it was coming from him.

"Jeez, Carmine, what the fuck? Are you cryin'?" asked the surpised and unfortunate Frankie Fontana.

With an agonized scream, Carmine smashed his fist into Frankie's face, knocking him to the ground. He leaped onto him and began pounding him.

One of the parents who'd been standing by the fence happened to look their way and saw it.

"Hey, what're you doin' there?" he called out.

Somehow, within his fury, Carmine heard it and realized he had to get out of there.

He got up and ran, tearing blindly through the park and then out onto the street. His old man, across the field in the middle of a jubilant throng, hadn't seen it. He never found out, and no one knew.

Shoving the memory aside, Carmine got back to business.

He'd left the park and found his way to Eddie's building, hoping to spot him hanging around outside.

Church had let out by now, and he had to be careful. He spotted a cop car cruising up Bay Parkway, so he ducked down the ramp. That's when he'd heard the Giant game coming through the Prestons' window and decided to stick around a while.

It wasn't always easy to catch what was going on. They were eating in the kitchen, so dishes would clatter around and at times their talking, or the crying of little Nate Junior, drowned out the radio.

But he was getting most of it; enough to know, for instance, that Whitey Lockman had just drawn a walk to load the bases. Bobby Thomson, Carmine's favorite player next to Sal Maglie, was stepping to the plate. Maglie was the only Italian on the team, but Thomson had been their best hitter since the turnaround began, and he was now firmly installed as Carmine's number-two guy.

Nate Preston's angry voice momentarily blocked out the play-by-play.

"James, Goddamn you! Watchoo doin' sittin' around when I tol' you to go sweep out the alleyway?"

To Carmine's surprise, the voice that answered was deeper than the father's.

"Can't I do it after this inning, Daddy?"

Deeper or not, it still had that old, familiar sound of parental fear in it.

"You're gon' do it right now, Goddammit!" Nate hollered in his shrill voice.

Time to get outta here, Carmine thought.

He started up the ramp and then quickly drew back into the doorway. A police car was double-parked outside on the street. Some fuckin' idiot had parked next to the hydrant there, and a cop was writing out a ticket.

Shit! He couldn't stay where he was because, any second now, James would be coming through the door. Then he remembered, further down the alley at the end of the building was a passageway leading to the rear courtyard. He and Vito had discovered it one time and had taken a kid in there and robbed him of 50 cents and an Archie comic book. Shit, he missed Vito.

Carmine hustled over to the passageway and stepped inside, but before he did, he took a quick look back and then did a double take. It was crazy, but he could've sworn he'd just seen Burl Ives coming down the ramp.

At least it was someone who was a dead ringer for him, a fat guy with a goatee, wearing a white, three-piece suit. He looked like one of those Southern plantation owners.

Daring another peek, Carmine put one eye around the corner and saw James nearly bump into the man as he came out of the basement door with a large broom, each of them surprising the other.

The man recovered first.

"You, boy," he said haughtily, moving back a step. He had a thick, Southern accent that made it sound more like "yew, bwah."

"Where's your daddy?" he bellowed, pointing a threatening finger at James.

"I don't think he home now," James said.

"You know who I am, boy?"

"Yes, suh, you's Mr. Beauregard in 4E."

"That's right." He waggled the finger again at James. "And that damn dumbwaiter cart was left next to my 'partment again, with a bag o' smelly garbage on it. You do that, boy?"

"No, suh," said James.

Carmine had to put his hand over his mouth to stifle his laughter. Leaving garbage on the dumbwaiter outside the asshole's apartment and stinking it up. He liked that.

Then he realized: Wasn't 4E right above where that little rat lived? Yes, it was; they lived in 3E.

He stuck his head out of the passageway a little further, which he could do safely because Beauregard was facing away from him and James was screened by the guy's bulk. Carmine looked past them to the street and was glad to see the cop car was gone.

He came out of the passageway and started edging along the wall toward them. Mr. Beauregard was now demanding to speak to James's mother, and James was telling him she wasn't home either, which was pretty silly because Carmine could hear Rosalie Preston's voice coming from the apartment, along with a Chesterfield commercial on the radio.

That meant either Thomson had made out and the inning was over, or that he'd gotten a hit and the Braves were changing pitchers, which would be great.

Carmine had the additional thought that maybe Beauregard was hard of hearing, which would also be great.

Picking up speed, he barreled into him, sending Beauregard stumbling forward.

James saw Carmine coming at the last instant and got out of the way, but he couldn't move the broom fast enough. He wound up tripping Beauregard, adding to his sprawl as he fell forward to the pavement.

He sputtered and rolled onto his back. Carmine stood above him.

"Stop pickin' on my friend here," he snarled.

"Wha…? Who are you?" Beauregard squinted up at him.

"Never mind who I am," Carmine said. "What matters is, I know who you are. And where you live."

He started to kick Beauregard in the ribs, making him flinch, then pulled it back at the last second.

"You ain't tellin' my friend's parents nothin', ya understand?"

He winked over at James, who held the broom in front of him like a defensive weapon and looked back at Carmine warily.

"Now get up," he said to Beauregard.

Still in shock, Beauregard slowly got to his feet, assisted at the end by Carmine, who gave him an evil smile as he delicately brushed some dirt from the man's vest, unsettling him even more.

"There ya go, Mister Beau-ree-gard from 4E. Now you go back upstairs and enjoy the lovely aroma. And if ya don't like it, ya can shut your nose, right along with your friggin' mouth."

Beauregard knew he considerably outweighed Carmine, and he realized this was a teenager, but still he was helpless in the face of such menace. He'd seen some tough young bucks back there in Mississippi; he'd even raised a little hell himself. But he sensed something different about this boy. This boy was capable of homicide, he was certain.

"All right, son," he said, starting to back up the ramp, keeping his eyes on Carmine, who continued to watch him like a snake watches a rabbit.

When he was half-way, Carmine took a sudden leap in his direction, making him turn and run.

Carmine cracked up laughing and looked over at James, who was still watching him carefully.

"That was fun, huh?" he said. "Us Giant fans gotta stick together. Here, let me help ya sweep up."

He reached out for the broom.

"Don't need no help," James said, turning and walking away.

He began sweeping up the dirt near the building wall, moving it toward the middle of the alley.

"Didn't need no help with that cracker, neither."

"Come on, sure ya did."

Carmine fell in step beside him as he wielded the broom.

"That guy had ya dead to rights and you know it." He chuckled again. "Puttin' garbage outside his dumbwaiter door, that's really funny. You ever do that to anyone else in the buildin'?"

"Jus' him," James muttered. "He a Goddamn cracker."

"Cracker, what's that mean?"

James stopped sweeping.

"You never heard o' crackers?"

Actually, James himself hadn't heard of them until two weeks ago, when he'd first met Beauregard. After that, his daddy had used the word lots of times.

"You don' know 'bout them rednecks from the South?" he asked Carmine, who shrugged.

"Well, he one o' them." James' voice was venomous. "Called my daddy 'boy.'"

He turned his head to the side and spat on the ground.

"Ain't got no respect for people who's colored. Thinks we's garbage. So I'm just showin' him some real garbage."

He resumed his sweeping.

"Well, good for you," Carmine said affably, walking alongside him. "And good for you for bein' a Giant fan, instead'a rootin' for the Dodgers like everyone else, just 'cause they got Jackie Robinson."

James stopped and gave him a cold look.

"Me, I love the Giants," Carmine continued, ignoring the look. "They play up in Harlem, right? Monte Irvin, Willie Mays, Hank Thompson, they're my favorite players."

James grunted and swept a large mound of dirt in his path.

"Watch your feet," he warned, as Carmine skipped out of the way.

"What do you do with all this crap after you sweep it up?" he asked.

"Put it in a garbage can; watchoo think I do?"

James started pushing the pile in the direction of the cellar door.

"Where is it? Ya want me to get it for ya?"

"No."

Carmine walked along with him in silence until they reached the basement entrance.

"Here, I got it," he said, holding the door open for him and then stepping inside before James could object. He looked around.

"Where's the garbage can you need?"

"Only got ten of 'em right there," James said, pointing to a group of cans that were piled against the far wall.

"Hey, I just thought maybe you needed a particular one, that's all."

Carmine walked over to a large metal door, set into the wall next to the cans.

"Is this the dumbwaiter?" he asked, opening the door.

Inside, the empty cart was sitting there. It was a little over four feet high and three feet wide, open on two sides and divided in half by a horizontal board, which Carmine took a closer look at.

"C'mere a minute," he said. "I wanna ask you somethin'."

"Got no time," James said, starting to roll the nearest garbage can in the direction of the basement door.

The movement was so fast, James didn't even see it. Carmine was suddenly in front of him, both hands on the can, blocking the way.

"I did you a favor just now." His eyes gleamed ominously. "That guy was gonna tell your old man, and now he ain't gonna say nothin'. So you better be my friend, or else I just might tell your old man myself. Am I gettin' through to ya?"

James started to say something, then slowly nodded.

"Okay, now tell me about the friggin' dumbwaiter."

Carmine pointed to the horizontal board that divided the cart in two. "Does this come out?"

"Yeah," James said, "when we need to haul somethin' big."

"How much can you put on it? I mean weight."

"Maybe a hunnert eighty, hunnert ninety pounds, maybe more."

Carmine nodded. He was going to have to wait a bit before he could do this, but it would be worth it. Man, would it be worth it.

"Ya know the good thing about dumbwaiters?" he said. "When ya ring the front doorbell, people ask who it is before they open it, but when ya knock on the dumbwaiter door, they don't ask nothin'. They just think it's their neighbor."

He gave James a wicked grin.

"They don't know it could be someone waitin' on the cart to jump out at 'em, do they?"

He laughed and closed the metal door.

"All right," he said, "here's what you're gonna do. You're gonna stop sendin' garbage up to that guy for now; no sense in pushin' it. But tomorrow afternoon, we're gonna do somethin' even better, somethin' real sweet with this thing." He patted the door fondly. "Okay, Giant fan?"

James had been aware of Carmine and his friends over the years, just like everyone else. They'd never messed with him, maybe because they didn't know what to make of him, maybe because he was a big, strong kid. Physically, Carmine didn't scare him.

But what Carmine could tell his daddy sure did.

"Yeah," James mumbled softly, looking at the floor.

"Hey, cheer up," Carmine said, breakng into another grin. "Today's the day we win the fuckin' pennant!"

***

Barry took another sip from the thermos as Ralph Branca buzzed a fast ball by Tommy Brown for a called strike three and Campy whipped the ball down to Cox at third base to start it around the infield. It was the bottom of the third, two outs, and nobody on.

Eddie wrote a backwards "K" on his scorecard, as his inner scorecard registered that this was the sixth time his dad had gone to the thermos. The last time had been in the top half, after Reese's two-out triple off the right-field wall brought Branca home with the first Dodger run. But Snider grounded to first and that was that.

"Let me ask you something," Barry said, marking down his own "K" and turning to Eddie. His eyes were just starting to look a little red. "Why did you feel you had to accompany me to the refreshment stand?"

"I just wanted to see what they had there."

It was the best he could come up with, but he knew it was lame. He'd always stayed at their seats and kept score for Barry while he was gone. Now, for the first time ever, they'd actually missed something. They'd had to ask people how Branca got Jones to end the previous inning.

"What do you mean 'what they had there'?" Barry said. "It was only ice cream. And you got vanilla. Something's going on with you; what is it?"

Bill Nicholson was being announced as a pinch hitter, and Eddie wrote down his name, trying to buy time. His mind was blank. This wasn't the way it was supposed to happen.

"I thought maybe you could use the company," he managed.

Nicholson slapped the first pitch into center field for a base hit.

"I don't believe that," Barry said.

"Hey, Eddie."

He looked up and saw Lionel standing in the aisle at the end of their row.

"I just wanted to see if things looked any better from here," Lionel called out.

"They don't," Eddie called back to him. "We're still losing 4-1 no matter where you sit."

"That's what I suspected."

The crowd suddenly let out a moan, as Branca uncorked a wild pitch and Nicholson took second.

"Jeez, Ralph," Lionel yelled toward the field, "how many times I gotta tell you? The plate is that white thing with five sides."

"Down in front!" someone yelled, and Lionel went into a crouch.

"We can't give up any more runs," he called to Eddie across the people sitting in between. A peanut vendor coming down the aisle almost tripped over him.

"Hey, kid," he growled, "you're blockin' traffic. Go find a seat."

"See ya later," Lionel said, getting to his feet and starting up the steps.

Barry continued to look down at the field, where Branca had just followed the wild pitch with ball four to Granny Hamner, making it first and second.

"So what's going on with you?" he asked, resuming the inquiry.

Eddie watched Branca's first pitch to Andy Seminick, which was also wide for a ball.

"About what?"

"Come on, stop it," Barry said. "About the way you've been acting. For instance, why did you want to know about my watch the other night?"

"I just wondered how you lost it."

The next pitch was inside for ball two.

"I'd already told you how I lost it, but you insisted on upsetting your mother. Why?"

Branca threw a pitch in the dirt that Campy barely blocked. The count was now three balls, no strikes on Seminick.

"You were the one she was upset with," Eddie said, trying to take the offensive.

Branca's next pitch wasn't even close. Ball four, and now the bases were loaded.

"Shit!" Barry slapped the back of his hand against the sheet of paper with a loud crack, tearing it slightly and coming close enough to Eddie's leg to make him flinch.

"And don't talk back to me," he said. "It's none of your business what goes on between your mother and me; remember that."

His face was starting to become flushed.

"And it's also none of your damn business about my watch. Now why were you so interested in it?"

Eddie tried the only thing he could think of.

"We're bringing them bad luck, Dad," he said, pointing at the field. "Can't we talk about it after the inning? Look, the pitcher's coming up; we can get out of this."

Barry was about to say something, but then he shook his head bemusedly.

"Okay, Sport," he said with mock tolerance. "Whatever you say."

Branca tried. He got two quick strikes on Church, but then threw him a change up that Church blooped into right field.

For a second it appeared Furillo was going to get to it, but it kept sinking and hit the grass just short of his outstretched glove. With the bases loaded, the merry go round was in full motion, as two runners scored, and the Phillies had now blown the doors off the game.

Six to one.

People all around them were groaning in misery. Barry only tightened his jaw.

"So much for bringing them luck," he proclaimed. "Now answer me. Why are you so goddamned interested in my watch?"

He was trapped. Trapped by the question, trapped in this seat, trapped by his own stupid hopes. He'd actually believed he could find out something today, something that would help him prove his dad was innocent. And, by the way, they'd also see a terrific game, with the Dodgers clinching the pennant on the field right in front of them. That's what he'd hoped.

But just like everything else, it went horribly wrong. Instead of finding out anything, he was the one who was found out. Instead of seeing the Dodgers clinch a pennant, he was watching them get slaughtered. And it was only the third inning. The nightmare was just starting.

Meanwhile, this man, his father, who'd continue to drink from that thermos as this torturous game wore on, and get drunker and angrier until God knows what he'd do, was waiting for him to speak.

Disgust overwhelmed him. He hated it all. He hated the Dodgers. He hated his father. He hated his whole miserable life.

Shaking with the effort to keep from screaming, he put his lips next to Barry's ear.

"I know why you don't want me to ask about that watch," he said. "It's because they found it in Sandra's hand. After you killed her."

CHAPTER SIXTEEN

Ernie Harwell was doing the middle innings on the WMCA broadcast of the Giant game.

("Dark taking his lead from second,") his baritone drawl informed from Nick's portable radio, as he described the top of the fifth in Boston.

("Wilson delivers to Monte Irvin, and the pitch is swung on and lined into left field for a base hit! Dark is rounding third and heading home. There'll be no throw, and the Giants are now up 3-1!")

Unmarked cars only had police radios, so Nick had brought his portable with him, and it was now propped up on the passenger seat. The car was a Hudson this time, not the DeSoto he'd shared with Joe on Friday. It had been the only one available.

He was using it because Carmine would have recognized the family car. Through the windshield he had a clear line of vision down Bay 28th Street to the empty house.

After he'd calmed Teresa down and she told him about the missing money, clothing, and laundry bag, the first place he'd gone was the Bay Parkway station, where he had a chat with the change clerk.

There'd been very few passengers entering the station on this Sunday morning, and the guy had not seen a teenager with a laundry bag among them. That, of course, only eliminated the train, not the buses or the trolleys under the el, but Nick had a feeling Carmine was still in the neighborhood. He'd hardly ever been out of it, and his punk friends lived here. At 14, he still didn't know too much about what lay beyond. Nick didn't want to think about what would happen at 15.

He was on his way to the home of punk family number one, the Peccarinos, when he passed by the deserted house and thought it might be worth checking.

Ten minutes later, his flashlight beam had found the laundry bag under the porch. This was a relief because now he didn't have to let the whole fucking neighborhood know his kid ran away. Now it was just a matter of waiting.

***

At Shibe Park, as the Giants' third run went up on the board, it got barely a stir from the Dodger fans, who were, by now, numbly accepting the inevitable.

Eddie, wrapped in his turmoil, hadn't even noticed it going up.

Barry, surprisingly, had not gotten mad. In fact, Eddie didn't know what he'd gotten. He'd just stared at him for a second, then slowly shook his head and looked away toward the field.

Eddie, his own anger fading, replaced by shock at what he'd done, sat and waited, his insides wound tighter than the strings of a baseball. The explosion never came.

For a solid inning, Barry neither looked at him nor spoke.

The Dodgers scored a lone run in the meantime, to bring it to 6-2. Campy, while legging out his triple to deep center field, pulled up lame at third. When he eventually scored on a Phillie error, he limped the 90 feet to the plate.

As the Phillies made their last out in the fourth, Eddie finally couldn't stand it.

"I'm sorry, Dad," he said, starting to cry and trying to stop at the same time. "I didn't mean it."

Barry still didn't look at him.

"Sure you did. Otherwise you wouldn't have said it."

"No, no, I didn't."

The tears were winning again. They were 3-and-0 against him so far this weekend.

"I just got mad, that's all. I know…" He lowered his voice. "I know you couldn't do that; I just got mad, that's all."

Furillo, at the plate, lined a fastball into center field for a base hit, to a scattering of applause. Barry's eyes were still on the field.

"What made you think I did 'do that'?"

Eddie hesitated, because he knew how dumb this would sound.

"Carmine told me."

A group of kids in the next section were starting a "we want a hit" chant as Pee Wee Reese stepped in.

"Carmine?" Barry looked at him for the first time, a look of incredulity. "What's he got to do with anything? And why would you believe a stupid kid like Carmine?"

'Cause you threw the ball into that guy's face, he thought, unable to speak.

Reese slapped the first pitch into right field. Furillo never broke stride, as he rounded second and steamed into third. First and third, no one out.

"He told me..." Eddie started, as the "we want a hit" chant picked up and spread to their section. Duke Snider was stepping to the plate.

"...he must've heard Nick talking. 'Cause he knew you lost something, and he said Nick found it. He told me Nick was after you, Dad. Carmine said Nick knows things about you. What did he mean?"

Church delivered. Snider swung and missed.

"Nick's my friend," Barry said. "We all know things about each other."

"Bad things?"

He shrugged. "You always know good and bad about your friends."

The Duke sent a slow chopper up the middle. Pellagrini speared it behind second, flipped to Hamner for one, then on to first...not in time, as Snider beat it out by a cleat's length.

Furillo scored on the play and now it was 6-3.

"What did Carmine mean, Dad? What could Nick know? Keep talking; we're bringing them luck."

The crowd intensity moved up a notch as Jackie Robinson stepped to the plate.

"Here's Robby's chance to redeem himself for hitting into that double play in the first."

"Not about the game, Dad, about Nick. Seriously, what do you think he knows?"

Jackie Robinson settled into the right-hand batter's box, his arms high, hands at cap level, the bat pointing straight up.

"You haven't mentioned any of this to your mother, have you?"

Robby looked at a curve outside for ball one, as the crowd cranked it up yet another notch.

"No, of course not."

"Haven't been asking her any questions?"

Robinson swung and crushed it. It headed out in a rising arc toward the wall in right field, Nicholson turning in pursuit, the crowd surging to its feet.

It caromed high off the wall, bouncing into the right field corner. Snider came all the way around from first to score, as Jackie flew around the bases, sliding into third with a triple.

It was 6-4, and the Dodgers were back in it.

In the midst of the roar, the Phillie manager made his way out to the mound, signaling down the right field line toward the bullpen for Karl Drews. Barry repeated the question.

"No," said Eddie, "I never asked her anything."

He knew it was a lie, and he was telling it because he didn't trust his father. His eyes started to water again, and he had to fight it.

"That's surprising," Barry said. "You were so inquisitive the other night."

"She doesn't know."

"Hmm."

They watched in silence as Drews warmed up. Roy Campanella stood in the on-deck circle swinging two bats.

Barry again uncapped the thermos and took a long sip. Eddie thought about the half-finished scorecard, still in his back pocket, with the things he'd copied from Nick's notebook on it.

There'd been no time to study it, but one thing he remembered: Like B at some foreign sounding place. He leaned in close to Barry's ear.

"Could it be something from the war?"

This got a scrutinizing look.

"Where did you get that from?"

"I used to ask you about the war, and if you killed any Germans, and you never gave me an answer."

The crowd noise began to rise again, as Campy stepped in.

"I guess I did; it was hard to tell. The tanks and artillery did most of the damage."

They were silent again, a two-person island in a sea of fans yelling, whistling, stomping, clapping, and exhorting Campy to hit one out and tie the score.

Eddie tried to think. *Sandra was strangled. People don't get strangled in a war, do they?*

"Were you ever up close to a German?"

"What do you mean?"

"Like in hand-to-hand combat?"

"No," Barry scoffed, "that's in war movies. We shot at them and they shot at us. That was about it."

Eddie nodded, as Campy swung and hit a ground ball back to the mound. Drews looked Robby back to third, then threw to first for the second out.

Barry pointed toward Campanella as he made his way back to the dugout.

"Look how he's running. Campy can hardly move on that leg."

Close to Germans, Eddie kept thinking. *Getting close to Germans.*

"What about German prisoners?" he said. "Did you see any of them?"

Andy Pafko was settling into the batter's box.

"I saw plenty of them. We kept passing them going the opposite way, being taken down to the beach for processing."

"The beach?"

"Omaha Beach, Normandy. Whoa, there he goes!"

Robinson had taken off, apparently trying to steal home as Drews was delivering his first pitch to Pafko. A quarter of the way down the line, he slammed on the brakes and dove back toward third, making it in just ahead of Seminick's hurried throw to Puddin'head Jones, which nearly went into left field.

"Robby really knows how to unsettle a team, doesn't he?" Barry said.

"Sure does," said Eddie. A pause. "What were they like?"

"What were who like?"

"The prisoners."

Barry frowned.

"Why do you want to know about this? They were Nazis, that's all."

Robinson again took a big lead off third. As Drews eyed him, Jackie feinted right, then left, then right again, like a pedestrian in a road full of invisible traffic. Drews delivered to the plate.

"Did you ever talk to them?"

Pafko swung and cracked a sharp ground ball to the right of second, just past Pellagrini and into right field for a base hit. Jackie, now the calm jogger rather than the daring pedestrian, trotted home and it was 6-5.

All around them the crowd screamed and hollered, pouring out its clamorous approval. Eddie had to practically shout in Barry's ear.

"Did you ever speak to them, Dad?"

"You should be enjoying this," Barry said, "not asking me questions."

It had become deafening.

"We're bringing them luck, Dad, don't spoil it," Eddie yelled. "Keep talking. Did you ever speak to any Germans?"

Gil Hodges was digging in at the plate.

Barry's expression darkened.

"Speak to them? What would I say?"

His eyes began to smolder.

"Would I ask them to explain to me why they killed my grandparents? And my uncles and aunts? And all their children, your little cousins who'll never grow up, the ones you'll never know because they were all sent to Auschwitz?

"Would I tell them how sorry I was that they were prisoners now, and I no longer had the chance to kill them for what they did? Is that what you want to hear? Is that going to bring the Dodgers luck?"

Hodges swung at the first pitch and hit a ground ball to Pellagrini, who flipped to Hamner for the force, and the inning was over.

***

Mary, on all fours, reached under her dresser with the whiskbroom and swept up the last few pieces of glass she'd missed earlier. She was wearing jeans, something Teresa frowned upon of late. They were all right for cleaning her room but, now that she was 13, she was being told to dress more ladylike. Ordinarily, she'd have been instructed to change into a skirt.

But today Teresa was lost in her own problems. She'd been pacing around the apartment for three hours now, chain smoking and occasionally crying. Mary tried to stay out of her way, keeping mostly to the living room and watching a Bowery Boys movie on Channel 13, followed by Junior Carnival, then moving to her bedroom when it was over and there was nothing on but the Yankee-Red Sox game on Channel 11.

She had no interest in that, or in the Dodger and Giant games on the radio, since she no longer was an anti-Giant fan. She was more interested in trying to come up with that elusive shred of memory she'd had about the second watch.

She knew she hadn't seen someone buying it, because it wouldn't have meant anything to her at the time. No, the memory seemed to be more about the train ride coming home. She had a mental image of them all sitting on the West End train as it rumbled across the Manhattan Bridge, the trucks and cars moving along the roadway outside the window (which Carmine got to sit next to, she remembered that).

The two women were on the side seat talking, and Mary was listening to them because she was ignoring Carmine. They must've been talking about the watch, but what were they saying? She'd been only seven years old then, and it was all so hazy.

She didn't dare ask her mother. She could not risk Teresa mentioning it to Nick.

As for Eddie asking his own mother, he told her he'd done it twice already, which was probably once too many. She'd definitely know something was wrong if he did it again. So it was up to Mary to remember it on her own, which, unfortunately, wasn't happening. But maybe there was a way she could find out without saying anything about a watch.

She changed out of her jeans into her new navy blue skirt and went into the kitchen, where Teresa was sitting at the table with what must have been her fourth cup of coffee.

"How're you doin', Ma?" Mary asked her.

Teresa looked up through moist eyes.

"I was tryin' to read the paper to take my mind off of it." She waved at the Sunday *Herald Tribune* on the counter. "And what do they have in there? An article about missing children. Oh, God."

She sighed and looked vacantly out the window.

"He'll find him, Ma. Dad's good at that."

Teresa continued to stare out the window. Mary edged over, into her line of sight.

"Does this skirt look okay on me? Do you think it's too long?"

"It looks fine," Teresa said absently.

"I don't think they have a good enough variety in the stores around here. We should go to Macy's sometime. I bet they've got terrific skirts there."

"Mmf."

Teresa stood up from the table and carried her cup over to the stove, where she poured herself some more coffee from the percolator.

"Remember that skirt we got there the time we had to bring back the one Aunt Annabella got me? I loved that skirt."

"You did? I don't even remember it."

"It was gorgeous," she said, although, in fact, Mary didn't remember it either.

"You, me, and Carmine went. We took the train in together, and…"

"Merciful Jesus," Teresa moaned, "will we ever do anything together again?"

Oh, Jeez, Mary thought, invoking the Son of God in her own fashion. "Ma, don't worry; Dad'll find him. He'll be all right."

Teresa sat down heavily at the table and stared into the cup of coffee.

"C'mon, Ma," Mary said. "I'm tryin' to help you take your mind off it. Eddie's mother came along with us, didn't she?"

"If you say so."

"She wanted to get somethin' for him, 'cause he was in the hospital having his tonsils out."

"How do you remember all this stuff? You must'a been what, seven, eight?"

Mary shrugged.

"Then, didn't we have to stop someplace, 'cause of Eddie's mother? The perfume department, wasn't it?" She looked hopefully at Teresa.

C'mon, Ma, say it was the jewelry department. Say it was a watch. C'mon, Ma.

Teresa looked up at her with deep weariness.

"Oh, Mary, I know you're tryin' to be mature, but you're still so young. It's okay for you to spend time thinkin' about some skirt you had when you were little, but your brother is in trouble, don't you understand that? I never seen your father so angry, and nobody tells me nothin'. All I can do is sit here and pray to God with all my might that this won't end up in some terrible tragedy."

She started to cry.

Mary moved behind her mother and put her arms around her.

"Please, Ma, don't worry," she said.

As she did, the word "tragedy" seemed to ring a bell. Teresa was always using words like that, but this time it reminded her of something. Was it on the train that day? Yes, yes, it came back to her. Julia and her mother were talking about a woman they ran into at Macy's, someone they knew whose child had a tragedy.

It got Mary's attention because she'd never heard the word before and thought it was some kind of toy. She remembered piping up and asking Teresa to buy her a tragedy, which made both women laugh.

Carmine, even though he had no idea what they were laughing at, called her stupid. Yes, it was definitely on that train ride. But was she the woman who bought the other watch, or were they talking about someone else?

Ohh, it was so frustrating!

***

The feeling of rebirth for the fans in the upper left-field seats had died in its infancy. The Phillies answered immediately with two runs of their own, widening it to 8-5 and keeping it there. Karl Drews, as puzzling today as he'd been an open book to the Dodgers on Friday night, had retired seven in a row.

In the midst of it all, at 3:35 p.m. to be exact, the final score from Boston went up on the scoreboard, showing the Giants had won 3-2. Now, as they began the eighth against Drews, the Dodgers were only six outs from oblivion.

Eddie's efforts had been just as ineffective. Barry answered his questions, but in ways that gave him nothing.

He insisted again that he didn't know Sandra. He vaguely recalled buying Eddie the baseball glove but not who'd sold it to them. On the night she was killed he'd been out, but he said he didn't go anywhere special, just walked the streets. No, he didn't see anybody.

Eddie told him about his visit to Mrs. Weinstock's apartment, about seeing "Lunch B.F." on Sandra's calendar.

"Means nothing to me," Barry said.

But, of course, if she'd been his secret girlfriend, that's what he'd say.

He refused to talk any more about the war, saying the subject was closed.

From time to time, he'd sip at the thermos, which seemed to be bottomless. As usual, he showed no outward signs of intoxication. Eddie had no doubt that if he was still meaning to steal the car he'd be able to drive it, or at least he'd think he could.

Lionel provided some brief comic relief in the Phillies' half of the sixth. He came by and slipped into a temporarily empty seat in front of them. Carl Erskine had come in to pitch at the start of the inning, as Dressen was forced to use anyone he could to try and hold the Phillies where they were, even one of his beleaguered starters. There'd been a runner on first with two out when Lionel sat down in the seat. Nicholson was the hitter, and he blasted one deep to left, sending Pafko back and out of their sight line beneath the upper stands.

No one breathed. A home run would've made it 10-5, and that would've probably been it.

But the sight of Nicholson pulling up between first and second told them Pafko had caught it. Lionel put his hand inside his polo shirt, flapped his fingers like his heart was fluttering, and slumped down in the seat in a mock swoon.

As the Dodgers were trotting off the field, the seat's original occupant came back and Lionel made his exit, still rolling his eyes and wiping invisible sweat off his brow.

Eddie had been afraid his dad would tell him to go along with him, and switch seats with Ben for a while. There was no way he could've reasonably refused. Barry would be left alone for a few minutes, with a chance to leave.

But it didn't happen. Maybe he still wasn't sure about running away, who knew?

Now, as Andy Pafko opened the eighth by grounding out to Hamner and moving the Dodgers one out closer to completing the worst collapse in Major League history, Barry began to curse under his breath.

For his part, Eddie felt as if his insides were dying. What was the use? He had to face it. He'd gotten nowhere and learned nothing.

He remembered one other item on the piece of paper: "B–at Bath Ave. Tav." He hadn't even asked his father about that one.

Gil Hodges was stepping into the batter's box.

"Dad, did you see the article in the paper about the guy who got killed 'cause he was a Giant fan?"

The look Barry gave him was so ugly it almost made him gasp.

"Why do you want to know?" he said.

Hodges hit a chopper up the middle, as Hamner raced to flag it down behind second on the outfield grass. His throw was just wide of first, and Gil had an infield hit.

"I just happened to see it in the paper, that's all," Eddie said.

"You didn't just happen to see it. You don't even read the paper, except for the comics."

There was a stirring around them, as people murmured and pointed to the Phillie bullpen. The great Robin Roberts, who'd pitched eight innings last night, was beginning to warm up.

Billy Cox was stepping to the plate.

"Sure I do. We have Current Events in school…"

"Stop it!"

It was said loudly enough that people sitting near them turned to look at them. They looked straight ahead for a moment and said nothing, until the people had turned away.

"I read the article 'cause I saw you reading it," Eddie said in a quiet voice. "You know something about it, Dad, don't you?"

Barry gave a humorless laugh.

"Not as much as you'd think. Now I've got a question for you."

Cox swung and blooped one into short right field. Three Phillies went after it, but it fell just beyond their reach, just fair, for a base hit.

Hodges, on the move, made it all the way to third and now there were two on, with the potential tying run coming to the plate.

The crowd once again began to hope.

"You said they found a watch in her hand," said Barry, as Rube Walker was announced as a pinch hitter for Erskine. "That wasn't in the papers, whether you read them or not. How did you happen to know that?"

Oh, God, what could he say? He sat there in confusion.

Walker swung at the first pitch and missed, for strike one.

"You made up all that stuff about Carmine, didn't you?" Barry's voice was edged in bitterness. "You couldn't have found out something like that from him, so it's obvious where you did find it out. And the next time you see your beloved coach, you tell him what I told him yesterday. You don't use a man's son to spy on him."

What?

"But he didn't…"

Walker swung and missed for strike two.

"And you, what's your excuse? Are you mad at me 'cause I never came to your Little League games, 'cause I didn't teach you how to play ball, and he did? Is that it?"

Barry's eyes were bloodshot. A tiny thread of saliva clung to the side of his mouth.

"Dad, I'm not…"

The crowd erupted, as Walker lined the 0-2 pitch toward the gap in left-center field. It shot by Ennis and Ashburn and hit the wall on two hops, Hodges trotting home from third, Cox putting on the afterburners and scoring behind him, as Walker slid into second, just ahead of Ashburn's throw. The Dodgers had narrowed it to 8-7, and the tying run was at second base.

Everyone was on their feet now, screaming. Eddie stood too, unaware he was doing it, as he tried to figure out what to say. Spying for Nick? It was crazy.

"Nick didn't tell me anything, I swear to God," was the best he could come up with, as the crowd sat down again.

The P.A. announcer informed everyone of two new players in the game, Don Thompson as a pinch runner for Rube Walker at second and, coming in from the Phillie bullpen, the awesome Robin Roberts.

"Then why did you say they found a watch in her hand?"

He was tempted to tell the truth, to say he'd seen it in Nick's notebook after Mary found it, but something stopped him.

Maybe it was stubbornness, maybe it was because he was kind of angry himself. This man, his father, had lied to him all day, about the money in his pocket and who knew what else? And when he wasn't lying, he was evading questions. Why should he tell this man anything?

Roberts completed his warmups, as Eddie kept silent.

"Well?"

"I guess I was just trying to be dramatic," Eddie said in a tight voice. It was a term Julia always used. "Stop being dramatic," she'd tell him.

Barry snorted.

"Well, the show bombed, kiddo."

Thompson took his lead off second, as Roberts buzzed a fastball on the inside corner to Carl Furillo for strike one.

For some reason, those damn tears started again. "I don't care about Nick, Dad!" he blurted out. "I care about you! You're my dad, not him. I'm just trying to help you. 'Cause I know he's wrong. I know you didn't do it. You could never be a..."

"Murderer" was engulfed in the roar of the crowd, as Furillo lined one sharply into left for a base hit.

Thompson, with a good jump, was already rounding third, as Charlie Dressen, in the coach's box, nearly pulled his arm out of its socket waving him on.

The throw came in, too late, as Thompson slid head-first across the plate with the tying run. The Dodgers had finally come all the way back.

He stared at his father in the thunderous clamor that surrounded them. Tears flowed down his cheeks; he couldn't stop them.

Barry looked like he might cry as well, as he gave Eddie a strange sort of smile.

"You think we just brought them luck?"

Eddie couldn't speak. In the pandemonium, he looked at the worn expression on Barry's face and wished the Dodgers could somehow bring them some luck too.

But, of course, they couldn't, could they? No amount of luck can change the past.

Whatever had happened, nothing could undo it.

CHAPTER SEVENTEEN

"I don't fuckin' believe it! They tied it up!" Carmine wished he could punch the radio.

"Ssh!" said Vito from the other end of the couch as he looked up to make sure neither of his parents had come in at that moment. Then he giggled.

"Robin Fuckin' Roberts, and he can't get nobody out," Carmine complained. "What'a you laughin' at?"

"Nothin'." Vito giggled again.

Carmine regarded him a moment. He hadn't known what the reaction would be when he rang Vito's doorbell earlier, but evidently things were okay now. He'd either switched his anger over to Frankie or he'd completely forgotten about it. One of Vito's problems was his memory. Carmine often wondered if he'd been dropped on his head when he was little, which was entirely possible, knowing his parents.

Speaking of which, Vito's father was standing in the doorway.

Vincent Peccarino was a short, squat man in his 40's, with an extended gut and more hair on his body than on his head. All of this was in evidence since he was naked.

"What's goin' on in here?" he scowled. "I was just gettin' in the shower when I heard all'a this yellin'."

"Hi, Mr. Peccarino," Carmine said casually, as if everyone's old man walked around like that. "We were listenin' to the game."

"Well, watch your mouth. I don't want Josephina and Angelina to hear no cursin' in my house."

"Sorry, Mr. Peccarino."

Carmine could see the twin four-year-old girls sitting on the dining room floor behind Vito's father, having stopped in their play to stare up at him.

What a fuckin' zoo, he thought.

"What's the score?" asked Mr. Peccarino.

"Eight-all," Carmine said.

"Well, keep it down in here. Vito's mudder is takin' a nap."

He turned and padded back into the dining room past the twins, who seemed indifferent now, as he headed toward the bedroom where Mrs. Peccarino was, rather than the bathroom where the shower was.

Fuckin' zoo, Carmine thought again.

He also thought he should get moving. He'd taken a chance coming here because he had some business to do, so he'd better do it.

"Hey, Vito," he said, reaching into his jacket pocket and taking out the deck of porno playing cards he'd never gotten around to showing anyone on Thursday. "Pick a card, any card."

Vito eyed him narrowly.

"You're gonna try'n make me look stupid? I don't like card tricks, Carmine."

"You're gonna love this one; I guarantee it."

He held out the deck, which, from the backs of the cards, looked ordinary.

"C'mon, if ya don't like the card ya picked you can rip it up, how's that?"

Vito considered it a moment, started to take one from near the top, then switched to one near the bottom.

Carmine rolled his eyes.

Finally, Vito drew one out and looked at it.

"Holy shit!"

"Pretty good, huh? I got fifty-one more of 'em right here, and each one is different."

"Lemme see 'em."

Vito grabbed for the rest of the deck as Carmine pulled it away.

"Take it easy," he said. "First, we gotta make a deal. How would'ya like ta own this deck, for keeps?"

Vito gave him a sour look.

"Yeah? What do I gotta do for it?"

"Lend me your knife."

Vito flipped the card back at him disdainfully.

"Uh uh. I awready lent it to ya once; that's enough."

Carmine took the top card from the deck, turned it over, and placed it on the couch. Then he slowly turned the others over, placing them on the cushion between them.

"Look," he said as he exposed each one. "Look, look."

Vito couldn't help doing just that, as Carmine glanced up and noticed the twins standing in the doorway.

"Get back in there where yez belong," he growled at them.

"You can't make us," one of them began, and then they both ran squealing back into the dining room as Carmine jumped to his feet.

He looked past them to see if Mr. Peccarino would be coming out, but nothing happened, so he figured he was all right for the next few minutes.

He sat back down on the couch, where Vito had grabbed up the cards from the cushion and was greedily ogling them.

"Listen," Carmine said to him, "this is a deal ya can't pass up. I'm gonna *give* ya these cards, y'understand? For keeps. And all you gotta do is *lend* me the knife, okay? Just for one day."

Vito managed to tear his eyes away from the pornucopia.

"Lemme see the rest of 'em first."

"Sure, here ya go." Carmine fanned out the remainder of the deck, keeping it open for a tantalizing second or two, and then closed it up.

"Hey, I didn't get a good look," Vito complained.

"You're gonna get lots'a good looks," Carmine said, leering, "and ya got all the time in the world to have 'em. So whatta ya say?"

"Awight." Vito giggled.

He got up and went into his bedroom for the knife, passing through the dining room where the twins were staging a fight between two of their dolls, smacking them against each other and laughing gleefully.

Carmine sat back against the cushions and turned his attention to the radio, as Red Barber was giving the totals for the top of the eighth. It had just finished up with a double play to end the Dodger rally, which warmed his heart.

They're still gonna get theirs, he thought. *And tomorrow, while the Giants are restin' up for the World Series, Eddie Fein is gonna get his.*

***

Nick had the game on too as he sat in the car. Red Barber was amazed at what they were witnessing, as the new Dodger pitcher in the bottom of the eighth, less than 24 hours after pitching a complete-game shutout, was Don Newcombe.

Once again, it was Newcombe and Roberts, with the season on the line.

Nick's watch said quarter after four. He figured Carmine might be listening to the game somewhere and wouldn't show until it was over, so he was surprised to see him walking right toward him down the street.

Carmine was headed for the deserted house, his eyes scanning both sides of the street, not seeing Nick in the unfamiliar car at the end of the block.

He wasn't really concentrating anyway. He was thinking about the Giants and feeling pretty good about himself. The words "living a life of crime" went through his head. They sounded nice.

It took balls to live a life of crime, more balls than it took to be a cop, that's for sure. He could feel the knife pressing against the small of his back, tucked snugly under his shirt behind his belt, and he remembered how easy it was to take care of that Southern guy.

And this was an adult, don't forget, not some faggy little kid from school. He'd scared the living shit out of him, and didn't even need a weapon to do it. He had a talent for this kind of thing, Carmine knew. He was good.

The 30 bucks he'd stolen would be a start, and he could always get more. The world was filled with people who were just waiting to be robbed.

Right now, though, as soon as he picked up the laundry bag, he was taking the train into Manhattan to the Greyhound Bus Terminal on 34th Street, where they had storage lockers for a nickel, or so he'd heard. Someday, he might even take a Greyhound bus himself, to parts unknown. That sounded nice too: parts unknown.

Tonight, he'd either find a cheap hotel room or save himself some dough by riding the subways. Tomorrow, after he came back and took care of Eddie Fein, he'd be on his way.

Nick watched him retrieve the laundry bag from under the porch, sling it over his shoulder, and start walking back toward the 86th Street el. Then he put the Hudson in gear and pulled out into the street.

He drove up the block slowly toward Carmine's retreating form, pulled even with him, and stopped, opening the door and springing out in the same motion. Carmine was on the ground before he could even blink.

Nick sat on his chest and pinned his arms. "Some kind'a week you been havin', huh, smart guy? Where's the money you stole from your mother?"

Carmine struggled for a moment, then suddenly relaxed. A calmness spread over his face that Nick did not like at all.

"In the laundry bag," he said. "I didn't spend none of it."

Nick did not like Carmine's eyes. There was no fear in them, none.

He resisted the urge to smack that calm, assured face because he knew he wouldn't be able to stop there. "Get up!" he said.

He hauled Carmine to his feet and pushed him hard against the side of the building.

"You love that goddamn closet? Well you can spend your whole life there now, 'cause you're goin' to your room and you're stayin' there. No TV, no radio, no nothin'!"

He accentuated the point by shoving Carmine against the wall again, as Carmine limply allowed him to do it.

"The only time you're comin' out is for meals, the bat'room, and school. And speakin' of that, I'm takin' you in every day myself, to make sure you actually get there. The principal is gonna know that if you so much as open your yap, he's to call me at the precinct. And if he ever does, you goddamn, miserable piece'a shit, all this is gonna seem like a vacation compared to what I'll do to you. You understand me?"

Carmine nodded.

"Say it!"

"I unnerstand you," Carmine muttered.

"Every day," Nick continued, "your mother is gonna personally escort you home for lunch and again at three o'clock. You'll be the only kid in junior high whose mama takes him home from school, ya like that?"

Carmine said nothing.

"Then you're goin' right back to your room, and it's gonna stay that way 'til I say it ain't. Now pick up that bag and get in the car."

Carmine bent down and got it. Nick grabbed him by the neck and perp-walked him over to the Hudson idling at the curb, took the bag from him, and threw it in the back seat. He forced Carmine's head down and pushed him in after it.

The portable radio in the front was leaning against the passenger door, still on. Nick got into the car and reached across, just as Red Barber was describing Ennis's fly ball to Snider for the second Phillie out, and turned it off.

"Is it still tied?" Carmine asked.

"Shut up."

He did, and stayed quiet for the short trip because he knew he didn't have to say a word. He'd seen his future today, and no amount of humiliating shit was gonna change that. Not even if his old man had beaten the crap out of him just now, which maybe he couldn't do anymore. Carmine had found that out today too, hadn't he?

As he listened to his "punishment," he felt more and more confident. They had no power over him. He had only to wait for tomorrow afternoon.

He still had the knife.

***

"You blew the call!" Pee Wee Reese hollered at Lon Warneke, the second base umpire, as Robin Roberts stood on the bag, slapping the infield dirt off himself.

"My foot brushed the side of the bag. He was out!" Pee Wee pleaded, as Warneke shook his head and turned away.

Pee Wee shook his head too and walked toward the mound to give the ball to Newk, who looked disgusted.

It was the bottom of the 12th now, the field bathed in the lights from the towers, the sun having moved behind the home-plate stands three innings ago.

Newk hadn't given up a hit since the first batter he'd faced in the eighth, but the Phillies still managed to threaten in every inning, either by walks or a hit batsman.

The Dodgers had their chances too against Roberts, putting men on in the 9th, 10th, and 11th, but leaving them there. The shadows lengthened and the evening approached, as the two great righthanders battled on.

Newk had started off the 12th in trouble again, giving up a lead-off walk to Roberts, never a good sign when you walk the opposing pitcher. Pellagrini had bunted, harder than he would have liked, between the mound and first, and Newcombe was quickly on it.

"Second! Second!" Campy yelled, as he saw they had the lead runner dead to rights. But the throw was wide, pulling Pee Wee off the bag, or so Lon Warneke had ruled.

Now, as Pee Wee put the ball back in Newk's glove and gave him a pat on the rump, they were looking at first and second with nobody out.

Barry twisted the cap onto the thermos more forcefully than he needed to and slammed it down on the concrete beneath the seat. Eddie heard a faint tinkling of glass as its inner lining shattered.

They hadn't said anything about Nick or the murders since the moment the Dodgers tied it. Eddie had run out of questions, or at least out of energy, and it was just easier to get caught up in the game, which was nerve-racking enough.

Only last inning, he'd held his breath as Andy Pafko, below him, made a beautiful, running, game-saving catch of Seminick's drive down the line, with Hamner rounding the bases and about to score the winning run if the ball had dropped in.

But that was last inning's problem. Now, as the Dodger infield met at the mound to talk about how they'd play the next hitter, Richie Ashburn, Eddie couldn't stop thinking that, in everything his dad said today, he'd never once denied it. Never once did he say he was innocent.

The meeting ended and everyone went back to their positions, Hodges setting up even with the bag, Reese and Robinson at double-play depth, and Cox in at third to guard against the bunt, as Ashburn stepped to the plate.

"Thirteen-and-a-half games ahead," Barry muttered, digging the fingernails of one hand into the palm of the other. "They don't just lose, do they? They have to wait 'til they've squeezed every last drop of blood from your heart."

"Don't jinx them," Eddie said nervously, as Newcombe delivered a fastball on the outside corner for a called strike.

"Jinx them?" Barry said. "I can't jinx anyone but myself."

Newcombe's next pitch was a change-up down and in, and Ashburn hit it on the ground toward first. Hodges fielded it, turned, and fired to Reese for the force on Pellagrini, but the return throw was just too late to get Ashburn, flashing across first base.

Roberts moved over to third, and now the Phillies had first and third with only one out and Puddin'head Jones, their leading home run and RBI man, coming up.

"The best infield that ever played the game," Barry said, "and you see what they did wrong?"

It so happened, Eddie did. "Yeah," he muttered, "Gil should've stepped on first before he threw to second. He was right by the bag. It should've been a tag-out double play."

"And whose fault was it? Mine because I jinxed them?"

Eddie really couldn't say. But he wondered about the thing just before that.

"What did you mean when you said you could only jinx yourself?"

Barry gazed down at the outfield grass.

"Every time you do something you regret," he said, "you jinx yourself."

Campy was signaling they should intentionally walk Jones, filling the bases and bringing up Del Ennis.

"Did you ever do that?" Eddie asked softly.

"Don't we all?" said Barry.

Newcombe threw four wide ones. Jones flipped his bat aside and trotted down to first.

The crowd around them began to loudly implore Newk to either strike Ennis out or, God willing, get him to hit into a double play. Barry reached for the thermos.

"Dad..." Eddie said, grabbing for his arm, remembering the broken glass.

"What's the matter?" Barry unscrewed the cap and shifted the thermos to his other hand. "Are you going to give me a temperance lecture?"

"No, there's..."

It was drowned out by a roar, as Ennis swung at a fastball and missed for strike one.

Barry turned away and raised the thermos to his lips.

"Dad!"

He desperately reached over his father's shoulder, trying to slap at the thermos, but his fingertips couldn't quite get there. Barry put it to his mouth and tilted it back.

With one final lunge, Eddie got to it, pushing it away from Barry's lips, as scotch splashed onto his shirt.

"What the hell are you doing?" he said, glaring at him.

"There's broken glass in there. Shake it, you'll see."

Barry shook the thermos and heard the tinkling sound.

"Oh, f..." he started to say, then cocked his arm.

"Don't!" Eddie yelled.

He grabbed Barry's wrist before he could throw it. Barry froze for an instant. Then he pulled his arm free.

"Just leave me alone, okay?" He dropped the thermos under the seat.

People were standing now, the tension too great to bear sitting down. Ennis fouled off the next pitch for strike two.

Eddie stood up amidst the din. Barry remained seated, the only one in their section still doing so. Newcombe went into his windup and delivered.

A curve that Ennis checked his swing on, as it sliced across the outside corner. There was the briefest of pauses, and then the umpire's arm went up for strike three.

The crowd erupted.

The ovation played out, and then the tension resumed. There was still one more out to get, as Eddie Waitkus stepped to the plate.

He'd replaced Tommy Brown at first base during the fourth inning, a lifetime ago, and Eddie, like all kids who are aware of such things, knew he was one of three Phillies who shared his namesake.

There were none on the Dodgers, since Eddie Miksis had been traded to the Cubs earlier in the Andy Pafko deal. Somehow, it became crucial, on top of everything else, that the Dodgers not be beaten by a player named Eddie.

"C'mon, Newk!" he hollered through cupped hands, as Newcombe bounced a curve in the dirt that Campy blocked.

Eddie felt something whisper past his left side.

"What's this?" Barry said, unfolding the piece of paper he'd taken from Eddie's back pocket.

Unnoticed in all the standing and sitting, it had worked its way up and was visible. Barry had noticed it, grabbed it, and was now reading it.

Eddie lunged for it just as Barry got to the words "like B at St. Laurent" and knocked it out of his hands. It fluttered in the air and then fell between them.

They both dropped to their knees after it, as everyone else in the park watched Newcombe deliver to Waitkus.

Eddie got to it first. He snatched it up and tried to stand, but Barry reached out and pulled him down again by the shoulders.

His hands moved to Eddie's throat.

Waitkus ripped a line drive up the middle toward center field, as Eddie felt his breath being choked off for a horrifying instant that took forever. He tried to pull his father's hands off him, as Barry suddenly let go and pulled them away.

The crowd gasped. Then there was silence.

Barry stayed on his knees, staring downward. Eddie staggered to his feet in the eerie stillness enveloping the park. He gingerly touched his adam's apple and fought back a wave of nausea.

He couldn't look at his father. He looked instead where everyone else was looking, toward the field where, behind second base, Jackie Robinson lay on his stomach, motionless.

A long moment passed. Then Jackie rolled onto his side, as the stadium watched in muted awe. He held the ball up, flipped it toward Pee Wee, and then collapsed again.

Warneke lifted his thumb in the air, signaling the third out, as the rest of the Dodgers swarmed from the dugout and sprinted from their positions in the field to where Robby lay. They were joined by some of the Phillies and, for several minutes, everyone gathered around as Harold Wendler, the Dodger trainer, bent over him.

Eddie could hear bits of conversation.

"…incredible catch…" "What happened to him…?" "Landed hard…I think he's really hurt."

"Son, is this yours?"

It came from just behind him, along with a tap on the shoulder.

He turned to see a thin, elderly man in a three-piece suit and a Dodger cap, holding the piece of paper.

"I thought it might be what you were looking for," the man said with a kindly smile, as he gave it to him. "Did you ever see a catch like that one?"

"No," Eddie said hoarsely, "I never did." Then he added, "Thank you."

"My pleasure," said the man. "He just saved our season. I hope he's all right. We really need him."

Just then, Robby rose unsteadily to his feet and the stadium went crazy.

Barry stood silently, a haunted look in his eyes.

Jake Pitler, the Dodgers' first base coach, held onto Jackie's arm and helped him walk to the dugout, as he and the rest of the Dodgers left the field to a thunderous ovation.

Eddie's hand was throbbing under the bandage, as he folded the piece of paper and put it back in his pocket. He wondered if the stitches had come open. In a way, he didn't care.

His original scorecard was under the seats somewhere, he realized, but he didn't want to look for it. He couldn't keep score now anyway.

All he could think of was how Sandra must have felt in her final, terrifying moments.

That and the words "what'll I do?" Over and over.

CHAPTER EIGHTEEN

Red Barber described the scene as Jackie Robinson and the Dodgers walked off the field, and then let the crowd speak for itself. It filled the air waves and reverberated from the radio in Julia's kitchen.

They picked a great game, she thought. *They must be absolutely thrilled.*

She'd just finished writing up two weeks' worth of lesson plans, and now there were two less things to worry about. In the refrigerator was a rib roast she was going to cook for dinner, which she figured would take place about three hours after the game ended.

She'd been lucky to get it. Cohen and Levine, the kosher butchers on 86th Street who were normally open on Sundays, were closing early today, since Rosh Hashanah began at sundown. She'd showed up just in time to be their last customer.

Now she had the thought that, even if it hadn't gone into extra innings, the guys could never have driven home before sundown. This wouldn't have meant anything to her husband, but she was sure Ben Gluck had considered it. Evidently, the Dodger fan in him was more persuasive than the Jew.

The doorbell rang as a Lucky Strike commercial began on the radio. She looked through the peephole and saw Mary DiFazio standing in the hallway.

This is interesting, she thought as she opened the door.

"Hi, Mrs. Fein," Mary said with a shy smile. "Is Eddie home?"

As far as Julia could remember, Mary had never come over here looking for Eddie before. They hadn't been particularly close playmates when they were little. In fact, they hadn't had much to do with each other. At least not until yesterday morning.

"Hi, Mary," she said, "he's not here. He and his dad are at the Dodger game, but, please, come on in."

Mary seemed disappointed, and nervous.

"That's okay, Mrs. Fein," she said, edging back toward the staircase. "I was just on my way to the drug store to get my ma some aspirin. I thought I'd stop by for a minute, but if he's not home...well, just tell him I was here."

"No, no, wait," Julia said, "I wanted to ask you about something."

Oh shit, Mary thought. *I knew this was a bad idea.*

She'd made a snap decision to come over here after her mother sent her on the errand, but now she didn't know what she was thinking.

"I really should get that aspirin," she said.

"You don't have to go all the way to the drug store; I've got some here." Julia held the door open a little wider. "Come in and I'll get it."

"No, no, I couldn't."

This was getting sticky. How would she explain bringing home aspirin that obviously wasn't from the store?

"Please," Julia said, smiling, "it'll only take a second. Don't stand out there in the hallway; come in."

She had no choice. *Okay*, she thought as she stepped past Julia into the apartment, *I'll let her give me the aspirin but I'll still go to the store, so it won't matter.*

Julia turned off the radio and transferred her lesson plans from the kitchen table to the counter.

"Can I get you something to drink?"

"No, no thanks."

Mary stood awkwardly in the middle of the kitchen.

"Sit, sit," Julia said, pulling a chair away from the table. "How is your family?" she asked, as Mary complied.

"Oh, they're fine."

Sure they are. Considering her father had locked her brother up in his room, her mother had a headache from crying all day, and she herself was banned from speaking to Eddie and had to sneak over here, things couldn't be better.

"I wanted to ask you," Julia said, sitting down at the table with her. "What's all this going on between you and Eddie?"

Mary was ready for it. She knew they hadn't caught him coming back through the window or all hell would've broken loose by now, so his mother must only know about their meeting at Al's. That meant the social studies report story.

She launched into it, then noticed how Julia was shaking her head.

"Come on, now, what was the real reason?" Julia said with a tolerant smile.

"Well..."

She was starting to get a crazy idea. Should she try it? Why not?

"I wanted to see him..." Her face started to redden. "...'cause I really like him a lot, Mrs. Fein. In fact, I think I love him."

Her eyes turned away from Julia's surprised expression, and she stared at the table top.

For several seconds, the refrigerator's hum was the only sound in the room. Finally, Julia managed to speak.

"He's only twelve years old."

"I don't care." Mary was still looking down at the table top. "He's the nicest boy I ever met."

Was that true? Maybe it was. "And I think I love him."

Her face flushed again.

There was more silence, and then Julia stood up with such suddenness that she hit her knee against the bottom of the table.

"My goodness," she said. "Here we are just sitting around while your poor mother needs aspirin. Let me go and find her some."

She headed down the hallway and into the bathroom, where she began rummaging through the medicine cabinet.

All right, calm down, she said to herself. *You knew something like this was going to happen someday.*

But it wasn't supposed to happen yet, and not only was Mary DiFazio older than Eddie, but she wasn't even Jewish. It's one thing not to be religious, but to have a Gentile girlfriend...

She stopped that train of thought because it was absurd. They were both children, for God's sake. How was she supposed to respond to this?

In the meantime, Mary, at the kitchen table, was feeling pretty good about how she'd handled that and was starting to get another idea.

Julia appeared in the doorway holding a bottle of Bayer.

"We've got plenty here," she said, a bit too cheerfully, "so why don't I give you a half-dozen? That should be more than enough, don't you think?"

She moved over to the box of Kleenex on the counter and started emptying the pills onto a tissue.

"I hope I didn't upset you, Mrs. Fein."

"No, no," Julia said. "You just caught me a little off guard, that's all."

"We're young, I know."

Mary felt a tiny thrill as she said the words. It was like something they said in the movies.

"Yes, you are young," Julia said, sensing an opening, "and it's good that you realize it. Believe me, Mary, you've got plenty of years ahead of you to fall in love. You're only thirteen, after all, just starting to have life experiences."

Mary was nodding her head in response to this, when suddenly her eyes lit up.

"Wow," she said, "sorry to interrupt, Mrs. Fein. I'm listening to what you're saying, and it's true, I know, but when you said 'life experiences' it reminded me. I've got this assignment for my Sunday School class, you know, at St. Finbar's? I wondered, could you maybe help me with it?"

Julia had to laugh. Kids really knew how to change the subject.

"You mean, like you were supposed to help Eddie with his social studies report?"

"No, no, really," said Mary. "Next week the lesson is about how God helps people who suffer. We each have to bring in a story. Mine is supposed to be about someone whose child had something tragic happen, and I don't know anyone like that."

She looked earnestly at Julia.

"Do you?"

***

Jackie Robinson trotted out to his position at second base as the bottom of the 13th began, and the crowd went crazy again.

"Robbee!" Eddie yelled. He stood up and whistled through his fingers the way Lionel had shown him last year.

"Sport…" Barry reached for his arm but Eddie pulled it away.

He sat down again, angling his body to present as much of his back to his father as he could, given the limitations of the seat.

"It was an accident," Barry said. "You know that."

Eddie didn't answer him.

"Let's go, Newk!" he shouted toward the pitcher's mound, as Newcombe completed his warmups.

"Talk to me. Is your hand all right?"

Actually, it was. There wasn't any blood on the bandage, which meant he hadn't broken the stitches, and the throbbing had stopped. But he didn't want to say that or anything else to his father.

"Get 'im, Newk!" he yelled, as Nicholson stepped to the plate.

"If you want me to say I'm sorry again, I will."

Nicholson promptly grounded the first pitch up the middle. Robinson moved to his right and backhanded it, throwing smoothly across his body to Hodges for the first out.

"Way to go, Robby!" Eddie said. "Nothing wrong with him," he added, to himself.

"Way to go, Robby!" Barry echoed.

Eddie had never heard the word "irony," but was now aware of the idea. He could probably ask his father anything, at this point, but he didn't want to anymore.

Besides, he already knew the one answer that mattered, didn't he?

He looked toward the field, where Granny Hamner was stepping to the plate.

"Newwwk!" he cried out.

"Come on," Barry said, "you're not going to spend the rest of your life not talking to me, are you? I told you, my hands slipped. As soon as I realized, I let go. You know I'd never hurt you; stop being this way."

Hamner bounced another ground ball at Robinson. It was scooped up efficiently and fired to first for the second out, to louder cheers from the crowd, and Eddie.

"Have I ever laid a hand on you? Tell the truth."

He had, in fact. Eddie could remember times when his father would be physical with him, shoving him out of the way if he didn't want to be bothered, and some of those shoves were pretty hard. As for hitting him, or choking him, no, he'd never done that. But, shit, that wasn't the point!

"Why did you do it?" he said, facing Barry and lowering his voice to a fierce whisper. "How could you kill Sandra?"

Barry's eyes were bloodshot, but they looked straight at him and they didn't blink.

"I swear to you," he said. "It wasn't me."

Eddie didn't know what he was expecting, more silence or more anger, but not this.

"You mean, you didn't do it?"

He couldn't help but start to hope, even though it was stupid, even though he knew better.

"Sport," Barry said, "it wasn't me."

He tried to get his thoughts together, not be fooled by emotions.

"Why didn't you say that all along?"

Barry's gaze never wavered.

"I was angry at you. I shouldn't have been. So I'm telling you straight now, once and for all. It wasn't me."

God, how he wanted to believe that! But his father had lied to him all day. Why should he believe it?

"What about the money in your pocket?" he said. "It's not for Mom's new dress. What's it really for?"

Barry looked down.

"It's severance pay."

"It's what?"

"Severance pay. It's what they give you when you're fired."

A tear began to make its way down his face.

"Please, Sport, don't tell your mother about this. I'll tell her myself, I swear, but I want to find another job first."

He'd never seen his dad like this. It shook him.

"I know it's asking a lot, but will you promise me you'll keep it a secret?"

Why not? Eddie thought. *What's one more?*

"Sure, Dad," he said softly.

Newcombe, in the meantime, had walked Seminick and Roberts on eight pitches, his arm finally reaching its limit. Dressen came out to the mound and the crowd stood yet again, showing Newk their gratitude, as the seventh Dodger pitcher of the game, the seldom-used Bud Podbielan, made his way in from the bullpen.

Eddie thought about the dream of his dad on the subway tracks, looking up and saying, "Save me." The expression on his face right now was exactly like the dream.

His dad didn't have to tell him he was fired. He could've said he won the money in a poker game at the office, or anything else, but he didn't.

And really, he knew in his heart that his dad didn't try to strangle him. He knew how clumsy Barry could get when he drank; he'd seen it lots of times. He was right, his hands had slipped, that's all. No big deal.

He tried to play devil's advocate. His dad was at the tavern the night the guy was killed. What about that?

Well, so were a lot of people, and they were probably all madder at the guy than he was.

What about the home run ball?

That stopped him for a second. He thought back and tried hard to picture it again. It happened so fast and was such a shock. But like that thermos bottle and the beer bottle his dad knocked against the wall, maybe he was just heaving it blindly. Dangerous? Yes. Stupid? Definitely. But Barry could've just been flinging the ball away, not even noticing where it went.

He saw it again in his mind's eye and, for the first time, realized that's just what had happened. He was sure of it. And not just because he wanted it to be. Because it was. His dad would never knowingly hurt somebody. His dad was innocent. Innocent.

He reached into his back pocket and took out the piece of paper. "Dad, I want you to look at this," he said.

He told Barry everything, from the moment Carmine ambushed him, to his enlisting Mary, to Nick catching them coming out of Al's Soda Fountain and warning him to stay out of it. To the discovery of the notebook and the things he'd copied from it.

Meanwhile, the game went on. Podbielan got the third out, the Phillies took the field to start the 14th, Pee Wee fouled out to the catcher, and Duke Snider was settling into the batter's box as Eddie was finishing.

Barry listened to it all without a word. Sometimes he'd glance at the piece of paper, then just shake his head.

Now, with a look Eddie hadn't seen since that first moment Barry came bounding down the steps to the Bay Parkway station, home from the war, he said, "Do you want to know why I never came to your Little League games?"

His voice broke.

"It was because I was scared. I didn't realize what it would be like that first time. It was a thousand times worse than watching the Dodgers lose. It broke my heart."

His eyes began to fill with tears.

"Even after you became a good player, I was afraid to come back because I was afraid you would mess up and it would kill me. I was selfish, and it was wrong."

Now the tears were flowing down his cheeks.

"I don't deserve a son as wonderful as you."

Eddie was crying too.

"Dad…" he began.

"But listen, Sport," Barry said, taking him gently by the shoulders. "That's why you've got to stop. Nick was right; you've got to stop now. Before you get in serious trouble."

"I don't care if I get in trouble."

"I know you don't. But I do."

Barry put his arms around him and they embraced, as Snider swung and lofted a pop foul behind third. Jones settled under it for the second out.

The ovation began, as Jackie Robinson discarded the weighted bat he'd been swinging in the on-deck circle and approached the plate.

Eddie knew there was just one more question he had to ask. For whatever reason Nick suspected his father, it all came down to "Like B at St. Laurent."

"Dad," he said very quietly, as Robinson settled into the batter's box, "what happened at Saint Lowrent?"

Barry sighed, but he gave a tired smile.

"It's Saint-Laurent," he said, pronouncing it *San Lo-raun.* "And I'm sorry, Sport, I really am, but all I can tell you is how to say it."

"Dad…"

"Please, Eddie, believe me, I…"

It sounded like the crack of a rifle shot, but, of course, it wasn't.

The crowd was propelled to its feet by it, screaming in anticipation, as Eddie looked up.

There, illuminated by the field lights against the darkening sky, was the ball, a tiny white dot, growing larger and larger.

And it was coming straight at him. No, it would be just beyond him.

He scrambled up on the seat and grabbed onto his father's shoulder with his bandaged right hand. With a twisting leap, he launched himself, using the uninjured heel of his hand for leverage to give him that extra foot, like Duke Snider climbing the center field wall, and his left hand shot up.

Barry's arms held him steady. He could feel the sting, as the ball hit his palm, and then his fingers closed firmly around it. The roar of the crowd enveloped him.

Barry bore him aloft in triumph amid the delirious throng, as Eddie held the ball high in the air for all to see.

Then, with people cheering, clapping, and patting him on the back, he was gently lowered to his seat.

***

"Everyone thought we were a great hitting club," Charlie Dressen was saying to the cluster of reporters, who were crowding around so closely they were practically pushing him into his locker, "but it was our defense today that did the job…"

He was drowned out for a moment by a loud whoop from someone nearby. At the other end of the clubhouse, Jackie Robinson was emerging from the trainer's room. The sportswriters, noticing it, excused themselves and began to edge over in Robby's direction.

"How're ya feelin', Jackie?" one of them called out as they did.

"A lot better than Leo Durocher," he said, sitting down on a stool in front of his locker.

"What happened to you on the catch?"

Dick Young of the *Daily News* was, as usual, among the first to get there.

Jackie didn't like the man very much, believing, though others did not agree, that he was prejudiced.

"My right elbow jammed into my stomach and knocked the wind out of me," he answered briefly, then looked over at Roscoe McGowen of *The Times*.

"Were you thinking home run in the fourteenth, with nobody on?" McGowen asked him.

Now Jackie smiled.

"It's the only time he ever gives them up, isn't it? With nobody on."

"'S'cuse me, Mr. Robinson..."

A large, perspiring man in a security guard's uniform was standing behind the writers.

"The kid that caught your home run is outside. He says he wants to give you the ball, but I told him he couldn't come in here. He wouldn't let me take it; he says he wants to give it to you himself."

"Where is he, outside the door?"

"Just outside."

"Sure," Jackie said, and got slowly to his feet. "Give me a minute, fellas," he told the sportswriters.

He made his way across the clubhouse, getting pats on the back from tired teammates en route, as the reporters turned back to Dressen with more questions about the pitching rotation for the playoff.

The guard opened the door to a crowd of kids, with a few adults mixed in, who saw Robby standing behind him and surged forward.

"Jackie! Jackie!" they yelled, pushing autograph pads and scorecards in his direction.

"Move it back!" the guard barked at them, spreading his arms and using his bulk to persuade. "Where's the kid with the ball?"

"Over here."

Eddie was holding it in his right hand as he struggled to the front, from which he'd been displaced while the guard was inside.

Jackie Robinson, standing in the doorway watching his efforts, noticed the bandage.

"What's your name?" he asked him.

"Eddie F..."

"Eddie Fein is his name, Robby," said a taller kid who'd also pushed his way forward. "He plays shortstop for the Cougars, our P.A.L. team. I'm Lionel Gluck and I'm a pitcher. In fact, I'm the ace of the staff."

He grinned proudly, as did the tall man with glasses who was standing with him.

Robinson regarded them both for a moment, then he smiled.

"Glad to hear it," he said. He turned back to Eddie.

"How'd you manage to catch the ball with your hand like that?"

Eddie was surprised at how big he was, something he could never have imagined from seeing him in photos or on television. He was easily as big as his father.

"I caught it with my other hand," he said.

"He made a one-handed, leaping catch. Everyone in the stands saw it," Lionel put in. "Of course, we also saw your catch," he added.

This time, Robinson laughed.

"Glad to hear that too," he said. "Tell you what, Eddie. Since you made such a great catch, I think you should keep the ball."

Eddie's jaw dropped, as the kids around him started murmuring.

"If you have a pen," Jackie added, "I'll sign it for you."

"I've got one," said a man behind Eddie, as he took out a fountain pen and handed it to Robinson. "I'm his dad, Barry Fein."

"Pleased to meet you," Jackie said, smelling a whiff of alcohol. "How did you hurt your hand?" he asked Eddie, as he took the ball from him.

Eddie was about to say he'd slipped while holding a glass of milk, but he couldn't. There was no way he could lie to Jackie Robinson.

"I got mad when you guys lost up in Boston," he said sheepishly, "and I slammed a glass down on the table."

His father, Lionel, and Ben stared at him in surprise.

Robinson who'd begun to write on the ball, paused.

"You don't have to do something like that to be a fan, Eddie. If you're going to get mad, there are a lot more important things in the world to get mad at than us losing a game. Do you know what I'm saying?"

Eddie knew exactly what he was saying.

"You're right," he said, his face starting to flush.

Jackie resumed his writing.

"Nothing to be ashamed of in getting mad; I get plenty mad myself. The trick is to do it at the right time and about the right thing. And not to take it out on your hand, especially if you're a shortstop. Here you go."

He smiled at him and handed the ball over.

As soon as he did, he was besieged by autograph pads, pieces of paper, and scorecards.

"Only a couple," he told everybody as he took the nearest one. "I have to get showered so we can get out of here. After all, we've got a playoff game tomorrow, right?"

A loud cheer went up.

"And thanks for coming all the way down here to support us. It's great to play in someone else's park and have it filled with your own fans."

With a final wave, he turned back into the clubhouse, and the guard closed the door behind him.

* * *

"'Of course, we also saw your catch,'" Eddie said to Lionel from the back seat of the Packard, as they moved slowly across the Tacony Palmyra Bridge in the Sunday evening traffic.

Lionel, in the front passenger seat, turned and shot a look at him over his shoulder.

"I hope you'll remember I said that when they interview you for my life story," he said. "It'll be an amusing sidelight to the day a future Hall of Famer met Jackie Robinson."

Eddie stuck two fingers into his mouth and pretended to gag.

Lionel snickered and faced forward again.

"So, it's gonna be at Ebbets Field tomorrow," he said. "Last week they had a coin flip in case it finished in a tie, and Dressen won."

"I wouldn't'a done it that way if I was him," Ben said, as he slowed the car yet again and downshifted into second. "'Cause if it goes the full three, then two of 'em will be in the Polo Grounds. What do you think, Barry?"

Eddie glanced over at his father, who had his eyes closed and was snoring lightly, his head tilted back against the seat cushions.

"He's sleeping," he told Ben.

"Ah."

"Hey, Dad," Lionel said brightly, "can we go to the game tomorrow? We don't have school."

"Are you kiddin'? The only reason you don't have school is 'cause it's Rosh Hashanah. We're gonna be in shul tomorrow; we already missed it tonight."

"Aww!" Lionel grumbled.

They drove in silence for a while. Eddie hadn't realized tomorrow was a Jewish holiday. As a part of his dad's atheism, he'd always had to go to school on Rosh Hashanah and Yom Kippur, while other kids had stayed out and gone to synagogue.

His parents, for their part, didn't stay home either. They'd always gone in to work as usual. Except that tomorrow, his dad wouldn't be going to work. He'd only be pretending to, because he'd be looking for a new job.

So why, then, couldn't Eddie pretend to go to school tomorrow, and not show up? He had a Jewish last name, so Fartsworth would think he was out legitimately, and his parents would never know.

It would give him more time, and he needed it.

The guy in the bar was killed because he was a Giant fan. Was that why Sandra was killed? Eddie sat in the darkness of the back seat and imagined her, standing on the promenade, talking to someone, not his dad, never his dad, but someone else. Some other Dodger fan from the neighborhood, someone she knew well enough to be talking about baseball.

He looked down at the ball in his hands. It was too dark to see the writing on it anymore, but he knew what it said: "To Eddie. Don't lose sight of what matters. Jackie Robinson."

I'll try, Robby, he thought. *I'll try.*

CHAPTER NINETEEN

Monday Morning, October 1st

Nick slipped the notebook back into his desk drawer as he spotted Joe at the other end of the squad room.

"Great game yesterday, huh?" Joe called out, giving him a sly look as he came toward him down the aisle.

"Ya mean Jansen beatin' the Braves?"

This got a smile, as Joe sat down at his desk.

"I'll bet you figured you had it locked up. I read the Giants were already celebratin' on the train back to New York when they found out. I would'a loved to see the look on Durocher's face."

This morning, before Nick escorted his sullen kid to school, he'd noticed the *Daily News* sports pages, filled with yesterday's games and speculation about the playoff, and it had all gone right through him. He tried to remember now who was pitching, Hearn for the Giants and who for the Dodgers? Oh yeah, Branca. It was amazing how little he cared.

Except he did care.

"We gotta keep our eyes open today," he said. "Especially this afternoon, if things don't go right."

Joe laughed. "Did I just hear you say, 'if things don't go right'? I don't believe it. This has turned you into a Dodger fan."

Nick just shook his head.

"You're our resident sociologist. Explain to me why someone would commit murder over somethin' like this."

Joe picked up a pencil and idly bounced its eraser against the surface of the desk. "Think of it as bein' in love. You make the same emotional commitment, to allow something outside yourself to affect you in a meaningful way. When the team's goin' good it's like you're goin' good, and life is wonderful.

"But if they, for instance, blow a thirteen-and-a-half game lead to your arch enemy…" He gave the eraser a crisp bounce. "…it's betrayal. It's like findin' out the one you love has been screwin' the whole neighborhood."

He gave it one more and snatched up the pencil.

"Crimes of passion, that's what we're seein' here." He pointed the pencil at Nick. "You can understand it. You're a Giant fan and you're deleriously happy, 'cause they just came all the way back from the dead. How're you gonna feel when, and you notice I said 'when,' the Dodgers beat 'em in this playoff and they break your heart? You're gonna get mad, right? You might even want to kill somebody."

Nick laughed. "Only you."

Joe leaned back and gazed up at the photos on Nick's wall, "Our Best PALs." "Any of them dilettantes ever come to a Little League game?"

"What do you got against them? They're helpin' kids."

"No, you're helpin' kids. They're gettin' a tax deduction."

Nick shrugged, picked up the Forensics Progress report, and looked through it again. Clothing fibers found on Riccio's body were inconclusive, and the prints on his wallet didn't match any of the bar patrons they'd rounded up over the weekend and fingerprinted.

This included the two who couldn't come up with decent alibis for the night of the Weinstock murder and Max Herskowitz, the guy who cursed out Riccio after he left. Forensics was now moving on to their massive arrest-record files. He didn't envy them their job, spending all day squinting at swirl patterns. Barry's prints wouldn't be in there, he thought.

"They find anything?" Joe asked him.

"If they did, would we be sittin' here shootin' the shit?"

"He might not be in our files," Joe said, in echo of Nick's thoughts. "Like I said, crimes of passion. Most of the time, the guy doesn't have a rap sheet. He's just some regular schmo with problems."

Nick knew what would be next. After they'd exhausted their own arrest files, they'd start looking at other groups of people who'd been fingerprinted, like government employees or anyone who'd ever been in the armed forces. If it was Barry, that's when they'd find him.

How long would it take, two or three weeks?

Too long. He'd go over there tonight and tell Barry what he was about to tell him on Saturday, before it all turned crazy. To come down with him to the station house and be fingerprinted.

If he was innocent, it would clear him. If he wasn't…so be it. Better to get it the fuck over with.

***

Eddie peered through the plate glass door to Faber's Sporting Goods and wondered if the place was closed, since it appeared to be empty. He tried the door and it opened, so he carefully stepped inside.

"Mr. Faber?" he said. There was no response. "Mr. Faber?" he said again.

"Hold on a minute," said a voice from under the counter, followed by some muttered cursing Eddie couldn't make out.

After a few seconds, Mr. Faber's head appeared above the counter top, followed slowly by the rest of him.

"Ping pong balls," he said acidly, clutching one in his gnarled right hand as he got to his feet. "Why do they pack 'em in so tight that they explode whenever you open a new box?"

He looked at Eddie with even more distrust than usual.

"You notice I've got no bats on display anymore? Your friends planning on meeting you here again?"

"I hope not," Eddie said, looking behind him and seeing a rack of bicycle pumps where the bats used to be. "And they're not my friends."

"I have to keep the bats behind the counter now, because of you," Mr. Faber said. "And what's your excuse for not buying something this time, the Jewish holiday?"

"I'll buy something. I don't care about the Jewish holiday."

"You don't? You're all dressed for it."

Eddie was wearing the suit he'd changed into after he doubled back to the apartment when he was sure his parents were gone. It would let him blend in with the other Jewish kids. Anyone roaming the streets during school hours today without a jacket and tie would look suspicious. If he'd had a yarmulke to complete the effect, he would have worn it.

"I shouldn't have even bothered opening the store," Mr. Faber complained, "for all the customers I'm gonna get today."

Eddie remembered that Jews were not supposed to carry money on the High Holy Days, or listen to the radio or watch television. He wondered what Lionel and his father were going to do about the game today. More immediately, he wondered how he was going to get Mr. Faber talking about Sandra.

While he was wondering, Mr. Faber took the problem out of his hands.

"Business has been so rotten, I can't even afford to replace Sandra," he said, adding the ping pong ball to a jar of them that was sitting on the counter.

Eddie silently thanked Whomever.

"I'll bet you miss her," he said. "You probably knew her better than anyone."

"I certainly spent more time with her than anyone."

Mr. Faber reached for the stool he kept behind the counter and pulled it over. He sighed as he sat down.

"She was a very unhappy girl."

"She was?"

"I just said so, didn't I? Don't make people repeat themselves."

He gave Eddie a brief glower, then looked off into the invisible distance.

"She used to tell me how her mother was always nagging her. The latest thing was that cough she had. You remember how she used to cough?"

Eddie did, actually, now that he mentioned it.

"She said it was just a cold but her mother kept insisting it was gonna turn into pneumonia. Tell the truth, I thought her mother had a point, and I told her so. In fact, that was probably the last thing I ever said to her."

His eyes got distant again.

"But she told me she hadn't seen a doctor in years. Young people think they're gonna live forever." He looked at Eddie. "Do you think you're gonna live forever?"

"No."

He remembered wanting to throw himself in front of a train, and stopped the thought.

"Was that the only thing she was unhappy about?" he asked.

"If it was, then she was the happiest person on Earth," Mr. Faber scoffed. "Of course there was more, plenty more. She didn't like living here in Bensonhurst, for instance. Said it was boring. That's another thing about young people; they're always bored. She wanted to move back to Greenwich Village. Ah, finally a real customer."

The door opened behind Eddie and a man in a dark blue suit came in. He was obviously not Jewish, or at least not religious, because he was holding out a dollar bill as he approached the counter.

"Excuse me," he said, "could you give me four quarters?"

Mr. Faber rolled his eyes, but opened the cash drawer and obliged. After the man left, he shook his head in disgust.

"There's a newsstand right on the corner. Why do they come in here for change? Sandra actually used to make conversation with them. I'd tell her not to waste time talking to people who weren't customers, but she never listened."

"Maybe she just liked to be friendly."

"Better to be friendly with people who spend money. In fact, why am I sitting here talking to you? I'm doing the same thing she did."

"I'm gonna spend money."

"Yeah? Well, why don't you put some of it where your mouth is? You were looking at a Dodger cap the other day. They're $4.98. If you want to talk to me, buy one."

Eddie didn't have anything like $4.98. He reached into his pocket and pulled out all the change he had, which came to 75 cents.

"Can I give you this much?" He held out the coins. "I can come back tomorrow and give you the rest." Which was, of course, untrue.

"Good enough," said Mr. Faber. "I'll take what you've got there as a deposit. Pick out a cap and I'll hold it for you. If you don't come back tomorrow, you lose your money."

"Okay." Eddie glumly gave him the 75 cents.

He quickly picked out a cap, tried it on, then handed it to Mr. Faber, who put it under the counter.

"Now tell me some more about Sandra. Did she have any friends?"

"Not that I ever met, but that man coming in for change just now reminded me. One day last week, while I was out of the store taking care of personal business, some guy came in wanting change and, before you knew it, he and Sandra became buddies. She told me they had a lot in common. He'd also moved to Brooklyn from Manhattan, like she did, and he wasn't crazy about living here. She said he was erudite."

"He was what?"

"Erudite. It means 'cultured.'" He sighed again. "She was very big on culture."

"Which day was it?"

"Tuesday," said Mr. Faber.

Tuesday was her last day alive. Eddie tried not to get too excited, or at least not show it.

"How long were you out of the store? What time did you leave?"

Mr. Faber gave him a bemused smile. "I was out from three to four, like I told the police."

So it couldn't have been his dad. His dad was at work. Or, at least, that was where he should have been.

"Did she tell you his name, or whether she was going to see him again?"

"No, she didn't say anything more than what I told you," said Mr. Faber, still with the wry look.

Eddie, not realizing he was thinking out loud, said, "Maybe he was…" He stopped himself before he did something monumentally stupid, like saying "B.F."

"Maybe he was what?" asked Mr. Faber.

"Nothing."

"Why are you so interested?"

"No reason," said Eddie as he backed toward the door. "Thanks, Mr. Faber."

"Don't forget, you gotta buy that cap tomorrow or you lose your deposit."

"I won't," Eddie said as he stepped outside.

"Won't what?" Faber muttered to himself. "Won't forget or won't buy the cap?"

He picked up a rag and began to wipe down the counter.

Look what I've come to, he thought, *extorting money from children.* Sandra would have never let him get away with it.

He missed her terribly. No matter how foolish young people were, it wasn't fair for them to die.

***

Carmine didn't think life was fair either, as he sat in the rear of the sparsely filled classroom. Today had to be a fuckin' Jewish holiday. He'd thought he'd only have to take this shit until three o'clock. Then, while everyone was going out the door to the street, he'd go down to the basement and slip out through the boiler room entrance. While his old lady was standing out front waiting for him, he'd be running home and grabbing the small bag of clothing he'd hidden in the closet, as well as the 30 bucks she'd been dumb enough to put back in the coffee tin.

By the time she realized he wasn't coming out of the school, and found a phone to call the precinct, his old man wouldn't have time to do anything. He'd be finished taking care of Eddie Fein and be fuckin' outtahere!

He knew Eddie would be home alone in the afternoon because his old lady taught school somewhere. But that was on a normal day.

Today, he thought bitterly, *the whole fuckin' family's gonna be home, or out prayin' or whatever they do.*

After he'd been locked in his room, he'd spent the evening fantasizing that he was in prison. Remembering "San Quentin," on The Early Show the week before, he'd decided that if he ever had to spend some time in jail, which was possible since he was going to lead a life of crime, he'd have to be as tough as Humphrey Bogart was, even if Humphrey Bogart was supposed to be a nice guy underneath.

Carmine wouldn't be. He'd terrorize the weaker prisoners and make them his slaves, be the king of the cellblock, someone even the guards were afraid of.

After a while, he did pushups and situps until he was near collapse. Then he masturbated and slept like a baby.

Now, in his notebook, he put the finishing touches on the doodle he was working on, the bloody heart with a knife sticking out of it that was one of his favorites.

He was also practicing some NYs. When he'd made the joke about carving an NY in Eddie's face, that's all it had been then. Now, he really meant to do it.

He could think of no better way to say good-bye, and no better way of beginning his life of crime, than to leave Eddie Fein with a permanent reminder of Carmine DiFazio, something he'd see in the mirror for the rest of his life.

He looked up from his artwork toward the front of the room where that asshole Fartsworth was sitting at his desk writing something. Fartsworth wasn't one of his regular teachers, but they'd combined the classes today because there were so few people in school.

He was supposed to be either doing homework or the bullshit busy work everyone had been assigned. Fuckin' waste of his time.

Mr. Farnsworth, for his part, was equally unhappy. He didn't like having to spend the day watching over this assortment of other teachers' problems, rather than doing the job he was paid for.

I'm an educator, not a prison guard, he thought, as he discreetly glanced up from the letter he was writing to the editor of *The New York Times*, the latest in a series of missives that they never seemed to print, about Truman's timid Korean war policy.

He glanced toward the rear of the room to see what the DiFazio creature was up to.

When this rag-tag bunch had been assigned to him, the principal had taken him aside and told him that any misbehavior by DiFazio was to be reported to him immediately. And that Carmine's father was then to be contacted at the 62nd Precinct.

He hadn't made the connection before when it was mentioned in the papers, but Carmine's father was the detective investigating the Sandra Weinstock murder. It was yet another reason for concern.

Now, he noticed that Carmine was staring back at him with a kind of low-key hostility.

"Yes, DiFazio?" he said in a vaguely threatening tone. "Can I help you with something?"

Carmine was immune to vaguely threatening tones.

"Yeah," he said insouciantly, his eyes roaming the room with studied laziness. "How about lettin' us listen to the game this afternoon?"

Everyone, of course, jumped on it.

"Ooh, please, Mr. Farnsworth? Can we, can we? Pleeease?"

"Excuse me, Mr. Farnsworth."

The voice came from the open doorway and was not a teenager's but a woman's. It was soft and honeyed, with a sensuality its owner seemed to be unaware of, but which always brought Mr. Farnsworth to the brink of arousal, especially considering the face and body that went with it. Aah, the delectible Melissa Hollis.

He looked over at her with his most winning smile and held up a cautionary finger to indicate that he needed a moment.

Then he turned back to the still-yammering class and boomed out, "Quiet!"

The noise stopped in mid-entreaty, everyone snapping to again. Carmine continued to lounge in his seat, smirking.

"I'll give you my answer in a moment," Mr. Farnsworth announced. "And I warn you that it will be greatly influenced by your behavior while I'm speaking with Miss Hollis."

Rewards and punishments, he thought, *that's all this so-called teaching comes down to. Nothing is ever for its own sake, only to get a reward or avoid a punishment.*

He rose from his desk, put the smile back on, and crossed over to the doorway, where Melissa Hollis was waiting.

Standing behind her, he noticed, was a short, sulky boy, his acne-ravaged face set in a scowl. He recognized the kid. It was Vito Peccarino, the DiFazio ape's friend.

"I wonder if you could help me," Miss Hollis said softly, the vulnerablility in her voice exciting him. "Would you please take him into your class for a while? He's continuously disrupting mine."

Peccarino and DiFazio in the same room was not a prospect he relished, but he could hardly refuse her.

"Don't worry," he said, feeling a bit like John Wayne telling the "little lady" to stay inside the covered wagon. "He won't cause any trouble here."

"I really appreciate this," she said, as if it were "My hero!" At least, that was the way he heard it.

He looked over at Vito, who'd just spied Carmine inside the room, and whose scowl had now become a deranged grin.

"Where are your books, Peccarino?" he asked him gruffly.

"I ate them," Vito said, still smiling.

"He didn't have any books when he came in," Miss Hollis explained.

"Wipe the ugly smirk off your face," Mr. Farnsworth instructed him, "and go inside. Take that seat in front of my desk where I can keep an eye on you. If you so much as look at DiFazio, you'll be washing blackboards all day with a Kleenex; you understand me?"

"Sure, boss," Vito said cheerfully.

He shuffled into the room and sat down in the seat. Farnsworth watched him do it, and then issued a general warning.

"Remember what I said about that request you made," he told the class, "and behave yourselves."

He stepped back out into the hall, sensing an opportunity to get friendlier with Melissa Hollis, but knowing he had to make it quick before all hell broke loose in his room.

"How many kids do you have today?" he asked her.

"Eight, why?"

He tilted his head toward the open doorway.

"They don't know it yet, but I brought in a radio to listen to the game this afternoon. Why don't you bring your class over and join us?"

***

Eddie got to the school just before the kids were about to leave for lunch. From across the street, he spotted Teresa waiting in front of the building, so he hung back and watched.

He saw Mary come out amid a crowd of kids and join her mother. Then, with a jolt, he saw Carmine come out the door and join both of them.

He ducked behind a parked car. Nothing was working out. He'd gone over to Mrs. Weinstock's building after he left Faber's store. She'd told him through the intercom that she didn't want to speak to him and cut off the connection.

He'd snuck into the building behind someone, gone up to her apartment, and pleaded with her through the door. She yelled back that she'd call the police if he didn't go away.

And now this. He raised himself slightly and gave a quick peek through the windows of the car to the street beyond. Teresa and Carmine were crossing it, coming toward him, but only the two of them.

He scooted around the car, keeping out of their sight as they passed by, and glanced again across the street toward the school.

Mary was still there, but it didn't improve things much. Her back was to him and she was standing with Cathy Cangelossi and Donna Petragliano, two large, beefy girls, who, according to rumor, liked to beat the shit out of boys.

Setting his jaw, he started across the street toward them.

"So what's the deal, Mary?" Cathy was saying, her gum snapping on "deal." "What's your muddah doin' here?"

"She ain't here for me," Mary said dismissively. "It's Carmine."

"Yeah?" Donna said, smoke curling out of her nostrils from the cigarette she was holding clandestinely in her cupped hand. "What did he do now? Hey, get the fuck outta here!"

This last was directed at Eddie, whom she'd just seen approaching.

Mary turned, saw him, and smiled.

"Oh, hi there," she said.

"Hi, Mary."

The other two girls regarded him the way vultures regard road kill.

"This is my friend Eddie," Mary explained. "He's all right."

Their venomous expressions were unchanged.

"Whatta ya want?" Cathy Cangelossi said out of the corner of her mouth.

"I have to talk to Mary for a minute," he answered gamely.

"Get the fuck outta here!" This time it came from both of them.

"She's busy," Donna Petragliano said acidly.

"No, it's okay; I need to talk to him," Mary said, taking hold of his arm, as the other two turned their stares on her.

"I'll see ya later," she said, pulling on his arm and starting to lead him off.

"This better be fuckin' good, Mary," Cathy called after her as they strode down the street.

Eddie looked back over his shoulder.

"Nice meeting you."

"Shut up," Mary said, but then she giggled.

They turned the corner onto 20th Avenue, walked a little further, and then she stopped and stood facing him.

"Did your mother tell you I was there yesterday?"

Julia had, in fact, mentioned it but said very little else, no matter how much he'd pressed her.

"She told me something about helping you with a Sunday School report," he said.

"Is that all?" She had an odd look in her eyes.

"Yeah, why?" he said carefully.

"Nothing." There was an awkward silence. "If she ever tells you anything else, don't pay attention to it."

"What else would she tell me?"

"Nothing." Mary's face was starting to redden. "Anyway, how's your investigation going?"

He liked hearing her say "investigation." Most of the time it felt like he was just bumbling around.

"I found out something today." He told her about the "erudite" man Sandra had met in the sporting goods store on the day she was killed. "How about you? How are you doing on the watch?"

"I remembered some more about it," she said and filled him in on what their mothers were talking about on the train coming home from Macy's.

"They said something about a woman whose child had a terrible tragedy, and I'm pretty sure she was the one they ran into. They were talking about her because your mother didn't know how she felt about giving your dad the same watch that someone else would be wearing, but my mother said it didn't matter, 'cause men were different when it came to things like that."

"What about the woman? Who was she?"

"I'm gettin' there. When I was over at your place yesterday, I made believe I had a Sunday School assignment to bring in a story about someone whose child had a tragedy. I asked your mom if she knew anyone like that, and it worked.

"She told me this story, but she wouldn't give me the woman's name. She said, 'Your Sunday School teacher certainly wouldn't want anyone's privacy compromised.'"

Mary said it in such a dead-on impression of Julia that Eddie had to smile. It was very cute.

"I didn't know how to get around it," she continued in her normal voice, "so I let it go. Anyhow, this happened ten years ago:

"There was a woman who had a two-year-old baby boy. One day, her husband was sitting in the living room having a snack, eating some olives out of a jar. He was supposed to be watching the baby in his playpen, but something happened and he had to leave the room for a few minutes. So of course, that was when the kid tried to climb out.

"He never could do it before, but this time he did it. He went over to the coffee table and picked up the fork his father left there, one of those small, metal olive forks with the two prongs? Then he took it over to the electric socket on the wall and stuck it in."

"Wow!" Eddie grimaced. "Did he die?"

"No, but he almost did. He was in a coma for a while, and there was a lot of brain damage. He's in some hospital now."

He couldn't imagine what it would be like for two parents after something like that. He shook his head.

"That's a terrible story."

"I know."

"I'm amazed that my mother told it to you."

"Me too, but she said people don't realize how extra careful they have to be with kids."

"Ah," he said. "That sounds more like her."

"But it doesn't do us any good if we don't know who the woman is."

He had a thought. "You could ask your mother, since it's not about the watch. Just tell her the story and ask her if she knows the woman."

"Sure, I could do that," Mary said. "But I'll have to wait 'til later, when they put Carmine in his room. If my dad's busy doin' somethin' else, maybe I can get her alone."

Eddie didn't know what she meant by putting Carmine in his room, but it sounded good enough.

"You could leave your window half open if you find out anything," he said. "Then I'll know to stay in my room and wait. You can write down the name and show it to me. Until then, just leave the window closed."

She nodded.

"Good idea. But I'd better be goin' now. My mom's probably got lunch ready."

"Oh, okay."

They both stood there, Mary making no move to leave.

"Hey," she said, "how was the game yesterday? It must've been great to be there."

"It was, it was!" he said excitedly. "I even caught Jackie Robinson's home run."

"You what!? Get outta here!"

"It's true. We took it down to the clubhouse after the game and he signed it for me. I'll show it to you next time."

She gave him a funny look.

"I don't know if I believe you."

"Just ask Lionel or his father; they'll tell you. And, like I said, I'll show you the ball."

Mary's look slowly became one of amazement.

"How did it happen? Did it just come right at you?"

"No, I had to practically climb my dad to reach it, but he held me up and it stuck in my hand."

The excitement in his voice had now become a sort of wonder.

"Last year, we were there when Dick Sisler hit that home run and the Dodgers lost, and something terrible happened. But this time, it was the complete opposite. It was like we both caught the ball together, and it was like a sign.

"At that moment everybody knew the Dodgers were going to win. And I knew more than ever that my dad was innocent. And if it takes me my whole life, I'm gonna prove it."

His eyes started to water and, for an instant, he had to look away from her.

When he looked back, she was suddenly very close. Her hands reached out and gently touched his cheeks.

She gazed at him lovingly for a moment, then brought her lips to his. They were soft and warm, and their touch gave him a feeling he'd never had before, a sort of excruciating ecstasy.

Then she pulled away, turned, and ran down the street, disappearing around the corner.

CHAPTER TWENTY

Monday Afternoon, October 1st

Before the game, Roy Campanella told sportswriters he'd prayed to be able to walk this morning. His right thigh muscle, the one he'd torn running out his triple yesterday and then caught *ten* more innings on, was shot up with Novocain and heavily bandaged.

As he stiffly made his way to the plate with one out in the bottom of the fourth, the last thing he wanted was to hit a ground ball. A ground ball was a sure double play.

Jim Hearn, the pitcher he was facing, happened to make his living off of ground balls. He had a heavy, sinking fast ball that, when it was on, could drop in the strike zone like a rock.

It was on today. He'd made only one mistake, a pitch to Andy Pafko in the bottom of the second that stayed up, and Andy had gratefully deposited it deep into the left field seats.

The roar of the 30,000-plus fans who'd jammed into Ebbets Field on this sunny, autumnal day carried across three New York radio stations, WOR-TV Channel 9, and a national radio hookup. Across America, people were aware that the Dodgers were up one-nothing.

It didn't last. Ralph Branca, who'd pitched a solid three innings and was one strike away from a one-two-three fourth, got a pitch inside to Monte Irvin that clipped him on the elbow and sent him to first. Then a mistake to Bobby Thomson, a too-good fastball that he got a hold of and sent to the same general area as Pafko's shot and, just like that, it was 2-1, Giants.

But after one out in their half, the Dodgers were answering. Snider hammered one of Hearn's sinking fast balls up the middle on a hop. It glanced off the tip of the second baseman's glove and rolled into center field for a base hit.

Then Robinson ripped a line-drive single into right, sending the Duke to third, and setting the stage now for Campy.

Moving the dirt around in the batter's box and looking out over the infield, he took note of where Stanky and Dark at second and short were playing him. At least, with the possible double play, they had to move closer in. During his first at-bat, they'd practically played him on the outfield grass, knowing he couldn't run.

He resolved yet again that he would not hit a ground ball. He would wait Hearn out until he got a pitch that was up, and then he was going to drive it. Get at least a sac fly to tie the game.

Snider took a step off third, while Robinson, at first base, eyed Hearn carefully. If he could steal second, it would eliminate the possibility of a double play. In fact, they'd have to bring the infield in, or walk Campy intentionally.

He stared over at Hearn, calculating the chances. Hearn's move to first was average, but Wes Westrum, the Giant catcher, had an outstanding arm.

Hearn threw over to first and Jackie easily got back. Campanella stepped out again and looked over at the third-base coaching box, where Charlie Dressen was flashing him signs. They were just for show this time, no take sign, no hit-and-run.

He nodded and stepped back in. Big hole between first and second. If Hearn threw him something outside, he could get it through, even on a ground ball. But he knew he wasn't going to get anything hittable on the outside, unless Hearn made a mistake and left one there.

Jackie took his lead, and Hearn checked him one last time. Then the big righthander delivered to the plate. Fast ball on the inside corner that Campy let go by for strike one.

He stepped out of the batter's box again and looked over at Dressen. Still nothing on, and Campy was just as glad. He wanted to be patient, to wait until he got something good to hit.

He got it on the next pitch, a belt-high change-up that he turned on and drilled down the left field line. But his bat was a little too quick. The ball curved foul by six feet and skipped into the stands.

Now, he was in a hole. With two strikes on him, he'd have to swing at anything close, and hope to foul it off if he couldn't drive it.

Robinson took his lead again. Hearn checked him over his left shoulder, then suddenly whirled and threw to first.

Robby, who was starting to lean toward second, dove back. Whitey Lockman applied a sweep tag on his wrist, too late.

"Tell him to give up," Jackie said to Lockman, as he got to his feet and wiped the dirt off his uniform. "He caught me leaning and he still couldn't get me with that horseshit move of his."

Lockman shot him a hostile look. Like their fans, the players on both these teams had no love for each other.

Hearn checked Robinson yet again. Then, as he delivered to the plate, Robby took off for second.

Campy saw the pitch as a curve, hooking toward the inside corner, not good to hit, but he had to swing at it.

He hit it sharply on the ground toward Alvin Dark at short, who scooped it and tossed to Eddie Stanky for the first out, a split second before Robinson arrived.

Jackie slid hard, barreling into Stanky and radically affecting his throw toward Lockman.

Breaking from the batter's box, Campy saw it all as he tried to run. But like a bad dream, he was in slow motion.

He could see Stanky's throw floating off line, pulling Lockman way off the bag as he had to range over to catch it.

He dragged his right leg after him, straining with everything he had toward first base, which seemed miles away.

In any other game, he would've been easily safe, with Snider scoring from third, the score tied, and the rally still going. Now, struggling down the line, he could only watch in pain as Lockman took the throw, moved nonchalantly back to the bag, and stepped on it.

Double play. Inning over.

***

The *Brooklyn Eagle*'s headquarters on Johnson Street, near Borough Hall, was only five stories high, and fewer than 700 people worked there.

But it produced a newspaper that did an annual business of nearly six million dollars and was, at one time, the most widely read publication in the country. Its previous editors had included Thomas Kinsella and Walt Whitman.

Samuel Boyleston, its present-day city editor, leaned back and absently ran his fingers through his thinning white hair as he shifted the cigar in his mouth, bits of ash falling unnoticed onto his desk.

He glanced away from his guest, to the 10-inch RCA TV perched on top of his file cabinet. He'd been distracted by Snider's hard ground ball up the middle, glancing off Stanky's glove for a base hit.

He looked back at his visitor, who was also watching the screen.

"Sorry," he said to him, smiling, "but this falls under the heading of breaking news."

"I know," Barry said. "I'd be watching it myself, ordinarily. Thanks for seeing me on such short notice."

"Please, please," said Boyleston, holding up a hand. "My door will always be open to Mike Fein's son."

"I appreciate it."

"Your father and I started out together, you know. We were a couple of naive cub reporters at the old *New York World*." Boyleston took another puff on his cigar and gazed over at the TV, where Jackie Robinson was settling in at the plate.

"That was back in 1915, before they merged with the *Telegram*."

Barry nodded. Boyleston was still looking at the screen.

"Now it's the *World Telegram and Sun*," he remarked with a bit of scorn. "Crappy name, too unwieldy. Seems like all the papers in this town are either folding or buying each other up. Pretty soon there'll be just two left, *The Times* and an amalgam of names that'll take ten minutes to pronounce." He sighed and shifted the cigar again.

"We've been having problems ourselves, not with circulation, but with the damn unions."

Barry nodded again and, this time, Boyleston happened to look away from the TV and saw it.

"Mike Fein's son!" he said, taking the cigar from his mouth. He gazed at Barry in an avuncular manner. "I can see him in your face. How long has it been since your dad passed on, about ten years?"

"About," Barry said.

"He was the cream of the crop, bar none," Boyleston said. "Never met anyone before or since who had such instincts for a story. If you're half of what he was, you must be a helluva reporter."

"I'm not…"

A flurry of activity on the screen suddenly drew Boyleston's attention. Robinson had just lined one past a diving Whitey Lockman into right field. Don Mueller was heading over to field it, as the camera switched to Snider rounding second and heading into third.

"We've got something going here," Boyleston said.

On the TV screen, Charlie Dressen could be seen giving the Duke a congratulatory pat on the rump as he stood on third. Boyleston narrowed his eyes and gave Barry a look of mock severity.

"You're not a Giant fan, are you?"

Barry laughed. "That's the last thing I'd be."

"Your dad was a Giant fan," said Boyleston. "That's the only bad thing I'll ever say about him." He chuckled. "But you're not, eh? Well, good for you. Shows independent thinking."

"You could call it that."

Roy Campanella was making his way to the plate.

"No one could smell a story like your father could," said Boyleston, putting the cigar back in his mouth. "In fact, he was right there the night Arnold Rothstein was killed. Did he ever tell you that?"

Barry didn't have to answer because it was rhetorical.

"Arnold Rothstein, a.k.a. Mr. Big, a.k.a. The Fixer, The Brain, and a dozen other things. The man who invented organized crime in New York. Taught Legs Diamond and Lucky Luciano everything they knew. Had Tammany Hall in his hip pocket and wore Mayor Jimmy Walker on his watch chain."

Hearn threw over to first, as Robinson got back.

"People credited him with masterminding the Black Sox scandal but, according to your dad, that was a fallacy. The gamblers used his name to influence the crooked ballplayers and Rothstein allowed them to do it. His only part in it was to bet sixty thousand on Cincinnati and win himself a quarter mill'. Your dad knew this because Rothstein was fond of certain reporters, and he happened to be one."

As he spoke, he kept his eyes on the TV set. Barry was doing the same.

"Rothstein used to use Sardi's as his 'office,'" he continued, as Campanella took a fast ball for strike one. "On the night he was killed, this was back in November of '28, he was sitting at his table with a gambler named Jimmy Meehan when he got a phone call. Your dad was sitting nearby, and he heard Rothstein tell Meehan that it was from George McManus, and that he was going over to the Park Central Hotel to see him. He said he'd be back in a little while.

"Well, your dad's ears perked up because George McManus, a few weeks before, had hosted a high-stakes poker game in which Rothstein lost three hundred grand. But he'd never paid off because he claimed the game was rigged. So if Rothstein was going over to see McManus, your dad was very interested. Whoa, baby!"

Campanella had just blistered one down the left field line that had curved foul.

"Damn! Thought that was a double for sure."

He glanced over at Barry, who was looking sourly at the screen. He felt a Dodger fan's affinity for him.

"Anyway," he went on, "your dad waited at Sardi's for a few minutes after Rothstein left, then grabbed a cab over to the Park Central. He was just getting out of the taxi in front of the hotel, when he heard a 'clunk' on the roof of the car. Something had fallen onto it and bounced off. He looked down at his feet, and there was a gun lying on the sidewalk.

"It had been tossed out of one of the hotel room windows. Well, your dad was smart enough not to touch it. He ran straight-away into the hotel lobby and asked the desk clerk for George McManus's room. It turned out McManus had checked in under another name, so there was no help there, but your dad had another idea. He knew the guy was a big tipper and popular with the hotel staff wherever he stayed, so it was possible one of them had recognized McManus no matter what alias he was using.

"So your dad went back out and headed for the employees' entrance."

He glanced at the TV screen, where Hearn was throwing over to first, causing Robinson to dive back in, just barely.

It distracted Boylan for a moment, then he continued.

"There he was, at the employees' entrance, questioning one of the bellhops, when who comes staggering down the service stairs clutching his stomach, but Arnold Rothstein!

"'Mike,' he says, seeing your father, 'get me a cab. I need to go home.'

"So your dad grabbed a hold of him and helped him outside onto the sidewalk, not knowing what to do. He couldn't just put the guy in a cab, but Rothstein was insisting that he didn't want an ambulance, he only wanted to go home.

"At that moment, your dad spotted a cop walking down the street. He steered Rothstein over to him and practically dumped him into the cop's arms.

"He told him it was Arnold Rothstein and he'd just been shot, and that he was Mike Fein, a reporter for the *New York World*. Then he left the cop holding Rothstein, ran to the nearest public phone, and called the story in to the paper before the ambulance even arrived. It was the biggest scoop we ever had. I tell you, they don't make 'em like your father."

Sudden movement caused him to look at the TV, just in time to see Campy hit the ground ball to Dark. He watched as Stanky's throw wafted toward Lockman, pulling him off the bag.

"C'mon, Campy. C'mon, Campy," Boyleston exhorted the screen. Then…"Shit!"

He turned to Barry, who was still looking at the TV.

"Why are they playing him? The guy can't run."

Barry didn't say anything.

"Ah, well." Boyleston waved a dismissive hand at the set. "On to more immediate business. So you want to be a reporter for the *Eagle*, eh?"

Barry shook his head.

"I think there's been a misunderstanding. I'm not a reporter; I'm a proofreader."

"Really?" said Boyleston, confused. "Don't I remember seeing your byline for the *World Telegram*? That was you, wasn't it?"

"That was me ten years ago," Barry said. "Now, I'm a proofreader."

His voice was calm enough, but Boyleston could sense the effort to keep it that way. It made him a bit uneasy.

"A proofreader," he mused. "I don't understand. The job pays next to nothing. Kids who are just out of college do it."

"That's right."

Boyleston shook his head.

"I don't even know if I can help you, if that's the kind of work you're looking for. Proofreaders are hired by the type shop. Why aren't you a reporter?"

Barry chewed on his lip.

"Let's take that story you just told me," he said, leaning forward, as Boyleston, for the first time, noticed the alcohol smell.

"Here was my father," said Barry, "who was rarely home, who I hardly ever saw, spending his time sitting around Sardi's with the likes of Arnold Rothstein and his friends."

On the TV, the game had come out of commercial and Ralph Branca was back on the mound, preparing to face Wes Westrum to start the fifth.

Neither man was looking at it.

"He happens to hear a little nugget of info that someone who cares about gangsters might call a 'news story,' and he goes scurrying off. While he's sniffing around for the room number of another lowlife named George McManus, by an incredible stroke of luck, Rothstein comes staggering down the stairs, and there's your story: 'One Piece of Crap Shoots Another.' And it's as if my father deserved a Pulitzer for it."

Boyleston was starting to be concerned now.

"There, there," he said uneasily. "No need to get upset…"

"You sit there romanticizing about some gangster getting shot?" Barry's voice had gotten louder. "In the war, I saw a lot of people getting shot, and worse. And they were people, incidentally, whose boots Arnold Rothstein and my father weren't worthy of licking!"

He glared at Boyleston, his mouth twisted in a snarl. He was about to say something else, when Boyleston abruptly got up. He cut a quick glance through the window and wondered if anyone in the city room beyond was noticing, in case he needed help.

"Well, thanks for stopping by," he said. "I'm sorry I couldn't be of more assistance to you. Now, I'm afraid I have to get back to putting out this paper."

Barry began to speak, then stopped and lowered his head.

"Right," he said softly. "Listen, I'm sorry. It was a mistake coming here. I shouldn't have bothered you."

"No, no," Boyleston said, moving around the desk toward the door, pulling it open. "No trouble at all."

He stood there waiting.

"Right," Barry said again. His eyes drifted over to the TV screen, where they lingered.

Boyleston, despite all, couldn't help but follow his gaze. Branca was delivering ball four to Westrum, who tossed his bat away and started to jog down to first.

"Perfect," said Barry, getting up. "Start off the inning by walking a .220 hitter."

Boyleston remained by the door. He gave Barry a wide berth as he passed by.

"Good luck," he said.

"Yeah," said Barry, stepping out into the city room.

An hour from now, he'd scheduled another interview with yet another old friend of his father's, at the *Journal-American*. The thought of it made him nauseous.

There was a bar he'd seen on the way over here, on Fulton Street. Maybe he'd go there. Beyond that, he had no ideas.

***

Carmine should've been enjoying himself. After all, the Giants were winning and he was getting to listen to it, but he couldn't stop thinking about the bombshell Fartsworth had dropped. It was right after they'd come back from lunch, and he'd casually mentioned, like it was nothing at all, that the fuckin' Jewish holiday was going to last through *tomorrow*!

That meant, his original plan of only having to take this shit for a few hours had grown to two days. Two days of this until he could get to Eddie Fein.

It was almost enough to make him say "fuck it," just get outta here this afternoon, and screw Eddie Fein. But he couldn't do that; it just wouldn't be right.

His hatred now encompassed the entire Jewish religion. Selfish bastards. They gotta have their own separate New Year's, and it's gotta take two fuckin' days?

Well, he'd just have to make the little prick pay for the extra time and suffering, wouldn't he.

And then there was Vito. Carmine had been just as sorry to see his stupid, smiling face this morning as Fartsworth had.

Because he knew he was trapped. There was no way to avoid what would happen at lunch time.

He'd tried. He charged down the stairs to the street as fast as he could, shoving kids out of his way, but Vito kept shoving them out of the way after him, babbling like a fuckin' idiot about wanting his knife back, for Christ's sake. Then they reached the street, and there she was, his old lady. Waiting to take him home from school like a fuckin' first grader.

He did the only thing he could, which was grab the little cocksucker by the shirt and hiss in his ear that if he ever said one word about this, he'd get his fuckin' knife back right through the heart.

He could feel it now against the small of his back, as he sat in the last row staring at Vito's greasy head in the front and listening to the play-by-play coming out of Fartsworth's radio on the teacher's desk.

It was tuned to WMGM, the Dodger station. He would rather have been listening to Russ Hodges or Ernie Harwell on the Giant station but, no, he had to listen to the Dodger suck-up Connie Desmond. It was a good thing the Giants were winning.

Two seats in front of him sat James Preston. As a Giant fan, he also should have been enjoying himself, but he wasn't. When Miss Hollis had told them they'd be going over to Mr. Farnsworth's room to listen to the game, he'd felt great. But it all dissolved when he saw Carmine sitting there in the back.

Then they had to go and put him just two seats in front of him.

Carmine had winked at him as James moved up the aisle, but he kept his face impassive and sat down. To anyone else in the room now, he looked okay, but, inside, his stomach was doing flip flops.

He'd hardly slept last night, tossing and turning and finally deciding to confess to his daddy about sending the garbage up to Beauregard. That way, he wouldn't have to do what Carmine wanted. But this morning, he couldn't go through with it.

Whatever was supposed to happen would happen this afternoon. Carmine didn't know it, but he'd picked a good time. Beauregard usually took a nap in the afternoon. He knew this because that's how it all started.

Two weeks ago there'd been a radiator leak somewhere in the building, and he and his daddy had gone up to Beauregard's apartment to see if it was coming from there. The goddamn cracker got real mad, 'cause his nap was being disturbed. He kept saying that he always took a nap in the afternoon and, where he came from, n_ggers knew better than to disturb a white man's privacy.

It was the first time James had ever heard anyone talk like that to his daddy. And his daddy just took it!

On the way back down to the basement, his daddy was so mad that James was afraid to utter a word for fear of getting smacked.

The memory caused a surge of hatred to rise within him. It was almost overwhelming, and he had to force himself to calm down.

So, yes, he thought, this afternoon would be a good time. He had a gratifying vision of Beauregard being awakened from his damn nap by a knocking on the dumbwaiter door. He'd start to open it and Carmine would smash the door open the rest of the way, hitting Beauregard in the face, bloodying his nose.

Then Carmine would leap off the cart and beat the living shit out of him. Maybe even kill him? This time, the surge was so strong, it took a full minute before James could think straight again.

When he did, though, the doubts began to creep back in. Why would Carmine do it? Why would he go through all that just to get someone he didn't even know?

The stirring of the kids around him intruded on his thoughts. Something had happened in the game for the Dodgers, and Campanella was coming up. As he tried to listen, he thought he could feel Carmine's hot breath tickling the back of his neck, even though he was a full two seats behind.

The scariest thing, he thought, was not knowing what you're getting into. In a way, it was as scary as his daddy.

At the front desk, Melissa Hollis was uncomfortable. She'd intended to move about the room, sitting in various empty seats, but Bruce Farnsworth had made a public display of pulling up a chair for her and placing it next to his. It would have been awkward to refuse, so there she sat, only slightly interested in the game and more than slightly uneasy about Bruce Farnsworth.

The only reason she'd brought Vito to his room this morning was that she was desperate. Because of his reputation as a disciplinarian, kids hated to be sent to his classroom. So much so that the mere threat of it could often turn a rotten apple into a little angel.

But with a hard case like Vito, nothing short of actually doing it would work, so she'd had to follow through. Then, she was so caught off guard by his offer to combine their classes that she couldn't come up fast enough with a reason not to.

It wasn't his reputation as a disciplinarian that worried her, of course; it was his other reputation. Bruce Farnsworth was a notorious lecher.

She was used to men paying attention to her, being solicitous, standing close when they talked to her, but with him, there was always a little more to it, a subtle aggression. Maybe he'd smile too much, or put his hand on your arm for a moment, a seemingly innocent, unconscious gesture that you knew was calculated.

The other women teachers felt the same way. They talked in the staff room about how he'd suggest having coffee after school, or getting together privately somewhere for "lesson coordination." There was even a rumor that he secretly rented a room nearby. Melissa didn't really believe it, but she wouldn't have been surprised.

Everyone knew he was married. In fact, Melissa had met his wife. Dora Farnsworth worked in a millinery shop on Bay Parkway, called Bo Peep's. A lot of neighborhood women bought hats there, and Melissa had stopped in one day on another teacher's reccomendation. She'd found Dora to be an attractive, knowledgeable and friendly woman, whose friendliness noticeably diminished when Melissa mentioned she was a colleague of her husband.

She was accustomed to other men's wives being standoffish with her, but the change in Dora Farnsworth's demeanor was striking.

The poor woman, she remembered thinking.

Now, as she shared the front desk with him, nodding automatically and only half listening to his sotto-voce explanations of baseball strategy, she was aware that his leg was touching hers.

Nodding her head once again, she managed to move her chair while pretending to adjust her skirt. She knew she could deal with this kind of thing, because there were limits to what he could try in a classroom full of kids.

And it was a well-behaved classroom, she had to admit. Vito Peccarino had, in fact, become a model of good deportment. He'd come in this morning without books, but when he came back from lunch he had a whole briefcase full of them. As it turned out, it was unnecessary because the ballgame would take up most of the afternoon, but it was an unexpected step in the right direction.

The kids were sitting quietly, listening together with only occasional outbursts, most notably after the Dodger home run and, again, after the Giant home run.

Farnsworth had allowed the first one to happen without comment, but he'd told them to knock it off after the second one, even though it hadn't been nearly as raucous as the first.

She was most surprised at the behavior of Carmine DiFazio, who would've been expected to take advantage of a situation like this. But there he was, sitting in the back row minding his own business. Even when the Giants took the lead and some of the other kids had reacted noisily to it, he'd only smiled, unlike Vito, who couldn't help jumping out of his seat in celebration.

But now, evidently, something important was happening in the game.

She sensed this because Bruce had stopped talking to her and was, instead, giving all his attention to the radio. That was one thing she never understood about men, how their libidos always played second fiddle to sports.

("...swings and sends a sharp grounder to short. Dark up with it, over to Stanky for one. The throw to first...is wide and pulls Lockman off the bag! But he's got time to recover, and he touches first before Campanella, with that leg injury, can get down the line.

Oh, my. An unusual double play by the Giants, but it snuffs out the Dodger rally.")

You could hear the disappointment in Connie Desmond's voice. "Yeah! Yeah!"

Vito was up out of his seat, about to dance in the aisle. Farnsworth slammed both fists down on the desk, startling Melissa. He rose from the chair.

"I've had it with you, Peccarino!" he said.

In two strides, he was around the desk, grabbing Vito by the arms and shaking him.

"You'll keep your ignorant mouth shut, and stay—in—your—seat!"

Each word was accompanied by another, more violent shake. He shoved Vito backward onto what would have been his seat, if it hadn't been raised. Vito fell through the empty seat well onto the floor, where he sat, his legs splayed into the aisle.

Some of the other kids laughed self-consciously.

"Get up," Farnsworth said sharply, glaring down at him.

Melissa could not see what happened next because her sightline was blocked by the desk, but Farnsworth could, and his heart froze.

Rather than getting to his feet, Vito was reaching into the briefcase on the floor next to him. He was pulling out a German Luger.

With a sharp intake of breath, Farnsworth stepped back, stumbling against the teacher's desk, as Vito stood up from the seat well, training the gun on his midsection.

"Whatsamatter?" he giggled, as screams rang out all around him and kids dove under their desks. "You don't like me?"

For a long moment, the only sound in the room was the Schaefer beer commercial playing on the radio, along with a soft whimper from Melissa Hollis, who crouched in terror behind the teacher's desk.

"How come you're not talkin', Mr. Fartsworth? Why don'tcha tell me to sit down?"

Farnsworth could only stare wide eyed at the gun.

"Turn around," Vito ordered him. "Go over to the blackboard and put your hands up against it."

Farnsworth did as he was told, aided by a hard push in the back by Vito.

As soon as he'd assumed the position, Vito looked away from him and surveyed the room. All the kids were cowering under their desks. All but one.

"Nice Luger," Carmine commented.

He was still slouched nonchalantly in his seat, his arm draped around the back of it.

"I never seen it before. Did your old man get it off a German?"

"Fuck you, Carmine."

Vito strode up the aisle toward him, the gun leveled at his head.

Carmine, with monumental effort, looked back at him placidly.

His first reaction, like the others, had been to dive for cover, but he'd stopped himself. He knew his only chance was to not show fear, just as it had been when Vito pulled the knife on him over that stupid nickname.

Thinking of the knife, he was again aware of it against the small of his back. He didn't know how much good it would be against a Luger.

"What are you mad at me for?" he asked in a reasonable tone of voice. "I said I'd give you back that thing today, and the day ain't over yet."

"Don't be a wiseass," Vito said icily. "You know what you did. You're always makin' fun of me and treatin' me like shit, but today, you went too far. You put your filthy fuckin' hands on me."

He took another step toward Carmine, his finger tightening on the trigger.

"Your filthy fuckin' hands!"

It was all Carmine could do not to flinch.

"Hey, Vito, man," he said soothingly.

"You, too, Fartsworth!" Vito yelled, glancing over there. "You did it too, and you're gonna get it right after him."

Carmine had always known Vito was crazy, of course. It was what he liked about him. But he'd never realized just how completely nuts "Mad Dog" Peccarino was. In other circumstances, he would've admired it, but right now, he was trying not to die.

"Vito, Vito," he said, struggling to keep his voice steady, "I'm sorry, man, I really am. I know how you feel about people puttin' their hands on you, and I shoudn't'a done it. I just lost my head for a minute, that's all. It was 'cause…" He looked embarrassed. "Shit, I don't wanna say this in front of all these jerks. C'mere."

Vito's eyes narrowed in suspicion.

"C'mere," Carmine said gently. "You got a gun; what are you afraid of? I just gotta say this softly."

Even though his mind was racing, he had no real plan. He just knew that if Vito was more than an arm's length away he had no chance at all.

"Please," he said, sensing Vito might be wavering. "It's hard for me to say this."

Vito walked the rest of the way up the aisle and put the gun against the side of Carmine's head.

"What?" he demanded.

"It was 'cause of my old lady," Carmine whispered, noticing out of the corner of his eye that Farnsworth was moving. He was slowly inching along the blackboard toward the door, although he still had a long way to go.

Vito's back was to Farnsworth. For the moment, he was intent only on Carmine.

"She comes to pick me up at school now," Carmine continued softly, "'cause my old man's punishing me. I was ashamed for you to know that, so when you saw her, I must'a flipped out."

He could feel the cold tip of the gun, pressed against his temple.

"But I'm your friend, Vito. And I'm gonna prove it to ya right now by tellin' ya somethin'." His voice got even softer. "Fartsworth's tryin' to leave."

"Huh?"

Vito looked toward the front of the room. He took the gun away from Carmine's head and started to aim it in that direction.

Carmine's hands shot out and grabbed his arm. He wrenched it backward and slammed it against the desk.

Vito let out a howl of pain, but held onto the gun. He flailed at Carmine with his other arm.

Carmine slammed the gun arm down again.

Vito let out another howl as his wrist hit the corner of the desk. The gun slipped from his hand and clattered to the floor, skittering down the aisle and coming to a stop in front of a surprised James Preston, huddled under his desk. He reached out and snagged it.

Carmine yanked Vito's arm behind his back and marched him up the aisle toward the front of the room.

"Ow, ow, ow!" yelled Vito.

"I'll put my filthy fuckin' hands on you anytime I want, ya little moron," Carmine said, approaching Farnsworth, who gaped at him.

"Stop it, you're hurtin' me!" Vito complained.

"Here ya go." Carmine pushed Vito at Farnsworth. "Now, get him outta here, so we can listen to the game."

***

Eddie let out a soft groan of disgust, as Monte Irvin circled the bases after belting Branca's eighth-inning slider into the seats, extending the Giants' lead to 3-1.

He'd wound up back at the apartment watching the game after all, since he'd decided to go someplace for a while and think.

And it wasn't just an excuse to watch the game, but it worked out because it was one of those games that you just knew they were going to lose, even though they were only down by a run for most of it. Hearn was having his way with them, and after Campy's double play in the fourth, the Dodgers did very little to distract.

A much greater distraction was the memory of that kiss. He'd stood there in the middle of the street for several stunned moments, before he finally recovered and walked home.

He'd changed out of his suit and made himself a peanut butter and jelly sandwich, being careful to wash off the dish and butter knife he used and put them back.

His mother, of course, thought he was at school, so he had to hide any evidence that he'd eaten at home. He assumed she hadn't counted the number of bread slices in the loaf or measured the amount of peanut butter and jelly in the jars.

Another thing he made sure of was to move the step stool back in front of the dumbwaiter door where it belonged, after he'd used it to reach up into the dish cupboard. Another little detail. And it would be nice if he grew a little taller one of these days.

Mary's kiss. He couldn't stop remembering the warm feeling of her lips on his and the closeness of her body. Why had she kissed him? And why was she so worried about what his mother might've said to him?

He realized he was distracting himself again, and, instead, tried to picture the "erudite" man Sandra had met on the day she died.

The man must have been in the store talking to her for some time, since they'd gotten so friendly. Customers could have been coming in and out and they would've seen him, although Faber's never seemed to have many customers. But it was possible Sandra gave him her phone number, and he might have given her his.

He wished for the thousandth time that he knew as much as the cops did.

Mr. Faber had said he'd told them about the man, so they must be investigating it. But for all he knew, they might have already found his phone number among Sandra's things, checked it out, and he's nobody.

He couldn't think like that.

He'd only had a few minutes to look through Nick's notebook, but he didn't remember seeing any mention of it, so he couldn't assume anything either way. As far as he was concerned, it was still a "hot lead," like they say on Racket Squad.

If they're still looking for him, does Nick connect him with B.F., or does he assume, like Eddie did at first, that the initials were his dad's?

Whatever Nick thought, Eddie knew they weren't. So until proven wrong, he was going to believe the "erudite" man could be someone with the initials B.F.

The Dodgers had gone down meekly in the bottom of the eighth and the Giants were now batting in the ninth. Eddie couldn't sit on the couch any more. He got up and began to wander through the apartment.

Once again, he thought about Mary. He had to admire how she'd been able to remember so much about the watch, and get his mother to tell her that story.

Mary.

Even when he took his mind away from the kiss, he couldn't take his body away from it. Before his mother came home, he'd have to find some way of losing the almost-constant erection.

But never mind; the important thing was that Mary would try and get the woman's name out of Teresa in the way he'd suggested. With any luck, he'd know who bought the watch by tonight, and that would be a big clue. A huge clue. Something he could actually tell Nick.

He'd never had any illusions about doing this without going to the police at some point. He'd have to be careful not to involve Mary, of course, but he'd known all along that, once he found something that proved his dad's innocence or pointed to the real killer, Nick would take it from there.

He'd tell Nick he found out about the second watch from his mother, which was entirely believable. It would all work out, if Mary could get the name of that woman.

By now, he'd wandered through the kitchen, down the hall, and into his room. He could faintly hear Red Barber's voice wafting through the apartment from the TV, saying that the Giants had been retired in the ninth, and that the Dodgers would be coming up for their last chance after this word from Lucky Strike.

"L.S.M.F.T.," he was saying. "Lucky Strike Means Fine Tobacco."

"Loose Stomach Means Full Toilet" was Lionel's version of it, something Eddie always thought of whenever he heard the commercial, and wished he didn't.

Looking into his closet, he noticed that he hadn't hung up his suit very well. The pants had slipped off the hanger and were lying on the closet floor. As he reached down for them, his hand brushed against paper. It was his original Inca report, the one on which Farnsworth had written "plagiarism" along with a note to his mother, that he'd hidden in the closet. It all seemed to have happened long ago on some other planet. He picked the report up and moved the top page aside, revealing Farnsworth's note, which he'd barely bothered to read before.

"Dear Mrs. Fein," it said. "Due to Edward's dishonesty, he has been instructed to rewrite his report. Would you please ensure that he does so, and sign the bottom of this one? In that way, I will know you are aware of the situation. Thank you. Sincerely, Bruce Farnsworth."

The first letters of each name were large and flowery, if it wasn't obvious enough. His signature, to Eddie, was like a neon sign screaming at him, B! F! B! F! B! F!

He hadn't known Farnsworth's first name, hadn't ever thought about it.

According to Mr. Faber, "erudite" meant "cultured." Fartsworth sure talked that way. And the time would've been right too, sometime between three and four, just after school.

"Hey, anybody home?" said a voice from the kitchen. "How come the door's unlocked?"

If it hadn't been Lionel's voice, it would have scared the shit out of him. He'd left the door unlocked again! His mother was always getting after him for that.

"I'm in here," he called out, shoving the report back into the closet and closing the door.

One good thing, at least; with the surprise at what he'd discovered and Lionel's arrival, the erection was gone.

He hurried into the kitchen. Lionel was standing there in his Rosh Hashanah suit, along with Ronald Herschfeld, who was similarly attired.

"Why aren't you watching the game? What's the matter with you?" Lionel demanded, as Red Barber's voice continued to float out of the living room.

"They're doing lousy. I just went into my room to get something."

"Lousy, whatta ya mean, lousy?"

Lionel strode into the living room to see for himself.

"They're losing 3-1," Eddie said, following him, "and it's the ninth inning."

Lionel had stopped in the middle of the room and was staring intently at the TV set.

"3-1? That's not so bad," he said. "Here you are, being rewarded for your Godlessness, and you're not even watching the game. Meanwhile, good, pious Jews like me and the Yankee Doodle Dumbo over there..." he indicated Ronald, who had now joined them in the living room, "have to wait 'til our fathers finally give us a break and spring us from shul. Then we have to sneak up to this unholy place to watch even a piece of it."

The three of them stood silently for a moment, looking at the TV.

"See?" Lionel said. "They're not doin' lousy. We've got Pee Wee on first with one out and the Duke is up. Tying run at the plate. Come on Doook!" he brayed, just as Snider swung and sent a two-hopper right at

Stanky, who flipped to Dark, then on to first for the Giants' fourth double play of the game, and it was over.

The Giants swarmed out of the visitors' dugout to join their mates in the field as they converged on Jim Hearn in celebration.

"Fuck!" Lionel screamed.

"You shouldn't say that word on Rosh Hashanah."

Ronald had spoken for the first time. His voice sounded shaky and Eddie noticed that he looked kind of pale.

"Are you all right?" he asked him.

"It's cold in here," Ronald said.

"Fuck!" Lionel repeated. "Now we have to beat them two in a row. At the fuckin' Polo Grounds!"

Strangely enough, Eddie could not bring himself to be mad. The feeling that he was getting close to something was that strong.

"I can't stand it!" Lionel said, walking over to the TV and turning it off. "I'll never watch another game in this jinxed den of sin. Let's get outta here."

He turned to Eddie. "You coming?"

"Where are we going?"

"Out. Out into Brooklyn. Maybe we'll play some stickball, even in these goddamn suits."

"Are you allowed to play stickball today?"

Lionel looked like he wanted to take a swing at him.

"Of course not, you imbecile, but I'd rather play stickball and go to Hell than sit around here, where the Dodgers lose. Now, are you coming?"

Why not? Eddie thought. Besides, there were things he wanted to ask Lionel, and Ronald too, for that matter.

"Sure," he said. "Should I bring a broomstick and a Spaldeen?"

"No," Lionel said sarcastically, "just bring your imagination. Of course you should bring a stick and a Spaldeen. In fact, bring a whole bunch, because I plan on hitting them over several rooftops and losing them for you."

He strode to the door and pulled it open.

"Give me a second," Eddie said.

He went back into his room, dug into his dresser drawer, and got out two Spaldeens, the pink rubber balls that said "Spalding" on them when they were new but whose name quickly rubbed off with use.

He threw on a jacket, stuffed the balls in his pockets, grabbed the broom handle he kept in the corner, and joined Ronald, who was waiting by the open door.

Lionel was already half-way down the stairs.

They stepped out into the hallway and Eddie made sure to lock the door behind him with his key. He didn't know why he'd been forgetting to do that. Probably because of so much on his mind.

"Hey, slow down!" he called after Lionel, once they were outside the building and heading down Bay Parkway toward 86th Street.

Their ultimate destination was Bay 29th Street, the next block over. It was where they always played because, unlike Bay Parkway, it was a one-way street and had much less traffic.

Eddie was hustling to keep up. Ronald was about ten yards behind and fading.

"We can't start until Ronald catches up to us anyway," Eddie pointed out. "So what's the hurry?"

The logic finally seemed to get through to Lionel. He reluctantly slowed down, making a disgusted face. Eddie pulled alongside him.

"How much do you know about Fartsworth?" he asked.

Lionel gave him a funny look.

"What do you mean?"

"His personal life, where he lives, that kind of thing."

"He probably hangs upside down in some attic. How do I know?"

By now, Ronald had caught up to them.

"Who hangs upside down in an attic?" he panted.

"He asked me if I knew where Fartsworth lives," Lionel informed him.

"Bay 31st, near Cropsey."

Lionel glanced sideways at him.

"And how in this wide, wide world would you know something like that?"

Ronald was still trying to catch his breath, but he managed to wheeze out between gulps of air, "'Cause his wife...works at a hat store, see?

...And my mom bought a hat there that some of the fringe was falling off...so she called the store and Mrs. Farnsworth...told her she was sorry about it, and to have me bring it over to their house...which is on Bay 31st near Cropsey...'cause it's closer to us than the store...and more convenient...so my mom put the hat back in the box...and I..."

"Stop!" Lionel shouted. "For God's sake, have some mercy on your fellow human beings!"

"I was just answering the qu..."

"Stop!"

It could work, Eddie thought.

Bay 31st and Cropsey wasn't far from the promenade where Sandra was killed, and going past the sporting goods store was one of the routes he could've taken on his way home from the school. If he'd lived in any other direction, it wouldn't have been as likely.

"What's the address?" he asked Ronald.

"I'm not sure, but it's a red house near the corner."

It didn't matter; he could look it up in the phone book.

"When did you do this? Was it on a weekend or during the week?"

"It was one day last week, after school."

"Could it have been last Tuesday?" It was worth a shot, why not?

By now, they'd turned the corner onto 86th Street and were approaching Al's Soda Fountain.

"Holy shit, would you look at that?" Lionel said.

Al always made up hand-lettered signs that he'd tape to his window. They'd announce new ice cream dishes he'd concocted or special promotions, like "Frappe-Happy Fridays" or "Half-Price Sundae Sundays."

Today's sign read, "Giants—3, Bums—1. Just One More And Then They're Done. Free Egg Creams To All Non-Dodger Fans."

"This is an outrage!" Lionel sputtered. "Who the hell does he think he is? We can't allow this; come on, guys."

He stomped over to the entrance and yanked the door open.

"Hey, Al!" he called out, stepping inside. "Somebody better clean off your window. It's got a piece of trash stuck to it."

Al Schaefer looked up from behind the counter at the three of them standing in the doorway. His eye was drawn to the broom handle Eddie was holding.

"What is this, the Storm Trooper Scouts?" he said. "Whatta ya think you're gonna do with that?" He pointed an accusatory finger at the stick.

"What? Oh, nothing," Eddie said. "We were just on our way to play stick ball."

Lionel indicated the empty place with a sweep of his arm.

"I see all the non-Dodger fans are slurping up your egg creams."

Al grinned.

"Give 'em time; I just put the sign up. Meanwhile, why don't you boys come in? I know at least two of you don't qualify, but what about you?" he asked Ronald. "Who do you root for?"

"The Yankees," Ronald answered.

"There you are," said Al. "You've earned yourself a free egg cream. And after we beat you in the World Series, you can have another one."

He pulled out a glass from under the counter and began squirting chocolate syrup into it from a dispenser.

"The only way the Giants are going to the World Series," Lionel said, defiantly approaching the counter, "is if they buy tickets. Who do they have pitching tomorrow, Sheldon Jones? He's six and ten. We'll kill him."

"Who do you have?" Al Schaefer riposted. "You're down to Clem Labine, the rookie Dressen gave up on weeks ago."

"When did you take the hat over to Farnsworth's house?" Eddie asked Ronald again, as Lionel and Al continued to go at it. "Could it have been last Tuesday?"

"I don't know. What happened last Tuesday?"

It was a good question, but he remembered in the same way he remembered a lot of things, by tying them to the Dodgers. That was the day they lost the twi-night double header in Boston and his dad threw the beer bottle.

"The weather was nice outside," he said. "We had to finish our reports on the Incas and turn them in on Wednesday."

"Oh, yeah," Ronald said. "That's right, it was Tuesday. In fact, after I got back from dropping off the hat, Lionel was waiting for me. He gave me two Joe DiMaggio cards for letting him look at my report."

Lionel, on hearing his name and "Joe DiMaggio cards," paused just long enough to mutter, "Sucker," and then resumed the war of words with Al.

"What time did you bring the hat over to Farnsworth's?"

"I guess it had to be around three thirty."

"Was he home?"

This was a big one. If Farnsworth was home, he wouldn't have been in the sporting goods store getting friendly with Sandra.

"No, nobody was home. I had to leave it with the downstairs neighbor."

Yes, yes!

Of course, it didn't prove Farnsworth was with Sandra, or anything else, but each little fact that kept the possibility alive gave him hope.

"Did you ever see him on the street after school?" Eddie asked. "Do you know which way he usually goes home?"

Al was about to say something to Lionel, but instead looked up at Eddie.

"Who are you talking about?"

"Mr. Farnsworth, our social studies teacher. He's a tall guy who talks sort of erudite."

"Nice word," Al Schaefer said, "and I think I know who you mean. Does he have thick, black hair and wear a tweed sports jacket with leather patches on it sometimes?"

Eddie nodded.

"Yeah, I see him a lot. Stops in here in the afternoons and picks up a *Journal-American*."

This was getting even better. So Farnsworth walked down 86th Street on his way home after school, which meant he passed by the sporting goods store.

Al resumed his concoction of the egg cream, adding a splash of milk to the chocolate syrup and then putting the glass under the pressurized tap that squirted out the seltzer, creating the frothy chocolate drink that contained neither egg nor cream. He swished a spoon vigorously around in it and leveled the excess foam off the top.

"Here you are," he said to Ronald, placing the glass in front of him. "I'll be doing this after every Giant victory from now on. So drink up; this is the first of many to come."

"Yeah, drink up," Lionel said. "This is a one-day opportunity that will never be repeated."

Ronald lifted the glass and took a sip. Judging by the look on his face, he didn't like the taste.

"What's the matter," Al said, "not strong enough?"

"No, it's fine. I just don't feel very good; I have a headache."

He took another sip and then put it down. His face had gotten pale again.

"I don't think I can finish this."

"Aha!" Lionel said. "Even someone like Ronald, who, as everyone can see by his shape, loves a good egg cream, can't buy into your evil offer. Good man, Ronald." He patted him on the back.

"And now, Al, I'm gonna jinx your Giants good and proper. If this accursed egg cream is finished off by a Dodger fan, or better yet, two Dodger fans, the spell will be broken forever."

He grabbed the glass, took a substantial gulp, and passed it over to Eddie, who'd only been half paying attention.

"Listen, Ronald," he said, as he took the glass from Lionel, "do you know the name of Mrs. Farnsworth's hat shop?"

He quickly drank the rest of the egg cream and put the empty glass on the counter.

"What's all this about Fartsworth?" Lionel said. "Are you starting a fan club?"

Then he snapped his fingers, reminded of something.

"Hey, you remember my Spider Jorgensen card?"

"Yeah?" Eddie said with a touch of antagonism. This was the baseball card that Farnsworth had confiscated before he doubled Eddie's Inca assignment.

"Well, I was walking in the hall later that day," Lionel said, "and I passed by the room and saw him sitting there alone. So I figured maybe I'd turn on the charm and see if I could get my card back."

Al took the empty glass from the counter, muttering, "Broke the spell, huh? You should call Dressen and tell him his worries are over."

"I went into the room," said Lionel, "and I explained that he was punishing the wrong person by taking that card, that it was mine, and the only reason you had it was because you took it from me."

"That's a lie!"

"No, it isn't," Lionel explained patiently. "I slid it to you under the seat and you took it from me. In any case, he gave me one of those stupid, know-it-all smiles and said I could find it in his waste basket, although it wasn't exactly in perfect condition. So I looked in there, and it was all cut up into pieces. Now, here's the interesting part."

He reached into his suit pocket and took out his wallet.

"You're not supposed to carry money on Rosh Hashanah," Ronald said.

Lionel opened the wallet and held the empty billfold compartment under Ronald's nose.

"Look, Rabbi, no money," he said. From another compartment he pulled out the four pieces of the baseball card.

"I was gonna show this to you yesterday at the game but it slipped my mind."

He laid out the pieces on the counter and put them together.

"Pretty creepy, huh?"

With a sharp, pointed object, probably the tip of the scissors before he'd cut up the card, Farnsworth had obliterated the NY from Jorgensen's cap and the word *Giants* from his shirt. Then, with two deep and angry slashes, he'd gouged a large X mark across Jorgensen's face.

CHAPTER TWENTY ONE

Monday Evening, October 1st

Carmine looked around his room and, step by step, imagined how he'd destroy it. First, he'd take the top drawer from his dresser and fling it through the window. He could almost hear the glass shattering and the heavy drawer crashing down onto Bay 29th Street. Then he'd throw the rest of the drawers out the window after it. Then he'd tip over the whole fucking dresser. Then he'd grab the mattress from his bed...

He stopped himself. He was better than this.

Dropping to the floor, he launched into a furious series of pushups, grunting fiercely. *The Giants won! The Giants won! The Giants won!* he thought.

Of course he didn't get to hear the rest of the game, but he found out the score afterwards. Just thinking about it now was helping.

Here he was, a fucking hero, and his old man could care less. Vito, it so happened, was planning to go out in a blaze of glory, with two more ammo clips in his briefcase. Carmine had not only saved his own life and Fartsworth's, but everyone in that classroom.

But did that get him out of being locked up again? Nooo! Well, fuck his old man. He increased the tempo of the pushups.

One good thing, he realized as he strained in the effort, was Vito, with all his raving about wanting to kill him and whatever else he told the cops, didn't mention the knife. He might eventually, but now that it was hidden away, Carmine could always claim it was Vito being crazy.

Earlier, he'd crawled under his bed and pried loose a section of the molding from where the wall met the floor, used the knife to hollow out a hole in the plaster, and then put it inside. He'd pushed the molding back in place and disposed of the plaster dust out the window. Everything looked normal, even if someone crawled under the bed and looked, which nobody would.

Of course, a gun to go along with the knife would be even better, and he envied Vito for stealing a Luger from his old man. He'd imagined himself many times doing something like that, sneaking into their bedroom while they were sleeping and taking his old man's service revolver. But it was always locked up, and his old man slept with the key in his pajama pocket.

Never mind, the knife would do for a start, and there were plenty of guns out there. Once he was out in the world, he was sure he could buy or steal one.

He wasn't going to blow it now. The whole thing depended on his ability to stay tough, to take all their shit, make 'em think he was behaving.

Another day and a half, that's all.

In the living room, Teresa sat on the couch, crying softly.

"I don't understand you," she said, as Nick paced the room. "Why do you hate him?"

Nick thought bitterly about how they had to get Carmine's closet soundproofed so they wouldn't have to go into the living room to have a conversation.

"Jeez, how many times do I have to say it? It was his fault what happened today. His own goddamn fault. I talked to the guys who took the call, and they gave me the whole story. The only reason the Peccarino kid brought the gun in to school was 'cause'a him."

"But he saved everybody."

Nick rolled his eyes.

"Yeah, like one of them arsonists that set fires and then help the firemen."

"Come on!" she said. "You know he did more than that. And look how he's been behavin' himself. Don't that count for anything?"

Nick shook his head in frustration. All it counted for was to make him surer that Carmine was faking. But how could he explain that?

"What's the matter with you?" she pleaded. "Why do you gotta keep treatin' him like this? Your son could'a been killed today."

The anger drained from his face. He sat down on the couch and took Teresa's hands. "I know how much you love him." She saw tears in his eyes, something very rare for him. "I love him too. But there are things inside'a him that I can't change.

"You remember when he was little, and I used to take him up to the Polo Grounds? He yelled and cursed at people if the Giants were losin', and I couldn't make him stop. Even when they were winning, I couldn't stop him from screamin' and botherin' people.

"I've tried talkin' to him; I've tried bein' firm with him; but now I don't know what to do.

"What happened in that classroom today was a stupid fight between two bad actors, and everyone else got caught in the middle of it. All the kids are scared shitless of our son, did ya know that? He beats them up, he steals from them. He's got no friends, except for Frankie, who's mentally retarded, and Vito, who's a psychopath. And he craps all over them too. I spoke to the Peccarino kid at the station house, and he told me…"

Mary appeared in the doorway.

"I finished my homework," she said. "Can I watch Paul Winchell and Jerry Mahoney?"

"Your mother and I are talkin'."

"But I always watch it," Mary pouted. "It's not fair."

"That's okay, let her watch it," Teresa said. "Don't punish her too. We can talk about it later."

"Are ya sure?"

Teresa nodded tiredly.

"Okay," he said, getting up from the couch, "I gotta take care of somethin' at the precinct anyway, so I may as well do it now." What he had to take care of was getting Barry to come with him and be fingerprinted. "I'll be back in a little while."

As he passed by Mary, he gave her a kiss on the cheek, surprising her.

"You're a good girl, honey, and I love you. Are you gonna be okay, babe?" he asked Teresa as he took his jacket off the coat tree.

"Yeah, sure, I'll be all right."

Mary turned on the TV set and switched to Channel 4. Paul Winchell was sitting in front of a curtain with his dummy, Jerry Mahoney, on his lap.

"I love you, Teresa," said Nick.

"I love you too."

He blew a kiss to her as he stepped out the door.

"Ma," Mary said, joining her on the couch, "I heard a story the other day about somethin' interesting. It happened ten years ago; maybe you know about it. There was this woman that had a two-year-old baby…"

"Dear God!" Teresa wailed. "What's gonna happen to us?"

She stood up.

"Mary, I can't just sit here. I feel too miserable; I gotta lie down." She turned and headed for the bedroom.

"But Ma," Mary called after her, "I need to find out about this."

It was no use. Teresa was already in the bedroom and closing the door.

("Stop moving your lips,") Jerry Mahoney said.

***

Nick paused outside the Feins' apartment. He'd used the "let's take a walk" excuse last time. Maybe he could say his car was making a funny noise and ask Barry to take a listen to it. Barry had been pretty handy with cars in the Army, once jury-rigging a jeep's air filter in the middle of a field under enemy fire.

What the hell, it was as good a ruse as any. Nick rang the bell.

Julia opened the door a crack and peered out at him over the chain.

"Oh, hi." She closed the door momentarily to undo the chain and then let him in.

"Barry isn't home yet," she said, as he stepped inside. "He's working late again."

Nick smiled. "Rakin' in the overtime, huh? What time did he say he'd be back?"

"He didn't. He called a little after five and said they were still working on that Saturday supplement and he'd call me when he was leaving, if it wasn't too late and I wasn't already in bed."

Nick remembered Barry's "bullshit story about having to work late, some crap about a supplement to next Saturday's edition."

Eddie appeared in the doorway to his room, where he'd gone to see if Mary's window was half-way open, which it wasn't.

"How're ya doin' there, Sport?" Nick asked him. "How's your hand?"

"It's okay. "

Eddie eyed him carefully. His mom had already told him about his dad's phone call. He couldn't be looking for a job this late.

"Doctor Glazer is supposed to check on the stitches tomorrow," Julia said. "Would you like some coffee, or a beer? I assume you're off duty."

"Actually, I'm on duty," Nick said, making Eddie's stomach tighten. "I was just on my way over to the precinct, so I'll have to take a rain check on the beer. And coffee sounds great, but I really should be goin'."

With an apologetic smile, he moved toward the door.

"I only stopped by to ask Barry a quick question about my car. No big deal, but would you tell him to call me when you hear from him, even if it's late?"

"Sure, Nick," Julia said, smiling. "Are you raking in the overtime too?"

"No overtime where I work. Just all the time."

He opened the door.

"G'night, Eddie," he said pleasantly.

"G'night, Coach," Eddie murmured.

***

It was shortly before 11 p.m. when the phone rang. Unlike the Feins, whose phone was in the living room, the DiFazios had theirs in the kitchen, so Nick had to spring from the couch to get it before it woke Teresa.

One difference between them was that, while problems kept him awake, her way of dealing with it was sleeping.

He'd been sitting in the darkened living room ever since Mary went to bed, the TV screen flickering and the sound almost inaudible. Boston Blackie was winding up, but Nick couldn't have told you anything about it.

He moved quickly and grabbed the receiver on the second ring.

"H'lo," he said quietly.

"Nick," said Julia, "I know it's after ten, and I hope I'm not waking you, but you said Barry could call late, so I thought…"

Her voice trailed off, but the distress in it was apparent.

"No, no, Julia, it's all right. I'm up."

He lifted the phone by its cradle and carried it as far from the wall between the kitchen and Carmine's closet as the wire allowed.

"What's the matter?" he whispered, facing away from the wall for good measure.

"Just now, I tried to call Barry, since he hadn't phoned, and they told me he doesn't work there anymore. That he hasn't worked there since Friday." Her voice was creeping up on panic. "What should I do?"

"Okay, now, just take it easy," he said reflexively.

This was not news to him. He'd already called the *World Telegram and Sun* himself. It was why he'd been sitting in the dark living room.

"When he called before, did it sound like he'd been drinking?"

Julia let out a sigh that almost became a groan, before she stopped herself.

"I couldn't tell. You know how he is; his voice doesn't get slurred. He sounded a little tired, so I guess he might've been drinking."

She started to cry.

"Who's kidding who, of course he'd been drinking. Where is he, Nick? Couldn't the police look for him?"

Not yet, he thought, *at least not for this.* If they went out looking for every husband who didn't come home when he was supposed to, it would use up the whole force. A guy had to be gone at least two days before they'd consider him a missing person, but he didn't want to tell her that.

"Don't worry," he said. "Either he quit or he got fired, but he probably couldn't bring himself to tell you, so he went on a binge. Listen, it's only eleven. He might walk in the door any minute, or, if not, then he's somewhere sleepin' it off and he'll come home tomorrow. Where's Eddie, in bed?"

"Yes, he doesn't know."

"Okay, that's good. Why don't you get some sleep? It ain't gonna help for you to stay up and stew about it."

"I can't," she said. "I wouldn't be able to."

Nick knew the feeling.

"Give it a try anyway," he said. "When he gets in, call me, no matter what time it is. If I don't hear from you, I'll call tomorrow. What's the number at your school?"

"I'm not going in tomorrow if he's not here by then. I couldn't possibly function."

"Then I'll call ya at home."

There was a pause, as if Julia didn't want it to end, but there seemed to be nothing more to say.

"Thanks, Nick," she said wearily. "Good night."

"G'night, Julia. Stay strong."

He replaced the receiver. "Barry, you prick," he said softly.

***

As Nick was hanging up the phone, Al Schaefer was pulling the shade down on the front window to his place. He'd put in all 16 hours without any help today, since the short order cook who came in at lunch time and worked in the evenings had been out for the Jewish holiday.

He didn't mind. He liked being here, where he could talk to people.

He particularly liked the give and take with the Dodger fans that came in, especially the kids. He'd never had any kids of his own. His wife Emma died of an aneurysm nearly 20 years ago.

He'd been thinking about her even more these last few weeks. The place they'd met was the Polo Grounds, at Game Five of the '22 World Series against the Yankees, when their seats behind third base happened to be next to each other.

She knew all about Giant manager John McGraw and his strategies, how he'd invented the hit and run, how he used the bunt in ways no one else did.

She knew as much about it as he did. She even knew that McGraw was the first manager to hire pinch hitters, and the first to have specialty relief pitchers.

They talked about baseball, they talked about themselves, they talked about life. By the ninth inning it was as if they'd known each other for a long time.

The Giants came from behind to beat the Yankees that day 5-3, winning the World Series, as Babe Ruth wound up hitting only .118.

Six months later, they were married.

They'd moved to Brooklyn, of all places, after her grandfather died and left her his house in Bensonhurst. It was mortgaged, but they were hoping this soda fountain would enable them to save up enough money to start a family. They never had the chance.

He immersed himself in work. Working hard was good. It made him tired, and it was easier to go back to an empty house when he was tired.

He hadn't worked very hard today. It was another byproduct of the Jewish holiday, but that was good too, because he was able to listen to the game, and that had been wonderful.

He felt happy for Jim Hearn, who'd labored in the shadow of Maglie and Jansen, and who'd always been tagged with the reputation of someone who couldn't win a big one. Very satisfying.

As he lowered the shade past his homemade sign, he had a brief thought of taking it down, since it was the end of the day, but he decided to do it tomorrow. Tomorrow, hopefully, he'd be putting up an even bigger one.

He moved over to pull down the door shade, when he saw a face inches away from his on the other side of the glass. A man in a dark suit with an open shirt collar was standing there, peering through the door.

It took Al by surprise, but then he recognized him.

"Oh, hi," he said, opening the door. "You're out late. I was just about to close, but what can I do for you?"

"You think you've got one more egg cream?" the man asked. His eyes seemed to be pained, like he had a headache or something.

"Why not?" Al said. "I feel magnanimous today."

He turned and walked back behind the counter.

"I'm gonna have to charge you for it since I know you're a Dodger fan." He laughed. "I'm not that magnanimous, at least not yet. Maybe tomorrow I'll be."

The man didn't reply. He closed the door behind him and stepped over to the magazine rack near the entrance.

Al put his head down and rummaged around for the bottle of milk in the refrigerated chest beneath the counter.

"What a game!" he said, coming up with the milk and not noticing that the door shade had now been pulled down.

He took a glass from the shelf and squirted chocolate syrup into it.

"I'll bet Leo must've felt especially good. There've been only two times in National League history that they needed a playoff, and he managed in both of 'em. The Dodgers in '46, when they tied the Cards and then got beat in two straight, but I guess you remember that." He chuckled. "Now, he finally wins himself a playoff game."

Al poured the milk into the glass and moved it under the seltzer tap.

"And who's it for? The Giants. And who's it against? Who do ya think? Ironic, ain't it? Ironic and very sweet."

The lights went out.

At first, he thought it was a power failure, but then he saw that the Coke sign on the wall was still on, although it shed very little light. For all intents and purposes, the place was in darkness.

"I think you must'a brushed against the light switch," he said, as he squinted, trying to get his eyes accustomed. "It's near the door."

He was about to come out from behind the counter to help the man find it, when a large shape suddenly loomed in front of him.

Hands clamped around his throat, as the egg cream glass fell to the floor and shattered.

He felt himself being dragged down behind the counter, the man on top of him now, pressing his full weight upon him. He tried to struggle, but he was rapidly losing strength.

As the darkness was swallowed up by blackness, his last thought was of Giant first baseman George Kelly stroking a line drive to center in the bottom of the eighth, scoring Frankie Frisch and Irish Meusel to give the Giants the lead, as Emma shrieked in delight and impulsively threw her arms around him.

CHAPTER TWENTY TWO

Tuesday Morning, October 2nd

Eustace Britchforth Beauregard, known to his friends and family in Greenwood, Mississippi, as "Buddy," strode down the basement ramp with a hard glint in his eye and a resolute set to his jaw. Ever since his encounter on Sunday with that young hooligan, he'd been cursing himself for his cowardice. This morning, he'd decided to regain his self respect.

He was not a man who looked for trouble, but he was not someone who ran from it either. The only reason he was here in this wretched city was to take his daughter home.

Fourteen years ago, she'd run off with a Yankee college boy who'd been passing through town on an Easter vacation jaunt. Beauregard and his wife only knew the fellow's first name, and they thought they remembered the name of the large university he'd attended, but they weren't sure. It was enough to compel them to spend their life savings on a series of private detectives.

His insurance business had nearly gone under and they'd had to refinance their home, as the trail grew hot and cold over the years, but it was finally worth it. Two months ago, the latest private eye had struck paydirt.

And so he'd journeyed to Brooklyn, the first time in his life he'd been outside of Mississippi, and rented an apartment a few blocks from where his daughter and the college boy, who'd since become her husband, were living.

He'd signed a one-year lease, but he had no intention of staying that long. One of the things he'd learned about this city was that people changed where they lived as easily as they changed their clothes. Moving out before a lease was up was not only commonplace, but landlords were known to encourage it. There was always someone else ready to move in, and at a higher rent. No, he wasn't going to stay here for anything close to a year. If he couldn't convince his daughter to come back home with him, by God, he'd kidnap her.

He passed through the basement area where the garbage cans were stored, giving the dumbwaiter a dirty look as he went by, and then turned right, into a room whose walls were lined with fuse boxes and electricity meters. At the far end was the door to the Prestons' apartment.

These n_ggers have it good, he thought, *a free place to live and a decent amount of separation from the garbage cans.* He figured the landlord didn't necessarily have to set it up that way, so they should appreciate how fortunate they were. He knocked heavily on the door.

In his bedroom, James Preston was just getting dressed for school when he heard the knocking and the door opening, followed by a loud, angry voice from the kitchen. Little Nate Junior, who shared the room with him, started bawling in his crib.

"Shh," James said futilely, trying to hear what was going on.

What he was able to make out over the baby's crying made him feel like joining the baby. With sickening dread, he heard the goddamn cracker light into his daddy, saying all kinds of things, words James never heard of before but he knew were insults, threatening to have the landlord kick them out on the street. All he could hear his daddy say was, "Yes, suh," and "No, suh," and "Sorry, suh."

He waited for the bedroom door to burst open and either his daddy or his mama to come in there and haul him out to the kitchen. He reached into the crib and picked up Nate Junior, hoping to use him as protection, knowing they wouldn't hit him while he was holding the baby. All it did was make Nate Junior cry even louder.

Holding the squalling infant and afraid to move, he heard the cracker leave and the front door close. His daddy was gonna kill him. He'd take the strap to him for sure, and then beat on him with his fists, like he did a couple of years ago, when James had been foolish enough to try and fight back.

He clutched the baby tighter as he saw his door opening.

It was his mama.

"What'choo doin' to that child?" she yelled at him, her eyes blazing. "Give that baby here!"

Rosalie Preston was a woman who weighed nearly 250 pounds. When she was in a good mood, her infectious cackle could make everyone around her break out laughing despite themselves. When she was in a bad mood, everyone around her would do well not to be around her.

"You goddamn piece'a trash!" she said, as James meekly handed over the baby, who immediately stopped crying. "You get your worthless behind into that kitchen!"

She reached out and slapped at his face with her free hand, as he tried to duck away.

James slunk toward the kitchen.

"Fool!" his mother added from behind him, the baby now gurgling happily.

His daddy was standing by the table with the strap in his hand, folded in half and ready for action.

"Take that baby outta here," he said ominously to his wife, who turned and carried Nate Junior out of the room. Nate Preston glared at his son.

"You come here, boy," he told him. James reluctantly moved closer. "You know what you done?"

"Daddy, I didn' mean to…"

WHAP!

James cried out in pain, but it was imaginary pain. His father had brought the strap down onto the table, just missing him.

"You deaf, boy? I ast if you know what you done."

James gulped in relief at not being hit, although he didn't understand why.

"Yessuh," he stammered.

WHAP!

Just missed him again, but even closer.

"You lyin' to me, boy," Nate said. "You just sayin' what you think you s'posed to say. Now, I'm gon' ask you one mo' time." His words were slow and measured. "Do you know what you done?"

James knew there was only one answer left.

"No, Daddy," he said in confusion.

"Tha's right, *No, Daddy,*" Nate said mockingly. "You got no idea 'bout nothin' do you? Now, sit in that chair, boy!"

James did as he was told and sat down at the table, as his father stood behind him with the strap. He knew if he looked over his shoulder he'd get hit for sure.

"You got no idea," Nate repeated. "If we was back in Geo'gia, that cracker would'a come in here with his friends, pulled you out, and strung you up on a damn tree."

He was tapping the folded strap lightly against his open palm, making James more and more unsettled with each tap.

"Then they'd be takin' yo mama, yo baby brother, and me, and doin' the same thing. They would'a had themselves a big ol' party about it."

Tap, tap.

"But you don' know 'bout things like that, do you?"

Tap, tap.

"No, you wasn't bo'n in no Geo'gia, you was bo'n up here. Y'all even get to play baseball wit' them white kids."

The tapping got louder.

"Tell me, boy, you sorry for what you done?"

"Yes, Daddy."

WHAP!

This time it wasn't the table, it was right across the shoulder blades.

James cried out, but more from surprise than pain. It still wasn't as heavy as his daddy usually dealt out.

"You doin' it again, boy. You just sayin' what you think you s'posed to. You best NOT be sorry for what you done, you hear me? You best NEVER be sorry!"

James couldn't believe it. He looked back, even if it meant getting hit again.

"I don' understand," he said.

"No, you don't, so I'm gon' tell you."

Nate came around the table and sat down in the chair facing him. He put the strap down and looked over at his son. His eyes held no anger.

"Standin' up to his kind ain't never a cause to be sorry," he said, "and don't you ever forget it. You might'a heard me sayin' a lot'a 'yes, suh' and 'no, suh,' but all I was doin' was gettin' by. I was jus' makin' him think he was 'complishin' somethin', so he'd believe me when I said you was already in school, and I'd take care of it later. Worked too, the fool."

"But Daddy, he said the landlord was gon' throw us out on the street."

Nate scoffed.

"Landlord ain' gon' do no such thing. He knows how I help him when that buildin' inspector comes 'round. That cracker ain' even been here a month. All he's gon' get from the landlord is some mo' yes, suh and no, suh, and it ain' gon' mean nothin'. You should never trust a white man, son, but some's better'n others. And they's all better than that cracker."

"So you ain't mad at me?" It was all James could think to say.

His father shook his head.

"No, I ain't. Now get goin'. You late for school."

James practically floated to his room in relief. Nate Junior was asleep again in the crib, and his mother was somewhere else in the apartment.

As he got his books together, his relief began to fade into something else. He thought about what his daddy said about Georgia, that they would've all been hung from a tree for what he did. It amazed him.

People like that cracker, he realized, people who'd kill a whole family over nothing, weren't fit to be called human beings.

Carmine had whispered something in his ear yesterday, after that whole scary experience. "Wednesday," he said. "We're gonna do it Wednesday."

He'd never liked Carmine, but man, he sure had to admire how he took that gun away. He knew Carmine had nothing over him anymore, since it all came out with his daddy, but now he wanted it to happen, and more than ever.

Never trust a white man, his daddy said. Well, he didn't need to trust Carmine. He still didn't know why Carmine was doing it, maybe just to beat someone up, but it didn't matter. James could control it now.

If it wasn't like he wanted, he didn't have to do it. But if it was, then oh, man! Carmine would be his weapon.

James would do a lot more than just say "yes, suh" and "no, suh." He'd make his daddy proud.

***

In Eddie's dream, Mary was standing in a field. She was wearing the blue dress she'd changed into on Sunday and holding a shepherd's crook.

"Which one are you, Mary Had a Little Lamb or Bo Peep?" he asked her.

"He didn't come home," she said, looking stricken.

"Who, your sheep?"

"He didn't come home last night." Her voice had become his mother's.

He opened his eyes and saw Julia standing at the foot of his bed.

"Your father didn't come home last night," she said, her face looking as distraught as Mary's in the dream. "I don't know what to do. I'm at my wits' end."

"Where is he?" he asked stupidly, still half asleep.

"I'll tell you where he isn't," she said. "He's not at work, because he either quit or got fired on Friday. When you were at the game with him, did he say anything?"

Now Eddie was fully awake.

"No," he said.

It wasn't so bad, he hoped. His dad had done this before. A few months after he came back from the war, he didn't come home one night and his mother was frantic. He, at age six, was terrified.

It was strange because, the whole time his dad was in the war, Eddie had never thought of him dying. Only on that day. But he was home the next afternoon, and nothing was ever said.

It could be like that now, he thought, or it could be something else. Maybe he knew Nick was coming over last night to arrest him. Maybe he remembered where he was the night Sandra was killed, and he needs time to find people who saw him. Once he does, he'll come back and prove he's innocent.

Eddie knew he was just wishing this, that it was the stuff of movies, but there was nothing he could do about his dad. There was plenty he could do about Farnsworth, and he was going to do it today.

"I'm at my wits' end," Julia said again.

The alarm clock on his dresser read 7:30. This was not good. She should have left by now to catch the subway to Greenpoint.

"Aren't you going in?" he asked, already knowing the answer and realizing how much this was going to screw him up.

"No, I'm going to stay here in case your father comes home, or at least calls. Now, get up and brush your teeth. I've got breakfast ready."

He trudged into the bathroom and brooded about it as he wielded the toothbrush. He sure didn't want to go to school today. What he really wanted to do was take his raffle tickets over to Bo Peep's, where Ronald said Mrs. Farnsworth worked, just before they'd tried to play stickball but couldn't because Ronald was too sick.

He'd intended to go there today and tell Mrs. Farnsworth that his friend had found a watch near the school, then ask if her husband had lost one. See her reaction.

His mother being home changed things, but maybe not that much. He could still fake going to school. He just wouldn't be able to wear the suit, which would mean he'd look suspicious to a cop or a truant officer, but he'd have to take the chance.

He rinsed his mouth and went into the kitchen, where Julia was pouring milk over his Rice Krispies.

"You're supposed to see Dr. Glazer today during lunch time," she told him, as she put the bottle of milk back in the refrigerator and picked up her cup of coffee from the table. She remained standing, taking sips and alternating with puffs on her cigarette.

"I wrote a note to your teacher saying you're not going to be eating lunch at school. It's right there." She pointed to a piece of paper next to the cereal bowl.

He was always amazed at how, even at her wits' end, she could still think of everything.

"I was going to leave a sandwich for you in the refrigerator, but now I guess I'll be here to make it for you personally."

She was about to say something else, but sighed instead.

He suddenly felt terrible. All the lies he'd told her, all the things he was keeping from her. But if he could find out just one more thing about Farnsworth, he'd be able to spare her so much grief.

"Dad's probably okay," he said. "Maybe he doesn't want to come home until he finds another job."

She looked at him for a long moment, with so much love in her eyes that he had to turn away or he'd start crying again.

"Oh, Eddie," she said, "you're always such an optimist. I don't know where you get it from."

***

The beat cop on the 8 a.m. shift followed his usual route, taking him past Al's Soda Fountain at 9:30. The shades were down, which wasn't right. A lot of other places on the block were closed for the Jewish holiday, but he knew Al's wasn't one of them.

Maybe he's sick, or just didn't feel like coming in, the cop thought, as he turned the door handle and found it unlocked.

He put one hand on his gun holster.

"Police!" he called out. "Anybody there?"

He slowly opened the door.

Stepping to the side as the daylight spilled in ahead of him, so as not to make an easy target framed in the doorway, he peered into the dim interior. Nothing seemed out of place, except for a large, crumpled sheet of paper on the floor.

He reached into his belt compartment for the flashlight and flicked it on, playing the beam into the corners and around the darker areas, seeing nothing out of place.

Taking a cautious step inside, he moved the beam over to the counter, gradually bringing it down to floor level and revealing the foot sticking out from behind it.

***

As usual, things were not going the way Eddie thought. After stashing his school books behind some bicycles under the first-floor staircase, he'd put the raffle tickets in his pocket and headed for Bo Peep's, to find that it was closed.

The sign on the door said it opened at 10:00, which meant he had an hour and a half to kill. He'd be conspicuous on the street for that long, so he walked the couple of blocks to the the J.C.H. Synagogue on 79th Street, hoping maybe to blend in.

He wasn't wearing a suit but he did have a tie for school, and maybe the absence of a jacket wouldn't matter that much.

It didn't, but for other reasons. They wouldn't let him in without a ticket. To his amazement, he learned that synagogues charge money, paid in advance of course, to get in on the High Holy Days.

He managed to swipe a yarmulke from the box of spares at the entrance, however, and was able to stand out front, along with the changing groups of people taking a break from the service.

Ninety minutes of crushing boredom later, promptly at 10 o'clock, he was back in front of the hat shop, which was closed.

It was still closed when he came back at quarter after, and then again at 10:30.

About to give in to utter despair, he saw a middle-aged woman hurrying down the street toward him with a key in her hand.

"Mrs. Farnsworth?" he asked, as she arrived at the door.

"No," she told him breathlessly, "Dora's home sick with the flu. That's why I'm so late in opening the shop. I wasn't supposed to be here 'til this afternoon." She put the key in the lock. "Can I help you with something?"

"No, that's okay," Eddie said, already starting down the street. He knew Farnsworth's address because he'd looked it up yesterday in Al's phone book. Bay 31st and Cropsey was over a mile from the shop, and even further to walk since he had to keep to the side streets.

Twenty minutes later, he was standing in front of a red brick two-family house with a front stoop common to both entrances. He climbed the steps and rang the bell that said "Farnsworth."

Several seconds passed, and then the door on the right opened a crack. Eddie could see half of a woman's pale face peering through it, and a thin hand clutching the top of a pink bathrobe.

"Yes?" she said.

"Hi, I'm Eddie Fein," he replied brightly. "You must be Mrs. Farnsworth. I'm one of your husband's students and I'm selling raffle tickets for the P.A.L. I wonder if you'd be interested…"

"This is a bad time," she interrupted. "I've got the flu and I wouldn't want to give it to you. Maybe if you came back tomorrow or, better yet, in a couple of days. I really do apologize."

With that, she shut the door.

He stood there. This was supposed to be easy. Just talk to her at the hat shop where, even if she didn't want to buy a ticket, she'd at least speak to him. It would be no problem to say, "Oh, by the way…" and launch into the story about his friend finding a watch. Nothing to it.

Instead, he was staring at a door. Was he jinxed or something?

Screw it, there was nothing left but to try again. Forget the raffle ticket this time and go straight to the watch, which he should have done in the first place.

But as his finger was poised over the doorbell, he heard the angry sound of a man's voice coming from just the other side of the door.

"…a no good womanizer! You've told me yourself what a roving eye he has, how he looks at other women. What makes you think he hasn't been cheating on you?"

The voice had a southern accent, like Red Barber's, although with none of the gentility and charm of the Ol' Redhead. Maybe it would be how Barber would sound if he was really pissed off, but, in any case, Eddie thought he recognized it. You don't get to hear southern accents in Brooklyn, and this one sounded exactly like his recently-moved-in upstairs neighbor, Mr. Beauregard.

He saw the door knob start to move and dove down the steps, ducking to the side of the stoop and crouching there, out of sight. He heard the door open, as the voice continued from above him.

"Get back in bed, or you'll never get well. You're lucky you've got your daddy here to go out and get you your medicine. Your worthless husband certainly doesn't take care of you."

The door closed and Eddie saw the man's brown, pointy shoes going down the steps. He made a right turn toward Bath Avenue, and, as Eddie had thought, it was indeed Mr. Beauregard.

He considered things. He could wait until Beauregard was out of sight and then ring the bell again, taking his chances with Dora Farnsworth, who wouldn't be too happy about being pulled out of bed again in her flu-ridden state. Even if she gave him the opportunity to blurt out the watch story, what could he tell from her reaction? She'd probably just shut the door in his face again. But maybe there was another way.

He stepped out onto the sidewalk.

Beauregard had already gotten a good distance down the block, so Eddie had to walk briskly until he came up alongside.

"Mr. Beauregard?" he said.

The man stopped and looked down at this youngster who had materialized beside him.

"Yes?" he said.

"I'm Eddie Fein, your downstairs neighbor."

There was no response whatsoever.

"I thought it was you," Eddie went on, smiling.

"Yes?" Beauregard said again, a little impatiently this time.

"I saw you coming out of that house back there. I didn't realize you knew Mrs. Farnsworth."

"She's my daughter," he said, squinting at him suspiciously. "How do you know her?"

"Her husband is my social studies teacher."

"Hmp," Beauregard grunted. "Well, don't disturb her. She's got the flu."

He turned and started up the street again.

"Oh, I'm sorry," Eddie said, falling into step next to him. "I hope she feels better."

Beauregard said nothing, as Eddie kept walking along next to him.

"Can I tell you something, Mr. Beauregard, just between you and me?" he said softly. "I like her a whole lot better than I like him."

"You do, eh?"

Beauregard was keeping up a pretty good pace, and Eddie was hustling to stay with him.

"She's a really nice lady. My mother buys hats in her shop all the time," he improvised. "But Mr. Farnsworth is a different story. He's a lousy teacher; everyone says so. All the kids hate him."

"They hate him, huh?" Beauregard was starting to slow down, just a bit. "How come?"

"'Cause he's the worst teacher in the school. He makes you feel like you're a moron if you don't know the right answer. You can tell he likes to punish kids. He gets a kick out of it."

Beauregard was nodding at all this, even smiling a little.

"And I think he's doing something else that's even worse, that's…" He paused. "No, never mind; I shouldn't say anything."

"Say anything about what?"

"I don't know; he's your daughter's husband and all. I'd feel funny."

Beauregard stopped and looked down at him.

"If this concerns Dora, young man," he said sternly, "then you'd better tell me what it is right now."

Eddie felt a quiet thrill, a subdued version of the feeling he'd had when he got his first Little League hit.

"Well—" he said, drawing out the word as if reluctant, "a friend of my dad's came over the other night, real mad. He didn't know I could hear him from my room, but I could. He told my dad he thinks his wife is seeing another man."

"Really."

"Yes," Eddie said. "He found a man's watch on the floor behind his bed. He told my dad it was a Hamilton Martin."

He shifted from leg to leg, nibbling at his lower lip in seeming discomfort at having to talk about this.

"But here's the thing: I sit up front in class, and I've always noticed Mr. Farnsworth's watch, 'cause it looked so fancy. Then last week, he used it as part of a lesson; I think it was about free trade laws or something. He held it up and said, 'This is a Hamilton Martin, and it's a very fine watch.'"

Eddie didn't know how he came up with stuff like this, but there it was, full blown in his mind's eye, vivid and believable, just like it really happened.

"The day after I heard what my dad's friend said, I went in to school and looked to see if Mr. Farnsworth was still wearing it, and he wasn't. For the first time all year, he had a different watch."

"Hmm." Beauregard thought about it. "There could be an innocent explanation. He could have two watches and he was just wearing the other one."

"Right, absolutely," Eddie said, nodding his head in vigorous agreement. "And I hope that's what it is. Gee, I wouldn't want it to be anything bad for Mrs. Farnsworth. But still…"

"Still, what?"

"I don't know, you probably wouldn't want to do this, but if you asked her if he lost a Hamilton Martin watch recently…"

Beauregard mulled it over.

"I suppose I could," he said. A brief smile flickered across his lips.

Wouldn't it be something, he thought, *if I could nail that rogue dead to rights? Then she wouldn't be so anxious to stay here.*

"I will," he decided.

"Great," said Eddie. "And I hope you don't mind me asking, but would you let me know what she says? If it turns out to be true, I know my dad would want to tell his friend."

Eddie saw that brief smile again. *Boy, he must really hate his son-in-law,* he thought.

"He would, eh?" Beauregard said. "All right, we'll just wait and see. A Hamilton Martin, you say."

"Yes."

Eddie continued to shift his weight uncomfortably in pretend awkwardness.

"I mean, I really hope we find out it isn't true," he said.

"Oh, so do I," said Beauregard. "Of course."

"When could you let me know?"

"Let's see, I'm going to get my daughter's medicine now, and then I'll be leaving her place at three o'clock." Eddie wondered if that meant he wanted to be out of there before Fartsworth came home. "Then I take my afternoon nap, so why don't you come upstairs sometime after six?"

"That sounds terrific, Mr. Beauregard. And thanks."

"I should thank you. You're a good boy, Teddie."

"It's Eddie, Eddie Fein."

"Eddie, yes," Beauregard said, resuming his progress toward Bath Avenue. "See you later."

Even though it was out of his way, Eddie moved off in the opposite direction, not wanting to be in Beauregard's company one moment longer, now that he'd done what he had to.

Again, it didn't prove anything yet, but it was another step. Farnsworth's "roving eye" made it even more possible that he'd want to get friendly with Sandra.

Eddie noticed that it was nearly 11:30, time to walk over to the school and wait out front while the kids were being dismissed for lunch, trying to see Mary, like yesterday.

The thought of it made him start to daydream again about that kiss, and he was lost in a reverie as he made his circuitous way through the side streets. Finally, he found himself on 86th Street approaching Bay Parkway, the kind of busy intersection he'd been avoiding.

But it was okay now, he realized. It was close enough to lunch time that he didn't have to worry about running into a cop or a truant officer.

That's why, when he spotted the people and the police cars in front of Al's Soda Fountain, he didn't shy away. He hurried over to see what was going on.

***

"All yours," said the medical examiner as he packed up his kit. "You can move him out anytime you want."

Joe nodded while Nick furiously stared ahead at nothing. All around them the Forensics team was still busy dusting the place for fingerprints, of which there were hundreds everywhere.

They'd gotten a nice, clear index print from the inside door handle that might be a match for what they found on Jimmy Riccio's wallet. It would be useful once they caught the guy, but it didn't help them now.

"When the hell is our luck gonna change?" Joe asked Nick, who didn't answer.

The precinct, of course, had been on the alert for something just like Al's sign and the trouble it could bring. And as Nick had pointed out, it was especially crucial after four o'clock if the Dodgers lost.

But a combination of events conspired against them, not the least of which was the Jewish holiday.

The regular beat cop who walked the 4 p.m.-to-midnight shift had been off duty because of it. His replacement from the 20th showed up just in time for the shift change and was unaware of the alert. To him, the sign was kind of amusing. He was a Giant fan anyway.

Still, they should have caught it. A squad car went past Al's Soda Fountain four times during the seven hours that the sign was up. But each time, their view was blocked by a large plumbing supplies truck parked in front of the store, again because of the Jewish holiday.

The truck's owner, Sol Lefkowitz, was not working, so there it sat the entire day. The cops in the car could see there was a sign in Al's window but couldn't read what it said. They were used to Al's signs, and they assumed it was just another one of his crazy promotions.

It was Nick's own part in it that was eating at him now. If he'd taken 86th Street rather than Benson Avenue last night when he was walking to and from Barry's, he would have seen the fucking sign himself. But it was exactly the same distance either way, and he'd just happened to take Benson.

And, of course, choosing the wrong street was the least of it if Barry had done this.

"Who's his next of kin?" Joe asked, intruding on his spiral of recrimination. "Does anyone know?"

"He lived by himself." Nick couldn't keep the tightness out of his voice. "His wife died a long time ago, and he never mentioned any relatives."

"Poor stiff."

Nick said nothing. The guys from Forensics, doing their quiet work around him, were starting to get on his nerves, and it felt like there was no air in the place. He looked down at Al Schaefer's body and suddenly wanted to start smashing things, not a good urge to have at a crime scene.

"Listen," he said to Joe, "I just need to step outside for a minute, okay?"

"Sure, go ahead," Joe said. "Jeez, I understand how you feel. I knew the guy, too, maybe not as good as you did, livin' right around the corner."

The words stuck in his craw as he made his way toward the door. It had been left slightly open so you could get in and out without touching the handle, which had been bagged to protect the prints until they could lift them.

He stepped out onto the street. Wooden saw horses had been set up on three sides, denying access to the sidewalk immediately in front of the store. Onlookers had gathered at curbside, standing in the gutter between the parked cars.

At the sight of Nick they became energized. A group of men in the front waved press credentials at him and started shouting a cascade of questions.

"Can we have a word with you, Detective?" "Does this have anything to do with the killings last week?" "Was there something about a sign in the window yesterday?"

He shouted over the ruckus.

"There's nothin' to say right now, okay? We'll have a statement in a little while."

It had no effect. The questions rained down on him.

"When did it happen?" "One of the officers said it was strangulation like the others; is that true?" "Do you have any leads?"

Why the fuck did I come out here? he asked himself.

He started to turn back inside when he spotted Eddie, standing alone at one of the side barricades, a look of devastation on his face. He moved over to him.

"Go home," he said softly.

"It wasn't my dad…" Eddie began.

"Shut up," Nick warned him, "and go home."

The reporters had noticed and were already moving toward them.

"I'll talk to ya later," Nick said. "Get outta here."

Eddie quickly moved away, walking in the opposite direction from Bay Parkway.

Smart kid, Nick thought.

"Who's that?"

The reporters had arrived in virtual unison, except for one, who was starting to follow Eddie.

"You!" Nick yelled after him, making him stop. "What paper are you from?"

"*The Mirror,*" the guy said, his eyes shifting back and forth between Nick and Eddie's retreating form. He was a young, skinny guy in a rumpled brown suit, and he had a hungry look about him.

"C'mere," Nick said. "I got a statement for you."

The reporter reluctantly took his eyes off Eddie and moved back toward the others.

"That's my friend's kid. He's got nothin' to do with anythin'. I told him to go home just now because this ain't no place for children."

Eddie had turned the corner onto Bay 29th Street and was out of view.

"So you ain't gonna follow him and you ain't gonna bother him," Nick continued, "'cause anyone that tries is not only gonna be wastin' his time, but his paper is gonna be suckin' hind tit on this story."

He looked at them all to make sure they got it.

"Now, like I said, we'll have an official statement in a little while, so keep your pants on."

He turned and walked back inside.

The medical technicians had put Al's body onto a stretcher and were covering it with a sheet, as Joe looked on.

"Lemme have a word with you," Nick said, drawing him aside.

They both moved to the far end of the counter.

"I got a friend named Barry Fein who's a diehard Dodger fan, and I been worried about him. He was always a big drinker, but lately he's been depressed and drinkin' even harder than usual. He didn't come home last night, and his wife still doesn't know where he is."

He reached into his jacket pocket and took out Barry's picture.

"It might be worth our while to find him."

CHAPTER TWENTY THREE

Tuesday Afternoon, October 2nd

"Come in," said Lenore Glazer, ushering Eddie into the examining room. "This is turning out to be quite a busy day."

"The flu season usually doesn't start for a couple of weeks," Aaron Glazer said, drying his hands after washing them at the sink. "Maybe these are just a few isolated cases, but I've been making house calls all morning." Back in the '50s, doctors actually did that. "Hop up on the table, and we'll see how those stitches are looking."

Dr. Glazer began to snip away at the bandage with a pair of scissors, as Lenore Glazer remarked, "I noticed some police cars down at 86th Street. Do you know anything about it, Eddie?"

"They're at Al's," he said, fighting the urge to gag. "Somebody killed him."

It was the first time he'd told anyone. He hadn't told his mother. Even under normal circumstances, he wouldn't give her upsetting news unless he absolutely had to, and this time, it seemed especially important not to.

Julia had been in no mood to talk, anyway, lost in thought, not noticing how he was forcing himself to eat the tuna sandwich she'd made him. Now, he'd actually said the words.

"*What?!*" both Glazers exclaimed.

Lenore's face was wide-eyed with shock; Dr. Glazer's hand froze in mid-air as he was about to snip Eddie's bandage.

"My God!" he said. "That's horrible, absolutely horrible!"

He shook his head, as if trying to absorb the news.

"Was it robbery?"

"No," Eddie said, and then he couldn't help it. He burst into tears.

"It was 'cause of that sign in his window!" he moaned.

He'd been so hot on the Farnsworth trail in Al's store yesterday, questioning Ronald, looking up the address of the hat shop, and then the impact of the Spider Jorgensen card. He'd completely forgotten the sign. In fact, he'd been trying to ignore all that stuff between Al and Lionel.

What was he thinking? He'd been incredibly stupid, and now Al was dead.

"There, now, take it easy," Dr. Glazer said, putting a comforting arm around him. "Get us some tissues, would you, Lenore?"

"Here you are, dear," she said gently, handing him a bunch. He buried his face in them.

"What's all this about a sign?" Dr. Glazer asked him.

Eddie looked up from the tissues, trying to get a hold of himself.

"He had a sign in his window yesterday after the game, making fun of Dodger fans. I should've warned him."

He started to cry again.

"Okay, okay," Dr. Glazer said, his arm still around him, holding him even closer.

He felt foolish, blubbering like this. He took a long, deep breath and composed himself. Then he looked up and nodded to Dr. Glazer.

"I'm all right," he said.

The doctor slowly took his arm from around Eddie's shoulders.

"I don't understand," he said. "What could you have warned him about?"

"There was a Giant fan who got killed Friday night after he made fun of Dodger fans in a bar. Did you see it in the papers?"

They both shook their heads.

"Well, he was strangled, and the police think that was the reason," said Eddie. "And a couple of days before that, a friend of mine, Sandra Weinstock, was killed."

He was afraid that talking about it would start him crying again, but it didn't.

"Did you know Sandra?" he asked them. "She lived a couple of blocks from here, on Cropsey."

"I did see her name in the paper," Dr. Glazer said. "I noticed it because she lived in the neighborhood, but I don't think I ever met her. Did you know her, Lenore?"

"No," she said. "But what about her, Eddie? Do they think the same person did it?"

"She was also strangled. And she was a Giant fan."

"My God," Dr. Glazer muttered.

"This is terrible," said Lenore. "We're supposed to be living in a safe neighborhood."

"Unfortunately, lunatics can live anywhere," Dr. Glazer said, shaking his head sadly.

He returned to the task of removing the bandage.

"These stitches look all right," he said. "I think we can take them out on Friday."

Eddie suddenly had a thought.

"You were talking about the flu before. Did you happen to make a house call to Dora Farnsworth?"

"Dora Farnsworth," Lenore said. "I just realized, we play Mah-Jongg at her place on Tuesday afternoons and she's sick today."

"Today's Rosh Hashanah," Dr. Glazer gently reminded her.

"Of course it is; what's the matter with me?"

"Did you see her this morning?" Eddie asked him.

"Yes, I did, why?"

"Her husband is my social studies teacher. Do you know him?"

Dr. Glazer nodded.

"Well, let me show you something."

With his good hand, Eddie reached into his back pocket and extracted his wallet. He'd had to do a lot of convincing yesterday, but he finally got Lionel to give him the four pieces of the baseball card. Now, he took them out and put them on the table, arranged in the proper way.

"This is what Mr. Farnsworth did to my friend's baseball card."

"My goodness," said Lenore.

Dr. Glazer let out a low whistle.

"Bruce Farnsworth did this?" he said. "I'm surprised."

He put a fresh gauze pad on Eddie's palm and was beginning to tape up his hand when he paused. He looked back again at the slashed, smiling face of Spider Jorgensen on the baseball card.

"You know, he was in here last week for his physical, and his blood pressure was very high, much higher than usual. I took it a couple of times and it wouldn't go down."

"What does that mean?" Eddie asked.

"Sometimes it's a sign of stress. Although he said everything was fine when I asked."

"When was he here? What day of the week?"

"I'm not sure, but would you check our appointment book, Lenore? This is interesting."

"Give me a second." She stepped out of the room and over to her desk.

"It was Wednesday afternoon," she said, coming back.

"Sandra was killed the night before," Eddie told them.

There was silence in the room. Then Lenore gave a nervous laugh.

"Aren't we going a little overboard here?"

"Maybe," Eddie said. "But is it okay if I tell Nick DiFazio about it? He's my Little League coach, but he's also the detective in charge of the case."

Dr. Glazer didn't look so sure. "Technically, we're not supposed to be talking about our patients. I really shouldn't have said anything." He thought about it another moment, then seemed to decide.

"Go ahead, tell him. I don't suppose it'll do any harm."

He wrapped the last piece of tape around Eddie's hand.

"There you go. Keep that hand out of trouble and I'll see you Friday."

***

As he walked in the door, Eddie saw Nick standing in the kitchen along with a tall, redheaded man who was leaning against the sink. His mother was sitting at the table.

"Hi, Eddie," Nick said. "I want ya to meet my partner, Detective Joe Flannery. Joe, this is Barry's son, Eddie."

"How're ya doin'?" Joe said, giving him a smile. "I hear you're a real slick shortstop."

"I'm okay," Eddie said warily.

He looked over at Julia, wondering what they'd told her. She seemed calm enough.

"Nick says they're going to find your dad," she said, a small note of optimism in her voice.

"I was just explainin' to your mom," Nick put in before Eddie could say anything, "that on missing persons cases, if it's an adult male, we usually don't take action for forty-eight hours. But I managed to pull a few strings, and we're gonna start lookin' for your dad as of right now. How about that?"

"That's great," Eddie said, hoping it sounded like he meant it.

"Why don't you sit down?" Joe said, moving away from the sink and pulling a chair from the table. "I hear you and your dad are real big Dodger fans. Your mom says you were at the game in Philly on Sunday. I'm a huge Dodger fan myself, so I'm jealous. That must'a really been somethin', huh?"

"He caught Jackie Robinson's home run," Julia said.

"What?" Joe said. "Go on, is that true?" He turned to Nick, and Nick shrugged.

He turned back to Eddie.

"Do you have it? Where is it?"

"In my room, do you want me to get it?"

"You bet I do," said Joe, suddenly sounding like a big kid.

Eddie stepped down the hall and into his room. The ball was on his desk by the window and as he picked it up, he automatically glanced across at Mary's window.

He'd just missed her at lunch time because he took a longer route to the school. When he'd turned down Bay 29th it wasn't to fool the reporters, he didn't even think about them, but to fool Nick. The only problem was, by the time he got to the school it was too late.

Now, as he looked over at Mary's window, not expecting to see her, there she was, looking right at him.

But he couldn't do anything. He was expected back within seconds.

With a look of helplessness he held up the ball, knowing that she wouldn't know what to make of it, and then he stepped back into the kitchen.

"Here it is," he said, giving it to Joe, who handled it like the Hope diamond, turning it delicately with his fingertips.

"I wouldn't have caught it," said Eddie, "except that my dad held me up. It was like we both caught it."

Somehow, he felt the need to say that.

"Were Ben and Lionel goin' for the ball, too?" Nick asked, trying to picture the scene.

"No, just me and my dad. It was so crowded that we couldn't all get seats together. Ben and Lionel were sitting a couple of sections away."

"Ah," said Nick.

"What does he mean by 'Don't lose sight of what matters'?" asked Joe, looking at the writing on the ball.

"I guess it's that there are more important things in life than your team winning. It was crazy in front of that clubhouse door, kids mobbing him. He was terrific, though. He thanked everybody for being there, said it was a great feeling to come into another team's park and have it filled with Dodger fans."

"Now you're really makin' me jealous," Joe said, giving him back the ball. "Your dad must'a been very happy for you."

"Sure."

"But how was he before that? Did he seem unhappy? He'd just lost his job on Friday; did he say anything to you about it during the game?"

"No, we mainly just talked about the game."

"It couldn't'a been much fun talkin' about it early on," Nick said. "Your dad must'a been pretty mad when they were down by five runs."

"I guess he was, but we all were."

"So what did he say to you then?"

"Nothing. We just kind of sat there."

"Keepin' score," said Nick.

Eddie felt his stomach lurch.

"That's right," he said, trying to hold his voice steady.

"Him and his dad are fanatics about keepin' score," Nick told Joe. "Eddie makes up special scorecards on notepaper before they go to games, right Eddie?"

"Usually."

He knew where this was heading, and he didn't know what to do when it got there.

"No kiddin'?" said Joe. "Boy, that turned out to be some special scorecard, huh? Where is it; can I see it, Eddie?"

"I don't have it," he said.

"What?" Nick said. "Why not?"

"Because my dad has it."

Nick gave him an appraising look.

"Your dad had his own scorecard at the game, right? Where's yours?"

He needed time to think, to come up with something, but he had no time.

"I only made one of them, so I let my dad use it and I bought one for myself."

"That's unusual, ain't it?" said Nick. "Why'd you only make one?"

"I wanted to get a scorecard at Shibe Park, for a souvenir," he ad libbed.

"So where's that one?" Joe asked.

"I lost it."

Now they both were giving him appraising looks. So, for that matter, was his mother.

"How'd you happen to lose it?" Nick asked.

It all flashed through his mind, the struggle under the seats, the feeling of Barry's hands around his throat.

"I don't know," Eddie managed, stumbling. "It got kind of confusing there at the end of the game. I think I dropped it somewhere while we were going down to the Dodger clubhouse."

They looked at him for another long moment.

"That's too bad," Nick said. "You would'a wanted to save that scorecard for the rest of your life, wouldn't ya?"

"I guess so."

"You guess so?"

"I mean, yeah, I would."

There was another moment of silence, and then Joe said, "Eddie, I want you to think back, now. You and your dad were sittin' together for a long time. You must'a talked about somethin' besides the game."

"Let me try and remember," he said, trying to come up with something, anything. "We talked about how I was doing in school. He mentioned something about Mom wanting a new dress and that maybe he'd surprise her by buying it for her." This got a raised eyebrow from Julia. "I don't know; we mainly watched the game."

Yet another moment, and then Nick and Joe exchanged glances.

"Okay, Eddie, thanks. That's fine for now," Nick said. "Let's get things started."

He moved toward the door.

"Julia, you take care, and if Barry calls, you got my number at the precinct. They'll track me down wherever I am."

"It was nice meetin' ya both," said Joe. "We're gonna find your dad, Eddie, don't worry. And it's gonna be life or death today, right?"

"What?"

For a horrible instant, he saw his father dying in a hail of police bullets.

"The game. We've gotta win or there's no tomorrow, so root hard. I guess you'll catch the end of it when you get home from school."

"Oh, yeah, I will."

Astoundingly, he hadn't even thought about the game today.

"Why don't you stay home this afternoon?" Julia said suddenly, as Eddie looked at her in surprise. "They don't accomplish much at school during the Jewish holiday, do they? I'm going nuts here by myself. Let's watch the game together."

"Wow, okay. Great!"

What was he planning this afternoon? Nothing, as far as he knew. Everything he could do was done. All kinds of forces were in motion and, if it worked out right, either Mary or Beauregard, or both of them, would give him the final piece he needed to make the case to Nick. Then they could arrest Farnsworth, and his dad would read about it in the papers and come home.

"So you get to watch the whole game, huh?" Joe said. "Now I'm really jealous."

He smiled again, as he and Nick stepped out the door.

Eddie looked at his watch and saw that it was almost five of one. Mary would be leaving for school any minute.

"Let me put this ball away," he said to his mother, quickly stepping back into his room.

Miraculously, she was there. She must have kept coming back and looking for him after that confusing moment, for which his heart soared.

She saw him now and nodded. Then she began to write something in her loose leaf book. This was going to be it, the name he'd been waiting for: Dora Farnsworth. He held his breath as she held it up.

I'm trying. You don't know how hard it is.

***

"That's a kid with a lot on his mind," Joe said, as he and Nick walked along Bay Parkway, heading back toward Al's, "and he don't want us to know what it is."

"I'm goin' back there later," said Nick. "If I can get him alone without his mother around, maybe he'll open up."

"What was all that stuff about losin' the scorecard? He wasn't fakin' that they were at the game, was he?" Joe asked, and then answered his own question.

"No, that ball was for real. I'd know Jackie Robinson's autograph anywhere, and if he'd'a gotten it before Sunday his mother would have to be in on the lie, which don't figure. So what's the deal?"

"The deal is there's somethin' out of place. Normally, when he and Barry come home from a game they've got two perfect scorecards of it, and I'm talkin' perfect. Everything down to the number of putouts and assists. And a game like that one...he wouldn't'a just lost his scorecard. And if he did, he'd be a lot more upset about it.

"No, somethin' happened, somethin' important enough to make them stop keepin' score. Or, if he did lose it, he lost it in a way he don't wanna tell us."

They were now turning the corner and approaching the crime scene. The barricades were still up and would stay that way for at least another

24 hours. When the Forensics team was finished with their work the store would be sealed.

They took a quick look around the interior.

"Things seem to be under control here," Nick decided, "don't ya think?"

"Yeah," Joe replied dourly. "Time to start ringin' doorbells to see if anyone saw anything last night, and start spreadin' your friend's picture around the bars and liquor stores."

"And the newspapers. If he was lookin' for a new job yesterday, that's where he'd go."

"Yeah, them too. I'm gonna miss the whole fuckin' game."

"Relax. Maybe you'll wanna miss it," Nick couldn't help saying.

"Don't start, all right? When are ya goin' back there for round two with the kid?"

"I'll wait 'til the game's over. It'll be easier to get him alone after that."

"Good. Maybe he'll tell ya where his old man is and save us a lot'a trouble," Joe said. "But even if he don't, he sure knows something."

Yes, he does, Nick thought. He just hoped it didn't include Saint-Laurent.

***

Dodger rookie right-hander Clem Labine had not only been relegated to Charlie Dressen's doghouse, he'd been sent to the back of it. It was ironic that he was pitching the most important game of the year only because no one else was left.

He was a rookie who was also a veteran, a veteran of World War II. He'd made 24 parachute jumps before the age of 20, and any nervousness about today's game paled in comparison to what he'd felt before every single one of them.

In July, he'd been called up to the Dodgers from St. Paul and been brilliant, winning his first four games in dominating fashion. It only took one loss, however, to land him in Dressen's pound.

On September 21st, he was facing the Phillies at Ebbets Field. They'd loaded the bases on him in the first inning, and Puddin'head Jones was at the plate. Dressen signaled from the dugout that he wanted him to work from a full windup, but Clem knew he felt more comfortable working from a stretch position. He ignored the sign, went into his stretch, and delivered to Jones, who promptly planted one in the left-field seats for a grand slam.

It will be forever unknown whether the same home run would have resulted from a full windup, but that moment of insubordination cost the Dodgers dearly. Had Dressen not lost faith in Labine because of it, he would have used him in the rotation during the final ten days, giving some needed rest to the tired arms of Newcombe, Erskine, and Roe.

But what was done was done, and now, Clem Labine stood on the Polo Grounds mound in the third inning of a pressure cooker, finding himself not in managerial trouble, but in good old-fashioned baseball trouble.

He'd been given a 2-0 lead before he even left the dugout, on a first-inning single by Reese and a line shot by Robinson into the lower left-field stands, that just cleared the wall at the 315-foot sign.

He'd made the lead stand up for two innings, but the third wasn't going very well. Stanky's leadoff ground ball had taken a bad hop on Pee Wee for an error, to put a man on first. Pee Wee made up for it on the next play, with a lunging, backhand stop of Dark's sharp grounder in the hole, forcing Stanky at second by an eyelash. But Mueller got a bloop single, and, after Irvin popped up for the second out, Whitey Lockman worked out a walk to fill the bases.

It was the first bases-loaded jam Clem had faced since the infamous pitch to Jones two weeks before. The batter this time was Bobby Thomson.

Thomson, who'd moved from center field to third base earlier in the year to accomodate the arrival of Willie Mays, had been the Giants' hottest hitter during the second half, and the playoffs hadn't cooled him off one iota.

Yesterday, he'd hit what proved to be the game-winning home run, and Clem could easily recall a ringing double Thomson had smacked off of him, since it happened only last inning.

Working carefully, not giving him anything good to hit, Clem found himself maneuvered into his present situation, a full count.

Some games are decided in the bottom of the ninth inning. This one, as it turned out, would be decided on the next pitch.

He stared in at Rube Walker for the sign. Walker had been his catcher when he gave up Jones's home run, as Campy was being rested that day. He was in back of the plate again now, this time because of Campy's injured thigh, and he was flashing the sequence of signs for a curve ball.

It so happened Clem had a dandy curve. As a kid in Woonsocket, Rhode Island, he'd broken the index finger on his throwing hand and it had never healed properly, leaving the finger with an unnatural bend at the first knuckle that enabled him to put a wicked spin on the ball.

He reached back now and uncorked a beauty, a big, sweeping rainbow that broke down and away, out of the strike zone but fooling Thomson, who flailed at it for strike three.

And did Clem Labine deliver that pitch from a full windup? You bet he did.

***

"Yes!" Julia cried out from the couch as she watched Thomson swing and miss. "Your ball is really working, Sport."

"Don't jinx it," Eddie said, cutting a nervous glance at the Jackie Robinson ball sitting on top of the TV set. He'd placed it there in the first inning, just as Robby was coming to the plate. The home run had followed on the next pitch.

"I didn't mean that!" Julia said loudly, cupping her hands around her mouth and tilting her head toward the ceiling. "Don't pay any attention to me!"

She could never understand all the superstition in baseball. At the end of last inning, for instance, Russ Hodges had pointed out Bobby Thomson leaving his glove on the ground near third base and Durocher, on his way to the coaching box, picking it up, tapping it three times, kicking third base and then tossing the glove into the coaching box, as he'd done after every inning for weeks.

Amazing, Julia thought. *But it didn't do them any good this time, did it? Maybe Eddie's baseball is more powerful than Thomson's glove.*

She suddenly felt guilty about making fun of him.

"I'm sorry, honey," she said, looking over at Eddie as he sat in his father's chair, the size of it making him look even more diminutive. "I know you and your dad are superstitious. He doesn't believe in God, but he definitely believes in jinxes."

"Why doesn't he believe in God?"

He'd never quite gotten an answer to that from his father. Anytime he'd asked, he'd get some variation of "You either do or you don't."

"He was never very religious," Julia said. "We only went to synagogue on the High Holy Days because everyone else did. But after he came back from the war, he insisted that we not go. He once said that believing you've got a personal relationship with the creator of the universe was the height of all arrogance, and more people were killed because of religion than for anything else."

Like for being a Giant fan, Eddie couldn't help thinking.

"Do you believe in God?" he asked her.

Julia stubbed out her Chesterfield in the ashtray and, again, addressed the ceiling.

"I do right now, if it'll help them find your dad."

Eddie said nothing, as, in fact, a Chesterfield commercial played on the TV screen. He didn't know if he believed in God or not. He knew he couldn't believe there was a heaven and a hell just because people said there was. Maybe you died and just became nothing.

And that wouldn't be so bad. You'd never know, so what would it matter? He'd heard people call themselves religious, but he didn't see how they could be so sure of the unknown.

But whether or not he believed in God, he was sure of one thing. Nick would be coming back, and he'd better be ready for him.

It was embarrassing how he'd botched that part about losing his scorecard. Nick didn't buy it at all, he knew, and it made him feel like an idiot. Well, he'd have to come up with something.

It was strange, though, how they pretended they were looking for his dad as a missing person, instead of a suspect. Maybe that's how cops worked; the less people know about what they're doing the better.

In any case, he had an idea.

"Mom, did you know that Mr. Beauregard upstairs is Mr. Farnsworth's father-in-law?"

"No kidding," she said, as, on the screen, Billy Cox stepped in to lead off for the Dodgers in the top of the fourth.

"Dora Farnsworth does have a southern accent like his," she mused, and then leaned toward him in interest. "How did you find it out?"

"When I was selling raffle tickets on Thursday," he said, making it the day she knew he was selling tickets, not this morning, never this morning, "I was working my way down Bay 31st and I noticed one of the doorbells said 'Farnsworth.' So I rang it, and Mr. Beauregard came to the door."

"That's really something."

"You never told me you knew Mrs. Farnsworth."

"I haven't seen her in a while," Julia said and gave a grim chuckle. "She works in a hat shop and you don't notice me buying many hats lately. Which reminds me, what was all that about your father buying me a dress?"

Oh, crap.

"I don't know; it was just something he said." *When he was lying to me about that big wad of bills in his pocket,* he remembered, and pushed it aside. "He never told you?"

"No, and I have no idea what dress he might have been talking about."

"Neither do I." He gave a shrug, hoping that would end it. "It was interesting to see where Mr. Farnsworth lived. I guess kids are always curious about their teachers."

"They are that," Julia said. "I know my fourth graders always ask a lot of questions."

"Do you tell them about me?"

"I never tell them anything."

Eddie nodded. "I wonder if Mr. and Mrs. Farnsworth have any kids," he said. "Do you know?"

"They don't," she said with a finality that sounded a little too final. Or was he imagining it?

If they were the parents in the story, she'd want to keep it a secret and say they had no kids. If he was going to get anywhere, he'd have to take a chance.

"Really?" he said. "I thought I heard Mr. Beauregard say something about seeing his grandson in the hospital, but maybe he was talking about something else."

She looked at him skeptically. "You did, huh?"

"Yeah, but, like I said, I could be wrong."

Was his face reddening? It was always so hard to fool her; it was like she had radar or something.

He looked away, at the screen where Clem Labine, a batter this time, had just popped one up into the spacious foul territory off first base. Lockman was taking care of it for the third out.

He looked back at his mother who was still measuring him with her gaze.

"This is about that story I told Mary DiFazio, isn't it?" she said. "You're trying to find out who it's about."

"No, I'm not..." he said in confusion. "What story?"

Julia laughed. "Forget it, Sport."

Tell her, he thought. *Just tell her everything right now and you'll get the answer.*

But no, he didn't have to. He only had to wait a little longer, that's all, just a couple more hours until he spoke to Beauregard. And if Nick came by before that, he'd try to get him up to Beauregard's with him. He didn't have to tell her.

So he didn't, and as they watched the game, with the Dodgers scoring another run in the fifth, and then seven more as it went on, Labine now unhittable, he was more and more sure he'd made the right decision.

Because of that decision, someone else would soon find out what does, in fact, happen after you die.

***

Mary peeked into the living room at Carmine sitting on the floor watching the TV screen. His back was to her, but she knew how furious he was by the low, animal sounds he was making, and the way his fingers were clawing at the carpet. She hoped he'd pull out a chunk of it and get in even more trouble.

Before he could sense she was there, she pulled back from the doorway and moved down the hall. Halfway to the kitchen she had to stop, as it hit her again that Al Schaefer was really dead.

It was incredible to believe. On her way back to school, she'd seen the cops in front of his store. Her father wasn't there, but the people milling around told her what happened. Feeling sick to her stomach, she went on to school, where it was all they could talk about.

Cathy Cangelossi claimed she saw them carrying out the body, said his eyes were staring right at her. Mary knew she was full of it because they covered bodies over before they carried them out, but she couldn't bring herself to say anything. She was too much in shock.

Then, as they were walking home from school with Teresa, there was that thing Carmine whispered in her ear.

"What?!" Mary said, astounded.

"I didn't say nothin'."

"Yes, you did. You said, 'Barry Fein strikes again!' What's that supposed to mean?"

"Whatever ya think it means," he said with that stupid grin of his.

Teresa, walking behind them, gave him a shove in the back.

"You shut up!" she said, surprising Mary.

Carmine just kept on smirking.

Now, she resumed her progress toward the kitchen where Teresa was making up a grocery list for her, reflexively thinking how unfair it was that her brother should be let out of his room to watch the game. It meant her mother couldn't leave the apartment, and that meant she had to do all the shopping.

She thought of Eddie. From out of nowhere, he came into to her mind, as he seemed to lately. After she'd kissed him, as she was running home, she couldn't believe what she'd done. But his face was so beautiful at that moment, and then, when he looked away like he was about to cry, she couldn't help herself. He was the first boy she'd ever kissed.

It was funny, but as smart and caring as Eddie was, it wouldn't be the same if he were older. His little-boy quality was what she loved about him.

Was that crazy? She had no idea, but she knew older boys repelled her. They might not be as cruel and horrible, but they were too much like her brother.

Her mind recoiled from the thought, and moved to Eddie's father. She tried to imagine him with his hands around Al's throat, and found she could actually do it.

Barry Fein was someone she'd never really been comfortable with. He wasn't all there. It was like part of him was somewhere else, thinking about something that was much more interesting than she was. She could count on one hand the number of times he'd actually spoken more than five words to her.

But Eddie believed in him, and so she was going to do everything in her power to help. She was going to get that woman's name from her mother if it was the last thing she ever did.

And it might be. It was amazing how frustratingly hard it was to find even the tiniest opportunity. Last night, after she'd tried to bring it up and her mother disappeared into the bedroom, her father had come home, so that was that. From then on, there had been no more chances.

This morning the whole family was sitting there at breakfast; at lunch Carmine was around; and this afternoon, when she was counting on him being locked up, he wasn't.

But now, finally, with the stupid jerk in the living room wrapped up in his ballgame and her mother alone in the kitchen, she had her shot.

Teresa was staring into the cupboard, getting more and more angry as she searched for the goddamn jar of mayonnaise. She was sure she had one in there, why wasn't she seeing it? Everything, absolutely everything in her life, was conspiring to make her miserable.

Since Thursday morning, when Nick dropped that bombshell on her about Barry and then clammed up, getting him to tell her anything was like squeezing a rock. Suddenly, this man who was so open, who even talked with her about his cases, for God's sake, didn't trust her anymore.

She had to practically beg him to tell her what his fight with Carmine was about, and if he didn't want to talk about that, she could just imagine how he felt about Barry. No, she couldn't; that was the trouble.

It was really two separate friendships, hers with Julia and Nick's with Barry.

In the early days, when the kids were very little, it wasn't that way. They all saw a lot of each other, Julia or Teresa often making dinner for everyone. On summer evenings, they'd take their beach chairs down to the street and sit in the gathering dusk, talking while the neighborhood kids played stick ball, ducking the occasional Spaldeen that bounced their way.

Then the war came, the men were gone, and Carmine started to have what she called "his problems." It became clear that he had a lot of trouble getting along with other kids, and especially with Eddie. Just when she and

Julia needed each other's companionship the most, they found themselves cut off, reduced to talking on the phone for the most part, because they couldn't bring their kids together.

Teresa still recalled with shame and horror the day they tried to take them to Coney Island. They were standing, waiting their turn at the carousel as it moved by them, gathering speed, when Mary dropped her ice cream cone.

In that one second of distraction, Carmine had Eddie on the ground and came this close to pushing him under the carousel. That was the end of outings with the children.

The memory of it tore at her now.

What's going to happen to him? she thought, almost overcome with helplessness and grief. She prayed for him all the time, even if Nick didn't, and she truly believed he was a good person. It was hard for him to show it, but he was trying, wasn't he? Look how he accepted his punishment, not a word of protest.

And yesterday in school he was a genuine hero. Not according to Nick, but she knew better. Her heart would always go out to him. That's why she was letting him watch his game today, despite the wisecrack he made on the way home from school. She could have killed him for that.

And what about that wisecrack; was it true? She knew Barry hadn't come home last night because she'd just gotten off the phone with Julia, who was a nervous wreck. That's how she found out Nick had been over there and was now looking for him.

She'd almost said something about Al Schaefer, but stopped herself. Julia obviously didn't know, and Nick obviously hadn't told her. Their phone conversation was brief because Julia didn't want to tie up the line in case Barry called, and Teresa found herself relieved to be hanging up.

Now there was more guilt, added onto what she already felt. This was crazy. There had to be some other explanation for why Barry was missing. He might also have "his problems," but she couldn't imagine him murdering people.

But just because she couldn't imagine it didn't mean it couldn't be. She'd been married to a homicide detective long enough to know that killers are very often people their friends don't suspect.

But Nick did suspect him, and right away too. And he was not only Barry's friend, he was his best friend.

Oh, Julia. Oh, God, what's going to happen to us?

"Ma?"

It startled her. She turned and glared at her daughter.

"Mary, don't sneak up on me like that."

"What'd I do?" Mary said petulantly, and immediately regretted it. She wanted things to be relaxed, so they could talk.

"I'm sorry, Ma," she said, softening her tone. "You got the shopping list for me?"

"I had some mayonnaise in here," Teresa complained, turning back to stare into the cupboard, "but I can't find it."

Mary looked past her and instantly saw it, sitting right behind a can of peas.

"Here it is," she said brightly, moving the can aside.

Teresa covered her face in her hands and began to sob.

"I'm losin' my mind," she groaned.

"No, you're not, Ma," Mary said anxiously. She was used to Teresa's emotional outbursts, but there was something extra to it this time that made her nervous. "You ain't losin' your mind; c'mon, Ma."

She knew she should comfort her, put her arms around her, but she was afraid to. For all she knew, hugging her mother would make her cry more.

"You want some coffee?" she tried. "I know how to make it."

With a deep sigh, Teresa took her hands from her face and looked at Mary, her eyes filled with desperation.

"Why can't people just be nice to each other?" she implored. "Why is there so much anger and hate in the world?"

She searched Mary's face as if she had the answer.

Mary felt her own tears well up as she was reminded of Al Schaefer.

This is no good, she thought. She had to get a hold of herself. She had to find out that woman's name.

"You know," she said, "we were talkin' about anger and hate in the world today at school, in Current Events."

She could usually get to her mother, or any adult, with something about school.

"Yeah?" Teresa said, only half interested.

"Did you know that, with all the soldiers dying in Korea last year, more people died at home from accidents?"

She had no idea if this was true, but it sounded like it could be.

"I think I heard that somewhere," Teresa said, never wanting to seem ignorant to her daughter.

"Can you imagine," Mary said, "being safer in the Korean war than your own home? My friend Donna told me this story one time, about a two-year-old kid? His father was supposed to watch him, and…"

In the living room, it was the sixth inning and Carmine was no longer sitting on the floor. He was up on his feet, moving about the room, stalking back and forth between his old man's chair and the wing chair in the corner.

Each time he reached one of them, he'd stop and drive his fist into it, as the fucking Dodgers took batting practice against his Giants.

Punching the furniture was something he did if he found himself alone in the living room and the Giants were losing. So far, the chairs hadn't popped any stuffing, and no one had caught him at it because he was quiet.

Just a short, sharp right hook to the cushion. Sometimes, he imagined his old man sitting there. This time, it was Eddie Fein.

He'd gone into school this morning expecting to be treated like royalty. Last night, he couldn't sleep, fantasizing about how they'd practically fall on their knees and give him blow jobs for what he did yesterday.

But everything was as crappy as ever. Kids still stayed away from him, like they always did. The only difference was, before, they were too chickenshit to look him in the eye, and now they were too chickenshit to thank him. Well, fuck 'em all.

Fartsworth, at least, showed some change in attitude, but only a little. He called him by his first name, instead of DiFazio, and when Carmine suggested they listen to the game on the Giants' radio station, he agreed, which made it easier to take when they fell behind two-nothing just like that.

He wasn't bothered because he was sure they'd get to Labine. This was just a rookie, after all, the last pitcher the Dodgers had, and the Giants kept getting men on base against him.

Then, Thomson struck out to end the third and Carmine got so pissed, he slammed his notebook down on the desk.

Even at that, Fartsworth just smiled and said, "Take it easy, Carmine." Like they were supposed to be pals.

Then there was the Al Schaefer thing. Speaking of chickenshit, that would be his old man, for not having the balls to arrest Barry Fein right away. And now someone else was dead because of it.

Not that it was any great loss. Carmine never liked Al Schaefer, even if he was a Giant fan. He was a son of a bitch, who used to yell at him for hanging around the magazine rack and stealing comic books. Why should he care about Al Schaefer?

What he really cared about was that his old man, who couldn't even arrest Barry Fein, was a big-shot cop, while he, Carmine, a hero, was treated like dog shit. Like fucking dog shit!

At that moment, Duke Snider ripped a single into right field, scoring Rube Walker and putting the Giants down six to nothing.

A cry of rage welled up inside him. He strode across the room to the wing chair and unloaded one that came all the way from his shoe tops.

It slammed the chair against the wall, one leg catching under the edge of the carpet and breaking. The chair collapsed sideways, onto the table next to it, sending a large crystal lamp crashing to the floor.

In the kitchen, Teresa was paying rapt attention as Mary finished the story.

"I don't know how your friend Donna could'a known," she said, "but what you're tellin' me is just like..."

The sound of something shattering came from the living room.

"Oh, dear Jesus!" Teresa cried out, bolting from the kitchen.

Mary stared for a moment at where she'd been, and then hurried down the hallway after her.

"No, no, no!" her mother was wailing as she stood in the living room doorway. "My beautiful Tiffany lamp!"

Carmine was standing defiantly over the wreckage.

"Lock me up!" he screamed at her. "You think you can punish me?"

He took a menacing step toward her.

Mary, seeing it happening over Teresa's shoulder, began to back down the hallway.

Teresa just stood there, wide eyed.

"Go on, lock me up!" he shouted, still coming forward.

Mary was amazed at how much bigger he looked, how he seemed to loom over their mother. In a lifetime of being afraid of him, she couldn't remember being more scared than now.

She backed further down the hall, as Teresa finally found her voice.

"That lamp was a wedding gift from my mother!" she hollered in Carmine's face. "I let you watch your goddamn game, and this is what you do to me?"

"Blame the fucking Dodgers," he said, shoving her aside.

She gaped at him, speechless, not only at the shove but the obscenity, as Carmine strode down the hallway toward Mary, who turned and ran into the kitchen.

She pulled open the knife drawer, whimpering, and grabbed the biggest one she could find. She looked back toward the doorway.

He wasn't there.

Slowly, she moved across the kitchen and looked down the hall.

Carmine had stopped at his room. He had one hand on the doorknob and was looking back toward Teresa.

"Go ahead, tell the old man!" he taunted her. "He ain't gonna do nothin' neither. You people are gonna learn about me."

Then he turned toward Mary and his eyes fell on the knife in her hand.

He smiled. It was the most evil, cold blooded smile she ever saw. It shook her so much, she almost dropped the knife.

"Don't play with toys ya don't know how to use, sis," he said. "You're lucky I don't take it away and then give it back special delivery."

He shoved open the door to his room.

"And tell your twerpy little friend that after tomorrow, he's gonna be a Giant fan forever."

With a meaningful look that meant nothing to her, he stepped into his room and slammed the door so hard the hallway shook.

Teresa immediately hurried over, fumbling the key out of her housecoat pocket, and locked the door behind him.

As she did, Carmine banged on the inside of it for good measure, making her jump.

Mary tried to breathe normally, as she walked back into the kitchen on wobbly legs and returned the knife to its drawer.

"Why did he go back in his room?" she asked Teresa, who seemed drained of emotion. "Why didn't he run away again?"

"I don't know," Teresa said in a monotone. "Get a broom and help me clean up the living room."

As she was pulling the broom out of the closet, Mary knew she had to give it one more try.

"You were startin' to say somethin' before, Ma, weren't you? About that story?"

Teresa was getting the dust pan from under the sink. She stood and faced Mary, fury in her eyes.

"After what just happened?" she said in a thick, tight voice. "You want me to tell you about *babies electrocuting themselves?!*"

"I…"

Teresa slapped her across the face. The sting of it was nothing compared to the utter shock.

"You're just like your brother!" Teresa spat out at her. "You got no feelings inside you at all!"

Tears were streaming down Mary's cheeks.

"Ma, I never meant…"

"Clean up the living room yourself!" Teresa ordered, shoving the dust pan into Mary's hands. "And don't you ever, ever, EVER! say another word to me about that disgusting story."

She stomped out of the kitchen.

***

At exactly ten after six, Eddie bounded up the steps toward Beauregard's place, feeling like a kid on Christmas morning. He'd already gotten one gift, unexpectedly, from his mother. She'd provided him with an excuse to get out of the apartment.

All afternoon, amidst the joys of watching the Dodgers clobber the Giants, he'd tried to figure out how to do it, but as six o'clock approached, he was drawing one blank after another. There it was, the final connection he needed, waiting for him only one floor above, and he was stuck. Then, from out of nowhere, Tropicana orange juice came to the rescue.

It was a brand new product, in the grocery stores for the first time just a couple of weeks ago. Orange juice in a cardboard container that was practically as good as fresh-squeezed and far better than the frozen stuff. It was so appealing to Julia that she became almost addicted to it. She had to have it first thing every morning.

As they were about to sit down to dinner, she reached into the refrigerator for the ketchup and, to Eddie's delightful surprise, realized they were almost out of Tropicana. And the store was closing at six-thirty.

It was just another sign of what a great day this was going to be.

With a bounce in his stride, he reached Beauregard's landing and rang the doorbell.

From the other side came the shuffling sound of slippered feet and then the door opened. Beauregard stood there wearing a maroon silk bathrobe with the initials EBB embroidered over the breast pocket. It looked like one of those bathrobes David Niven or Cary Grant would wear, as they glided about a luxurious penthouse in some movie.

Except, Beauregard's apartment wasn't luxurious. Eddie could see that behind him was a bare room with a bridge chair and a card table, which supported an old radio. And aside from the bathrobe, Beauregard looked nothing like David Niven or Cary Grant. He looked like an angry Burl Ives.

"You connivin' little hooligan," he snarled. "You got some nerve showin' up here."

Eddie was at a total loss for words.

"Huh?" was the sound that came out of his mouth.

"You think I'm a fool? Let me tell you somethin', boy. I came all the way up north to this Godforsaken place, with its uppity n_ggers and Mafia gangsters, for just one reason, to take my daughter home. I don't know what your game is, or who put you up to it, but you ain't gon' stop me, y'hear?"

"But…didn't you ask her about the watch?"

"My advice to you," Beauregard said acidly, "is to keep that nose of yours out of other folks' affairs."

With a final contemptuous glare, Beauregard rendered Eddie once more on the wrong side of a closed door.

CHAPTER TWENTY FOUR

Tuesday Evening, October 2nd

"I'm just gonna talk to ya, okay?"

Nick leveled his gaze at Carmine, who'd jumped up from the bed at the first click of the lock and was now standing in a semi-crouch on the other side of the room. He looked like a catcher waiting for a runner coming in from third.

"Relax," Nick told him. "I'll be calm if you will. We got a deal?"

He's scared, was Carmine's immediate impression.

"Say what you're gonna say," he rasped out.

He liked how it sounded, like an order.

Nick was working very hard to control himself. "Why did you do that to your mother?" he asked in an even tone.

"I didn't do nothin' to her," Carmine said defiantly. "It was just a stupid lamp."

"Why?" Nick asked again, harder.

"Whatta you care?" said Carmine. "Why are you even here? Ain't there a murderer out there you're supposed ta catch?"

Nick laughed, but only to keep down the anger. "I'd be doin' that," he said, "if I didn't have to take care of a little punk who don't know how to live with other humans."

The fatigue was gaining on him. This had been a helluva day, and it wasn't over.

They'd been typically unable to find a witness who saw anyone go into or out of Al's last night, at least so far. When they called the newspapers where Barry might have gone looking for a job, they eventually found Samuel Boyleston, who told them Barry had been in his office yesterday around two o'clock.

They drove over there, and just about the time Boyleston was telling them how the game had been on the TV set and how he'd gotten nervous about Barry's behavior, Nick began to feel tired.

They'd hit the street and showed the picture around the bars near Borough Hall, finally getting an I.D. from a bartender on Fulton Street.

Barry had been there, drinking scotch and watching the game, hadn't said much, hadn't bothered anybody, left when it was over. After that, nothing.

"I'm really tryin' here," Nick said, locking eyes with Carmine, who determinedly stared back. "Are we gonna talk or what?"

Carmine kept the stare, then shrugged and looked away.

"Okay." Nick's tone softened. "It must'a been hard watchin' the Giants lose like that, huh?"

Carmine didn't know why, but tears came to his eyes. He looked fiercely at the floor, before his old man could notice it.

"Yeah, so what?" he said.

"Hey, listen," said Nick, "if you're gonna lose, ya may as well lose by ten runs, right? They got all that hittin' out of their system, and now we got Sal the Barber tomorrow."

Carmine was totally thrown by this change of direction. "Yeah?" he said, trying to figure out what was happening.

"And they got Newcombe goin', who just finished pitching fourteen innings. He ain't gonna have nothin' left."

"And Sal's on his normal three-day rest," Carmine surprised himself by saying.

"That's why Leo was smart not ta start him today."

Carmine thought this was so weird, him and his old man all buddy-buddy like this, jawing about the Giants. For his whole life, it seemed, his old man was off being a soldier, or a cop—or a fuckin' Little League coach. Or else he was home, and pissed off at him.

No, this wasn't real; this was bullshit.

"So what?" he said, finally recovering from the lapse. "You ain't gonna let me watch it."

"I don't know," said Nick. "Depends on how nice you tell your mother you're sorry. And whether we believe it."

Carmine almost grinned. His old man had no idea, none at all.

He didn't need permission to watch the game. Starting tomorrow, he wouldn't need anyone's permission to do anything ever.

"Sure," he said, with an equitable smile, "I'll tell her I'm sorry."

Nick scrutinized him a moment.

"You're bullshittin' me."

Carmine shrugged, smile still in place.

"Okay, I won't tell her, and I won't watch the game either. Who cares?"

Nick didn't need this, any of it. Six years ago, he'd come home to discover the baby boy he left behind was now an eight-year-old brat. Teresa said it was because he missed him and he needed a father. Nick sensed it was more than that, but he tried, God knows he tried.

He got Carmine involved in the Little Leagues. The kid played pretty good, but could not stop getting into fights, even with his own teammates. After a while, it was hard to find a team that would take him.

Of course, Nick himself did the final honors after he saw Carmine punching that poor kid at the end of the game.

As for taking him up to the Polo Grounds to watch the Giants, it was like he'd told Teresa. Whether Carmine was eight-years-old or thirteen, he'd be screaming at the top of his lungs if things didn't go right. Sometimes he tried to throw stuff on the field. Half the time, Nick wound up taking him home by the seventh inning.

Tonight, he was only gonna grab a quick bite before he went over to the Feins', and Teresa greeted him at the door in hysterics.

She shouldn't have let the kid out of his room in the first place, was his opinion, but he kept it to himself. They could always get the chair fixed, and Nick secretly never liked that lamp anyway. It looked like it belonged in a French whore house. He had so many other things to take care of.

"I don't got time for this," he told Carmine. "You just stay here and work on bein' sorry."

It got yet another shrug.

Disgustedly, Nick shook his head, stepped out, and locked the door behind him.

There was a moment there, he thought, *when we were almost a normal father and son.*

He didn't know what caused it, or why it didn't last, but it filled him with an unbearable sense of loss. Not every kid whose father was in the war turned out like this. Barry, with all his demons, was the lucky one.

Inside the room, Carmine threw himself onto the bed and buried his face in the pillow so they wouldn't hear him laughing. In all his fantasies about what he'd do to Eddie Fein tomorrow, the game was never a part of it, because no one knew there'd be one until the series got evened up today.

Eddie Fein probably thought he'd be coming home from school to see the end of it, but he didn't know he'd have company.

Actually, he wasn't going to watch very much, what with Carmine sitting on top of him and the knife up against his adam's apple.

And he wasn't going to root very loud for the Dodgers, or scream for help either, because of the handkerchief stuffed in his mouth.

Then, as Carmine lovingly imagined it, just as the Giants were winning the pennant, Eddie would get his farewell gift, the interlocking NY.

He'd been practicing on pieces of paper, holding the pen the way he would a knife, and he'd gotten real good at it now. He could whip one off in under five seconds.

Still, just to make sure the little creep wouldn't move his head and spoil it, he'd grab Eddie by the hair. Then he'd carve a permanent New York Giant symbol into his pathetic, ugly face.

***

On Channel 5, Al Hodge as Captain Video was explaining his new atomic rifle to Don Hastings, the Video Ranger, as Eddie fidgeted on the couch.

He'd been sent there by his mother and Nick, who'd arrived and said he wanted to talk to her privately in the kitchen. They'd been talking for ten minutes now. He had no idea what they were saying, just as he had no idea why Beauregard shut the door in his face.

It still didn't mean he was wrong. He tried to picture any of the thousands of things that could've happened this afternoon.

What if Dora Farnsworth denied it, got angry, even kicked Beauregard out? So what? All it could mean was she didn't notice the watch was missing, or she knew it was but Farnsworth had made up an excuse about it, or else she just didn't like her father butting in.

There were lots of ways he could still be right, and he had to hang onto that. It would be nice, though, if just for once he could actually know something.

He wished he could go to his room and look for Mary, but it was way too risky, not with Nick right there in the kitchen. Why was she having problems finding out the woman's name? All she had to do was tell her mother the story, so why was that so hard? He felt like he was swimming in a sea of molasses.

("Holy Hyperion, Captain Video!") exclaimed the Ranger. ("That's some weapon!")

"The minute I found out he lost his job," Julia said to Nick in a low, anxious voice, "I knew it was going to be different this time."

"Well, we know he was out there lookin' for one yesterday. Maybe he's got it in his head that he doesn't wanna call ya 'til he finds a new job."

She gave him a wan smile.

"That's what Eddie said. I thought it was cute how naive he was."

"So I guess I'm naive," Nick said, shrugging. "Nobody ever accused me of bein' cute."

He'd been having thoughts that Barry might kill himself. It occurred to him now. If there wasn't a note...

God, his instinct for survival disgusted him sometimes.

"Can I ask ya a favor?" he said. "Would it be okay if I talked to Eddie alone?"

He expected her to ask why, be suspicious, but she wasn't at all.

"Yes, you should do that. Maybe he'll talk to you. How should we work it; should I go into the bedroom?"

The eagerness in her voice made him feel even more rotten.

"Nah, let me take him outside for a while."

"Okay, good," she said.

He moved over to the living room door and opened it. Eddie looked up anxiously from the couch.

"C'mon, kid, let's get some air," Nick said. "It's your last chance to give it to me about the Giants before we beat your brains in tomorrow."

***

Eddie didn't even wait until they were out of the building.

"I think I know who did it," he said urgently, as he walked down the stairs ahead of Nick, looking back up at him and stumbling down the next two steps.

"Jeez," Nick said, reaching out and grabbing his arm, "take it easy."

"No, no, I really do," Eddie said, regaining his balance.

"Wait 'til we get downstairs, okay? I don't want ya to accidentally trip and get knocked out before you can tell me."

"I'm not kidding."

"I know," Nick said soothingly, "let's just wait 'til we get outside."

They walked slowly up Bay Parkway in the direction of 86th Street. Nick listened as Eddie told him what he'd learned over the last two days, leaving out the parts that involved Mary.

He started with the "erudite man," and, for a moment, had a vague sense, a tickling in the back of his mind, that Faber had said something that wasn't right, that didn't add up.

But it was only a feeling, and he couldn't connect it with anything.

He went on, telling Nick why Farnsworth could have been that man, about his snooty way of talking, how he normally passed by the sporting goods store on his way home, how, in fact, he wasn't home during the time Sandra was talking to the man in the store.

He told him about Beauregard, said he'd bet that if Nick talked to him he'd tell him what Dora Farnsworth said about the watch. Or, better yet, Nick could talk to Dora Farnsworth.

He paused and looked up for a reaction.

"That it?" Nick said.

"No, no, there's lots more."

He took out his wallet as he moved over to the light of the next lamp post.

"Mr. Farnsworth did this," he said, displaying the pieces of the defaced Spider Jorgensen card. "I showed it to Dr. Glazer and he said that, last Wednesday when he examined him, Mr. Farnsworth's blood pressure was way higher than usual. Last Wednesday was the day after Sandra was killed."

Nick squinted at the card.

"Seems to me," he said, "like evidence of you not liking your teacher."

"No!" Eddie wailed in double frustration, that he wasn't being taken seriously and that he couldn't tell Nick the most important thing.

Without knowing for sure that the other woman in Macy's was Dora Farnsworth, he had nothing. He couldn't even tell Nick about the possibility.

After all, how could he know the killer's watch came from Macy's? Only if he'd seen it in Nick's notebook.

He stood there, tongue-tied.

Nick felt pity for him, followed by another stab of pity for himself. He sighed and put his arm around Eddie's shoulders.

"C'mon," he said gently, as the two of them started walking again. "I know I told ya to stay out of this, but I understand why you didn't, and I know it's 'cause you love your dad. That was a good job gettin' the story outta Mr. Faber. And I'm surprised at Dr. Glazer for talkin' about another patient, but that was good detective work too.

"I gotta be honest with you, I ain't convinced about this teacher'a yours, but I promise I'll check into it. But only if you're honest with me. I know you and your dad didn't just sit there at the game and not say anythin' about this. You gotta tell me the truth. Will you do that?"

Eddie nodded. "Okay," he said, "but then you have to tell me what happened at Saint-Laurent."

He pronounced it correctly this time, the way Barry had.

It was as if someone had casually handed Nick a high-voltage wire. He jerked his arm from Eddie's shoulders like it was in spasm.

"Whatta you talkin' about?" he said.

"It's why you suspect my dad, isn't it?"

He hoped he could pull this off. He'd had plenty of time to think about it, to plan what to say to keep Nick from realizing he'd gotten the name from his notebook, and now he launched into the made-up version of events.

"I kept asking him questions and he wouldn't answer me. I asked him why you suspected him and he didn't say anything, so I kept at it. Finally, I guess just to shut me up, he said, 'Because of Saint-Laurent.' But that was it. That was all he'd say."

Nick gave him a hard stare.

"What do you think he meant?"

"I asked him to spell it," Eddie lied, "and then, when we got home, I looked it up in my encyclopedia," which was true. "It's a town in Normandy, so I figure it had something to do with the invasion, and maybe my dad killed someone there. But it was war, wasn't it? Doesn't that make it okay?"

"Good question," Nick said, "and we'll talk about it, I promise ya. But first, let's get back to you and your dad at the game. What did he say when you asked him about Sandra Weinstock?"

"He said he didn't do it!"

It came out louder than he intended.

"He said he didn't do it." Eddie lowered his voice. "He said, 'It wasn't me.'"

Nick's stride stiffened imperceptibly, then was back in rhythm.

"That's what he said: 'It wasn't me'? Those were his exact words?"

"Yeah," Eddie said carefully. He didn't understand the change in mood, but there definitely was one. "He said it a couple of times."

"Not 'I didn't do it,' or anythin' like that? Think careful."

"No, he said, 'It wasn't me.' Why does it matter?"

Another wave of exhaustion washed over Nick. He felt like he could go home and sleep for days.

"'Cause it's important to get the exact words right," he said wearily, as they turned into 86th Street. "Now, tell me what else happened at the game."

Eddie told him most of it, because most of it was harmless. He didn't mention that, for a time, he thought his dad was guilty, or about how his dad accused him of being Nick's spy, and certainly not about the piece of paper and that moment under the seats.

He again described catching the home run ball and said he couldn't have done it if his dad hadn't held him up.

"And...I guess that's all."

"You're forgettin' somethin', ain't you? How did you lose your scorecard?"

Oh, God.

"I told you, I…"

"I know what you told me. How did you really lose it?"

As so often happened, the story just appeared in his mind, as clear as the truth, which it actually was, in part.

"He had a thermos bottle with him." Eddie didn't want to say what was in it. Nick would guess anyway, and he still couldn't talk to anyone, not even Nick, about that.

"One time, he put it down hard accidentally, and I heard glass breaking inside. I thought he heard it too, but he didn't, 'cause a little later, he picked it up again.

"I grabbed his arm to stop him and he got mad at me. Even after I told him about the broken glass, he was still mad. I guess he was just mad at me for everything.

"He said I should leave him alone, and that if I was going to keep bothering him and asking him questions all day instead of watching the game, then I didn't need to keep score. Then he took the scorecard out of my hands and ripped it up."

It was plausible, just the kind of thing he wouldn't have said in front of Julia, and it worked.

"I guess the Dodgers were losin' at the time," Nick commented. "So, all this happened while he was still not answerin' your questions, right? Before he finally said, 'It wasn't me.'"

"Maybe after he tore up my scorecard, he felt bad," Eddie improvised, "and that's why he finally started talking to me."

"But you asked him about Sandra Weinstock a few times, and he didn't say nothin'. Why did it take him so long to deny it?"

"I don't know," Eddie admitted.

They walked on in silence. As they did, Eddie came to a decision.

He had no more time to wait for Mary. As soon as he got home, he'd ask his mother about that woman in Macy's, even if it meant telling her everything. There was no other choice.

Nick was also making a decision. Maybe it was all the years of forcing his mind away from it. Or the hundreds of nights when he suddenly woke up sweating, afraid to go back to the bloody carnage in his dreams.

Maybe it was sheer exhaustion, the kind he hadn't felt since that first day on Omaha Beach, catching up to him, overwhelming him, eclipsing all better judgment.

He looked down at the kid, this wonderful kid who'd do anything for his father, and he realized if there was one person he owed the truth, it was Eddie.

And, God help him, it was now.

"Okay," he said, his throat suddenly bone dry and his voice ragged, "here's what happened at Saint-Laurent."

CHAPTER TWENTY FIVE

It was D-Day plus two, June 8, 1944. The survivors of the 16th Regiment, 1st Infantry Division had emerged through Hell to take the beach and the cliffs above it. Now they were stepping into the next circle of Hell, the terrain known as the bocage.

The Germans hadn't set up any barriers here, as they did in the shallow waters and on the beach. All the barriers they needed had been in place since the Middle Ages. The Normandy countryside was a crazy quilt of small grazing fields, enclosed to keep flocks from wandering by high earthen embankments, topped by giant hedgerows. Each field was surrounded by walls of trees, bushes, and vines, that provided excellent cover for German machine gun nests, mortars, eight-millimeter artillery, and camouflaged Panzer tanks.

A field was its own fortress, accessible only by an entrance in one corner of the hedgerow. The Germans could have a clear line of fire, sometimes from three sides, as infantrymen were forced to go in one behind the other and try to deploy across the shooting gallery.

Tanks weren't much help. It took time to smash through the foliage, and they became noisy targets, announcing their positions, exposing their underbellies as they climbed over the embankments.

Artillery wasn't either. Many of the fields were too small for its use without shells falling on G.I.s and Germans alike. It would be six brutal weeks before specially modified tanks with hedge cutters, known as "bocage busters," combined with ever-increasing Allied numbers and German attrition, finally secured the region.

But on June 8th, it was largely up to the infantry, and it was field by lethal field.

"Me and your dad were in one of the few rifle squads that made it through the beach landing intact," said Nick. "Some units had thirty percent casualties in the first hour alone. We were incredibly lucky. There were twelve of us, and we'd been through North Africa and Sicily together and never lost a man.

"Your dad was one of the reasons. We were on a road in Sicily one night, just outside'a Ragusa, and a grenade landed right in the middle of us, but it didn't go off.

"Everyone froze except your dad. He never hesitated. He reached down and grabbed it, then heaved it back toward the woods. It went off in mid-air, maybe two seconds after he let go of it. I don't know how many of us would'a died if it wasn't for him.

"Then there was Omaha Beach, which was a thousand times worse than anything we'd ever seen. When we even made it through that without losin' anyone, it was like a miracle."

They were walking slowly along 86th Street and Eddie was hanging on every word.

"Our squad was part of a platoon that was workin' with another platoon, and we had to take this field. They were softenin' up the Germans before we tried it, lobbin' mortar shells into the far hedgerow, but they were doin' it blind. Nobody really knew where the Germans were. They had tunnels everywhere, and they could dig into the embankments and just sit there. The only thing the mortars did for us was give us some cover while we moved out into a field. After that, we were on our own."

There was no way to tell if the mortars had done anything at all. They could only send out the first few men and see where the firing came from.

"We were the guinea pigs this time, the first ones, which meant we had to get to the middle of the field. If we made it, we had to hold our position 'til everyone else got there."

Crouching low, the squad moved through the calf-high grass, ready to dive to the ground at the first sign of enemy fire. There was none.

There was still none, as both platoons followed and spread out beside them. They all began moving forward, parting the grass ahead of them, looking for mines even as they scanned the hedgerows.

Behind them, once enough ground was clear, two M4 Sherman tanks began smashing through the entanglement, rolling over the embankment onto the field and joining them, pounding 75-millimeter shells into the far hedgerow.

There was still no answering fire, as the infantrymen moved through the field alongside the tanks. They reached the far embankment.

Above them, the bushes and trees smoldered with smoke and dust from the mortar and tank gun assault. There had been no opposition.

"We could hear the noise comin' from other fields, but ours was dead quiet and, lemme tell ya, it was strange," Nick said.

Their lieutenant radioed back that they'd secured the area. The men sat in the grass, sheltered by the embankment, and grabbed a breather.

"Now, I gotta tell you about somebody," said Nick. "Someone in our squad, a kid named Tommy Hyland. Farm boy from upstate New York, twenty-one years old, with this cowlick that wouldn't stay down. He could be wearin' his helmet for five hours straight, but when he took it off, there was that cowlick.

"Nicest guy in the squad; give ya the shirt off his back. And he could play ball! If things had gone different, you would'a seen him, not Carl Furillo, out there in right field today for the Dodgers."

Eddie gave him an 'are you kidding?' look.

"It's true," Nick said. "He was in spring training with them in '41. Would'a made the club except he was eighteen and they thought he was a little too young. So they sent him to Montreal for the season, and all he did there was hit .350 with thirty-two homers. He was gonna be in the majors the next year, but then Pearl Harbor happened and he enlisted.

"He used to tell us stories about Pee Wee Reese, Dolph Camilli, Dixie Walker. Great story teller. Never bragged; I don't think the kid was capable of braggin'; just real interestin' stories. And you never seen an arm like he had, Eddie. He could throw a grenade further and more accurate than anyone in the whole First Infantry. We said it was like he was nailin' German runners at the plate."

It was all absolutely amazing to Eddie. There'd been nothing about any of this in his dad's letters.

"So, we were sittin' there with our backs up against the embankment."

Tommy, Nick, Barry, and two others decided they had time for a couple of quick hands of poker. As they were moving into a circle, Tommy moved the furthest and, for a moment, became visible from the bushes if anyone was looking.

Someone was.

A shot rang out, and blood spurted from Tommy's neck. With a look of bewilderment, he fell backward and lay sprawled in the open.

Barry and Nick jumped out after him, exposing themselves as well, as they took hold of him and tried to pull him back. Everyone grabbed their rifles.

"Nicht schiessen, nicht schiessen! Don't shoot; I surrender!"

The voice came from above them, from the smoke and dust of the hedgerow.

All rifles swerved in that direction as, out of the haze, stepped a short, stocky man. He was wearing an SS Panzer Corps Major's uniform and holding a sniper's rifle high above his head. His hat was gone, revealing close-cropped blond hair.

"I am unarmed," he said, flinging the rifle dramatically aside, leaving his hands still in the air. He directed his blue-eyed gaze toward the empty side-arm holster on his right hip.

"See? Unarmed."

"SS Major Gerhardt Schmidt." Nick's voice was so filled with loathing, it was like he was spitting a bad taste out of his mouth.

They'd stopped now and were standing a few doors down from Al's Soda Fountain, darkened with its Crime Scene notice on the entrance.

"There was Tommy, bleedin' to death, and your dad and me tryin' to stop it, knowin' we had no chance. Screamin' for the medics and knowin' they couldn't help either. I could feel his life flowin' outta him, right through my fingers."

There were tears in Nick's eyes, glistening in the light of the street lamp.

"You wanted to know if killin' someone in a war makes it right? Not that time. Not when a kid like that dies, just 'cause some Nazi slime wants one more before he packs it in. That's called murder."

First Lieutenant Richard Selvy, the platoon commander, was a man five years their junior. He was from Cleveland and, in another world, he'd worked in an accounting firm. Nowadays, he couldn't believe he'd ever been worried about things like missing invoices and rush hour traffic.

"Hold your fire!" he ordered.

He cast his gaunt eyes up at the German on the embankment.

"Keep your hands in the air and come down slowly," he told him. "You speak English?"

"Yes, yes I do," the man replied deferentially as he clambered down the slope, his boots slipping in the dirt as he struggled to keep his balance. "I lived in America for two years, Herr Lieutenant," he said, pronouncing it *Loy*tenant. "Milwaukee, Wisconsin."

Selvy seized his arm and roughly pulled him down the rest of the way, then threw him on the ground.

"Never been there," he said, "but I'm sure it's much nicer now that you're gone. Lie on your stomach and keep your hands behind your head or, so help me God, I'll blow it off."

Several of the squad moved toward him then, ready to smash their rifle butts into him, kick him, or worse, but Selvy stood over him and ordered them away.

"You want to do something useful," he said, "toss some grenades up there, then check to see if there are any more like him."

The men muttered a few curse words, but moved off and did as they were told. They searched the hedgerow and found no Germans, at least no live ones. One of the dead ones was the sniper from whose body Major Schmidt had appropriated the rifle.

"There were a lot'a fresh Panzer tracks in the field on the other side," said Nick, "from at least six or seven of 'em. They were headed out in different directions. We didn't know what Schmidt was doin' there. The Germans must'a been in a hurry to get out, and maybe he got caught away from the tanks when our mortars started. He had a lump on his forehead, so he might'a gotten knocked out for a while in the bushes, and they couldn't find him. Or they thought he was dead. Didn't matter. We now had an SS tank commander on our hands."

They couldn't take him with them, nor did they want to. More importantly, he knew where those Panzers were headed.

Lieutenant Selvy grabbed a length of rope, pulled Schmidt's hands behind his back and tied them together. Then he ordered Nick and Barry to escort him to Battalion Headquarters for questioning. Headquarters had been set up temporarily in the town hall at Saint-Laurent, which had been taken after the first day and was a mile back.

"I don't know why he picked us. Maybe 'cause we were the only two that didn't try and hurt the guy, even though it was only 'cause we were tryin' to save Tommy. Maybe he remembered I was a cop in civilian life and your dad was a police reporter, although that kind'a stuff don't seem to matter in the Army. In any case, we were the ones."

The sun was getting low on the horizon. Rather than try to return at night, they were ordered to remain at Headquarters after dropping Schmidt off, then rejoin the platoon the next morning.

Their M1s slung over their shoulders and Major Schmidt between them, they started walking back across the field.

"I can't tell ya how many perps I've escorted in my life," said Nick. "Most of 'em, if they're smart, clam up, but not this guy. We were gonna let him talk if he wanted to 'cause he might say somethin' useful, but this was just a lot'a nothin'. 'Nice countryside, gentlemen, don't you think? Lovely day for a stroll.' We just ignored the fucking sonofabitch."

He knew he shouldn't have said it like that to Eddie, but it was way beyond that now.

They exited the field through the corner they'd come in, onto the dirt road outside. What roads they had in the bocage country were muddy and narrow, and the steep embankments on each side made it feel like you were walking in a long trench.

It was crowded with soldiers and tanks that had moved up from the beach and were heading inland. The infantrymen parted for them, staring at Barry and Nick as they moved in the opposite direction on either side of an SS Major.

Most of them had come ashore after the beach was secure. They hadn't seen action yet, and this was their first live German. They gawked in silence at Major Schmidt, who was now silent himself, his eyes downward.

"It was slow goin', since we were movin' against the traffic, but it was no big deal. We just had to follow the road 'til it came to another one (None'a these goddamn roads had names), and then take it into town. We got maybe a quarter mile, when there was a big explosion up ahead, and everyone hit the dirt, includin' us and the Nazi."

A tank had run into a mine. Other tanks had gone over the spot before it, but their treads had passed to either side. This one wasn't as lucky.

"Now we had a problem," Nick said, "'cause all movement on the road was stopped."

Consulting a map they'd sketched out earlier, copying from the lieutenant's, they saw they could cut through the field on their left and one other, and it would take them out on the second road.

They pulled the German to his feet and started looking for a break in the hedgerow. When they found one, they shoved Schmidt ahead of them up the embankment and through it to the other side. They began the diagonal trek across this new field, and Major Schmidt once again found his voice.

"Your President Roosevelt, he is Jewish, no?"

They ignored him, as before, but Barry gave him a sharp look that the German caught.

"Most Americans do not realize this. I am telling you something your government has kept secret from you."

By now, the sky had turned a darker blue and the first few stars could be vaguely glimpsed. A crescent moon and Venus peeked out from over the trees on their right.

"That is why you are in the war, you know. You could have spared yourself all of it. The Fuhrer has great respect for the American people. He knows they are being fooled by the Jews."

"All right, that's it," said Barry. "Hearing a talking pig has been very amusing up to now, but it's time for you to shut up."

It made the German laugh.

"Me? Shut up? But you don't want that, do you? You're waiting for me to, how do you say it...'spill something.'"

"When he said that," said Nick, "the first thing I thought of was Tommy's blood. It was all over us, on our hands, on our faces. I could smell it."

They'd resumed their progress along 86th Street and were walking slowly, approaching the corner of Bay 29th. It felt better to be moving, Nick decided. He could look straight ahead, not have to see Eddie's reaction.

"Nein, nein, gentlemen," Schmidt teased them. "You should encourage my talking."

He laughed again.

"What will be the topic? Not my Panzers, I think. You will not find them, but they will certainly find you."

He glanced over at Barry.

"Maybe you should be the topic, my friend. I heard your *loy*tenant refer to the both of you as DiFazio and Fein. You must be the one called Fein, because you didn't like it when I spoke of Jews. You are one of them yourself, yes?"

Nick jabbed his rifle butt into Schmidt's side, making him cry out in pain.

"This ain't your show, pal," he informed him.

"Turns out," Nick said to Eddie, "it was the worst thing I could'a done."

They continued across the field in silence. Ahead of them, the stone ruins of an old shepherd's cottage stood near the embankment.

Schmidt was slightly bent now, but apparently still unbowed.

"It is typical what you just did," he said to Nick. "Jews always find someone else to fight their battles, don't they? It is the perfect example of why you are in the war."

Barry was the one, this time, who jabbed his rifle butt into Schmidt's side, sending him to the ground.

"Hey, take it easy," said Nick. "We don't wanna have to carry the guy."

"Bullshit!" Barry was glaring at him in cold fury.

It took Nick completely by surprise.

"Listen…" he started to say.

"He's *my* fucking problem!" Barry yelled at him. "And you stay the fuck out of it, you hear me?!"

Nick had stopped once again. He had to look at Eddie now, whether he wanted to or not, because he was about to try to explain the inexplicable.

"Ya gotta understand, we hadn't slept in three days. We'd seen things I could never describe. There must'a been a hundred times when we thought we were gonna die. It was crazy, that's all. Nobody who wasn't there could ever know what it was like."

The shepherd's cottage was just a few yards away from them. Only the shell of it remained, the four walls of piled stones. Its thatched roof had collapsed and rotted away ages ago.

Barry took off his helmet and then slung his rifle to the ground, as well as his ammo belts.

"What the hell are you doin'?" Nick asked him.

"If he gets anywhere near these, shoot him."

He pulled the German to his feet and marched him into the cottage. He began to untie the ropes around his wrists.

"Jesus Christ, are you nuts?" Nick said, but made no move to stop it.

"I want him to be able to defend himself," Barry said through gritted teeth.

From the distance came the unrelenting sounds of mortar and artillery explosions, punctuated by the intermittant, crackling staccato of machine gun and semi-automatic rifle fire. A mere hundred yards away from them, across the adjacent field, was the second road, clogged with personnel and tanks moving up from the beach, as the first had been. But in the ruins of the hut on that ancient, deserted field, it was as if they were on an island of their own, surrounded by a churning sea of men and military power that was entirely unaware of them.

"I been in lots'a situations before and after that," Nick told Eddie, "where my partner wanted to get personal and hurt some mope we had in custody. I never let it happen, 'cause I knew there was a right way and a wrong way. Except for just that once."

"Come on, Ubermensch," Barry said, spinning the German around to face him, "let's go."

With that, he punched him in the jaw.

The blow stunned Schmidt, but he recovered quickly, moving away from Barry with a feral look in his eye, as the two men circled each other.

Nick watched from the entrance, his rifle at the ready, not saying anything.

Barry was much the taller and heavier of the two, and he knew how to box. He kept just enough distance between them so that Schmidt could only flail at him with occasional, futile punches, while Barry pumped stiff jabs into the German's face each time he tried.

"What's the matter?" he said. "This should be easy for you, a member of the Master Race, up against an inferior being like me."

"I watched it," Nick told Eddie, "like it was Louis and Schmeling all over again. Your dad kept hittin' him and makin' fun of him, and I wanted it to just keep on goin'."

Eddie was in complete awe. He'd never loved his dad so much. He waited for Nick to go on, but Nick was gazing in the direction of the trolley tracks, his eyes focused on nothing.

"What happened then?" Eddie asked.

"He just kept hittin' him," Nick said, almost dreamily.

Barry's words had stopped being taunts now.

"Where are my grandparents?" he said, pounding Schmidt with lefts and rights, shoving him away if he got too close. "Where are my uncle and aunt? Menachem and Rachel Fein. They had five kids and they lived in Dusseldorf. What did you fuckers do to them?"

Schmidt grunted with each blow but was still upright, his breathing labored.

"You can be sure," he said, gasping, "that wherever they are, they are being put to good use."

He lowered his head and charged into Barry, who, for the first time, was caught off balance.

They careened across the hut, clutching at each other for leverage. Then...

"Your dad got him by the throat and lifted him clear off his feet," said Nick. "He put him up against the wall and pinned him there with his body while he choked him. The Nazi's feet were dangling, and he tried to kick your dad and pry his hands loose.

"I knew I had to stop it, right then and there, before he killed him. But I couldn't do it. I felt...glad.

"'Cause your dad was doin' what I really wanted to do, for Tommy. So I just watched it. The guy's feet never touched the ground. Even after he stopped strugglin', your dad still held him there. I don't know where he got the strength. Finally, he let him drop."

As Schmidt's body slid down the wall to the dirt floor, the life seemed to drain out of Barry as well. He sank to his knees, his eyes as vacant as

Schmidt's, as he stared at the wall. His head drooped forward and came to rest against it. He began to moan softly.

Nick remained in the doorway.

"Like I said, it was crazy," he told Eddie. "I watched it all happen, and I wasn't even sorry afterwards. I just knew we were in trouble, and I started thinkin' about how we were gonna get out of it."

It took some coaxing, but he got Barry to his feet and led him outside. They sat down in the grass. Dusk had deepened to violet, and soon it would be dark.

"Your dad didn't say a thing, just went along with what I told him. I said we had to make it look like Schmidt worked his hands free and tried to get one of our weapons. Then he got shot durin' the struggle. And it had to be in a way that would destroy any evidence of strangulation.

"So we hauled him out, and your dad held him upright while I put my rifle to his neck. I have'ta confess, I thought it was poetic justice, since that's where he shot Tommy. An M1 at close range can practically blow your head off, and that's what it did to him."

Eddie winced, his mind recoiling from the image.

"Sorry," Nick said softly.

The rope was still on the floor of the cottage, so Nick went in and got it. Then he threw it in the grass near the body, and the two of them climbed the embankment and crossed the next field to the road. They walked the rest of the way into Saint-Laurent.

"I think Schmidt wanted us to kill him all along. He was yellin' 'don't shoot' when he surrendered, but he didn't have'ta hold up that sniper's rifle. It was like he wanted us to know he was the one that used it. Maybe he thought he was gonna be tortured once we got to Headquarters. If it was the other way around, the Nazis sure would'a tortured one of our guys. Maybe he saw the writin' on the wall like a lot'a them did, and he was such a fanatic, he didn't wanna live if Germany lost the war. Who knows?"

When they got to Headquarters, it certainly didn't seem like the writing was on the wall. They found it in near turmoil.

The Allies had been unprepared for what they were encountering in the bocage, and plans were constantly being revised, and then re-revised, as the situation kept changing. Nick and Barry told their story to an MP who seemed anxious just to take it down and get rid of them.

On the beach below, more Germans than expected had surrendered after the first day, and it was stretching the MPs to their limit to guard them all. The C.I.D. man who was the next to interview them was just as disinterested, asking very few questions.

"The feelin' I got was that it wasn't gonna be much of an investigation."

They spent the night on the lobby floor in the town hall. The next day, they ran into more bureaucracy when they tried to make arrangements to get back to their squad. The largest invasion force in world history was in danger of getting bogged down, and reconnecting two PFCs with their unit was not a priority.

A day and a half went by before they were able to find out, from a staff sergeant they'd befriended, that the platoon was now three miles southwest of where they'd left it, near the Aure River outside Trevieres.

"But we can't get you there yet," the sergeant said. "It looks like something's happened."

Something had. The fields were narrower in that region and were surrounded by deep woods. The Shermans had been forced into single file along the road and wouldn't be able to support the infantry until they'd secured a larger portion of the field. And that's where the Panzers were waiting.

From the woods on either side, they trapped both platoons in the open, inflicting heavy casualties. Lieutenant Selvy was killed, along with every other member of Nick and Barry's squad.

Eddie didn't like the look in Nick's eyes. He was staring again at the trolley tracks, with the same expression his dad had after that moment under the seats.

"But it wasn't your fault!" he said, wanting that haunted look to go away. "You said they didn't care, right? They wouldn't have got it out of him anyway."

Nick shook his head.

"I told myself that. But it would'a been a lot different if we'd showed up with him alive. The reason they didn't care was 'cause he wasn't any use to them anymore, and they didn't have the time to knock themselves out lookin' into our story. Besides, they might'a gotten it outta him or not, but we'll never know. We never gave them the chance."

Eddie understood now. Who could blame his dad for being the way he was? What a horrible thing to carry around inside.

But still, *still!* It didn't mean he killed Sandra, or Al Schaefer.

He was about to say this, but Nick was speaking again.

"When we were goin' along that road into town, your dad finally talked to me. He said, the whole time it was happenin', he knew better. He wanted to stop, but he couldn't. It was like someone else had taken control of him.

"I said that's just how I felt. Like it was someone else just standin' there watchin' and lettin' it happen, not me.

"It was like the two of us, walking down that road, were two different people than the ones back there in the shepherd's hut. We didn't know who those other two were, but they sure weren't us. Not really.

"So we kept sayin' it. After a while, it was like some magic incantation, that if we said it enough it would make it true. 'It wasn't me,' we kept sayin'. 'It wasn't me.'"

They'd been walking again, and were now half-way down Bay 29th, in front of Nick's building.

"D'ya understand?"

There was a moment when Eddie thought his heart stopped. Nick and everything else disappeared, and he saw only blackness.

Then Nick's face came back into focus. It was filled with pity, a bottomless well of it, enough to drown in. And he was drowning.

Of course his dad had done it. He'd known that all along, hadn't he? And now he must face it, for once and all time. His dad was a reporter; words were important to him. He knew exactly what he was saying at the game. Eddie thought he was denying it, as his dad meant him to. But he was confessing.

Now Nick's face was melting, because he was seeing it through a film of tears. He tried to breathe, but it caught in his chest and became a sob.

Nick put his arms around him. He held him, as Eddie buried his face in the soft leather of Nick's jacket and wept. It felt like he'd never be able to stop, that he'd just keep on crying for the rest of his life.

"I know," Nick said, starting to cry himself now, not trying to hold it in or disguise it. "I know."

***

Carmine was down on all fours, pen in hand. His school notebook was open in front of him, with a pillow underneath to simulate Eddie's head. He was practicing his NYs, gripping the edge of the notebook and the pillow as if they were Eddie's hair.

NY, NY, NY, with the curlicues on the edges of the letters, to distinguish them from the Yankee NY. That was the toughest thing about doing it fast, but he'd even gotten that down now. He wished he could use the knife to practice with, but there was no way of doing it without cutting up the pillow.

Through the door he heard the sounds of the TV show his old lady and his bratty sister were watching.

Milton Berle. He hated Milton Berle, if only because everyone else liked him so much. Besides, what was so funny about a faggot dressing up in women's clothing and prancing around? He probably would've stayed in his room tonight anyway, so they weren't really punishing him at all.

He felt proud of himself. The end was in sight.

He thought about whacking off, but it didn't appeal to him. After his old man had left, while he was lying on the bed fantasizing about what he'd do to Eddie Fein, the fantasy had turned into a woman that he was sitting on top of, holding the knife to her throat.

He didn't know who she was, sort of a combination of Ava Gardner and his sister's friend Cathy Cangelossi. Anyhow, he'd whacked off then, so he wasn't really up for it again so soon.

He got off the floor, stretched, and wandered over to the window, giving a casual glance at the street below.

It was as if someone had punched him in the stomach, kicked him in the balls, and laughed in his face, all at the same time.

For a moment, he thought he was imagining it. It was so much like that terrible jolt, that unbelievably awful moment, when he'd seen Eddie Fein leap into his old man's arms after the triple play.

But it was real. They were both standing there, right under his window, right where he could see them. They were hugging each other!

He turned away, his gorge rising inside him. He retched, and vomit spewed from his mouth, onto his notebook and the pillow. The room seemed to tilt.

He retched again, but it was a dry heave this time. There was nothing left inside him to bring up. Nothing except rage.

It was slow and simmering. It began in his gut and spread through his chest and arms, up through his throat and into his brain, until he was practically vibrating from it. It had to be released or he'd explode.

He let out a short, barking scream, which went unheard in the living room, masked by a burst of loud laughter from the TV set.

And then the calm set in, that icy calm that always seemed to follow the rage. It was what saved him when Vito held the gun to his head, and it was saving him now, filling him with the resolve he'd need for tomorrow, telling him what he had to do.

One thing about it; he wouldn't have to worry now about Eddie Fein jerking his head and spoiling the NY he was gonna carve in his face. He could take all the time he wanted with those curlicues.

Because he was going to kill him first.

CHAPTER TWENTY SIX

Wednesday, October 3rd

Like the game and the season, the skies could go either way. The gray overcast could pour down rain any second, or never shed a drop, making people who'd taken their umbrellas to the Polo Grounds feel either foolish for bringing them, or wise in the knowledge that if you bring an umbrella it won't rain.

Either way. Like the pitching matchup, Maglie versus Newcombe. Sal had beaten the Dodgers five times already this year. Newk had done exactly the same to the Giants.

Just before noon, Duke Snider was taking batting practice in the cage, driving one ball after another deep into the right field stands, upper and lower, putting chips and dents in the ancient, green-painted wooden seats.

As a left-handed batter, he was less intimidated by Maglie than others were. He wouldn't be seeing the curve the way right-handed hitters like Gil, Jackie, Pee Wee, and Campy did, as coming at their heads. To him, the curve would break down and in. One little slip by the Barber, and it could break right into the Duke's wheelhouse.

As he was keenly aware, he hadn't homered in more than two weeks, which, to his way of thinking, meant he was way overdue.

Standing behind the cage as the Duke deposited his last couple were Reese, Robinson, and Branca. A reporter walked by them.

"Any butterflies?" he asked.

Pee Wee shrugged and said that the big ones always gave you butterflies, no matter how long you've played. Jackie, who'd been yawning earlier in the clubhouse, laughed, and Ralph merely nodded.

Music floated down from above them, mingling with the crack of the bat, the slap of leather, and the players' chatter. The reporter jerked his thumb in the direction of a speaker.

"Don't know who picks the tunes around here," he remarked.

The song playing over their batting practice was "Enjoy Yourself, It's Later Than You Think."

***

"Edward!"

Eddie looked up from the written questions he'd been trying to answer at the end of the chapter, the words swimming in front of him.

"I want to speak with you."

Mr. Farnsworth indicated the open classroom door and hallway beyond.

Eddie had to hold onto his desk to steady himself as he stood up. His head ached, his stomach churned, and his skin felt like thousands of needles were stuck into it. He thought this was how one of his dad's hangovers must feel.

It had taken him a solid half hour of crying last night, as he and Nick walked the nearly deserted neighborhood streets. Once again, it was Tuesday night and Milton Berle ruled the hour between eight and nine.

Finally, Eddie had no more tears to cry, and he could think clearly again.

Nick asked him if he was okay now, and he said he was. Then, Nick asked if he was going to say anything about what he'd just heard. He said no.

"Good," said Nick. "I didn't wanna make you promise before I told you. You decided for yourself, and that's good."

They started back to the apartment.

Eddie put on a great show for his mom, the performance of his life. He even managed to pretend to laugh as they came into the apartment, like Nick had just said something funny. After that it was straight into the living room where he sat staring at the TV screen, while they both talked softly at the kitchen table. He didn't know what was said, but Nick must have convinced her that nothing was wrong beyond what she already thought.

He got through the next hour and made it to bed. In a way, it was easier than most of the times he'd tried to fool her. He didn't need to make up any stories, just act like things were okay, which he was good at.

As he crawled under the covers, Julia came in and sat down on the bed beside him.

"I'm going into work tomorrow, Sport. It's not accomplishing anything to sit around here, and if your dad wants to call me, he has the number at my school. That's where he'd figure I'd be anyhow."

Eddie told her it sounded like a good idea.

"G'night, Mom," he said through a yawn, as his eyes closed of their own will. He was exhausted.

She sat there, watching him.

"I only wish you could've seen how your dad really was," he heard her whisper, as he drifted off to sleep.

If he had any dreams he didn't remember them as he awoke, startled, to the ringing of the alarm clock. He got out of bed woozily and dressed, almost falling over trying to put on his pants.

His mother had already gone. She'd left him a note that said "I love you" and a bowl of cereal, which he was unable to eat. He walked to school on rubbery legs.

Farnsworth gave him an ugly glance as he came in but said nothing, at least during home room. But now, just before lunch and while the class was otherwise occupied, he was being summoned to his fate.

Not that he cared.

School, Farnsworth, all of it meant nothing to him anymore. He stood in the hallway, which was swaying slightly, and Farnsworth's low and angry voice was just a drone, with occasional words reaching him. Something about lying. Something about how dare he interfere in someone's personal life?

Almost idly, Eddie wondered how Farnsworth had known it was him. Beauregard must have given Dora Farnsworth his name, he guessed, when she demanded to know who told him about this watch that didn't exist.

It was all just a stupid idea, but it didn't matter. Nothing mattered, except his dad. How long before they found him? What would happen if he resisted? Would they kill him?

He swore that if his dad was killed, he really would go up to the station platform and throw himself in front of a train.

No, he wouldn't. It would destroy his mother. What was he thinking? Just another stupid idea. That's all he ever had, stupid ideas.

He realized Farnsworth had stopped talking and was looking at him. He was supposed to speak. Should he say he was sorry? He wasn't, really, and what good would it do?

"You little brat," Farnsworth snapped. "Don't you even have the decency to answer me?"

It wasn't supposed to be an apology yet, he thought. *It was a question.* He looked up at Farnsworth blankly.

"Why are you staring at me? What's the matter with you?"

"I feel sick," Eddie said. Boy, was that true!

Farnsworth gave him a long, critical look, then reached out suddenly for his face.

He ducked instinctively, making him lose his balance and have to grab for the wall to keep from falling.

"Hold still," Farnsworth said. He felt Eddie's forehead and cheek, looked into his eyes, and then gave a grunt of disgust.

"It's the flu. Don't your parents know better than to send you to school like this? Do they want everyone to get it?" He gave a snort and then muttered, "That's Communists for you."

Stepping back into the classroom, he called out, "Lionel Gluck. Take your friend here to the nurse's office. And don't get too close to him."

***

With a sour expression on her face, Rosalie Preston strode down 21st Avenue, pushing little Nate Junior ahead of her in his stroller. Walking beside her was James, who turned and glanced back over his shoulder at Eddie, gamely struggling to keep up behind them.

"You keep yo eyes fo'ward," Rosalie instructed her son. "Don' want you breathin' no air that's got flu in it."

Theirs was the emergency phone number on file with the school in case anything happened to Eddie, a throwback to when he used to stay with them after school.

"Hey, Eddie," James called out, not looking back in obedience to his mother, "you a lucky stiff. You gon' get to see the whole game." This made him the second person to express that sentiment.

The first had been Lionel, on the way to the nurse's office.

"Man, I haven't had a chance to talk to you lately," he said breathlessly, as soon as they'd started down the staircase. "You heard what happened to Al? Wow, I still can't believe it. Who could'a done a thing like that?"

Eddie said nothing, but Lionel wasn't expecting an answer. He was already going on.

"And we saw him just that afternoon, when he made the egg cream for Ronald. Say, I'll bet that's how you got the flu. Ronald had it while he was drinking the egg cream, and then the two of us drank from the same glass."

He left unspoken that it had been his idea.

"How come you didn't get it?" Eddie murmured.

"I must'a drunk from the other side of the glass," Lionel said with a shrug. "You lucky stiff. Now you get to see the whole game."

Rosalie, because she really was concerned about Eddie, looked back at him to make sure he was okay. She held her breath while she did it, though.

She was going to get paid for this, was what she was thinking. Mr. and Mrs. Fein always paid her to take care of Eddie in the afternoons. This year it had ended, which was too bad because they needed the money. Now she was risking her family's health, so she not only deserved to get paid, but paid more. The Feins were nice enough people, at least Mrs. Fein was. Mr. Fein was too, she guessed, although he'd hardly said anything to her in all these years. She'd talk to Mrs. Fein and make her understand how much of a risk she was taking here.

"When we git home, Eddie," she said without looking back, "you head straight upstairs and go to bed. Drink a lotta water like the nurse said. Your mama gits back in just a little while, so you wait for her."

The little while was actually more like four hours, but what difference did it make?

"Okay, Mrs. Preston," Eddie said to her ample backside.

James, in the meantime, was thinking about other things. This was Wednesday, and that meant Carmine was coming over to take care of that cracker. He didn't know why he waited this long, but no matter, just as long as Beauregard got what was coming to him.

He'd seen Carmine in the hall this morning while the classes were changing, caught his eye, and got a nod and a wolfish grin in return. It was what James had been hoping for, but it still gave him the heebie jeebies.

He couldn't explain why. He had no physical fear of Carmine. In fact, he knew his own strength, and that he could fight any kid in the school if it came to that. It was just the feeling that if Carmine ever really got mad at him, being strong wouldn't be enough. Not nearly.

***

Eddie did not go straight to bed when he got home, although he sure felt like doing it. The nurse, after she took his temperature, had said it was 102.

It was just that the game started in 45 minutes and, since he'd be watching it in the living room, it didn't seem worth it to get into bed. Besides, he might fall asleep, and he didn't have the energy to reset the alarm.

He had to watch the game, every moment of it, with the Jackie Robinson ball sitting right on top of the TV. They had to win today, because his dad wouldn't be able to control himself if they didn't. He'd kill again, some other poor Giant fan. And they'd be easy to spot, celebrating all over the place.

Please, Eddie asked God or Whomever, *let the Dodgers win*.

Maybe if they do, his dad would walk into a police station and give himself up. His dad never wanted this to happen; Eddie knew that in his heart.

He got himself a large glass of water at the kitchen sink (he'd at least do that much if he wasn't going to bed), took it into his room, and half fell into his chair at the desk. He gazed across at Mary's window.

She was there, searching through a bookshelf for something, not looking toward him. He stood up, which he had to do slowly, to make himself visible in case she did.

She finally turned his way and spotted him. Waving and smiling, she mouthed the word "hi."

He waved "hi" back, albeit more weakly.

She wrote something down in her loose leaf book and showed it to him.

I'm sorry, it said. *I messed up. She won't even talk about it now.*

He opened his own loose leaf book to a blank page and wrote,

It doesn't matter. My dad did it.

Tears poured down his cheeks. He felt ashamed, not for his father, but that Mary was going see him cry. It was dumb, but there it was. He tried desperately to camouflage it, keep his face expressionless, as he held up the piece of paper.

She gasped.

How...? she thought. He was so sure. What happened?

She looked across at him, her eyes wide in questioning. He was crying, she saw, and he was trying not to show it. She suddenly felt more love for him than for anyone ever in her life.

"Mary, come on!" Teresa shouted from the hallway. "Carmine's ready to leave."

She glanced helplessly back toward the doorway, then, just as helplessly back at Eddie.

"Arrrrgh!" she said, in frustration.

Grabbing the pen, she quickly wrote *I want to see you!*

Then, before she could stop herself, she added, *I love you.*

She looked at it for a moment, then held it up to the window. For only a few seconds. Then she crumpled it and ripped it into tiny pieces.

Eddie was looking back at her in wonder.

Mouthing the words "See you in school," she grabbed her books and turned away.

He continued to stare at her empty window. *Wow*, he thought. *Wow.*

It was all he could think, as he looked down again at the words he'd written, the shaky letters wet from his tears. It was strange how the pain was still there, but accompanied now by a new feeling. A quiet, mysterious excitement.

Wow, he thought again.

***

The last strains of the National Anthem gave way to an anxious hum, as the Giants replaced their caps and turned away from the flag. Whitey Lockman tossed soft grounders to the other infielders, while Irvin and Mays played casual catch in left and center. Mueller did the same in right with the bullpen catcher.

On the mound, dark growth of stubble, angry scowl and all, Sal Maglie was throwing his final warmup pitches.

In the on-deck circle, swinging two bats, Carl Furillo waited to step in against him.

During the average game, over 250 pitches will be thrown, and the first one is rarely the most important. But in big games, and this was the biggest, fans don't think that way.

Furillo settled into his stance and peered out at Maglie, as the voices of 34,000 people, exhorting both pitcher and hitter, rose in thunderous crescendo as the ball left Maglie's hand.

Fast ball, outside for ball one.

Half the crowd fell silent. The other half cheered.

Maglie missed outside with the next one, to a similar crowd reaction, but then found his control for two identical fastball stikes.

Then that curve, the one that looks like another inside fastball until it's too late to adjust.

Carl barely adjusted, fouling it off and staying alive.

Another one, breaking sharply toward the outside corner. At the last fraction of a second, Furillo decided it would miss, as he checked his swing.

It didn't. One out.

***

Eddie had the choice of watching the game on any of five channels. Every one on the dial was carrying the game except Channel 5 and Channel 13, the Newark station that showed movies and cartoons and always came in snowy.

It wasn't much of a choice, really, because picture and sound were exactly the same no matter which one you tuned in to. It was the regular Giant home game coverage, with Ernie Harwell alternating with Russ Hodges doing play by play. It was also being carried by the Dodger station and all three national networks.

He picked Channel 11, the Giant station, only because that was the channel it was on yesterday when the Dodgers won 10-0. The Jackie Robinson ball was in place atop the TV set, as Eddie sat sprawled on the couch, his head pounding worse than ever and chills periodically making him shiver. He pulled a blanket over his legs and sipped from a glass of water, as he watched Maglie walk the next batter, Pee Wee, on five pitches.

He began to dare hope the Barber might not have it today, as Maglie missed on the first two to Snider. He tried not to jinx it by hoping too hard. Maglie, the catcher, and the second baseman had a meeting on the mound.

It didn't do them much good, as Sal threw two more balls to Snider, who trotted to first as Reese did likewise to second.

Now, Robinson was stepping up to the plate.

"Take it easy," Eddie told him, leaning forward carefully, as sudden movements tended to make him dizzy. "Don't get too anxious."

He knew, after two straight walks, Maglie's first pitch was going to be a fat one, and, of course, Jackie was aware of it too. He'd seen hitters get overanxious and pop up pitches like that.

Not Robby. Not this time. Fast ball right down Broadway and he jumped on it, ripping a line drive past third and into left field. Pee Wee came around to score without a throw.

One-nothing, Dodgers.

Eddie was immediately on his feet yelling, "Yeah! Yeah!" and it almost made him lose consciousness.

He fell back onto the couch as the room spun around him. As it finally steadied, he told himself what he'd just told Jackie Robinson. He had to take it easy, no matter what happened in this game.

And nothing much did for a quite a while after that, if you're a fan of runs and hits.

Durocher visited the mound in the wake of Robby's single, and then Maglie settled in. He got out of the inning without further damage and, with one exception, the game turned into the tight Newcombe-Maglie duel everyone expected.

The exception happened in the Giant second. With one out, Lockman singled to right. Up stepped Bobby Thomson, who'd had the thought the night before that if he got three hits today the "ol' Jints" would do all right.

He got his first one right there, a shot down the left field line that had "double" written all over it. At least, that's how it felt to him.

It didn't feel that way to Lockman, who saw how quickly Pafko was getting to the ball and knew he'd be a dead duck if he tried to make third. Thomson, his head down, never slowed as he rounded first and flew toward second.

Three-quarters of the way there, he looked up and saw, to his shock, his roomie standing on the bag and staring at him in disbelief.

The throw from Pafko to Reese to Hodges got him by plenty as he vainly tried to get back. There was nothing left but to trot off the field, before God and a national TV audience, who, because it was in black and white, couldn't see his red face.

Newk quickly got Mays on a fly ball to end the inning, and Eddie had to chuckle from the couch.

Thank you, Bobby Thomson.

In the third, there was Billy Cox's great stop on Stanky's hard grounder to start an inning-ending double play, and, in the fourth, Hodges' leaping catch of Don Mueller's line drive, but other than that, the innings slid by in a semi-haze.

From time to time, the camera would focus on Maglie as he stared in for the sign from Westrum. It wasn't an actual close-up like the TV cameras could get in Ebbets Field (yet another reason why he thought the Dodgers had it over the Giants), but medium distance. Even so, the intensity in Maglie's eyes, his dark stubble, the sour downturn of his mouth, were all powerfully vivid.

He'd seen other pictures of Maglie in the papers, smiling after a win, so he knew he didn't always look that way. But on the mound, Maglie's face was a study in evil, as malevolent as any villain he'd ever seen in the movies. The face of a killer.

He glanced at the sepia photo of his dad on the credenza. It had been taken in a studio after the war, and Barry was in uniform, looking seriously at the camera, not smiling.

But there was none of the evil in his face that there was in Maglie's. Eddie tried to find it, but he couldn't.

His eye went to the Jackie Robinson ball on the TV set. The light from the screen flickered against the bottom of it like a soft, blue flame, and the last two words faced out at him, "…what matters."

Well, all that mattered today was this game, despite what Jackie said about there being much more important things in the world than whether the Dodgers win or lose.

For him, for his dad, and for that Giant fan who'd be the next to die, this game was everything.

He shivered as another chill took hold of him.

***

The tall, heavyset man could not avoid the game. It was all around him as he walked through the streets. He could not escape it no matter how hard he tried.

The play-by-play came blaring out of radios in open windows, sometimes Red Barber, sometimes Russ Hodges, depending on the station. Even housewives were out on their stoops with portable radios.

He tried to blot it out, but it filtered in. The Dodgers were up one-nothing, and it was the seventh inning.

The man did not want to know that. There was no joy in it, only fear.

One-nothing could be gone in an instant. He tried to shut his mind off. It was crucial that he not watch, listen to, or even think about the game.

He'd find out eventually, he realized, sooner rather than later. But it would be over, and if they lost…well, maybe, just maybe, if he didn't actually see, hear, or experience it, he could control this thing.

It was really his only chance.

In the window of a TV and appliance store, *five* TV sets were showing the game. He wished he could reach through the glass somehow and turn them all off. Wrap up the box five times. He remembered how, on the promenade, Sandra had thought he was so clever when he used his private expression "wrap up the box" instead of "turn off the TV," and how good it made him feel. Just before it all turned horrible. Now, here he was, wanting to wrap up the box on a Dodger game.

He hurried past and turned into a side street. It was quiet for the moment, not a radio in earshot. He neared the corner and the light turned red, stopping him from crossing the street.

A "Sky-View" DeSoto taxi cab pulled up next to him. Coming through the driver's window, was ("...off the left-field wall! Irvin pulls into second for the Giants with a leadoff double.")

He let out a moan and tried to cover his ears as he stepped off the curb, nearly being wiped out by a bus in his desperate lunge for the other side.

***

Bobby Thomson would later say it was his at-bat in the seventh inning, not his most famous one in the ninth, that was the toughest of his career. He'd already gotten two of the three hits he'd wanted, and they'd amounted to nothing.

The first one, of course, had been cancelled out by his brain lock in the second inning, and after the next one, a genuine double this time in the fifth, he'd been left stranded.

Now, with Irvin on third, Lockman on first, and nobody out, he'd been given an opportunity to make up for his second-inning boneheadedness.

Newcombe quickly got ahead of him with two strikes.

Thomson tried to keep his emotions in check. "See the ball, hit the ball," he told himself.

The next was a fast ball that he barely fouled off.

Then another fast ball, a perfect pitch on the outside. He was forced to swing, so he did.

"I didn't think I hit it that good," he was later to say. "Newk's power must have provided the distance."

It was a lazy fly ball, lofted to straightaway center, just deep enough for Irvin to score after the catch.

Thomson had done his job, and the game was now tied.

As Irvin's foot hit the plate, Ralph Branca was already warming up in the left-field bullpen, throwing next to Carl Erskine.

Ralph had not expected to pitch today. He figured he'd be among the last pitchers Dressen would use, since he'd pitched nine full innings in Game One on Monday after pitching in Philly the day before.

When called upon to warm up in the fifth inning his arm felt stiff, and he threw gingerly. But now, in the seventh, it was loosey-goosey.

His curve had that satisfying snap to it, and his fast ball was exploding into the catcher's mitt. He felt strong.

***

"Shit," muttered Joe Flannery as Irvin scored. "I knew one run wouldn't be enough in a game like this."

Nick just nodded as he sat at his desk, rereading witness reports of people who hadn't witnessed anything, looking for something he could've missed. Maybe it was a question he didn't ask, maybe something wrong with what they'd answered.

The manpower was beefed up. There were almost twice as many cops on the street. They'd interviewed everyone they could find by now, and Barry's picture was being shown around all the bars, liquor stores, and flop house hotels they could get to.

He wondered when the brass upstairs would take him off the case. It could be anytime now. Barry was only a person of interest, not a suspect, but it was bad enough. They wouldn't let his best friend go on being lead detective much longer.

And he had other problems. He'd written a sanitized version of his interview with Eddie, the only true part being Eddie's ignorance of his father's whereabouts. The rest was bullshit.

He'd never in his entire career knowingly written a false report. And when they discovered the "lunch B.F." to "lunch B.P." switch on Sandra's calendar, he'd get fired altogether, if not brought up on charges.

Meanwhile, Joe was wrapped up in the game, happier than a pig in shit that there was nothing else to do but listen to it, though not so happy now that the Giants tied it up.

Nick, his team possibly capping off the greatest comeback in Major League history, was sorry the game of baseball had ever been invented.

"Excuse me, are you Detective DiFazio?"

A short, rotund man who looked to be in his early 50's, with thin, graying hair combed unnaturally over a large balding area, was standing on the other side of the desk. A cigarette dangled from his mouth.

"Yeah?" Nick said. "Can I help you with something?"

"The sergeant over there told me you were the one to talk to," the man said, removing the cigarette and looking about for somewhere to tap the ash. Nick slid an ashtray over to him.

"Thanks. My name is Charlie Rojek. I noticed in the paper today about that murder on Monday night, the soda fountain owner? The paper said he was killed around eleven o'clock, is that right?"

Joe turned down his radio a little and leaned in closer.

"That's right," said Nick. "Have a seat, Mr. Rojek."

"Thank you. Well, when I read that, I realized something. On Monday night I was just coming home from work, getting off the train at the Bay Parkway station." He took another drag on the cigarette. "Now, one thing I hate about the subways is you're not allowed to smoke, so the first thing I do when I get off the train is light up. Tell the truth, it's all I think about the whole trip. Anyway, that night, I'm coming down the stairs to the street when I discover my lighter is jammed. So I need to find someone with a match."

"What time was this?" Joe put in.

"A little before eleven; it's the time I always get in. So I look around, and there's this guy standing in front of the soda fountain place, and he's staring at a sign in the window, I mean really staring at it. I can tell by his face that he's steamed. He's muttering to himself, he's got his fists clenched, and his eyes are just glaring at that sign."

"You remember what it said?" Nick asked. This was important. They hadn't released the wording of the sign to the papers, only that it made fun of the Dodgers losing to the Giants. So far, the guy could be making this up.

"I can't remember the whole thing, but it said something about 'just one more and then they're done.'"

Joe moved his chair in closer.

"Go on, Mr. Rojek," Nick said.

"Well, I started to go over and ask him for a light, but at the last second I stopped. The guy looked so mad. He looked almost, I don't know if I should say this, homicidal. I didn't want to get near him, even to go past him into the store; that's how crazy he looked."

"So what did you do?" Joe asked.

"I shoved the cigarette back in the pack and went home. I only live two blocks from there, on Bay 32nd, and I figured if I could wait through the subway ride, I could wait a couple minutes more." He stubbed out the one he was smoking, reached into his shirt pocket, and withdrew a pack of Camels.

"I've gotta quit someday," he said.

"You think you could recognize this guy if you saw him again?" asked Nick.

"Absolutely. I specialize in people's faces."

He took out his wallet, extracted a business card, and slid it across the desk. It said "Charles Rojek, Portrait Photography," with an address on DeKalb Avenue.

"Well, Mr. Rojek," said Nick, "we got some lovely head shots to show ya, and if none of 'em look familiar, we got a young sketch artist who's workin' his way through art school, and he's just dyin' to help out. So make yourself comfortable."

"I hope it won't disturb you if I turn up the game," Joe said to him. "You a baseball fan, Mr. Rojek?"

"Yankees," Rojek replied.

"Ah," said Joe. "So you're not."

***

Carmine let himself into the apartment with the key they didn't know he had, the copy of the one he'd lifted from his old lady's key ring a couple of weeks ago while she was at the beauty parlor, and then put back. One thing he was going to miss about his old lady was how stupid she was.

Speaking of which, he checked the coffee tin. The household money was still there. He pulled it out, counted it, and was pleased to see it had grown to fifty dollars. He stuffed it into his pants pocket.

In his room, he crawled under the bed and removed the knife from behind the baseboard molding. It was all going to happen quicker now than he'd originally planned. He wouldn't get the chance to watch the end of the game while sitting on top of Eddie Fein with the knife to his throat. Now that he was going to kill him, things had to go much faster.

He wouldn't do it with the knife, for one thing. Too messy, and he'd have blood all over himself afterwards. The knife was just for carving the NY symbol into Eddie's face afterwards, and the little rat wouldn't bleed very much then. No, the way he was going to do it was even better, almost perfect, in a way.

He was going to strangle him. Just like Barry Fein did to those Giant fans, for whom Carmine now felt enormous sympathy. Sympathy was a good feeling, especially when it led to revenge.

As soon as Eddie opened the dumbwaiter door, he'd jump out and grab him by the throat before he even knew what happened, and then pull him to the floor. It would be over in less than a minute.

And if that moron super's kid didn't believe he was only stopping off to tell Eddie about the little trick they were gonna play on Beauregard, then fuck him. Carmine wouldn't waste time with it. He'd climb up the fire escape and go in through the kitchen window, which, he could see across the courtyard right now, was open.

It was just that the dumbwaiter would be so great, even if the idiot super's kid had to be involved. If he went in through the kitchen window, Eddie wouldn't be right there in front of him, surprised, easy to get a hold of. He'd be in the living room or someplace else in the apartment. He might yell for help, or run, or fight back. It could get complicated.

Carmine wasn't worried about the super's kid. He wouldn't be able to tell what was happening. There'd be no noise, and he couldn't see up the shaft past the dumbwaiter cart. He'd be waiting for Carmine to get back on for the trip up to Beauregard's.

After a few minutes, he'd think there was something wrong, but it wouldn't matter. Carmine would be out the window, down the fire escape, and, keeping to the side of the building and under the cover of the bushes, into the next courtyard and the one beyond that.

There, as he knew from experience, was a building whose basement door had no lock. He'd slip in there and, finally, emerge onto Bay Parkway, two buildings down from the crime scene, right near the stairs to the elevated train. If he heard one coming, he'd run up to the platform and get on it. If not, he'd look for a bus and take it as far as another subway line. Hell, he could even take a cab.

Eventually, he'd find his way into Manhattan and the Greyhound terminal. Then he'd get on the next bus to anywhere, and after that, who knows?

His life of crime would be officially underway, and started off in grand style.

Everything was working so far. He'd slipped out of the school through the boiler room, as planned, leaving his old lady waiting for him out front.

He hadn't run all the way home because he realized it would attract attention, so it had taken him a little longer.

But that was okay. Knowing his old lady, she'd wait until every last kid was out of the school. Then she'd think he was being kept after class, and go inside and try to find his teacher.

So he knew he had some time before his old man found out. Of course, his bratty sister might not wait around with her, so he really should get outta here. But maybe he had a second or two to see how the game was going.

He hadn't missed much of it; that's what was so amazing. The game was everywhere. First, in school, where everyone was listening to it except in Fartsworth's room. Someone said his radio was broken or something like that. Tough titties for them, was his opinion. Then, as he hustled home, there were portable radios all over.

He heard Irvin's leadoff double in the seventh from an open first-floor window. Then Lockman's bunt, fielded by that hillbilly catcher for the Dodgers, Rube Walker, who thought he could get Irvin at third but couldn't, so everyone was safe. He'd heard that coming from a radio in a baby carriage. Unbelievable.

Even crazier was how he heard his guy Bobby Thomson hit the sac fly that tied the score. That was coming out of a radio in a police car parked by a curb.

But since then, he didn't know. Screw it, he'd flip on the TV and take a quick look.

He strode into the living room and turned it on. The Dodgers were batting, so it was the top of the eighth. Robinson was up. What was going on; did the Giants take the lead?

Ernie Harwell did him a favor and announced the score, still tied with one out.

He felt a stab of disappointment, followed by a stab of apprehension, as he saw the Dodgers had runners on first and third.

"C'mon, Sal, you sonofabitch," he muttered at the TV set.

Maglie promptly uncorked a wild pitch, a curve in the dirt that scooted by Westrum and rolled all the way to the screen. The foul areas in the Polo Grounds were immense (they once put on an entire rodeo there in foul territory), so not only did Reese score from third, but Snider moved all the way around from first to replace him there.

Two-to-one, Dodgers.

Carmine seethed in frustration, as Maglie walked Robinson intentionally and Pafko came to the plate.

"Double play, double play, you motherfucker," he said.

Yes!

Pafko hit a bouncer to Thomson's right. He went to backhand it but, as Carmine watched in horror, it ticked off the heel of his glove into left field. Snider scored, Robinson moved to second, and now it was three-to-one, Dodgers.

Stifling a howl of agony, Carmine lowered his shoulder at the side of the console TV and slammed into it. There was a flash, and then the screen went as black as his heart.

He stormed out of the apartment and down the stairs.

***

Eddie couldn't believe what he was seeing. They were shredding Maglie bit by bit. In a way, watching them score like that was even better than all at once on a home run.

Hodges popped up for the second out, which was a letdown, but then Cox drove another one down the third base line, a vicious one-hopper. Thomson tried to get his body in front of it, but couldn't. The ball took a high bounce over his shoulder into left field.

Robby, running on contact, came all the way around from second to score, and now it was *four*-to-one, Dodgers!

Rube Walker grounded out to end the inning, but no matter.

If Eddie could've gotten up and danced around the room, that's what he'd be doing. His head was swimming and the chills were back, but, man oh man!

Newk had a three-run lead, and we were just six outs away from the World Series!

As a Chesterfield commercial came on, the doorbell rang, followed by the sound of the handle being tried, then the door opening.

Oh shit, he thought. *I didn't lock it again.*

"Hello?" said a voice from the kitchen.

It was Dr. Glazer.

That's right, I forgot, he thought. The school nurse had called the doctor just before he and the Prestons had left.

"I'm in here," he called out.

Dr. Glazer stuck his head in the doorway and gave a cautious look at the TV set, where the commercial was just ending.

"Why are you out of bed?" he asked. "Aren't you supposed to be sick?"

"I am; I've got the flu. But I was watching the game."

"No, no," said Dr. Glazer, stepping into the room. He gave another nervous glance at the TV set.

"If you've got the flu, you don't belong in here. You belong in bed."

The doctor's tall, heavyset form towered over Eddie.

"Now, come on. Wrap up the box."

CHAPTER TWENTY SEVEN

Mary fidgeted as she waited impatiently with Teresa outside the school entrance, kid after kid streaming past them.

Carmine, goddamn it, where are you? she thought, getting antsier and antsier.

If her dopey brother would just get down here, they could all go home. Then he'd be watching the game, because her mother sure wouldn't be able to stop him from it, and Mary might get one more shot at finding out the name of that woman.

She knew she couldn't try it now. Teresa was too anxious, her eyes riveted on the door, from which the stream was becoming a trickle.

C'mon, you stupid jerk! she thought.

She'd tried to spot Eddie when their classes were passing each other in the hallway and realized he wasn't there, so she grabbed the arm of that creep friend of his, Lionel Gluck, and asked him where he was.

"He's got a case of the lucky flu," Lionel said, leering suggestively at her. "Maybe you want him to give you some?"

She'd almost smacked him in the face. How could an ugly kid with a dumb name like that be such an insufferable wiseass?

Anyhow, she was determined to find out that woman's name before she went to see Eddie, even if his father had done it and it didn't make any difference. She still felt like she'd let him down.

The least she could do now was the one thing she'd promised, whether it mattered or not. And who knows, maybe it did matter.

"I'm going in there to look for him," Teresa said. She reached into her purse and took out her household keys. "Here, you don't have to wait around. Why don't you go home?"

"That's okay, Ma," Mary said resignedly, "I'll stay with you."

***

Eddie didn't understand. "Wrap up the box? What do you mean?"

"I mean turn off the TV," Dr. Glazer said sternly, taking a step toward it, his hand reaching for the knob.

Newcombe had finished his warmup pitches and Bill Rigney was stepping in as a pinch hitter for Westrum.

"No!" Eddie cried out, launching himself from the couch as a wave of dizziness overcame him. He stumbled against the coffee table and fell to his hands and knees. He tried to crawl the rest of the way.

The TV had to stay on, or they'd be jinxed.

"Whoa, there," Dr. Glazer said, pulling his hand away from the TV knob and reaching for Eddie. "Take it easy."

"We can't turn it off," he told him, panting. "It'll be bad luck. They just scored three runs off Maglie and they're winning four-to-one!"

"Are they?" The doctor helped him back onto the couch.

He'd always liked the way Dr. Glazer's hands felt, strong but gentle. When Eddie broke his arm falling off the monkey bars at age five, Dr. Glazer had set the fracture. He'd been terrified, but one pull on his arm and the pain was magically gone.

Dr. Glazer gave an uneasy glance at the TV screen, where Rigney was taking a called second strike.

"What inning is it?" he asked, his voice trailing off.

"Bottom of the eighth," Eddie said. "I've got to watch the whole game, every minute of it, and we've got to keep that baseball right where it is on top of the set. It's my lucky Jackie Robinson ball."

Rigney, at that moment, waved at a Newcombe fast ball for strike three.

"See? Can't you just examine me in here? I'll stay calm, I promise."

From the expression on the doctor's face, it seemed like he was facing an agonizing decision. It scared Eddie that he might be sicker than he thought, but then, after a moment, the doctor nodded.

"All right, I suppose," he said.

He opened his bag and took out a thermometer, along with a bottle of peroxide and a piece of cotton, and began swabbing the thermometer tip.

On the screen, Henry Thompson was pinch hitting for Maglie.

"That's it for the Barber," said Eddie. "We won't see him anymore."

Dr. Glazer nodded again and started to shake down the thermometer.

"Ernie Harwell kept calling him the Giants' money pitcher." Eddie smiled at the TV. "I guess he isn't worth much now, is he?"

"Nope," the doctor said with a brief smile, "not even a two-dollar bill." He placed the thermometer in Eddie's mouth.

***

Shit! Fuck!

Carmine was just approaching the alleyway and ramp that led to the basement of the Feins' building, when he spotted a familiar-looking car parked across Bay Parkway. It was down the block a ways and facing him, and he recognized it instantly. It was the tan Hudson his old man had been driving on Sunday when he caught him trying to run away. There were two men in suits sitting in the front seat.

They're watchin' the freakin' building! Carmine thought helplessly. *Like Barry Fein is just gonna stroll in there!*

Well, he was really fuckin' screwed now. He couldn't just go down that alleyway right in front of them, and he also couldn't just stop and turn around, because they'd see it. He had to keep walking.

And, he realized in a fury, he had to keep on walking all the way around the block. He had to go all the way back home, and then out his own basement to the rear of the building.

Then he had to climb the fence into the courtyard of the Feins' building, slip through the passageway he'd waited in on Sunday when he'd overheard Beauregard bawling out the dumb super's kid, and get to the basement door that way.

Every fuckin' second of it would take up time.

He tried to look casual as he walked past the unmarked car and turned the corner onto Benson Avenue, where he started walking faster.

Halfway down the block, he passed a guy on a porch with a radio playing. Henry Thompson was grounding to Hodges, who flipped to Newcombe covering for the second out in the eighth.

Shit! Fuck!

***

"You've got a temperature of 103," Dr. Glazer told him.

Eddie nodded weakly, as he continued to mull over the curious thing the doctor had said.

He'd heard the expression "not worth a plugged nickel" or "not worth two cents" or even "not worth the paper it's printed on." There seemed to be lots of ways to say something wasn't worth much, but "not even a two-dollar bill"?

No one else knew about the Sal Maglie two-dollar bill except Nick and the police. It hadn't been in the papers.

Did he say something about it to Dr. Glazer yesterday in the office, when he showed him the Spider Jorgensen card and told him about Farnsworth?

No, he was sure he didn't.

"Pull up your shirt for a minute," said Dr. Glazer, taking a stethoscope from his bag, "and let's have a listen."

He did as he was told, as the doctor sat down on the couch next to him and began moving the stethoscope around on his back and chest.

It was probably just a coincidence, he thought, some expression he'd never heard of before.

On the screen, Stanky was in the process of lifting a pop fly that Pee Wee was taking care of for the final out in the eighth. Three outs away from the World Series.

"There's some mucous in your chest, but that's to be expected," Dr. Glazer said.

He got up and moved over to the TV during the commercial, taking a closer look at the baseball on top of it.

"You said this was your lucky Jackie Robinson ball?"

He reached out to pick it up.

"Don't touch it!" Eddie said.

It came out more panicky than he'd intended. Dr. Glazer's hand moved away instantly.

"It's got to stay right there," Eddie explained, more calmly. "It's the home run Jackie hit on Sunday. My dad and I caught it."

"Really? That's amazing." Dr. Glazer squinted at it more closely. "Did he sign it for you? I can't see everything he wrote."

"We went down to the clubhouse after the game," Eddie said, and then he began to tell the story.

By now, having told it to his mom and Nick and his partner, as well as Mary, it was almost routine.

"And then Robby thanked everybody," he said, using virtually the same words again. "He told everyone it felt great to come into some other team's park and have it filled…"

No one really knows how the mind makes connections, how a word or expression can trigger a host of complicated associations and bring them together in a flash of insight, but that's just what happened.

Eddie's mouth dropped open and he couldn't speak, as it all hit him at once.

"What's the matter?" the doctor asked, looking into his eyes with concern.

"Nothing," Eddie said, finding his voice again, looking away from the doctor. "Jackie just said it felt great to have the park filled with Dodger fans."

"Ah." Dr. Glazer gave him another long, appraising look.

Then he said, "I'm afraid you're going to need a penicillin shot, Eddie."

In the early '50s, penicillin was considered a "wonder drug" and was prescribed and administered for just about everything, including the flu. Sterilized disposable syringe packs had yet to be invented, and needles had to be sterilized before each use.

"I promise it'll hardly hurt, but I need to boil some water to sterilize the needle. Where does your mom keep her pots and pans?"

"In the cabinet next to the stove."

He tried to keep his voice steady, not give way to the panic growing inside him.

"Okay, thanks," said Dr. Glazer, stepping into the kitchen.

It was the words "have it filled."

He'd suddenly remembered the moment in Mrs. Weinstock's dining room when she was looking for her purse and a prescription had fallen out from between two magazines on the table.

"Oh look," she'd said, just before she started to cry, "it's the prescription for her bronchitis medicine. She never even got the chance to have it filled."

And that's what was wrong with what Mr. Faber said, the thing that had been bothering him about it. He said she hadn't seen a doctor in years, and she'd told that to him on the last day.

That meant, between the time she left the store and when she got home, she thought better about that cough and stopped at a doctor's office.

Eddie had looked straight at the prescription and seen the doctor's name, Aaron Glazer. But it meant nothing special. It wasn't surprising that Sandra would have the same doctor. He knew several families who saw Dr. Glazer.

He'd forgotten it, and hadn't even remembered yesterday, when Dr. Glazer told him he'd never met Sandra and had only read about her in the papers.

But now he remembered it. Oh, boy, did he ever!

"There we are, just have to wait a few minutes," said Dr. Glazer, returning from the kitchen. "What's going on in the game?"

"Huh? Oh, I don't know," Eddie said in confusion, looking over at the screen.

Larry Jansen was now pitching instead of Maglie, and Newk was at the plate as a hitter.

"I think the ninth inning's just starting."

This wasn't good. The doctor was looking at him funny again.

"You only think so, eh? I thought you were supposed to watch every minute of it or you'll jinx them. I guess a fever can make you lose your concentration."

He sat down in Barry's chair.

He was a large man, who filled up the chair every bit as much as Eddie's dad, and he was about the same age. But where his dad was powerfully built, Dr. Glazer was softer around the edges, his shoulders a bit rounder, his midsection a little paunchy, his manner more amiable. At least that was how Eddie had always seen him.

He tried not to look over there now, keeping his eyes on the TV screen, where Newcombe was grounding out to Stanky. His mind continued to race.

There was still something wrong. Lenore Glazer also said she'd never met Sandra. Why would she lie too? They both couldn't be in on it, could they? Something still didn't make sense.

Oh, God, yes it did!

Mrs. Glazer had been upset that Dora Farnsworth was sick because they always played Mah-Jongg on Tuesday afternoons, and Dr. Glazer had reminded her that it was Rosh Hashanah.

But it wasn't Rosh Hashanah the week before. Lenore Glazer had been out playing Mah-Jongg when Sandra stopped into the office. Dr. Glazer was there alone.

"You know, Eddie," the doctor said, startling him, "sometimes flu symptoms can actually be signs of other diseases."

On the screen, Carl Furillo was hitting a bouncer to Dark for the second out.

"A while ago, actually it's almost ten years now, I happened to save a woman's life, and you want to know how?"

"How?" Eddie asked.

It'll be okay, he told himself, *if I just act normal. I only have to wait 'til he's gone and then call Nick. It'll be okay.*

"I was covering for another doctor who'd left on vacation, and one of his patients called me, a young lady who supposedly had the flu. She said she felt silly, because he'd told her just to get some bed rest and drink lots of fluids, but she wanted to know if I could come over and take a look at her, because it seemed to have gotten worse."

"Uh huh."

Pee Wee took a called strike from Jansen.

"Well, I went over, and it turned out she had spinal meningitis. Her doctor had completely missed the diagnosis, and if I hadn't gotten her to a hospital right then and there she would've been dead within hours."

"Gee, I didn't know that could happen. That's pretty scary."

"You don't have to worry," the doctor said with a chuckle. "I'm sure what you have is only the flu, but do you know what the tell-tale difference is?"

Eddie shook his head.

"It's a swelling of the neck. And with flu symptoms, you always have to make sure."

He rose suddenly from the chair and moved toward Eddie, his hands outstretched, reaching for his throat.

Eddie couldn't stop himself. He cringed and tried to pull out of the way.

"What's the matter?" Dr. Glazer asked softly. "I'm only going to gently palpate your neck area. It's okay."

He reached for him again. Eddie's hands instinctively shot up, grabbing at the doctor's wrists.

Dr. Glazer squinted down at him.

"Are you afraid of me for some reason?" he asked.

"N...no," Eddie stammered.

He hadn't meant it to come out that way. He'd meant it to sound more like "Oh, no, Dr. Glazer, don't be ridiculous. Why on earth would I ever be afraid of you?", but his voice had a mind of its own.

"Then let me palpate your neck."

Again, the doctor reached out for him.

Let him do it! Eddie told himself.

But there was a part of him that was screaming like a fire alarm, saying if he let this man put his hands around his neck, he was dead. He could feel the air being cut off from his windpipe just as surely as if it were happening, and that's how he reacted.

He gagged, and violently pulled his head away, giving himself another wave of dizziness for his efforts.

The doctor withdrew his hands and gave him yet another long, searching look.

"You know, don't you," he said grimly. "I had to go and make that damn joke. Me and my private sense of humor. When you were playing junior detective in my office yesterday and said Nick DiFazio was your coach, I never dreamed he'd discuss the details of a case with a child. But I guess he did."

"He didn't tell me anything," Eddie said weakly. "Please..."

"Shut up," said Dr. Glazer. "You just sit there."

He looked at Eddie with a kind of weary regret.

"Now I have to think about what to do with you."

On the TV screen, Pee Wee had just flied out to Mays for the third out. The Giants were coming in and the Dodgers were taking the field. It was the bottom of the ninth.

CHAPTER TWENTY EIGHT

James Preston sat bent over the kitchen table, his ear tilted toward the radio on the window sill. He had to be careful it didn't get too loud because his mama and the baby were asleep in the next room.

Russ Hodges, describing Mays's bread-basket catch of Pee Wee's fly, was explaining that Willie didn't catch fly balls near his belt buckle just to show off; he did it that way because it felt the most comfortable. But the Major Leagues had never seen anything like it.

James didn't much care at the moment. Damn Dodgers were beating his Giants, and that Carmine punk never showed up.

And the timing would've been just right too. His daddy was at the plumbing supply place all the way over on Bath Avenue, trying to find some kind of special socket wrench. So, yeah, man, this would've been a helluva time to do it.

Suddenly, there was Carmine, standing right on the other side of the window.

"Where you been?" James whispered at him through the six inches of open space at the bottom.

Carmine felt a very strong urge to kick in the glass, but instead, he bent down and spoke just as quietly.

"Never mind where the fuck I been."

Where he'd been, until a minute ago, was standing in the shadows of his basement door, staring daggers across the courtyard at the fat old lady in the window just below the Feins. As long as she kept sitting there, he couldn't climb the fence.

It was Vilma Haberman, the 82-year-old younger, and by-far heavier, Haberman sister. Carmine didn't know her name, but he'd seen her around the neighborhood forever, and right now, he wished she would keel over and die.

He thought of bagging it, just getting the fuck out of there, but each time he did, he pictured that little prick watching the game, laughing his scrawny ass off.

He couldn't let that happen. He had to give it a little longer, and hope the old bitch got the runs or something.

Not one, but two radios competed for his attention. Red Barber and Russ Hodges were dueling each other to tell him about the game, as the top of the ninth trickled away.

Then, just as Reese was sending the fly ball to Mays, she not only got up and closed her window but *pulled the shade.*

To Carmine this was a sign from Heaven, and he was over that fence in a goddamn flash.

"C'mon, let's do it," he hissed at James, jerking his thumb at the basement door, indicating he wanted to meet him there.

James got up from the table and hustled around to where Carmine was waiting, just inside the doorway.

"Befo' we do anythin'," James told him, "I gotta know what's goin' on."

Carmine shot a quick look at the dumbwaiter and another one at James.

"I'm gonna do what you want," he said. "I'm gonna fix it so that friend'a yours don't bother you no more. Now, ya want me to, or not?"

He stepped over and pulled the door open. The cart was there waiting.

"Hol' on a minute," James said. "Why you doin' all this for me? What you get out of it?"

Carmine gave him a grin.

"'Cause I don't like the guy neither, and it'll be fun. So whattaya say?"

James kept picturing the look on that cracker's face. Man, he wanted this to happen.

"All right," he said, "but once you get off that cart, you on your own. I'm pullin' it back down and goin' 'bout my business."

Carmine spread his arms magnanimously.

"That's all I want ya to do."

James moved over to the dumbwaiter and grabbed hold of the horizontal board that divided the cart in half. He pulled it out, and now there was room enough for Carmine. Once he got in there he'd fit comfortably, as long as he squatted in a catcher's position.

"Just right," Carmine said. "Hey, don't Eddie Fein live underneath him?"

James gave him a guarded look.

"Yeah, so?"

Already, Carmine didn't like that. Maybe he should just forget this clown and go the fire escape route after all. He'd have to decide in the next few seconds.

"Shit, that's great!" he said. "Stop on his floor for a minute. Let's let him in on it."

The look became even more guarded.

"Why you wanna do that?"

"'Cause he'd love it. He hates the fuckin' son of a bitch as much as you do. Ya know what he told me?" James shook his head. "He said the guy called him a dirty little Jew kike."

Carmine watched him carefully, gauging how well this was going over. One thing he was good at was knowing whether or not people believed him. A lot of kids pretended to because they were scared, but he could always spot the phonies.

"C'mon," he said, "let's let him in on it. It'll just take a second."

James met his gaze as he thought it over.

"Yeah, awright," he said, "but you gotta make it quick. We ain't got all day."

"Don't worry," Carmine said, his judgment telling him James had swallowed it, "it'll be quicker'n shit through a goose."

You dumb fuck, he added in a silent postscript, as he climbed into the cart.

Back in the Prestons' apartment, coming through the radio and unheard by either of them, Alvin Dark was singling off Gil Hodges' outstretched glove to open the Giant ninth.

With a grunt, James began to pull hand over hand on the up rope. Carmine was heavier than what he usually had to haul, but he was managing it okay. The cart slowly made its way up the shaft.

Of course, he didn't believe any of the crap he'd just heard. He didn't know how Eddie Fein felt about Beauregard, but he knew he wasn't any friend of Carmine's. In fact, now he understood what was going on. Carmine wanted to get Eddie.

Well, James wasn't about to help him do that. But he didn't want to argue with him either, which is why he decided to do like his daddy and give him the old "yes, suh." It was just his own version of it.

He wasn't stopping this thing at Eddie's apartment, that was for sure. If Carmine wanted to beat up someone, it'd have to be the cracker. And when he came around later, James would just say he heard his daddy coming, so, change of plans.

Nuh uh, Carmine wasn't going to no Eddie Fein's. He was going to Beauregard's floor, and that's where James was leaving him.

***

"God damn you."

Dr. Glazer kept muttering it as he paced the living room floor. Eddie knew he wasn't talking about Alvin Dark on first base or Don Mueller at the plate. The doctor had glanced at the TV screen only once, when Dark hit the ground ball to Hodges' right that Robby probably would have handled, if Gil hadn't lunged for it and deflected it with his glove.

Eddie glanced futilely at the phone on the end table, right there in arm's reach, but it might as well have been in the Dodger bullpen, where Erskine and Branca were throwing. Before he'd even get the receiver off the hook, let alone dialing and the rest of it, it would be ripped out of his hand, and easily.

His head was swimming, his body was burning up, and his feelings were oscillating wildly between relief that his dad didn't do it and sheer, blinding terror.

He couldn't believe he'd ever thought for one minute about jumping in front of a train. Dying wasn't some idea you played with when you didn't like how your life was going. It was real, it was horrible, and it was final.

And it was going to happen to him.

It would be useless to promise the doctor he wouldn't tell anyone. That was what people said in the movies, just before they got killed.

His only hope, if he had one, was to somehow convince Dr. Glazer to turn himself in. He tried to speak.

"Shut up!" the doctor barked, not looking at him but glaring at the TV.

"They always do it to you in the end," he muttered.

It was the first thing he'd said in a while, other than "Shut up!" and the ever-popular "God damn you." The camera showed Alvin Dark taking his lead off first, Hodges holding him on.

"That's a mistake right there. They shouldn't be holding him on. His run means nothing, and they're giving the left-handed hitter a big hole on the right side of the infield."

Eddie could not ever remember talking about baseball to Dr. Glazer; he'd had no idea the man even cared. But now, it was probably good that the doctor was distracted from thinking of a way to kill him and make it look like an accident.

Eddie knew that was the doctor's problem. Otherwise, he would've done it already. In a crazily optimistic way, he thought if the Dodgers won, he'd have a better shot at convincing him to give himself up. It was like the fantasy of his dad walking peacefully into a police station.

Newcombe delivered a change-up, and Mueller, swinging too early, hit a bouncer to the very spot where Hodges would have been if he were not holding the runner on. It skipped into right field for a base hit, as Dark motored all the way around to third.

"Knew it," Dr. Glazer said venomously. "Knew it!"

He sat down heavily in Barry's chair and gripped both arms of it, his knuckles whitening.

"It's okay," Eddie said reflexively, "Newk'll get 'em. They haven't hit the ball hard, and we're still three runs ahea…"

"Shut up, God damn you!" the doctor yelled at him, combining his two favorites.

***

("Mueller swings and hits a grounder to the right side…into right field for a base hit! Dark rounding second, heading for third. He'll make it safely, and the Giants have first and third with nobody out!")

Carmine could clearly hear Russ Hodges reverberating through the shaft as the cart slowly ascended. It was coming from a radio one floor below the Feins, and it must have been right up against the dumbwaiter door, that's how loud it was.

They've got something going, he thought.

Now he was past the radio and nearing Eddie's floor. Carmine's body tensed in anticipation. Don't bang on it, just give it a nice, friendly knock like the neighbor would. Here it comes.

He brought his fist toward the door.

A sudden jerk of the cart threw him off balance, and his arm shot back so he could right himself.

What the fuck? he thought.

He brought his fist forward again, but the cart was picking up speed. In helpless disbelief, Carmine watched Eddie's door slip beneath him.

WHAT THE FUCK! he thought again. The cart continued to the next floor and then stopped.

("Dressen is on his way out to the mound, and the Dodger infield is gathering around Newcombe. A stunning turn of events here in the ninth inning, fans, and the Giants have a golden opportunity. The National League RBI leader Monte Irvin is coming to the plate as the potential tying run and, by golly, we're not dead yet!")

Carmine could hear it plain as day, coming from two floors below. He'd started to yell something down the shaft along the lines of "Hey, asshole, what the fuck ya doin'?" but he stopped himself.

First of all, everybody would hear him and it'd blow the whole thing. Second of all, maybe the moron would realize his mistake and lower him back down a floor. But third of all, and this was the weird thing, he wanted to listen to the game. Just for a minute.

He really wanted to see if the Giants were going to do it.

***

Red Barber described Alvin Dark's leadoff single off Hodges' glove in the same manner as he would've described a leadoff single by a Dodger. He was not a cheerleader; he was a reporter. Evenhandedness was a trademark of the Ol' Redhead, and evenhanded was how it sounded coming out of Joe's radio.

Joe, who was standing in front of his desk watching the sketch artist's progress, gave it a wary glance.

Nick, sitting at his own desk, was not listening. He was on the phone with Teresa, who'd just called from the principal's office to tell him Carmine was missing.

Rolling his eyes, he said, "All right, babe, calm down. There's nothin' I can do right now; we got a lot goin' on here." A pause. "I know this was my idea. I'm not blamin' you." Another pause. "I said I'm not blamin' you, okay? Just go home and don't worry; I'll take care of it. I gotta go now, bye."

It took a supreme effort not to slam down the receiver.

He got up and joined Joe.

"The eyebrows were heavier and the nose was a little flatter," Charlie Rojek was instructing the sketch artist.

They'd shown him six photographs, five other men and Barry, and he'd shaken his head at all of them. Nick still felt there was a chance he could be making it up. Sure, he'd gotten the sign in Al's window right, but a lot of passersby had seen it on Monday.

Yet, he didn't seem like one of those people who say they witnessed a crime just for the attention. There was something genuine about the guy.

"I'm sorry," Rojek said, looking away from the half-formed sketch, "I need to take a break. Do you mind if I use the john?"

"Be our guest," said Nick. "It's just the other side of this wall, but you gotta go out that door and around. Hang a right down the hall, and..."

He trailed off because Rojek wasn't listening. He was staring at the wall Nick had just pointed to, looking at the pictures of "Our Best PALs" in the center of it with a strange expression.

"Just a minute," he said, walking up to the photos and taking a closer look at one of them.

"That's him. Oh my God, that's him."

***

All right, that's it, Carmine thought, as he heard Monte Irvin pop up to Hodges in foul territory for the first out. The Giants were still going to lose, and it was all fucked. Everything had taken too long, and his old man must certainly know by now.

He had to forget about Eddie Fein and get moving. It took everything he had to make that decision, but he vowed to himself that he'd come back someday and take care of that little piece of shit if it was the last thing he ever did.

"Hey, asshole, pull this thing down!" he hollered down the shaft at the fuckin' idiot super's kid, the stupid sonofabitch who'd spoiled it. Maybe on his way out, he'd give the fucker something to remember him by.

There was no answer and the cart didn't move. The only thing he heard was Russ Hodges' voice.

I don't fucking believe it, Carmine thought, his fury climbing into blood-vessel bursting range.

"Hey!" he yelled, banging on both doors, Beauregard's and the one across from him. "Open up. Lemme out!"

It didn't matter which one did it first. He'd climb out and push his way past Beauregard or whoever the fuck it was, then get out of there.

He waited. Again, only Russ Hodges.

"Hey!" he yelled louder, pounding on the doors again. His legs were starting to cramp up from the catcher's squat, and the cart didn't smell too good besides.

Shit, what if nobody's home? he thought.

Nobody was home. Beauregard, rather than taking his usual nap, was at the Farnsworth household, making one last-ditch effort to pursuade his daughter. He was standing in their dining room pleading with her to come back with him for her mother's sake, while Farnsworth was in the living room trying to ignore it, watching the game and chewing his nails.

The apartment across the way was empty. The landlord was scheduled to show it to someone, but not until after five.

"Hey, you cocksuckers!" Carmine shouted at the top of his lungs. "Can anybody hear me?"

The answer was no. Eddie, for one, couldn't, and neither could the doctor. They were in the living room with the TV on. Sam Schwartz was at Myra's hospital bedside. The Haberman sisters, of course, were playing the radio that was drowning him out for them and everyone else, and they were hard of hearing besides.

"Shit! Fuck!" Carmine hollered, slamming his fists uselessly against the doors. "Shit! Fuck!"

("Whitey Lockman is the batter,") Russ Hodges informed everyone.

***

"Why couldn't you have minded your own business?"

The doctor was still sitting in Barry's chair, as Gil Hodges settled under Irvin's pop foul.

"Please," Eddie said, "you don't have to kill me. I know you didn't mean to kill those people."

Dr. Glazer glanced back at the TV screen.

"It wasn't a matter of meaning to," he said, his voice flat. "I had to. Just like I have to do something about you."

With that, Eddie's get-him-to-turn-himself-in fantasy dissolved into the sparkly dust of wishful thinking it had always been. He had nothing.

"Look at them." Dr. Glazer waved a hand at the screen, where Newcombe, Walker, and the Dodger infield were again conferring on the mound. "They're killing me. I try not to care; God knows I try. Why can't I stop caring?"

The only chance he had was the door. He was pretty sure the doctor hadn't locked it when he came in, so all he had to do was open it, if he could get there.

"Every year, they tease me. And then they kill me."

Even if standing up didn't make him fall down, there was no straight route to the door. He had to go around the coffee table before he could even make it out of the living room. His dad's chair was directly across from the kitchen entrance. As long as the doctor was sitting there, Eddie couldn't do anything without passing in front of him.

Dr. Glazer suddenly gave an insane, braying laugh that startled Eddie more than all the shut ups and God damn yous put together.

"What's so strange," he said, "is that they're the only thing in my life that can give me any pleasure at all."

Eddie's fear mixed in with the fever-and-chills cocktail raging inside him. He felt his bandaged hand begin to throb, which it hadn't done for days.

He peeked at his watch and it was quarter to four. His mother wouldn't be home for another 45 minutes, but the doctor didn't know that.

Should he say she'd be here any minute now? It might panic him. Eddie didn't know whether that would be good or bad.

"You heard about Mickey Owen dropping the third strike in the '41 World Series, didn't you?" The doctor looked over at him, as Lockman stepped into the batter's box.

"Sure, it was famous."

What else could he do but keep talking?

"It was famous, all right. It was also the day my father died."

"Oh, I'm sorry," said Eddie. "I know how I'd feel if my dad died." He sure did; he'd been thinking about it all day. "It must've been hard."

"Hard?" The doctor gave a snort. "It was hard enough when he was alive. My esteemed father was a God, the almighty chief pediatric surgeon at Mount Sinai. Me, I'm only a lousy G.P., taking people's temperatures, wiping their noses, and dispensing pills. All I do is listen to their complaints, feign an interest in their lives, and pretend it all isn't going to end badly."

He cut a sharp glance over at Eddie.

"And let me tell you from experience. It always ends badly."

He looked away again.

"My father was not a G.P. He was a specialist. His real specialty was pointing out my inadequacies, the bastard. I hated him."

His knuckles were whitening around the arms of the chair again.

"Yeah, Owen dropped that third strike all right, and my father had a stroke of his own; that was the beginning. But the next day…"

He stopped speaking. His head slowly lolled back against the cushions and he stared up at the ceiling. Then he squeezed his eyes shut.

"Ohh," he moaned.

Eddie still didn't dare move. Whatever this was, it would be too easy for the doctor to sense the movement, and then he'd be a dead duck.

A tendril of steam wafted through the air in the kitchen, from the pot of water boiling on the stove to sterilize the needle for the injection.

"I have a son your age," said Dr. Glazer, recovering, making Eddie glad he hadn't tried it. "You didn't know that, did you?"

"No," he said, although he did, of course, since the Glazers were the elusive parents from that story.

And he'd have known it yesterday, if only he'd told his mom the truth. He swore that if he ever got out of this, he'd never lie to her again.

"His name is Paul, and he has no idea who I am."

The doctor's eyes, filled with pain, had drifted to the TV again, where Lockman took one outside for a ball.

"I was looking after him that day because Lenore was out buying a dress for the funeral. She had plenty of dresses, and why she had to get a new one for a funeral is beyond me. But the game was on, and even though they lost Game Four that horrible way, they still had a chance. How could I not listen to it?"

Come on, get out of that chair, Eddie thought. Get up and start pacing again.

"Paul was in his playpen, but our radio was in the next room. I guess I could have brought it in, but the damn thing weighed a ton, and I thought if I turned it up enough I could hear it. But he kept making noise, and it was difficult."

Dr. Glazer was looking at neither Eddie nor the TV now. He seemed to be talking to a space somewhere in the middle of the room.

"They were down two-nothing, but they were rallying. They had first and third, and Reiser hit a long drive to right. I couldn't tell if it was gone or not, because Paul picked that moment to start yowling. So I got up and went into the kitchen for a moment, just to hear what happened."

Lockman fouled one off.

"It wasn't a home run, only a sac fly, so we got a run. But then he stopped crying, so I decided to listen for one more batter."

Sure, he stopped crying, Eddie thought. He was climbing out of the playpen.

"When I found him, he wasn't breathing."

Doctor Glazer's voice had gone flat again, matter of fact, like a stranger describing to the cops how he'd discovered the body of a vagrant.

"By the time I resuscitated him it was too late. There was already significant brain damage."

He looked over at Eddie, and his eyes held no pain, only deadness.

"So much for my son."

Lockman swung and drove one into left field for a base hit, as the crowd noise almost drowned out Ernie Harwell's description of it.

Dark came home to make it 4-2, as Mueller went all the way from first to third, sliding awkwardly, even though he was in there with ease.

Lockman pulled into second with a double, as the crowd, already on its feet, went wild. Bits of paper could be seen cascading from the stands, down onto the field.

Dr. Glazer was also on his feet now. The base hit had propelled him out of the chair.

"You're killing me!" he wailed at the TV set. "Killing me!"

At least Eddie had the first part of what he wanted, for what good it did. The doctor still had to move to his left, way to his left.

He did, but just slightly, taking a step closer to the TV as Mueller lay writhing in pain on the ground near third base.

Durocher had come over, and several of the Giant players had run onto the field. They were standing around him, as the trainer was arriving to examine his ankle. Off to the side, Dressen could be seen making his way out to the mound.

The doctor moved further to his left as he stared at the screen, but just slightly and still not enough.

A stretcher was being brought out for Mueller.

"They should shoot him, like they do horses," the doctor remarked. "When I was a medic in the army, sometimes I had to perform mercy killings."

Maybe he should try it now anyway. He'd have the element of surprise, and this might be his only chance. The doctor, muttering to himself, seemed to be almost unaware of him.

Then he realized it was useless.

Sure, he might make it out of the living room if he was lucky. But even if the front door was unlocked, he couldn't just barge his way through. It opened out into the kitchen. He'd have to stop, take a step back, and pull it open, and by then it would be too late. Unless…

***

Ralph Branca felt strong and ready, walking in from the bullpen across the outfield grass toward the mound. He was entirely focused on what he had to do. Two more outs, that's all, just two more outs. Throw strikes. Get ahead of Thomson on the first pitch.

He was the one making this walk, rather than Carl Erskine, because of a curve ball Erskine had bounced in the dirt just at the moment bullpen coach Clyde Sukeforth was speaking to Dressen on the phone. It was the most significant bounced curve in baseball history, and it didn't even happen in a game.

In short center field, Branca passed by Newcombe, who was headed in the opposite direction toward the clubhouse. Newk had pitched 21 consecutive shutout innings before the run he'd given up in the seventh, gotten through the eighth on fumes, and was now truly out of gas. The two men briefly embraced as they passed each other.

As Ralph reached the edge of the infield, where Reese and Robinson were standing, he remembered the reporter's question before the game.

"Any butterflies?" he asked them. He got two tenuous smiles in reply.

Don Mueller was being lifted onto the stretcher near third base, as the rest of the Giants looked on, but Bobby Thomson stood apart from them. He was near home plate, swinging two bats and in a world of his own.

Come on, you son of a bitch, he told himself, concentrate!

He'd made that boneheaded play on the base paths in the second inning and let two ground balls get by him during the Dodgers' three-run rally in the eighth, but now his teammates had given him an opportunity.

Wait and watch, he instructed himself. Give yourself a chance to hit. Be aggressive, but don't get overanxious. All of it interspersed with, Come on, you son of a bitch!

At one point during his intense reverie, he took a glance at the mound.

To his surprise, Newcombe was no longer there. It was Branca. He hadn't even noticed them making the change.

***

The doctor was staring at the TV screen, as Eddie slid the blanket off his lap and inched forward on the couch. He was now sitting on the edge, and he'd moved far enough to his right to be clear of the coffee table. He remembered what Nick told him about getting a good jump when you're trying to steal. You put your weight on the front foot and use it to push off, so you're already in motion before you take the first stride.

"Is Dressen nuts?" Dr. Glazer was muttering as his jaw clenched and unclenched. "Of all people, why bring in…?"

His heart pounding, Eddie launched himself toward the kitchen.

A wave of dizziness tilted the room, and turned what was supposed to be a sprint into a staggering lurch, but still, he stumbled forward.

Dr. Glazer reacted. He grabbed for him, but that lurch happened to take him just out of reach and got him to the kitchen entrance.

The front door was still three strides away.

Dr. Glazer had also lost his balance when he reached for Eddie. His hip bumped hard against a corner of the TV set as he recovered, making Branca jump as he threw a warm-up pitch.

Eddie was in the kitchen now, one stride from the door, but Dr. Glazer was behind him, reaching for him again.

Suddenly, he ducked and veered away from the door, toward the stove with its pot of boiling water. Grabbing the handle, which he knew was going to be hot and was ready for it, he swung it around and threw the boiling water straight into the doctor's face.

At least that was the plan.

It only worked up to the ducking and veering part. After that, it failed miserably.

His feet shot out from under him as the sudden change of direction made his equilibrium finally give up, and he fell to the floor, sprawled on his stomach, his face just missing a table leg on the way down.

It was all he could do; he kept moving.

He scuttled under the table as Dr. Glazer's clawing hand brushed against the bottom of his shoe. He pulled it away.

Desperately, he crawled. If he could get out the other side, he'd have a chance. The stove was right nearby.

He did. The doctor, in bending down to try and get at him under the table, had cost himself time. He was still on the other side and would have to come around, as Eddie hauled himself to his feet, staggered toward the stove, and reached out for the handle.

It was as far as he got.

Strong arms grabbed him around the waist, spinning him away from the stove and holding him in their grip.

"That's enough of that," said Dr. Glazer breathlessly. "But thank you for reminding me about the pot of water."

He half-carried Eddie over to the step stool by the dumbwaiter door and pushed him down onto it.

"Sit there and behave yourself," he said.

He moved over to the stove and turned off the flame, as Ernie Harwell's voice could be heard coming from the living room, giving Branca's statistics and reminding everyone he was the losing pitcher in Game One.

The doctor carefully removed the pot and poured the water down the sink.

Eddie sat terrified, shivering on the stool. His head felt like it was about to explode and every bone in his body was aching.

Dr. Glazer looked at him with a strange, cunning expression.

"And thank you," he said, "for reminding me of something else. When you and your mother were in my office, didn't she say you needed to stand on that step stool to reach across the dumbwaiter shaft? I think she did."

He had one more try in him, a mad dash for the door that lasted one step before the doctor was on him again, wrapping him up in an iron grasp he had no strength to fight.

"No…" was all he had time to say, before Dr. Glazer clamped a hand over his mouth. He whirled Eddie around and started walking him toward the dumbwaiter.

"I'll tell them what a terrible thing it was. You must've been trying to knock on the neighbor's door and lost your balance. Shouldn't have been doing something like that with the flu. When I got here, the apartment was unlocked, so I opened the door. Then I noticed the shaft was open."

Eddie tried to scream, but the doctor's hand was securely fastened to his mouth. All that came out were soft gurgling sounds.

A thump came from the living room, barely audible. When Dr. Glazer banged his hip against the TV, the Jackie Robinson ball had started to roll slowly toward the side edge.

Now, as Branca delivered his first pitch to Thomson, a fat, juicy fast ball right down the middle that Bobby, to his eternal chagrin, took for a strike, it dropped to the floor.

CHAPTER TWENTY NINE

Nick and Joe pulled up in front of Dr. Glazer's house at the very moment Monte Irvin was popping up to Hodges in foul territory. Joe was aware of this because he'd grabbed the portable radio from his desk and it was sitting in his lap as the car came to a stop.

"That's one," he said. "Now maybe Lockman'll do us a favor, hit into a double play, and end this thing."

"You are fuckin' unbelievable," said Nick.

Joe looked ruefully at the radio, then muttered, "Shit" and turned it off, stashing it under the seat.

"This is lousy timing, pal, that's all I gotta say. Also, I might add, you've got interestin' friends."

He opened the passenger-side door and swung his legs out of the car.

"He ain't my friend," Nick said as he got out the driver's side. "He's my doctor and he gives money to the P.A.L. We never discuss anythin' except my continued good health, and for all I know he roots for the St. Louis Browns."

Charlie Rojek, despite his claim of being an expert on faces, could still be wrong. But from a head shot, he didn't happen to pick out someone who was five foot seven. He picked a guy who was tall, heavyset, and, as Nick remembered, had big hands.

It certainly behooved them to ask Dr. Glazer a few questions about where he was on the nights of the murders. Maybe even ask him to come down and be fingerprinted.

He signaled to the two men in the unmarked car across Bay Parkway, who'd been watching the Feins' building but switched the surveillance to this address, a block away, after Nick had radioed them.

He walked across and talked with them a moment.

No one had gone into or out of the house during the few minutes they'd been there.

"All right, just keep watchin'," he told them over his shoulder, as he crossed the street and joined Joe.

"Let's go," he said.

They climbed the porch steps and tried the door, which was locked.

"It ain't office hours yet," Nick said, ringing the bell.

After a moment, the door opened. Lenore Glazer, in her nurse's uniform, looked quizzically from one to the other.

"Hello, Nick," she said. "Is everything all right?"

"Everything's fine, Lenore," he said. "This is my partner, Detective Joe Flannery." Joe tipped his hat and nodded politely. "Is the doc in?"

"No, I'm afraid he's making house calls. Is there anything I can help you with?"

"Can we come in?"

"Oh, of course," she said apologetically, stepping aside.

They entered the empty waiting room. The sounds of soft classical music came from an old console radio in the corner.

"He should be back in a half-hour or so."

"Maybe you can tell us where he is now," Joe suggested.

"What's this about?" Lenore Glazer asked, turning to Nick.

"Nothin' to worry," he said. "He may have some information that could be useful to us, that's all. Do you have a schedule of his house calls?"

"Yes, I do. Just a moment, I'll get it."

She opened the double doors to the examining room, went inside, and continued on into her office.

Joe, who'd been eyeing the radio, moved over to it and switched the station.

("Lockman swings and fouls one back against the screen,") said Red Barber. ("One and one is the count on Whitey.")

Lenore emerged from the examining room with a date book in her hands. She frowned at the radio, walked over, and changed the station back to the classical music.

"Uh, Ma'am...?" Joe began.

"If you don't mind, I can't stand listening to baseball games. All that talk, talk, talk," said Lenore. "Now, you wanted to know where the doctor is, let me see." She opened the book and started leafing through it. "Things have gotten so hectic, you know, what with this flu outbreak. No one in your family has gotten it yet, Nick, have they?"

"Not yet."

"Keep washing your hands, that's my advice. And don't use public phones. They're communications devices for communicable diseases."

She leafed through the book with painstaking thoroughness.

"Ah, here we are."

Her finger ran down the page. Nick and Joe leaned in and looked over her shoulder.

"It's hard to say exactly where he might be because some house calls take longer than others."

She glanced at her watch, turning her wrist and accidentally closing the book in the process.

"What time is it now, ten of four?"

She opened it again and found the page. "If he's on schedule, then he's either here...or here."

She pointed to two names and addresses.

Nick's heart started to race. He pulled out his pad and hastily scribbled down the second name and address, just in case. The first one he already knew.

"Come on," he said to Joe. "Let's get movin'."

They hustled down the porch steps.

"That's an interestin' place for him to be, wouldn't ya say?" Joe remarked, as he headed over to the car and reached for the door handle.

"Never mind that," Nick called out, already moving up the street. "It's only a block away."

"Yeah, but I think we should still take the..."

"Will you forget the goddamn game for Chrissake?!" Nick yelled, walking faster.

There was something about this that didn't feel good. Eddie had talked about the murders with Dr. Glazer yesterday, even mentioned Nick's name.

The doc had taken him seriously, not like he was talking to a kid. Seriously enough to tell him about Farnsworth's high blood pressure.

Nick had wondered about it, surprised that he'd give out private information like that. But if he was the guy, wouldn't he want to help throw suspicion on someone else if he had the chance?

It didn't prove anything, of course, but the more he thought about it, the less he liked the idea of the doctor and Eddie being alone. He'd never forget the look in that kid's eyes years ago, as he stood frozen in fear and uncertainty next to Albert Glanville in the deserted filling station.

He could hear his own voice. "Get away from him, son. GET AWAY FROM HIM!"

Joe had to struggle to catch up, as Nick suddenly started running.

***

Lockman's double, scoring Dark and moving Mueller to third, had interrupted Carmine's ranting and pounding on the doors. He'd been quiet since then, having shifted his painful squatting position to a more comfortable, if cramped, sitting position, and was now intent on the game.

He knew he wasn't in any danger. He wouldn't stay trapped there until he starved to death, or anything like it. Eventually, they'd have to use the dumbwaiter to collect the garbage, and way before that, the radio would probably be turned off and someone would hear him.

He didn't know what he was going to do after he got out; he wasn't thinking that far ahead. He was thinking that the Giants had the tying run on second with only one out, and his man Bobby Thomson was coming to the plate.

He listened as Russ Hodges talked about Mueller's ankle injury and how he was being taken off the field on a stretcher, followed by the announcement of Clint Hartung as the pinch runner and the more meaningful announcement that Ralph Branca was coming in to pitch.

Great, great, Carmine thought, remembering Thomson's home run and double off Branca in Game One, as well as at least two other homers he hit off him that season. He kills this guy.

("Okay,") Russ Hodges said, the tension creeping into his voice now, ("here we go. Branca winds and delivers. Fast ball, taken by Bobby for strike one.")

Carmine gritted his teeth.

"C'mon," he said softly, "hit one outta here."

A sliver of light appeared in the shaft below the cart. A dumbwaiter door had been opened, and Carmine heard something, or did he imagine it?

It was very brief, but he could have sworn that over Russ Hodges' next words, he'd just heard that little piss ant Eddie Fein yelling, "Help!"

***

The doctor had to take his hand off Eddie's mouth to open the dumbwaiter door, giving him that one "Help!" before it was clamped on again.

He struggled, kicking backward as he was lifted off his feet, trying to get Dr. Glazer in the crotch but failing.

The hand was taken from his mouth again, as the doctor tipped him over the edge. But he didn't yell "Help!" this time, or anything else. He was too terrified to make a sound.

He was going to die.

He looked down the shaft, four stories to the bottom, about to plunge head first. He'd be aware of every terrifying second, watching straight on, as it rushed up toward him and smashed him into oblivion.

("Lockman without too big of a lead at second,") said Russ Hodges, ("but he'll be running like the wind if Thomson hits one.")

The doctor tilted him further and then let him go.

***

Branca had done what he wanted, gotten ahead of Thomson, and now he was going to throw another fast ball, this one up and in. See if he'll chase it, foul it off, maybe pop it up. As he released the pitch, it seemed to be going exactly where it was intended.

Thomson saw it all the way. His eyes wide, he sprang out of his crouching stance and clobbered it.

***

Eddie's hands reached out and grabbed for the nearest rope, holding onto it with a strength he shouldn't have had. It was adrenaline and the will to live, momentarily trumping the flu. He wasn't even aware that the stitches under his bandage had come open.

His legs swung crazily under him, almost yanking his hands from the rope, as gravity turned him right side up. Dizziness almost overwhelmed him.

He swayed there, dangling for a precarious second. Then his feet found the rope and gripped it, just like in gym, where they made everyone learn to climb ropes. He was one of the best at it. Better than Lionel, who couldn't help looking down and then chickening out.

He sure didn't look down now. Dr. Glazer was right there above him, leaning out into the shaft, clawing at him.

He tried to move further down the rope, but started to lose his grip and just hung on. The doctor's fingertips were grabbing at his hands, trying to pull them loose. He looked up and saw the cart, hanging above him at the top floor.

When he and James used to play with the dumbwaiter, he'd learned the up and down ropes. He realized he must be on the up rope; that's why the cart was just staying there.

("Branca throws...") said Russ Hodges.

In the apartment, the doorbell was ringing. Nobody could hear it.

He had to try, it was all he could do. He let go of the rope and lunged for the other rope, five feet away.

("There's a long drive...")

He caught hold of it, his hands gripping one rope now and his feet the other, as the doctor leaned out into the shaft, gaping down at him.

("It's gonna be...I believe...")

He hung on as hard as he could, took his feet away from the up rope, and swung them under his body, transferring all his weight to the down rope. It caused him to immediately drop, as he desperately clung to the rope and pulled the cart down with him.

("The Giants win the pennant!")

He came to a jolting halt.

It almost cost him his grip, as his feet flailed about for a sickening moment. Then they found the rope again and grabbed it.

("The Giants win the pennant!")

For Carmine, the sudden fall and crunching stop of the cart cut right into his celebratory yell, rattling his teeth and making his stomach heave. The usual "what the fuck!" went through his mind.

("The Giants win the pennant!")

A droplet of blood landed on Eddie's arm, then another.

("The Giants win the pennant! Bobby Thomson hits it into the lower deck of the left field stands! The Giants win the pennant, and they're going crazy!")

Inside the apartment, the doorknob was turning. The door was opening.

"Eddie?" Mary called out.

("They're going cra—zy!")

The sound was muffled, but Mary's eyes went to the source of it, which seemed to be the dumbwaiter shaft.

"Oh my God!" she gasped.

("Whoa, ohh!") screamed Russ Hodges.

A man was wedged into it. She could only see the lower half of him, bent over the rim, his feet in the air and not moving. The rest of his body was hidden by the undercarriage of the cart.

She took a few tentative steps toward him, as, one floor below, the radio was turned off, Russ Hodges' primal scream echoing, then fading.

"Help!" Eddie cried out as loud as he could.

"Eddie?" Mary said, not believing her ears.

Was his voice coming from the shaft? She bent down and put her face into the small opening to the left of the doctor's bulk. She could hardly see into the chute, but one sideways glance at Dr. Glazer's face made her recoil in horror.

Gagging, she pulled back.

"Help!"

"Eddie!" she cried out in frustration.

"Sis?"

She thought she was losing her mind.

"Sis, get me outta here."

For the first time, she noticed the bottom of a trouser leg inside the cart. Its undercarriage and the doctor's bulk were taking up the rest of the opening. All she could see were Carmine's ankles.

"I'm stuck in this fuckin' thing," he complained

She didn't know what was going on here, but she knew her priorities. She forced herself to look back into the shaft and keep her eyes away from the doctor.

She could see Eddie now, just the top of him, one floor below.

"Help him!" she shrieked down the shaft in desperation. "Open the dumbwaiter door and help him!"

Nothing happened.

"They're old ladies," Eddie said. "I think they're hard of hearing."

"Oh, Jeez," Mary whined.

She made a decision. She turned, and bolted for the door, which she'd left open.

"Sis?" Carmine said, unable to see her but sensing she wasn't there anymore. "Where'd ya go? Get me outta here."

She took the stairs two at a time to the Habermans' apartment and pounded on the door, ringing the bell and screaming for them to open it. Please!

The door opened and Rose Haberman, the elder, and by-far thinner, Haberman sister stood there.

"Open the dumbwaiter!" Mary yelled at her. "He's in there. We've gotta help him!"

"Who? In where?" said the old lady.

She could see the dumbwaiter door, tantalizingly right there across the kitchen.

"I'm sorry," Mary said, moving the woman aside and rushing into the apartment.

As she disappeared into it, Nick and Joe were pounding up the stairs, past that floor to the Feins' apartment, finding the door wide open.

One look inside toward the dumbwaiter and they drew their revolvers.

"Dr. Glazer?" said Nick as they slowly entered, although he was pretty sure from the doctor's position that he was talking to a corpse.

"Eddie?" he said next, his eyes scanning the kitchen and hallway to Eddie's room.

In the shaft, Eddie couldn't hear him. He was losing whatever strength he had left, the adrenaline slowly being reconquered by the flu.

He silently held on, trying not to look up at the doctor's face, as the blood continued to drip onto him. He had no idea where Mary went.

Was this it? Was he going to die now after all?

"Wait a minute," said Rose Haberman, as Mary charged toward the dumbwaiter, running smack into the two-hundred-pound Vilma Haberman, who'd just emerged from the bedroom muttering something about why didn't Dressen bring in Erskine?

"Whoa, hold on there, girlie. Where you goin'?" she said, her large body blocking Mary.

With a monumental effort, Mary reached around her and pulled the handle on the dumbwaiter door.

It swung open. Eddie was framed in it, clinging to the far rope.

"Oy, mein Gott!" Vilma Haberman gasped, lapsing into Yiddish.

She let go of Mary and gawked, as Mary rushed over and stretched her arms out, reaching toward him over the shaft.

Eddie was just about to reach for her, when he realized what would happen if he did.

"I can't do it," he said. "If I grab onto you, you won't be able to hold me. I'll pull you in and we'll both fall."

"Ohh!" Mary moaned. And, of course, he was hanging onto the rope that was farther away.

"Can you grab this one?" she said, trying to push the up rope a little closer to him. If he could grab it, then maybe he could lean the rest of the way, and she'd pull him in.

Sure, he could, he thought. He'd just done it in reverse.

But then he looked up at the doctor and saw that he couldn't.

"If I do it, I'll drop down," he said miserably. "It'll lift the cart off him, and he'll fall on me."

"Ohh!" Mary moaned again.

Upstairs, Nick and Joe had just spotted the trouser bottoms and discovered they belonged, not to another body, but Carmine.

"What the hell are you doin' in there?" Nick said, peering up at him incredulously through the crack.

"Nothin'," was Carmine's reflexive answer.

"Where's Eddie?" Nick demanded. "What happened to him?"

"I dunno," Carmine lied. He'd heard the little fuck yelling in the shaft, along with his bratty sister. Maybe he was dead.

"Search the apartment," Nick told Joe, then bent over and put his face to the opening, to try and see whether the doctor was, somehow, still alive.

He saw the light below and looked down the chute.

"Holy Christ," he exclaimed. "Joe, wait!"

Downstairs, Vilma Haberman put her hand on Mary's shoulder.

"I'll hold onto you," she said.

"What?"

Mary was wild-eyed with fear, afraid to look away from Eddie, scared that if she took her eyes off him he'd be gone.

"I'll hold onto you while you get him. I used to be the captain of the tug of war team at our summer camp in Gdansk. We were the champs three years in a row, remember, Rose?"

"That was in the last century," Rose reminded her.

"So what? I ain't lost any weight. C'mon."

She put her arms around Mary's waist.

"Eddie!" Nick shouted down at him. "Try and hang on. I'll be right there."

"I don't think I can."

He was slipping, the bandage on his right hand now crimson.

"Girlie, whatta ya waitin' for?" Vilma Haberman insisted, planting her feet and gripping Mary tighter. Mary held her breath and reached out into the shaft.

Eddie let go of the rope and flung himself toward her. His hands grasped for her forearms as hers grabbed for his.

His arms were slippery with sweat and Doctor Glazer's blood, but she desperately held on, tightening her grip even more as his weight pulled at her.

"Rose, what's the matter with you?" Vilma hollered over her shoulder.

"Gevalt!" Rose said, as she attempted to wrap her arms around her "little" sister's enormous waist. She could barely do it, but she did, interlocking her fingers and trying to pull with all her diminutive might.

It was working.

Eddie could get his feet on the side of the chute, and he was using it to gain just enough of a tenuous purchase. Slowly, Mary was lifting him, as the two old ladies tugged and strained.

The top half of him was now in the opening. With one last heave, they pulled him into the room, as Mary and both Habermans stumbled backward.

They all toppled to the floor in a heap.

Nick arrived in the doorway at that moment. He stood there, surveying it all.

The Haberman sisters were sitting on the floor, nodding and panting and smiling big smiles. Eddie was lying on his back, with Mary all over him, smothering him with kisses and talking a mile a minute about how she'd finally screamed at Teresa that she'd explain it to her later, but she had to know that woman's name right now because it was life or death.

"I didn't think it really was," she said between kisses, laughing and crying at the same time.

Eddie lay in numb exhaustion, but he knew he liked those kisses, liked them a lot. He wanted to tell her to stop, though, because she'd get the flu, but he couldn't talk.

I'm alive! he kept thinking.

It was incredible. His dad might still be missing, but he was going to read about this in the papers and come home. Eddie was sure of it.

I'm alive, he thought again, almost in disbelief. *I'm alive! Everything is okay now. It's okay!*

Except for one detail. One thing he still didn't know. Something had happened in the game, and then it suddenly got turned off.

While he was desperately struggling to save himself, Russ Hodges' voice was just noise in the background. He looked up now into Mary's adoring eyes.

"Did the Dodgers win?" he asked her.

"What?" she said.

***

Upstairs, Joe had checked out the rest of the apartment, called the precinct for some uniformed help and the medical examiner, and was standing by the body now, waiting for Nick. His hand and the cuff of his suit jacket were all that were visible to Carmine through the three-inch crack at his feet.

"Hey, Joe?"

"It's Detective Flannery to you."

"Ya wanna know how the game ended up?"

This was obviously a joke, and Joe was in no mood for any crap. He'd gone into the living room and seen the TV on, tuned to Channel 11, but it was playing an afternoon movie by then.

"Whatta you know about it?" he said. "You been sittin' in a dumbwaiter cart. And, I might add, ya better make yourself comfortable in there. If ya gotta take a piss hold onto it, 'cause it's gonna be a while. Nothin's movin' till the M.E. releases the body to us."

"Body?" Carmine said. "What are ya talkin' about?" He still didn't know what made the cart stop, and could see nothing. Was it Eddie Fein? he hoped. "What body?"

"The guy you landed on."

Carmine considered it a moment, and it still didn't make sense.

But never mind that. He wasn't gonna be distracted from the important thing, the most important thing.

"The Giants won," he said.

"You're full of it."

"They did, you'll see," Carmine giggled. "Somebody had a radio on and I heard it all. We got four runs in the ninth. Bobby Thomson hit a three-run homer."

"Save your breath, kid. Nice try."

"You'll see," said Carmine.

It was astounding. Here he was, his plans blown to shit, stuck in this fuckin' cart, his ass in unimaginably huge trouble when they discover the knife in his pocket, not to mention the broken TV set and the fifty bucks he stole from the coffee tin.

But none of it mattered, and wasn't that something? None of it fuckin' mattered.

Life was good. Life was very good. Life was fucking beautiful.

The Giants win the pennant, he thought rapturously. *The Giants win the pennant!*

Gil Hodges stood on third base observing the scene going on 90 feet away. Davey Williams, the Giant second baseman, was screaming apoplectically at umpire Larry Goetz that he'd tagged Furillo out, while Carl, placidly dusting the infield dirt off his uniform, stood on the bag aloof to it all.

Bobby Thomson had let a double-play grounder get by him into left field for an error, to the joy of the Ebbets Field crowd, sending Gil from first to third.

Furillo, the hitter, had thought he could make it all the way to second and he'd been right, at least according to the ump.

Now, as Williams pantomimed how he'd made the tag, Gil wondered if anyone had called time out. He hadn't seen it. Looking over at Dressen in the coach's box, he thought of asking him, and then realized he didn't have to; he'd have nothing to lose. If time had been called, they'd just send him back.

So, without a word to anyone, he broke for the plate.

All the Giants, including Durocher, who'd been on his way out of the dugout to back up Williams in the argument, stopped what they were doing and gaped at him. Then they went nuts.

The whole Giant infield descended on plate umpire Frank Secory, Leo practically spraying saliva in his face with his fervor, as Secory backed away from it.

"What the hell's the matter with you?" Leo was fuming at him. "Of course we called time!"

Secory wasn't so sure.

He made his way out to second base, Durocher right behind, and approached Goetz. Had Williams, or anyone else, called time out before the argument started?

"Nope," Goetz replied.

"Run counts," said Secory, signaling to the scorer to put it up on the board. The game was tied at one.

In line at the refreshment counter under the third-base stands, Julia and Teresa could hear the crowd give out a surprised "oooh," followed by a lot of murmuring, and then a big cheer.

"Sounds like something good happened," Julia said.

"Maybe for your two," said Teresa.

The women were there getting sodas for everyone, since the concessionaires who roamed the stands did not sell soda. It only came in bottles, not yet cans, and was too heavy to carry around. The only liquid you could get from the comfort of your seat was beer, which was dispensed into cups from tanks strapped to the sellers' backs.

It made Julia nervous. She thought it was too soon for Barry to be at a game, where the smell of beer was everywhere. In fact, just last inning, a vendor going by had yelled, "Hey, getcha cold beer!" right at him.

"Not today," Barry had said.

On October 3rd, some seven hours after Bobby Thomson's homer, he'd been picked up for vagrancy, asleep on the D train, still wearing the suit he'd worn to the Samuel Boyleston interview two days before.

His wallet was gone and his only possessions were 35 cents in his pants pocket and, inside his jacket, a scorecard from the Polo Grounds. He had only a vague memory of being there.

The scorecard was filled in with complete accuracy, however, right up to the notation of Branca replacing Newcombe. The space for Bobby Thomson's last at-bat was empty.

While he sat in the drunk tank, one of the cops recognized him from his picture, and Nick was contacted. By then, they'd confirmed the doctor's prints and the case was virtually wrapped up, but Nick told them to put him in a squad car and bring him over to the 62nd.

There, after a shower courtesy of the NYPD, Nick presented him with a change of clothes he'd gotten from Julia, assuring her over and over that Barry was safe and in good health, and that he'd be home shortly.

He'd sat him down in the interview room and told him everything, except for one detail. He did not tell him that Eddie knew what happened at Saint-Laurent. He'd deal with that someday, but not then.

As Barry listened, he began to weep softly. Then he began to sob.

It had been nine months ago to the day, and he hadn't had a drink since.

"I wish this line would move," Julia said anxiously.

"Don't worry," said Teresa, knowing what she was thinking. "He wouldn't dare get a beer with Nick sittin' right next to him."

"A.A. told me that if someone wants to relapse, nothing will stop them."

"They never met Nick," said Teresa.

Julia allowed herself a smile.

It hadn't been easy, from the moment she'd arrived home to the scene in her kitchen and learned how close she'd come to losing Eddie, a stab in the heart now every time she thought of it; to Barry's tearful return in the wee hours of the morning; to the weeks and months that followed.

He'd gone to meetings, four and five of them a day. The people at A.A. said he'd be difficult to live with for a while, because recovering alcoholics have a lot of rage pent up, and they were right. But as angry as he'd get, it would pass. And then it was wonderful.

He was there for her now, not off somewhere in his head. As scary as his rage was, it was so much better than the silences.

And she had her own rage to deal with. In her mind, she knew alcoholism was an illness, but in her soul, she couldn't help blaming him for everything.

But she had to control these feelings, because if she didn't they'd have no chance at all. Sometimes she, herself, wanted a good, stiff drink.

"Carmine's comin' home tomorrow for the weekend; did I tell ya?" Teresa asked her.

She had, at least twice, but Julia said, "That's great. You must be excited."

"I am. You ought'a see how good lookin' he is in that uniform, and that crew cut."

"Ah, finally," Julia said as they stepped up to the counter. "Four Cokes, one orange soda, and a ginger ale, please."

In the stands above them, Mary was trying to take it all in. This was the first game she'd ever been to, and she looked over at Eddie as Secory signaled for the run to count.

"How do you score that?" she asked, her pencil poised.

"I'm not sure."

He leaned across the two seats vacated by his mother and Teresa, toward Barry.

"Dad, what did he do, steal home?"

Barry laughed. It sounded different than his laugh used to when he was drinking. Eddie never got tired of hearing it now.

"Gil probably wishes he did. It'd be the first time in his career, maybe in his life. But it's just a continuation of the play. He advanced one more base on the error."

"Ah," Eddie said, turning back to Mary.

"Okay, we put a little E-5 in the lower left-hand corner of the square, right here."

"Isn't that amazing?" Barry said, turning to Nick. "No matter how many games you watch, something will happen that you never saw before."

"And I hope I never see again," said Nick disgustedly.

He called over to Eddie. "Even the Cougars would'a known better, right?"

"I don't know," Eddie called back. "You never let us argue with the umpires."

"And that's why," said Nick.

He'd finally learned the rest of of the story later that day, saving his own questions for after the official ones.

He and Joe had taken Eddie's statement in the Coney Island Hospital emergency room. The doctor there had restitched his hand and given him hydration, aspirin, and the obligatory penicillin shot. Joe then went back to the crime scene, while Nick stayed behind.

"What did Mary mean by 'that woman's name'?" he asked, as soon as they were alone.

"Uh...I..." Eddie stammered.

"Listen, don't worry," Nick said. "I'm not mad at ya, even though I told ya not to involve Mary. Turns out it was a good thing you did."

In fact, at the moment, he felt kind of proud of his little girl.

"So what did she mean?"

Eddie told him how she'd remembered the other woman buying a watch at Macy's, but not her name.

"How did you know the watch we found came from Macy's?" Nick wanted to know.

There was another pause.

"Uh…remember, you're not supposed to be mad?"

Nick nodded his head.

"You sure?" Eddie asked him.

"Come on."

"Okay."

He told him about seeing Mary find the notebook, and how he'd gone over there by the fire escapes and persuaded her to let him look at it.

"Perfect," Nick said grimly. "It was 'cause'a that fight with Carmine that I lost it in the first place. Carmine again. Perfect."

Later that evening, he'd found out what his son was doing in the dumbwaiter cart with a switchblade in his pocket. Carmine wouldn't say anything, just gave him a lot of shrugs, but Nick didn't need to bother.

He knew he'd had help, and that James Preston, Nick's own Cougar first baseman, was either in on it, or, at least, knew something.

He and Joe had gone down to the basement and talked to James and his father. James was scared shitless, since he hadn't counted on anyone dying in all this, and was more than willing to talk. Nate Preston looked like he couldn't wait for the two detectives to leave so he could take a strap to the poor kid.

From all of it, Nick came away feeling that James was right. Eddie was Carmine's target, not Beauregard, which was pretty funny. By trying to hurt him, Carmine had saved his life.

But it was the last straw. As far as his son was concerned, Nick was throwing in the towel.

They'd always said military school, as a last resort, could straighten out even the worst of them. He'd been skeptical about it, but now he was out of ideas.

The New York Military Academy, in Cornwall-on-Hudson, was costing him half his salary, and Carmine, at first, did nothing but get into fights. But then he calmed down enough to stay out of trouble, for the most part.

His grades, however, were still awful. From the way his teachers described it, Nick could see that his kid was just playing the system, doing his time straight up like thousands of criminals before him.

Was he to blame?

He couldn't help it if he was away in the war. After he came home, he'd tried everything to reach the kid.

Was it his fault if being a cop kept him busier than most people and cut down on his time at home? It was his job, for Chrissakes. What was he supposed to do?

And was he to blame because it turned his stomach to see his kid acting like every piece of shit he ever arrested?

Well, maybe.

If he could've controlled his anger a little more, maybe it would've made a difference.

But then again, maybe not.

Like a lot of cops, he'd come to believe that some people are just born bad.

But why did it have to be his son?

As always, he made himself stop thinking about it.

"Hey, I was wonderin'," he said to Barry, softly enough so that Eddie and Mary couldn't hear, "when you're in A.A., you're suppose'ta yield to a higher power, right? But you're an atheist, so what do you do?"

"They've got that covered," Barry said. "You believe in A.A. as the higher power. You can call it GOD, but what you really mean is Group Of Drunks."

Nick nodded. "Not bad," he said.

No, not bad, Barry thought.

At that moment on the field, the Dodger batter, pitcher Billy Loes, swung and lofted a fly ball into right field. Mueller ranged over and caught it.

Barry glanced at Eddie, who was marking it on his scorecard while showing Mary, who was dutifully doing the same. He thought of Eddie whenever he wanted a drink, which was literally hundreds of times a day. His desk in the city room of the *Brooklyn Eagle* was crowded with photographs of Eddie, from infancy to the present, many of them in his Cougar uniform, a reminder of all those games he'd missed.

Another beer man happened to go by, the aroma wafting through the air, but Julia needn't have worried. He wasn't at all tempted, and not because of Nick being there. Because of Eddie.

It had taken six solid months of A.A. meetings before he'd been able to call Samuel Boyleston, apologizing, explaining his situation now, wondering if there was possibly a job opening.

Boyleston had been more than magnanimous, recalling Barry's dad as someone who also was in need of a second chance every now and then. He even repeated the line that if Barry were half the man Mike Fein was, he'd be a helluva reporter.

It made Barry wince on the other end of the phone, but it was nothing he couldn't handle now.

It was all a matter of proportion. He just had to remember how it felt in the back seat of that squad car, being taken to the 62nd Precinct to face what he was sure would be murder charges.

And he wouldn't have denied them, because, even if he didn't remember doing it, he must have.

That was the difference being sober made. It didn't take away the guilt; in fact, the guilt was more present than ever, which was why he'd get so angry, way beyond whatever little nuisance triggered it. (At least, that was how they explained it to him, not that it helped.)

But when he was drinking he couldn't see the world of things he had to be grateful for. Now he could, and he never wanted to lose them.

His job at the *Brooklyn Eagle* was virtually as a cub reporter, getting the stories no one wanted to cover, no byline, minimal salary at present. But it would change.

The other city reporters gave him a lot of respect for his experience, and he was the only one among them who could actually write a clean paragraph, with no spelling, punctuation, or syntactical errors. They were all nice guys, too, and he liked being with them. The only problem was that they drank, but he was handling it. So far.

When it really got bad, he was supposed to call his sponsor, who was Joe Flannery, as a matter of fact. But sometimes he didn't have to. He'd open his desk drawer instead, and take out the Jackie Robinson ball.

Eddie had given it to him on his first day at work. He'd heard that, after Thomson's homer, Robby had been the only Dodger on the field not to turn and begin trudging toward the clubhouse. He'd stood at his position and watched Thomson cavort around the bases, making sure he touched every one of them.

"Don't lose sight of what matters."

Barry would stare at the words until they sank in once again. He may not know about tomorrow, or even an hour from now, but as of that moment, he was still all right.

And that was all he needed to know.

Furillo took a short lead off second, as Jim Hearn toed the rubber, and Billy Cox stepped into the batter's box.

The distinctively harsh, stentorian voice of Tex Rickards, the public address announcer at Ebbets Field, was conspicuously silent.

"How come they're not announcing him?" Mary asked.

"'Cause they've gone through the lineup once now, and they stop announcing the batters after that," Eddie told her. "Only if there's a pinch hitter, or some other change."

"It's so strange actually being here at a game," she said. "The way it just goes along by itself. I keep waiting to hear Red Barber or somebody doing the play by play."

"That's just how I felt the first time."

"And all the colors. You don't realize it when you watch it on TV."

"I know."

They'd seen a lot of each other these past nine months. The word "inseparable" came to mind, particularly to the minds of their mothers.

Teresa thought they were a cute couple. Julia thought it was ridiculous to think of them as a couple, because Eddie was too young to have a girlfriend. But she could certainly understand why they wanted to be together. It was just another of the many things she had no control over.

The story had been in all seven newspapers, front page in some. The *Daily News* and *Daily Mirror* had shown pictures of Eddie and Mary.

They'd been treated like movie stars at school. Even Lionel was impressed.

He'd won the respect of Mary's friends Cathy Cangelossi and Donna Petragliano, who sidled over to him at lunch one day and promised to beat the crap out of any fucker who gave him trouble.

Mr. Farnsworth was also treating him with new-found deference. He still referred to him as "Edward," but no longer with that acid tone, and Eddie's papers were being graded now with a lenience shown to no others.

This was because of a secret gratitude.

Mr. Farnsworth was much relieved the case had been solved and the police would look no further. Now, they would never find out that he was going to meet Sandra Weinstock for lunch that Friday. It wouldn't have made him a suspect, necessarily, but it certainly would have added to his already substantial marital problems.

Billy Cox took a curve at the knees for strike one, but Mary wasn't looking in that direction. She was watching the five men who were wending their way through the stands, playing a slightly out-of-tune version of "Beer Barrel Polka" on trumpet, trombone, saxophone, cymbals, and bass drum.

This was the Dodger Sym-phony, pronounced with the accent on "phony," a group of amateur-musician fans who were a fixture at Ebbets Field. Eddie had told her about them.

Sometimes when an opposing player struck out, they'd play him back to the dugout with "The Worms Crawl In, The Worms Crawl Out," keeping it up until he sat down. Then, as his rear end hit the bench, they'd let out a loud, blatting chord for the finale.

If he tried to delay taking a seat, say by going to the water cooler, they'd interrupt the song long enough to play "How Dry I Am," before resuming it. Eventually, they got their man.

Mary loved it. In fact, she loved just about everything in her life these days.

It was unspeakably wonderful that Carmine had been shipped off to a military school. She dreaded the weekends he came home, but it was a small price to pay for the rest of the time, which was sheer bliss for his absence.

And then, of course, there was Eddie, who she still loved as much as ever. At least, she thought she did. Sometimes she wondered.

His voice was changing, and he'd grown three inches in the past few months, so that now he was a little taller than she was.

It sort of bothered her. That little-boyness she'd found so irresistible was fading a little more each day. She knew it was crazy for a thing like that to affect her, and what did she think was going to happen? After all, he wasn't Peter Pan.

But, still, it made her feel sad for some reason.

As for Eddie, he didn't know whether he loved Mary or not. He'd tell her he did, but only after she said it first. What was love supposed to be, anyway? He knew he liked being with her. She was beautiful and smart and really interesting, and he discovered the first time they played catch together that she could actually throw a baseball the right way, not from the elbow like a girl, but with a smooth overhand motion. It had been a revelation.

And the kissing was a revelation, too, although kind of frustrating because his body had certain urges. But love? He just didn't know.

His parents supposedly loved each other, but it was hard to tell sometimes. Since his dad came back, they seemed to touch each other more, and Eddie would catch them exchanging little glances now and then. But they still had loud arguments over money and all sorts of things, just as much as they ever did. Now, though, his dad would yell back instead of getting quiet and slamming things around.

As for Saint-Laurent, he would always believe Major Schmidt wouldn't have told where the tanks were in time for them to do anything. And he'd always remember how his dad had picked up that live grenade, and saved the woman on the subway tracks.

"Hey, I just noticed something," Mary said to him, as Billy Cox fouled one off down the right field line. "Did the Dodgers always have those little red numbers on the front of their uniforms?"

"No, this is the first year they've had them."

"I thought so. They're neat."

Julia and Teresa came down the aisle just then.

"Okay, here are the sodas," Julia announced, as she and Teresa moved past Nick and Barry and took their seats.

"Did we miss anything, Sport?" she asked Eddie, as she leaned across him to give Mary her Coke.

"We tied it up," Eddie said tersely, not wanting to explain any more than that.

His patience was very short with his mother these days. For instance, he didn't like her calling him Sport in front of Mary. He'd come to think of Sport as something you'd call a little kid. And her insistence on sitting next to him at the game today was typical of how she'd been lately.

He'd hoped that after all he did, she'd understand he could take care of himself now. That she'd stop worrying about him once and for all.

But it was the complete opposite. She was more smothering and protective than ever.

This was only the first game he'd been to all year, and why? Because, unlike Lionel, or even Ronald Herschfeld for God's sake, he was not allowed to ride the subway if an adult wasn't with him.

She'd even talked about quitting her teaching job, now that his dad was working again, so she could be home in the afternoons to "take care of him."

Not only didn't he need "taking care of," he could only imagine the fights they'd have about money then. Fortunately, his dad was the voice of reason, but Eddie was afraid she really might do it. Or, short of that, insist that he go back to staying with the Prestons, like a little child.

It was all too much. It made him so mad, he couldn't stand thinking about it.

He glanced again at the man sitting four rows in front of them, as he'd been doing on and off since the game started. He could only make out the back of his head, and he wished the man would turn around, so he could make sure it wasn't Dr. Glazer.

He knew that it wasn't, of course, but it would help if he could see the man's face. It was amazing how many people resembled Dr. Glazer, at least at the first, gut-wrenching sight.

Sometimes, the doctor invaded his dreams, appearing out of nowhere. Just last night, he dreamed he was stranded on a desert island, climbing a palm tree, trying to get at a coconut. Suddenly, there was Dr. Glazer, hiding in the palm fronds above him, reaching down to grab him as he froze in terror.

In the dreams, the doctor always said the same thing as he lunged for him: "I'm only going to gently palpate your neck area. It's okay."

Whenever Eddie had to walk past Dr. Glazer's house he'd give it a wide berth, keeping as close to the curb as possible. It was empty now. Lenore Glazer put it on the market before moving away to live with her family in Rochester.

No one had bought it yet. Maybe they were spooked that a murderer used to live there. If so, Eddie knew how they felt.

More and more, he wondered what people were really like under their friendly exteriors. How many of them had scary, secret inner lives?

The vendor, for instance, who'd sold them hot dogs last inning, smiling and winking at him and Mary. Was there something evil living inside him, a monster just waiting to strike?

Eddie couldn't help having thoughts like these about almost everyone he saw. It made him uneasy. What kind of a world was he living in?

The crack of the bat brought his attention back, as Cox hit a solid line drive into right field for a base hit. Furillo, on the move, rounded third and headed home. Mueller in right field came up throwing, launching a tracer toward the plate. The ball and Furillo arrived together, as the crowd leaped to its feet. Through the dust, amid the tangle of Furillo and the catcher, umpire Frank Secory spread his hands wide and bellowed, "Safe!"

"Yeah! Yeah!" Eddie and Mary shouted, jumping up and down with the rest of the faithful. From the upper center-field stands came the clanking sound of a cowbell.

"Is that Hilda?" Mary yelled into his ear.

He'd told her about the famous Hilda Chester, who came to every game with a large cowbell.

"It's either her, or someone snuck a cow into the bleachers," he yelled back, and just like that, the world was okay again.

The world was Ebbets Field. And it was two-to-one, Dodgers.